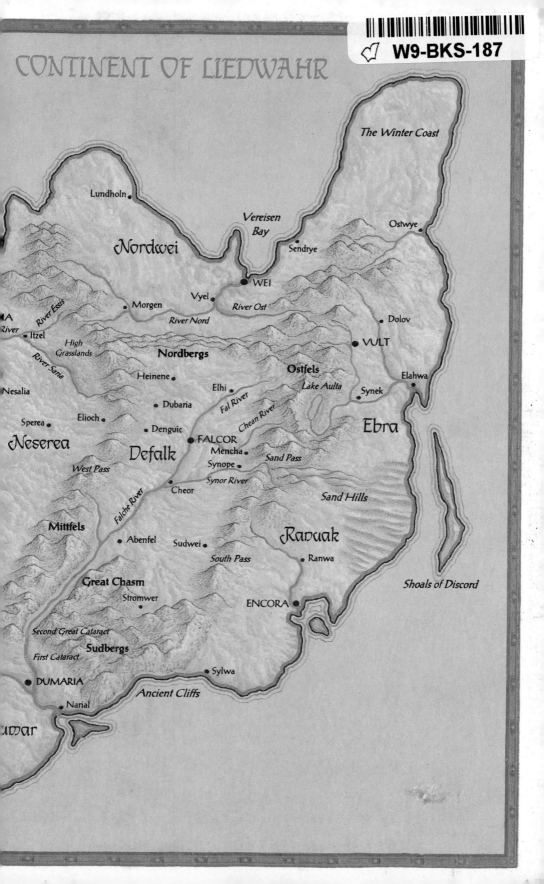

CONTINENT OF LIEDWAHR

W9-BKS-187

THE WHITE ORDER

L. E. Modesitt, Jr.

THE WHITE ORDER

TOR ®

A Tom Doherty Associates Book / New York

This is a work of fiction. All the characters and events portrayed
in this novel are either fictitious or are used fictitiously.

THE WHITE ORDER

This book is printed on acid-free paper.

Endpaper map by Laszlo Kubinyi
Interior maps by Ellisa Mitchell
Edited by David G. Hartwell

A Tor Book
Published by Tom Doherty Associates, Inc.
175 Fifth Avenue
New York, NY 10010

Tor Books on the World Wide Web:
http://www.tor.com

Tor® is a registered trademark of Tom Doherty Associates, Inc.

Library of Congress Cataloging-in-Publication Data

Modesitt, L. E.
The white order / L.E. Modesitt, Jr. —1st ed.
p. cm.
"A Tom Doherty Associates book."
ISBN 0-312-86645-3
I. Title.
PS3563.0264W48   1998
813'.54—dc21   98-11954
CIP

First Edition: May 1998

Printed in the United States of America

0 9 8 7 6 5 4 3 2 1

6/4

*For and to
my soprano sorceress*

OCEAN

Gulf of Austra

AUSTRA

Brysta

Valmurl

NORDLA

WESTERN OCEAN

Swartheld

Luba

Cigoerne

AFRIT

Atla

Swarth River

MEROWEY

HAMOR

GANDAR

Devalonia
Armat
Diev
Bleyans
Rulyarth
SUTHYA
West Cliffs
Dosai
HIGH STEPPES
Carpa
West
Horns
SARRONNYN
Jera
Bomt
Sarron
Lornth
the
Ironwoods
Middlevale
JERYNA R.
Rohrn
Berlitos
WEST-
WIND
Roof of the World
GAL
Biehl
DELAPRA
the
Stone
Hills
JERANS
Clynya
CERLYN
Fer
Ky
MILDR
Summerdock
Dellash
(Esalia)
Southport
SOUTHWIND
Copper
Mines
West
Horns
Stone
Hills
NACLOS
The Great Forest
GRASSLA
the
Empty
Lands
Rybalta
HIGH
DESERT
Diehl

GREAT
WESTERN
OCEAN

NORTHERN OCEAN

Gulf of Murr

Lands End

Black Holding

Extina

Alberth

Reflin

e Devalin

Spidlaria

Lydkler

IDLAR

Quend

leth

East Horns

Alaren

lparta

Tyrhaven

Gulf of Candar

Feyn R.

IRON WOOD

Rytel

SLIGO

Lavah

CERTIS

Matra Feyn

Wandernaught

Jellico

MONTGREN

Erstronn

era

Vergren

Clarion

ryna

Weevett

Fiven Freetown

Sigil

Tellura

Hydolar

Nylan

Southpoint

Meltosia

OHYDE RIVER

FREETOWN
(Lydiar)

RECLUCE

PHROS

Dasir

Telsen

HYDLEN

Renklaar

Pyrdya

Asula

a Arastia

ga

Faklaar

PAKLA RIVER

Sunta

BAL

HIGH DESERT

zor

Womak

EASTERN OCEAN

C.Mitchell 1995

THE WHITE ORDER

I

The brown-haired child clung to the long shadow cast by the ancient house as he edged toward the south end of the tailings pile. His eyes led him toward the barely shimmering oblong of light reflected from somewhere in the tailings against the rough planks of the doorless shed, a shed that had once held mining tools. His bare feet made no sound as he slipped from the shade into the late afternoon sunlight and over the rocky ground to the gray and reddish brown heap of stone and slag.

After he went to one knee, his fingers brushed away the thin coating of dust that had half-concealed the fragment of mirror, perhaps half the size of his palm. He teased it out of the dirt and laid it flat on half of a broken yellow brick. He turned his head toward the house, but the door was closed and the front stoop vacant. He glanced past the next closest tailings pile to the south, checking the other piles of earth and stone and slag, and the abandoned mineheads, but the only movement was that of scattered summer-browned grass waving in the hot afternoon breeze.

A lizard scuttled from where he had lifted the broken brick. The boy tensed until he saw the large brown stripe down its tan back. Then he smiled, watching as the lizard vanished behind a fist-sized chunk of slag. His eyes went back to the lizard hole, but no other lizards emerged.

The hot wind ruffled his clean but armless and ragged shirt as he squatted on the lower slope of the waste pile and gazed intently at the fragment of mirror. His pale gray eyes narrowed. The oblong of light cast against the toolshed winked out. Silver mists swirled across the glass, thickening into nearly a misty white. A faint smile crossed his lips, vanishing as he tightened them, concentrating on the irregular mirror.

"Cerryl! Stay away from that glass!" A heavyset woman, broom in hand, appeared on the clay-and-rock stoop of the house behind the boy.

Cerryl did not move, intent as he was on the image forming in the glass. His mouth formed a silent O, and his eyes widened at the sparkling white tower looming over a green park.

Abruptly, at the sound of heavy steps crunching across the ground, he looked up, his eyes flicking to the squat figure in clean but mottled gray trousers and tunic.

"How you found that . . . suppose it doesn't matter." The woman's big hand seized his shoulder, and she lifted him to his feet and twisted him away from the shard of mirror. Her booted right foot came down on the glass with a *crunch*. All that remained of the window that had shown Cerryl an impossibly beautiful white stone tower was a heap of sparkling dust. His eyes burned with unshed tears.

"Glasses, mirrors, they be tools of chaos and evil! Have I not told you that, boy?" Nall's free hand brushed a wisp of iron gray hair off her forehead, but her gaze remained fixed on him.

Cerryl's thin shoulders drooped, but his gray eyes met hers, looking up to a woman more than half-again as tall as he was, and far burlier than even most of the sheepmen and peasants around Hrisbarg. "It was only a little shard, Aunt Nall."

"A little shard. Like saying a little night lizard—one bite, one shard—that's enough to kill you, boy." Nall took a deep breath, then another. "How many times been that I told you to stay away from mirrors and shiny things?"

"Enough," Cerryl admitted in a low voice, his eyes still meeting his aunt's.

"You be the death of us yet."

"I wanted to help," Cerryl said. "They find things with the shimmer glasses. You told me that Da said so."

"Always yer da." Nall shook her head. "Poor I may be, child, but poor be not evil, and evil be the shimmer glasses. Even you know where that took yer da." She glanced toward the door of the house, swinging half-open in the light wind. "You come with me 'fore the soup boils over."

"Yes, Aunt Nall." Cerryl's voice was polite, level, neither apologetic nor begging.

"Child . . ." Nall sighed again. "Back to the house."

Cerryl walked across the dry and dusty ground, a pace to her left and a pace back. He glanced toward another tailing pile, farther eastward. If there had been a mirror in one pile, what about the others?

"No lagging, child."

Cerryl followed Nall to the stoop, where she reclaimed the broom. She gestured with it, as if to sweep him into the house. Cerryl stepped inside. At the end of the main room of the two-room house was the hearth, with the cook table to the right, the narrow trestle table with its two short benches before the hearth, and a weathered gold oak cabinet with cracked drawer fronts to the left.

"Not even enough sense to fool around where no one could see you," snapped the woman, closing the door behind the boy. "Your poor mother, no wonder she died young. Not a scrap of sense in you or in your worthless father. A white mage, he was going to be." Nall shook her head sadly. "Poor fool . . . thinking he was that them mighty types in Fairhaven would welcome him. Him a peasant boy from Howlett . . ."

Cerryl lowered his eyes to the spotless stone floor.

"How did you spy that glass?"

"I saw its reflection on the side of the toolshed. I had to look. I just looked."

"Aye, and that was because yer aunt was there afore you could do more, I'd wager, young fellow."

Cerryl remained silent.

"You men, even young. Syodor . . . even he . . ." Nall broke off the words abruptly and looked at Cerryl. "No sense in that. What be done be done." She pointed to the stool by her kitchen table. "Well, leastwise you can help. You're careful enough with the roots."

Cerryl climbed onto the stool and looked at the handful of bedraggled golden turnips. His eyes flicked to the open shutters of the single window and the other tailing piles, then back to the turnips.

II

All life composes itself of chaos and order. Yet too many forget that without chaos there is no life. Far within the earth, chaos abides, giving warmth and life to the depths beneath the lands and oceans.

The very light of the sun is white chaos, and it, too, brings life. Within the very sunlight are all the colors of white, the pure chaos from which springs all life . . .

The sun can be seen but by solely its own light, and thus all that is under the sun can only be because of the chaos of the sun. Even the wisest of mages cannot perceive any portion of all that exists on and under the earth itself except through the operation of chaos.

To claim that order is the staff of life, as some acolytes have done since the ancient heretic Nylan, is not only false but folly, for the sole perfect order in life is death.

Even a blade or a shield must be forged through the heat of chaos and wielded by a man whose very lifeblood is heated by chaos.

Chaos is the foundation of power and strength. Mastering chaos is the first step in controlling power. Power is the foundation of all lands and towns that would prosper, and those who would have their home-lands free of invaders and devastation must then seek the mastery of chaos . . .

Colors of White
(Manual of the Guild at Fairhaven)
Preface

III

In the corner where the hearth fire spilled light onto the floor, Cerryl looked at the book, eyes straining at the incomprehensible black symbols on the aged tan page. He turned the page. The symbols on the next page looked the same.

"Cerryl?" Nall continued to place the rolled-out biscuits in the battered tin baking pan on the table at her left.

"Yes, Aunt?" He did not turn, fearing she might see the book, afraid she might see the tears of frustration in his eyes.

"Your uncle be a-coming up the south path soon. Would you be fetching another pail of water?"

"Yes, Aunt Nall." He slipped the ancient tome inside his ragged tunic and forced his face into composure before standing and turning.

"And a cheerful face would be good. Days been hard for Syodor lately," she added. "Specially after he found that cursed white bronze . . ." The after-statement was whispered to herself, but Cerryl heard it as clearly as though she had spoken loudly.

He only nodded, knowing she would not want him to know what she had said, and walked quickly across the threshold, stopping by his pallet and slipping the book inside it before continuing and picking the ironbound wooden pail off the long peg set into the cross-timber behind the door. His bare feet carried him out the door and off the stoop and toward the path leading to the stream uphill and in back of the house.

He wished they could use the stream where it wound in front of the old house, but there it had turned orangish from the tailings. And it smelled like brimstone, sometimes rusty like iron as well. Cerryl's nose twitched at the thought of the odor as he trudged up the path toward the spring from which the smaller stream flowed.

A sharp *terwhit* slashed through the early dusk—a bird hidden somewhere in the scrub junipers that sprouted willy-nilly in the areas untouched by tailings or the orange leachings. Cerryl glanced to his right, in the direction of the stone arched tunnel with a foreboding name carved in the rock over the beams. While he couldn't read the name, he could sense that something left better alone lay deep in the tunnel. Still, the dusk that strained Nall's eyes, or his uncle's, was as bright as dawn just before the sun rose—something he'd tried not to let them know.

The bird did not call again, and the chirping of insects rose in the dusk. Cerryl wondered if they were crickets or something else. He shrugged. Insects had never been that interesting. He turned westward, heading up the foot-packed clay toward the spring.

The faint gurgling of the brook did not rise over the insects' chirping until he reached the end of the spring itself, dark silver waters nearly still, except where they flowed over the rock dam created years back and covered in thick green moss.

Cerryl edged along the south side of the spring until he reached the rock embankment from which the waters flowed. There, in the long shadows and the gathering dusk, he looked at the dark waters bubbling over the rock ledge and into the narrow basin, then at the mockgrape vines clinging to the reddish rocks above the ledge.

Where did the water come from?

He frowned and looked at the ledge, then at the dark-silvered and rippled surface of the pond, so much like a mirror, and so unlike it. Could he make the mirror trick show him where the water started?

He squinted at the twilight-dark springwater, imagining ... what? Was there a hole in the red sandstone that led to the depths of the earth? Cerryl took a deep breath, his lips pressed tightly together, the empty bucket at his feet forgotten for the moment.

Silver mists swirled across the pond, silver mists, Cerryl realized, that only he could see. "Nall and Syodor couldn't, anyway," he murmured under his breath, puzzled over why he had even to say that, but knowing that he did, knowing that his whispered words were a sort of defiance that were somehow important, if only to him.

The gray-haired image of Nall flitted through the mists, and Cerryl pushed it away, seeking the source of the waters. Darkness spilled across the water, only darkness.

After a time, as his head began to ache, he finally took another deep breath, a gasping one, before bending down to pick up the bucket and dip it into the spring. Water splashed across the ragged bottoms of his trousers, across his bare feet, and onto the dry clay of the path.

He lifted the heavy bucket and turned back downhill, bare feet sure on the beaten clay path. Once he slipped past the juniper barely his own height at the base of the trail, his eyes went toward the south path.

A deep breath followed when he saw the distant figure of Syodor, still more than a kay away on the lower part of the south path. Cerryl stepped up his pace, but slowly, so that the water wouldn't slosh out of the bucket.

"Uncle Syodor's on the bottom of the south path now," he announced as he stepped into the house.

"Cerryl . . . you took a time. Be not good woolgathering out in the twilight. The demons abide then."

"I am sorry, Aunt Nall," he said dutifully, lugging the pail across the room to the hearth.

Without looking at Cerryl, she checked the biscuits in the baking tin before replacing the tin sheet that served as a cover. "Bein' sorry like as not save you from bein' carried off."

"I got back before full dark."

"See as you do." She lifted the bucket and poured water into the gray crockery pitcher, then set the bucket on the floor to the right of the hearth.

"Put the pitcher on the table."

Cerryl carried the pitcher from the worktable to the eating table.

Behind him, Nall lifted the lid on the cookpot, stirring the heavy soup with the long-handled wooden spoon.

"Yes, Aunt Nall." Cerryl glanced at the corner where he had been sitting before he'd gotten the water. Then he waited.

Shortly, the heavyset woman turned as the door squeaked.

"Evening, woman." The one-eyed and gray-haired man set the heavy iron hammer on the rough, one-plank table inside the door and the patched canvas pack beside the table on the floor with a thud. Dust puffed from the fabric, settling slowly toward the polished floor stones that had come from an abandoned grinding mill.

"How was the day?" Nall replaced the tin cover on the ancient iron cookpot and stepped away from the hearth composed of battered yellow and brown bricks.

"Better since I'm seeing you." Syodor laughed, moving toward his consort. He hugged Nall, the gnarled and stubby fingers of his hands meeting for a moment before releasing her.

"Supper be a-waiting. The day?" Nall smiled, then bent and swung the iron arm and the cook pot back out over the coals, ignoring the squeal of the ancient iron swivel bracket.

"The day be fine. One bit of malachite, looks to be solid, and mayhap Gister will pay a copper for it. A fine pendant it would make for a lady, ground and polished."

"Aye, and he'll cut it and wrap it in two silvers and then sell it for a gold." Nall checked the biscuit tin once more. "Best you wash up."

"Wash up . . . that be all you think of, woman?"

"After all your grubbing through tailings and tunnels? Should I be thinking of aught else?"

Syodor turned and walked toward the pitcher and wash table in the corner on the far side of the room from the hearth.

"You as well, Cerryl."

"Right, lad," added Syodor with a grin.

Cerryl waited for Syodor, then washed his own hands with the heavy fat-and-ash soap, rinsing them with the clean water from the pitcher.

His hands still damp, Cerryl sat down on the bench across from Syodor, his left side to the fire.

Syodor lifted the crockery mug. "What have you done here?"

"Little enough," said Nall. "Arelta had some of the bitter brew. She said it wouldn't last. So I brought it home."

"Poor enough to take the brewer's youngest daughter's charity, are we?"

"Should I have let her pour it out?"

"No. Waste be worse than charity." Syodor laughed, not quite harshly.

"Don't be so hard on yourself," Nall said softly, slipping a pair of biscuits from the tin onto the chipped earthenware. "All know you work hard."

"Much good it did me when they closed the mines."

"It did you good. Who else has a patent to grub the tailings?"

Syodor shrugged, then grinned. "No man has a better consort. No man."

"You'll not be turning my head, either." Nall set the large tin bowl filled with steaming root stew before Syodor, then turned back to the cookpot and filled a smaller bowl with the wooden ladle. "Cerryl, here you go. You want more, let me know."

"Thank you, Aunt Nall." Cerryl offered a smile.

"No brew for you, thanks or no," Nall replied with her own knowing smile. She took the smallest of the tin bowls and filled it, setting it on the table. Then she slipped onto the bench beside Cerryl.

Cerryl took the biscuit and nibbled one corner, then took a mouthful of stew with the wooden spoon he'd carved himself. Another corner of biscuit followed the stew.

"Hot . . . and filling. Brew's not too bitter, either." Syodor smiled at Nall.

"Been a long day for you. Some brew might set well." Nall smiled. "There's enough for a night or two more."

"You be not having any, I'd wager."

"Not to my taste."

Though Nall smiled, Cerryl could sense the lie, the same kind of lie Nall always told when she gave something special to him or to Syodor and took none herself.

"Dylert, he said he needs a boy at the mill," Syodor said slowly to Nall, but his eyes crossed the table to where Cerryl sat on the bench beside her. "Wants a serious boy. Cerryl's serious enough. That be certain, I told him."

"Sawmill be a dangerous place for a boy," answered Nall.

"Mines were a dangerous place for a boy," Syodor said. "I was younger than Cerryl is, back then."

"You were stronger," Nall pointed out.

"I'm stronger than I look," Cerryl said quietly. His gray eyes flashed, almost like a jungle cat's, with a light of their own.

"Be no doubt of that, lad. You look like a strong wind would carry you all the way to Lydiar."

"He's not even half-grown," protested Nall.

"Got to grow up sometime. We'll not be here till the death of chaos." The former miner looked intently at his consort.

"Syodor! No talk like such around the boy." Nall made the sign of looped order.

"Chaos is, Nall." Syodor took a deep breath. "I see it all the time. Watch the tunnels crumble. Watch the folks sneak around mumbling about who courts darkness. Or who knows which white mage."

Cerryl's eyes slipped toward his pallet and the hidden book he could not read.

"You know, Cerryl, the mines here, they're older than places like Fairhaven . . ."

Nall's mouth tightened, but she only cleared her throat, if loudly.

"Older than the trees on the hills," Syodor added quickly. "When my grandda was a boy, the duke sent folk here, and they mined the old tailings piles, and then they dumped all the leftovers and the slag from their furnaces into the piles we got now."

"Furnaces?" asked Cerryl, mumbling through the last of his second biscuit. "What happened to them?"

"The duke took the iron fixings back, and the bricks, well . . ." The gnarled man laughed. "See the hearth—that's got some of the bricks. So's the west wall. Good bricks they were, 'cept some broke easy 'cause they got too hot in the furnaces."

"Bricks, they got too hot?" asked the youth.

"Anything can get too hot, if there's enough fire or chaos put to it. Too much chaos can break anything."

"Anyone, too," added Nall quietly.

"That, too." Syodor sipped the last of the brew from his mug. "Ah

...miss this the most from the days when I had two coppers a day from the mines. Now what have I . . . a patent to grub that any new duke can say be worthless."

Nall nodded in the dimness of harvest twilight.

"Shandreth, I saw him this morning," Syodor said after a time. "Said he'd be needing hands for the vines in an eight-day. Said you were one of the best, Nall."

"Two coppers for all that work?" she asked.

"Three, he said." Syodor laughed. "I told him four, and he said you were worth four, but not a copper more, or he'd be coinless 'fore the grapes were pressed."

"Four . . . that be a help, and I could put it away for the cold times."

"Aye . . . the cold times always come." Syodor glanced at Cerryl, his jaw set and his face bleak. "Remember that, lad. There always be the cold times."

For some reason, Cerryl shivered at the words.

"These be not the cold times, lad." Syodor forced a smile. "Warm it is here, and with a good meal in our bellies."

Cerryl offered his own forced smile.

IV

Cerryl glanced over his shoulder, down the long, if gentle, incline toward the road that led from Hrisbarg.

Syodor pointed. "Over the hill, another three kays or so, the road joins the wizards' road. A great road that be, if paved with too many souls."

"Paved with souls?"

"Those displeasing the wizards built the great highway." Syodor grunted.

Cerryl studied the distant clay road again, nearly a kay back from where he trudged on the narrower road up the slope to the sawmill. To the right of the road was a gulch, filled with low willows and brush, in which ran a stream, burbling in the quiet of midday. Puffs of whitish dust rose with each step of Cerryl's bare feet and with each step of Syodor's boots.

"How much longer?" asked the youth, looking ahead. The roofs of the mill buildings seemed another kay away—or farther. A trickle of sweat ran down the side of his face, and he wiped it away absently.

"Less than a kay. Almost there, lad." Syodor smiled. "This be best for you. Little enough Nall and I can offer. Be no telling when this duke will come and take my patent, and open the mines one more time, and leave us with naught. Too old, they'd be saying I am, to be a proper miner." He snorted softly. "Too old . . ."

Cerryl nodded, sensing the strange mixture of lies and truth in Syodor's statement, knowing that Syodor was truthful in all that he said, but deceitful in some larger sense. So Cerryl concentrated on putting one foot in front of the other.

"Stand aside." Syodor pointed toward the oncoming horse team and the wagon, then touched Cerryl's shoulder. "Back."

Cerryl stepped onto the browning grass on the shoulder of the road to the sawmill and lowered the faded and patched canvas sack to the ground. His feet hurt, but he did not sit down.

His gray eyes fixed on the four horses. Though each was a different color, all were huge, far bigger than those ridden by the duke's outriders or the white mounts favored by the lancers of Fairhaven. He'd seen the white lancers only once. When he'd gone to Howlett right after spring planting with Syodor and Nall, a company had ridden through, not looking to the right or left, every lancer silent.

The wagon driver grinned as he passed, and waved to Syodor. "Good day, grubber!"

"Good day to you, Rinfur!" Syodar waved back.

The long and broad wagon was piled high with planks and timbers, set between the wagon sides and roped down, and on the side board was a circular emblem with a jagged circular gray sawmill blade biting into a brown log. Under the oval of the design were symbols. Cerryl's lips tightened as his eyes ran over the symbols—the letters he could not read.

He stood there long after the wagon had passed, the sun pressing down on him through the cloudless green-blue sky.

"Cerryl, lad? It be but a short walk now." Syodor's voice was gentle.

"I'm fine, Uncle." Cerryl lifted his pack and stepped back on the road, ignoring the remnants of the fine white dust that drifted around them in the still hot air.

A fly buzzed past, then circled Cerryl. He looked hard at the insect, and it wobbled away. As he and Syodor neared the flat below the hillcrest, Cerryl's eyes darted ahead. The sawmill consisted of three buildings—the mill itself and two barnlike structures. Above the mill on the hillside were a house, what looked to be a stable, and a smaller structure.

The mill was of old gray stones and sat beside a stone dam and a millrace. The waterwheel was easily four times Cerryl's height but stood idle.

"Slow at harvest time," Syodor said, gesturing at the dry stone channel of the millrace below the wheel. "Folks don't think about building or fixing now."

The road they walked continued uphill and past the millrace, where it intersected a stone-paved lane that extended perhaps a hundred cubits from the open sliding door in the middle of the side of the mill facing the two lumber barns. Beyond the stone pavement, the road narrowed to a lane winding past the mill on the right and uphill toward a rambling long house, with a covered front porch. The wooden siding had been freshly oiled, and the house glistened in the midday sun.

An ox-drawn lumber cart was drawn up to the mill door, and a man taller than Syodor was checking the yoke.

"Brental?" asked Syodor.

The young red-bearded man turned from the oxen and glanced at the two dusty figures for a moment, then said, "Syodor? You'd be wanting Dylert?"

"The same."

"I'll be getting him for you, once I get the cart out of the door." Brental lifted the goad, but did not touch either ox, and called, "Gee-ahh!"

The oxen started forward, slowly pulling the heavy but empty log cart away from the open sliding door in the south side of the mill. Cerryl watched as the cart rumbled along onto the stone causeway across the intersection with the road.

Once the cart was clear of the intersection, Brental gestured with the goad and said mildly, "Ahh . . ."

The oxen obediently stopped, and Brental walked past Syodor and Cerryl, giving them a nod, and into the mill.

Cerryl stood, shifting his weight from one bare foot to another, his sack by his feet, ignoring the dampness of his sweaty shirt.

Syodor cleared his throat. "Dylert . . . he runs a good mill." After a moment, he said again, "A good mill. A good man."

Cerryl nodded, waiting.

Shortly, an older and taller man, taller even than Brental, over four cubits in height, his brown shirt and trousers streaked with whitish sawdust, stepped through the open sliding door of the mill.

"Syodor, Brental said you were here to see me." A broad smile crossed the man's face. "I have no coins, not until after harvest."

"I be not selling today," Syodor said slowly. He cleared his throat, then continued. "Ser Dylert, you said you wanted a boy—a serious boy." After a pause, he added, "Cerryl's serious."

"That I did say." Dylert fingered his trimmed, white-streaked black beard, his eyes on Cerryl. "And you need not 'ser' me, Syodor, not as one honest wight to another."

Syodor nodded.

Cerryl glanced up at the tall Dylert and met his scrutiny, not challenging the millmaster, but not looking away.

"Harvest time, it is now," suggested Dylert. "The mill is quiet, and few coins flow for timber and planks."

"That it is," agreed Syodor. "A good time for a boy to learn."

Dylert smiled. "A peddler you should have been, Syodor, not a miner and a grubber. Not with your silver tongue."

"You're too kind, mill master. Cerryl's a good boy."

"He is slight, Syodar, but he looks healthy. You and Nall took him as your own, Dyella says."

"We did." Syodor smiled. "Not a regret for that." He shrugged. "Time now for him to start on his own. No place to go in the mines. Not these days."

"True as a pole pine," answered Dylert. "No place for anyone in the mines, even back when the duke reopened them." He shook his head. "Folks say they're no place these days, with what's there." The millmaster looked hard at Syodor.

"Could be," admitted the one-eyed miner. "Cerryl'd do better here."

The boy looked at Syodor, catching his uncle's uneasiness. The mines had seemed fine to him, except for those places that anyone with sense had to avoid. Why were Dylert and Syodor talking as though anything connected to the mines happened to be dangerous?

"I did say I needed a mill boy." Dylert cleared his throat. "You sure about this, Syodor?"

"He be much better here, ser Dylert. Nall and me, we did the best we could. Now . . ." The miner shrugged apologetically.

"You think I'd do right by him, Syodor."

"Better 'n aught else I know."

"That's a heavy burden, Syodor." Dylert offered a wry smile before turning his eyes back to Cerryl. "Even for a boy, mill work is hard." Dylert paused.

After a moment, understanding that an answer was required, Cerryl replied, "I can work hard, ser."

"Mill work be dirty, too. You'd be cleaning out the sawpits, and the gearing. The blades, too. Not sharpening. I do that," Dylert said quickly. "And probably other chores. Feed the chickens, cart water—most things that need doing. Take messages." Dylert looked from Cerryl to Syodor. "Can he listen and understand?"

"Never had to tell Cerryl anything twice, ser Dylert."

Dylert nodded. "Good words from your uncle, boy. He may have a golden tongue, but his word is good. Some ways, that be all a man has."

Cerryl thought his uncle might say something, but Syodor gave the smallest of headshakes.

"Half-copper an eight-day to start. After a season we'll see. Get your meals with us." Dylert laughed and looked at Cerryl. "Dyella's cooking be worth more than your pay." The millmaster turned to Syodor. "You certain, masterminer?"

"Aye, as sure as I can be."

"It be done, then," Dylert said.

Syodor bent and gave Cerryl a quick hug. "Take care, lad. Dylert be a good man. Listen to him. Your aunt and I . . . we be seeing you when we can."

Cerryl swallowed, trying to keep his eyes from tearing, trying to understand why he felt Syodor's last words were somehow wrong. Before he was quite back in control, Syodor had released him and was walking briskly down the lane away from the mill, the sun on his back.

Cerryl felt as though he watched his uncle from a distance, even though Syodor was still less than a dozen cubits away. His lips tightened, but he watched, his face impassive.

For a time, neither Cerryl or Dylert spoke—not until Syodor's figure vanished over the nearer hillcrest.

Then the millmaster cleared his throat.

Cerryl turned, waiting, still holding on to the sack that contained all that was his.

"Your uncle, he was near right. We've got time to set you up." Dylert fingered his beard once more, then looked down to Cerryl's bare feet. "Need some shoes, boy, around here. Let's go up to the house and see what we got. Might have an old pair of boots." Dylert started up the lane to the freshly oiled house with the wide front porch.

For a moment, turning to follow the millmaster, Cerryl had to squint to shut out the brightness of the early afternoon sun.

Dylert waited at the top of the three stone steps to the porch, then pointed to the bench beside the door. "Just wait here, boy."

Cerryl sat on the bench, letting the sack rest on the wide planks of the porch, glad to be out of the sun. Not more than fifty cubits to the south, while occasionally *brawkking*, yellow-feathered chickens pecked the ground around a small and low chicken house.

Cerryl could feel his eyes closing.

"Boy?"

He jerked away and looked up at Dylert. "Yes, ser?"

"Long walk, was it not?"

"We left well before dawn."

"I'd imagine so." The millmaster extended a pair of boots, brown and scarred. "You be trying these."

"Yes, ser. Thank you, ser." Cerryl slipped on the worn leather boots, one after the other, wiggling his toes inside.

"Those were Hurior's 'fore he left. They fit?"

"Yes, ser. I think so, ser."

"Good. One problem less."

A dark-haired girl peered from where she stood in the doorway over at Cerryl. She wore a tan short-sleeved shirt and matching trousers, with a wide leather belt and boots that matched the sandals.

"Erhana, this be Cerryl, the new mill boy." Dylert laughed. "Don't be distracting him while he works."

Erhana stepped onto the porch, and Cerryl could see that she was taller than he was, and possibly older. She had her father's brown eyes and square chin, but dark brown hair, cut evenly at shoulder length. "He's thin."

"Your mother's cooking will help that."

"He'll still be thin," prophesied Erhana.

"Maybe so," said Dylert. "You can talk at supper. I need to get him settled and show him the mill."

"Yes, Papa." Erhana slipped back into the house.

Dylert led Cerryl back down to the nearest of the lumber barns to the west—or uphill—side, where three doors had been cut into the siding and rough-framed with half-planks. "These are the hands' room. The far one—that's Rinfur's."

Cerryl nodded.

"You know Rinfur?"

"No, ser. Uncle . . . Syodor . . . offered him a good day. He was driving the wagon."

"Your uncle said you listened." Dylert pointed to the second door. "That's Viental's." Dylert grinned. "You know him?"

"No, ser."

"He's the one does stone work and helps with the burdens. You'll know Viental when you see him. Let him go off and help his sister with the harvest. He'll be back in an eight-day. Now," continued the millmaster, opening the door nearest the mill, "this be yours."

Cerryl glanced around the bare room, scarcely more than four cubits on a side, and containing little more than a pallet, a short three-legged stool, and three shelves on the wall to the right with an open cubicle under them on the wall.

The bottom of the window beside the door was level with Cerryl's chin and a cubit high and half a cubit wide. It had neither shutters nor a canvas rollshade, just a door on two simple iron strap hinges with a swing bolt on the inside.

"Nothing fancy, but it be all yours. Put your stuff in the cubby there, boy, and I'll show you around the mill. You need to know where everything is."

Cerryl stepped inside and slowly eased the sack into the cubby, his eyes going to the bare pallet on the plank platform.

"Be sending down some blankets for you after supper. Mayhap have some heavy trews, too. Yours are a shade frail for mill work."

Cerryl swallowed, then swallowed again. "Yes, ser."

"Don't be a-worrying, boy. You work for me, and I'll see you're fitted proper. 'Sides, I owe your uncle. Little enough I can do. He be a proud man."

Cerryl kept his face expressionless.

"Not so he'd talk of it, but when he was the masterminer—that was years back, mind you—he was the one. Insisted that the timbers be right, and no shaving on their bearing width. Saved many a miner, I'd wager. Saved the mill, too." Dylert shrugged. "I offered him a share here. He'd have none of it." The millmaster looked at the youth. "Be ready to see the mill?"

"Yes, ser."

"Said, he did, that someone had to look after the mines, old or not, and that was his duty." Dylert led Cerryl around the back corner of the lumber barn and toward the mill.

A brief shadow crossed the hillside. Cerryl glanced up, but the small cloud passed the eye of the sun, and he had to look away quickly as the light flooded back.

Cerryl glanced toward the second lumber barn. The oxen stood placidly, still yoked in place, without their driver.

They stepped through the wide door to the mill. The entire mill was floored with smoothed stone, worn in places, cracked in others, but recently swept. An aisle of sorts—wide enough for the oxen and lumber cart—led to the far wall, where a raised brick-based platform stood.

Dylert gestured to the racks on either side of the cleared space. "Holding racks. Be where we sort the planks and timbers after cutting. Use some of the racks for special cuts. Special cuts—that's for the cabinet makers or the finish carpenters. Takes special work; charge 'em special, too."

Cerryl waited.

"There be the brooms. When the blade's cutting, you sweep, unless I tell you otherwise. Have to keep the mill clean. You know how fast sawdust burns? Goes like cammabark—faster maybe. Poof! Helps sometimes if'n you dip the end of the broom in water—specially if we're cutting the hardwoods. The dust there, it be specially fine." Dylert strode toward the platform.

Cerryl followed.

"This be the main blade, boy." The dark-bearded man pointed to the circle of dark iron. "Don't you be touching it. Or the brake here, either." His hand went to an iron lever.

Cerryl looked at the iron blade, barely managing to repress a shiver at the deep blackness within the iron that almost felt as though it would burn his hands. "No, ser."

"Good. Now . . . see . . . this drops the gear off the track, so the blade stops even if the mill turns. Up there, that's the water gate. Most times, the blade's on gear track when the gate opens. That way, we fret less about breaking the gears." Dylert fingered his beard. "Cost my father more coins to have the drop gear put in, but it's better when a house has two doors. That's what he said, and it's saved me a blade or two along the way—and blades, they're dear. Black iron, you'd best know."

Cerryl nodded. "That's hard iron?"

"The hardest. Not many smiths as can forge it, even with a black mage at their elbow." He laughed harshly. "Good smith and a black mage—few of either, these days, or any times."

Cerryl managed not to frown. Why couldn't white mages help a smith? Why did it have to be black mages?

"Here . . . the entrance to the sawpit. You'll be cleaning that." Dylert frowned. His voice hardened. "You never go under the blade less the water gate's closed and the drop gear's open. Stay away from the blade even so. You understand that?"

"Yes, ser."

"No one but me tells you to clean the pit. Understand? Not Rinfur, not Brental, not Viental. No one but me. You understand?"

The gray-eyed boy nodded.

"First time, I'll show you how. Not today." Dylert smiled. "Be taking you a mite to get used to us. Let's go to the barns." He turned and started toward the big door. "Good days, we open the swing windows on the west. More light."

Cerryl's eyes went to the iron blade, and he shivered. Black iron? Why did it feel so . . . dangerous? Then he turned and followed Dylert out of the mill and toward the first of the two barns.

Dylert slid back the door, the same kind as the main mill door, and stepped inside into the middle of an aisle between racks of wood that stretched the length of the barn. "Some mills—like in Hydlen—they just put a roof over their cuts and say that's enough. Lucky if the mill lasts from father to son. You want wood to last . . . then you have to season it right—lots of air, but you don't let it get too hot or too cold. Our cuts are the best. Last season, a mastercrafter sent a wagon all the way from Jellico for my black oak. Something for the viscount . . . suppose that's all he does now that Fairhaven . . ." Dylert shook his head. "There I go, woolgathering again."

Cerryl wanted the mill master to keep talking, and he nodded, without speaking, as Dylert continued.

"This first barn here. See—it's smaller. Mostly hardwoods—oak, lorken, maple. Some fruitwoods, like cherry and walnut and pearapple, when we can get it. Crafters, cabinet makers—they're the ones who use it—and the builders who work for the duke or the white wizards. Fairhaven—they want a lot of white oak." Dylert walked over to one of the racks on the left of the aisle. "See. You can touch it."

Cerryl let his fingers brush the wood, white, but with a trace of yellow or gold that would darken with age, like the chest Syodar and Nall shared. The white oak felt cool to his touch, reassuring, unlike the black iron of the saw blade.

"People think there's no difference between lorken and black oak." The millmaster shook his head. "Not seen a blade struggle through lorken, they haven't. Here." He pointed to a stack of thin, nearly black planks, no more than a span wide and three cubits long. "Pick up the top one."

Cerryl had to strain for a moment. "It be heavy." The dark wood felt warm to his touch, smooth as polished silver, yet prickly beneath the patina, and he quickly eased it back onto the pile.

"That's lorken. Not more than a handful of crafters can handle it. One big lorken log, and even the keenest mill blade needs sharpening. Got some logs on the back racks, seasoning till a buyer comes. No sense in blunting a blade."

Dylert led Cerryl to the next set of racks, also bearing dark narrow planks. "Lift one of those."

Cerryl complied. "Not so heavy."

"What else?" prompted Dylert.

Cerryl replaced the plank. "I don't think it be quite so dark, and it seems rougher."

Dylert nodded. "Black oak. It be hard, not so hard as lorken, not so heavy, not so smooth." He snorted. "And folks say there be no difference."

Cerryl nodded. The dark oak hadn't seemed so warm to the touch, either.

The tall man walked toward the back of the barn. "Sometimes we get virgin logs, the big ones. If I've the time, I'll crosscut a section. Takes a different blade, and a lot of care. But some of the cabinet makers like bigger wood sections. Can charge them as much as a silver a section that way." He wiped his forehead. "Work, though. A lot of work, and the sections are brittle—break just like that if you drop 'em. Only do a few a year."

Cerryl hurried to keep up with Dylert's long stride.

"A lot of guessing if you be a millmaster . . . keep the wide planks back here. Charge more for them, but a lot of folks rather'd use more of the narrower cuts . . ."

The gray-eyed youth found himself struggling to take in all the words as Dylert turned at the rear wall and walked back toward the door.

"Folks always want some lumber. Some years, we couldn't cut and season enough . . . hate to let go of green wood . . . even if you charge less and it splits, folks don't forget . . ."

As soon as Cerryl stepped into the sunlight, Dylert shut the barn door and strode quickly toward the second barn.

Again, the youth had to hurry to catch up.

"This barn—it's where we put the rougher cuts and the heavier timbers used for bigger buildings. Not that simple, but you'll learn." The millmaster opened the door and stepped inside, between another set of racks.

Cerryl followed, his eyes adjusting to the dimness and taking in that the racks in the larger barn seemed fuller.

"The racks on the right—they're for planks, smaller timbers, that aren't as good as those in the first barn. On the left here . . ."

Cerryl squinted, concentrating on every word, even though his stomach growled, and sweat continued to ooze down his back.

After going through all the racks in the second barn, and then escorting Cerryl back out onto the stone causeway that connected both barns and the mill, Dylert grinned. "Lucky I'd be if half of that stuck in your head, young fellow. But you'll learn. Yes, you will."

Cerryl tried to look attentive.

Dylert fingered his beard. "Now . . . for the house."

Cerryl could feel the weight of the new boots and his feet dragging as he followed Dylert back up the lane to the house, up the three steps that felt even steeper, and to the door in the middle of the porch.

Dylert gestured, and Cerryl stepped inside. The kitchen ran most of the length of the space behind the front porch. At the left end of the kitchen was a hearth—of yellow bricks—that held two separate niches for fires and three iron oven doors for baking. Out from the hearth area were two large worktables, and two large cabinets were against the side wall nearest the hearth. A narrow many-drawered chest stood between the cabinets.

At the right end of the kitchen was a long trestle table with a bench on each side and a straight-backed chair at each end.

A woman looked up from a large wooden bowl on the worktable and smiled, dipping her hands in the wash bucket, then wiping them on a gray rag. Her brown hair was piled behind her head in a bun, from which wisps escaped in every direction.

"Dyella, this be Cerryl, the young fellow raised by his uncle Syodor you heard me talk of." Dylert patted Cerryl on the shoulder. "Dyella, she cooks so well you'd think I'd be twice my size."

"How could that be?" answered the thin-faced and black-eyed woman. "Never be said that you stopped long enough for the food to settle." She glanced at Cerryl. "White, he is. You've run his legs off, Dylert, and he's scarce arrived." She lifted a knife and turned toward one of the long tables. When she turned back to Cerryl, she handed him a thick chunk of bread. "Here. Eat it, so Dylert doesn't have to scrape you off the planks, boy."

"Thank you, lady."

"No lady. I be Dyella, first, last, and always."

"Thank you, Dyella."

"Polite young fellow." Dyella looked at Dylert. "Blankets."

"Oh . . ." Dylert nodded and stepped out of the long kitchen.

Cerryl ate the bread slowly, feeling strength returning, his hearing sharpening.

"Mind you, don't try to keep up with Dylert. None I know can. Just do your best, boy, and that'll be better than most. More bread?"

"Ah . . ."

"Don't be shy. You walked all the way from the mines, and I'd wager not a morsel to eat since dawn." Dyella thrust another chunk at him. "Now . . . why don't you eat it and wait on the porch? Dylert's fetching your blankets, and supper be needing my hand."

"Thank you."

Dyella smiled as she held the door.

Cerryl sat on the bench and ate, slowly, trying to digest both the bread and the day.

V

A pair of pine logs lay on the three-axled timber wagon. The six draft horses, their breath like steam in the chill afternoon, stood facing south. The ox-drawn log cart faced north, toward the open mill door. The bed of the log cart was nearly a cubit lower than that of the timber wagon.

Broom in hand, Cerryl stepped to the side of the mill, well away from the door, and back far enough that he would not be in the way of drovers or the loaders.

"The first log, Viental," said Brental.

"First it be." Viental half-dragged, half-lifted one end of the huge log, its girth more than two cubits, and swung the end from the timber wagon onto the ox-drawn log cart. Then he walked to the front end of the wagon, where he and Brental lifted the weight-bearing end and struggled to ease it onto the cart.

The log cart groaned as the full weight of the pine log came to rest on it. Cerryl watched the rear axle bow ever so slightly, a stress that less-fine eyes and senses would not have discerned.

Brental slipped the log wedges in place on the side closest to Cerryl, knocking them solid with his long-handled hammer. Then he walked around the oxen and, standing where the beds of the cart and wagon nearly joined, placed the forward wedge. The redhead had to walk around the cart again to place the rear wedge.

Viental released his hold on the log.

Brental reclaimed his goad. "Ge-ahh!"

The log cart creaked forward and into the mill, and Cerryl stepped back into the doorway to try to finish getting the sawdust out of the door tracks before Brental brought the cart back.

Viental half-shrugged, half-flexed his broad shoulders, swinging his arms. "Heavy, that one." He grinned at Cerryl, yellow teeth flared out of the ginger beard braided below. "Ever think you could lift that, mill boy?"

Cerryl shook his head.

"Best you know that. Not one in a score dozen be lifting as I do."

"Not one in score of scores as bald, either," called the lumber wagon driver from where he stood beside the lead horse.

"Rinfur . . . I don't see you handling the logs."

"I don't see you handling the teams. You have to be smarter than the horses."

"Someday I be strangling you with that tongue."

The teamster grinned. "Not while I run faster and ride better."

Viental shrugged, then grinned. "And talk longer."

"Go see your sister," suggested Rinfur amiably. "You do whenever you feel like it anyway."

"So? No one else lifts as I do."

Cerryl and Rinfur exchanged glances. Viental disappeared for days on end, always returning with the explanation that he had had to help his sister. Dylert refused to pay for the missing time but said nothing.

"That right? Even the mill boy knows that. Right, Cerryl."

"No one lifts like you do," Cerryl agreed.

"See?"

Rinfur continued checking the harnesses.

Cerryl's eyes flicked up to the house and then to the trees beyond, gray-leaved, almost brooding under the hazy clouds and waiting for winter and the snows and cold rains. A gust of wind stirred the leaves that had fallen, lifting a handful, then dropping them.

The mill boy frowned. Why did the trees drop but half their leaves every fall? No one had been able to tell him—just, "That be the way it is, boy. Always been so."

There was too much that had always been so.

With a gust of wind, Cerryl shivered, not because of the chill but in anticipation of the cold rain he felt would fall before night. His eyes went uphill once more.

Behind the house, Erhana dipped a bucket into the well. Cerryl smiled. Close up, after all the practice with the scraps of mirrors and the flat sheets of water, he could do without either and catch glimpses of people just beyond his sight.

He watched, first with his senses, then with his eyes, as Erhana carried a bucket of water from the well up the steps and onto the porch, each step precise.

"Better start sweeping," said Viental. "Dylert be coming from the second barn."

Cerryl picked up the broom.

VI

Clang! Clang!

At the first bell, Cerryl peered out from the blankets, shivering. His breath was a white cloud that billowed into the air.

"Darkness," he murmured, trying not to move, not to let any of the cold air slip inside his blankets. There were no cracks in the heavy planked walls; the door fit snugly; and the window door was shut tightly—frozen shut, Cerryl suspected. But his cubby room had no hearth, not even a warming pan, though Dylert had sent him back down to bed the night before with two fire-warmed bricks.

Clang!

Cerryl clambered out from the blankets and began to shiver. His feet were cold and stiff as he wedged them, one by one, into his boots. Then he struggled into the patched canvas-and-leather jacket Nall had made for him. It was getting harder to tie shut. Had he grown that much over the fall and early winter?

He lifted the two warming bricks—cold as ice—then tucked them under one arm. He opened his door, stepped outside, and shut it quickly, trying to keep the little heat in the room from escaping. Beside the path that led across to the mill and then up to the house the snow was more than knee deep, sparkling despite the lack of direct light in the moments before dawn.

The smoke from the house's kitchen chimney was a thick white plume that climbed through the still air into the clear dark green-blue sky of predawn. A smaller plume escaped from the chimney at the far end of the house, the one Cerryl thought was the hearth for the mill-master's bedchamber.

One foot skidded on the packed snow of the path, and Cerryl staggered, trying not to let the bricks slip from under his arm as he tried to catch his balance. He walked uphill carefully, eyes on the slick and icy surface, hands thrust inside the bottom of his jacket. Even the porch steps were slick, with a thin coating of the more recent snowflakes over the ice.

Cerryl stamped his boots on the porch planks, trying to knock off all the snow, then reached for the boot brush. He could feel his toes jammed against the ends of the boots. He needed new boots, but the nine coppers he had saved wouldn't pay for them.

Bundled in a heavy leather jacket and leather trousers, Erhana opened the door. "Come on! Breakfast is ready, and you've a lot to do, Da says."

Cerryl stepped into the kitchen, letting Erhana close the door. For a moment, he stood there, letting the warmth fill him. Then he walked to the hearth and set the bricks by those brought up by Rinfur. "Thank you," he said, nodding toward Dyella.

"Little enough," answered the millmaster's consort with a smile. "This be going on, and you all sleep in the kitchen."

Cerryl slipped onto the middle of the bench, with Rinfur on his left. Viental, once more, had left to see his "sister." Dylert sat at the end of the table, eating his gruel. On his right sat Erhana, still wrapped in her leather jacket.

Dyella ladled the steaming gruel into the chipped bowl in front of Cerryl. "Seen your uncle recently? Before the snow, I be meaning," she asked pleasantly. "Or your aunt?"

"Aunt Nall, she stopped by coming back from Shandreth's vineyard last fall." Cerryl took a sip of water from the cracked cup that was his. "I saw Uncle Syodor an eight-day ago, before the snows started. He'd been helping Zylerant raise a barn." He quickly swallowed some more of the gruel, welcoming the warmth, and took a small bite of the muffin beside his bowl. He held the muffin for a moment, enjoying its warmth on his cold fingers.

"They see you a lot more regular than some," observed Dyella, adding another ladle of the hot gruel to Cerryl's bowl.

"They've been good to me," said Cerryl. "Good as they could be." He ignored the glance from Dylert to Erhana, as well as Dyella's raised eyebrows as she glanced at the millmaster. Instead, he concentrated on eating, and before he could finish the last of the porridge in the bowl, Dyella had added more.

"You be needing this today. No sense in wasting it. Forgot Viental was gone."

"Thank you, Dyella." Cerryl smiled.

Rinfur cleared his throat. "I best be checking the horses, ser. Extra grain, you think?"

"Half cup, no more," said Dylert. "No telling when I can get another barrel. Not in this weather. Can't hardly get to the road, except with the sled, and that's not much for carrying."

"Half cup each, that be it." The teamster stood, stretched, then fastened his jacket and tromped out of the kitchen and onto the porch.

Erhana, despite the heavy coat, shivered as the chill air washed over her. "Cold out there."

"Be thankful you only have to fetch water, child," said Dyella.

"I have to get more?"

"I have to cook, if you want to eat," pointed out her mother.

"Mother . . ."

Cerryl smothered a grin by looking down at his bowl.

"Erhana—not another word."

Cerryl slowly ate the second bowl of hot gruel, saving the rest of the muffin, but he finished the last bite of the warm muffin all too soon.

"Cerryl?" said Dylert.

"Yes, ser?"

"I was going to have you clean the pit today, seeing as things are slow." He coughed. "Dyella, though, she pointed out how the roof of the chicken shed is sagging, and my bones tell me we might yet see more snow. I'd like you to clear that afore you come down to the mill."

"Yes, ser."

"Got an old pair of mitts." Dylert glanced toward the narrow table by the door to the porch. "Need those, you will, lest your fingers chill." He coughed. "Best you keep them till the weather warms."

"Thank you, ser." Cerryl nodded and smiled, trying to show that he appreciated the gesture. "Thank you."

"Can't have you getting frozen hands. Darkness, this been a cold winter. Coldest in years."

"Coldest I can recall," added Dyella.

Cerryl eased off the bench and nodded to Dylert and then Dyella. "Thank you. The porridge was good."

"Stick to your bones," Dyella said.

After slipping the mitts on and easing out the door onto the porch, Cerryl took the slick steps carefully. Once his boots were on the packed snow of the path, he glanced at the mill. A thick plume of smoke billowed from the chimney.

At least the mill would be warmer than his cubby. He trudged toward the chicken shed, conscious of how much warmer his hands were in the heavy leather mitts, mitts big enough for a grown man.

Before he reached the chicken shed, his toes were cold, jammed as they were into his boots. The path went to the door of the chicken house, but the roof was slanted down to the left. Cerryl struggled from the path through the knee-deep snow around to the left side of the building, where he could reach the lower edge of the slanted roof.

The bottom edge was but chest high, and Cerryl stretched and used his right arm to sweep the snow clear—except the powdery stuff swirled into the air and came down on his face and hair, and sifted down the back of his jacket.

He brushed off his hair and face, then swept another heavy armful off the lower roof. More snow swirled around him and drifted down his neck, inside his jacket and shirt. Grimly, he swirled aside more snow, and more of the powder sifted around him, even getting into his nose and mouth.

He stepped back, all too conscious of cold dampness down his back and toes going numb, looking up at the snow beyond his reach.

"Here! Use this," said Brental, handing Cerryl a small timber—quarterspan by quarterspan—perhaps six cubits long.

"Thank you, Brental." Cerryl gratefully took the timber.

"No thanks. You be getting it done sooner this way. Da wants the sawpit cleaned later. Said he'd tell you, but Ma feared for the hens if'n the roof went." The redheaded young man grinned. "I'm off to clear the barn roof."

"Lucky you."

"When you're taller, you can help." Brental laughed. "Make sure you brush off that snow 'fore you go into the mill. It be getting warm there now, and you won't be wanting wet clothes."

Cerryl nodded. No . . . he wouldn't be wanting wet clothes. He took a firm grip on the end of the pine timber and began to sweep the rest of the snow off the chicken house roof.

VII

Cerryl lay on his back, the heavy coarse blankets up to his chin, looking up through the darkness at the wide planks overhead. He could sense, rather than see, the heavy timbers that rested on those planks—the end of the finish timber rack holding oak beams. Almost a dozen score were stacked above Cerryl, seasoning, waiting for a buyer.

Even in designing where his workers' rooms were, Dylert wasted nothing, not even barn space, since any storage where the rooms were would have been almost inaccessible. Cerryl frowned, thinking about the three men—his father, his uncle, and Dylert. One had failed and died; one had failed, but not died; and one had succeeded. Was it luck? Order? Or had chaos just struck down his father and crippled Uncle Syodor?

He recalled something Syodor had said to Nall—one night when they had thought Cerryl was sleeping—something about his father screaming he could have been High Wizard of Fairhaven had he only come from coins. Somehow, Cerryl didn't think that being High Wizard was something coins could purchase. Or had his father meant something else? Or had Syodor really recalled what his father had said?

Cerryl inhaled deeply, then exhaled slowly with no answers. His breath no longer steamed like hearth smoke, and the worst of winter had passed, or so he hoped. One eight-day had been so cold that both he and Rinfur had slept by the hearth in the millmaster's house. The gray-haired woman who tutored Erhana on her letters had not been to the mill in four or five eight-days.

It had taken Brental a two-stone black oak timber to break the ice in the well. Cerryl shivered at the memory, glad that only an eight-day had been that chill.

His eyes went to the board under the cubby, the one he'd spent eight-days loosening. Behind it was the book he'd brought, the one he still kept puzzling over when he could.

That, too, he could sense behind the wood, in a different way, with a faint white glow, not so reddish as a fire, but with the same hidden depths. The book held a key, that he knew, but how could he find it when he couldn't even read?

He sighed again, his eyes blank, fixed on the planks over his pallet.

VIII

A light but chill spring breeze blew through the open mill door, carrying the scent of damp earth and pearapple blossoms, and the hint of the words Dylert exchanged with a crafter in brown near the mill door.

Cerryl was on his knees, a relief to be off his feet, half under the fresh pine cuts rack, half-pushing, half-sweeping sawdust clear from underneath the lowest rack, using the side of the broom. He tried to ignore the itching in his nose and across his bare forearms, an itching that was worst around the pine sawdust.

"Cerryl!" called Dylert from the center aisle. "Where are you?"

"Yes, ser?" Cerryl straightened and stood, using his left hand on the rack to keep his balance. "I was cleaning out under the pine racks."

"Good." Dylert nodded as though he had personally ordered Cerryl to clean there. Beside him stood a burly man in brown, black-bearded with a dour look upon his face.

"There's a handcart in the second lumber barn. Use it to bring three dozen of the narrow rough floorboards from the second barn. The best ones we have there, mind you."

"Yes, ser." Cerryl set the broom carefully against the rack, watching Dylert.

The millmaster turned toward the man in brown. "What will you be needing for timber? We have . . ."

Cerryl eased himself away from the rack, walking as quickly as he could toward the mill door, each step sending a knife jab up his legs.

Outside was a cart, and between the traces was a brown mule, thin and bony. The mule's leads, and a halter rope as well, were tethered to the ring on the millrace side of the causeway.

Cerryl glanced up at the thickening clouds, then staggered and put his hand on the door frame to steady himself.

"Gee-ahh!" Brental guided the empty log cart back toward the mill, gesturing for the oxen to stop as they neared the mule cart.

With a pleasant smile plastered in place, Cerryl tried not to limp, but his toes and calves knotted with every step.

"Cerryl, what's the matter?" asked Brental.

"Nothing. I was sweeping under the pine racks. I'm stiff."

"Cerryl . . ." said the redhead firmly. "Sit down on the wall there. Next to the hitching post. Right now."

"Dylert said I was to use the handcart and bring him three dozen of the narrow rough floorboards from the second barn." Cerryl stopped beside the hitching post but did not sit.

"I'll help you if it comes to that. Sit down," Brental insisted.

Cerryl sat.

"Off with the boots."

The youth looked stolidly ahead, as if Brental had not spoken.

"Off . . ." Brental reached down and eased off one boot and then the other.

Cerryl did not look at either his feet or boots.

"Your toes are bloody." Brental shook his head. "Darkness . . . how long you been like this?"

Cerryl looked at the stones of the causeway, his face blank.

"Your feet are too small for those boots."

Cerryl kept looking down.

Brental sighed. "You get chaos blisters there, and you'll not work again. You'll not walk again."

"Your da said I'd not go unshod, not in a lumber mill." Cerryl managed to keep his jaw firm. "I almost have enough coppers for boots."

Brental laughed, not harshly but ruefully. "Lad . . . Cerryl . . . you'd not ask for anything, would you?"

Cerryl met Brental's gaze evenly. "I'd rather not."

"There are times to ask, and times not to. When you cannot walk, it be time to ask." The redhead shook his head. "I've got an old pair of boots. They'll do better than these. Wait here."

"The boards . . ." Cerryl glanced toward the mill door.

"All right. You get the boards—barefoot. I'll meet you here before you go back into the mill." Brental stood and gestured. "Rinfur! Watch the oxen for a moment."

Rinfur crossed the road. "Have to get the team."

"I'll be back in just a moment."

"Yes, master Brental." Rinfur shook his head.

Before Rinfur could see his feet, Cerryl stood and began to walk slowly, if more quickly than if he had worn boots, to the second lumber barn. The handcart was inside the door, and he pushed it to the right. The floorboards were on the low rack on the far right, and barefooted as he was, he was glad that he'd swept the second barn the day before.

He inspected each board, letting his eyes check it, and holding it a moment, trying to get a feel of the wood before stacking it on the handcart. Sort of a golden oak, somewhere between black oak and white, floor oak wasn't bad. Three lengths he set aside because the knots were obvious, and two because he could sense, somehow, that the boards were weak.

Once he had the golden oak floorboards stacked in four short piles, he pushed the cart slowly back out of the barn and along the cool stones of the causeway back toward the mill.

Brental was standing by the oxen by the time Cerryl and the handcart reached the mule cart beside the millrace wall.

"Da . . . he's still jawing with master Hesduff. Got some boots here, and a bucket of water. Sit back down."

Cerryl sank onto the wall.

Brental took a soaking rag and sponged away dust and blood. His eyes widened. "Darkness . . . what you did." The redhead shook his head. "Cerryl. You have to wash your feet several times a day, no matter what. Till these heal. You understand?" Brental's brown eyes bored into Cerryl. "And wash 'em right 'fore you go to bed."

"Yes, Brental."

"Cerryl?" called Dylert.

"You stay here." Brental stood and pushed the handcart toward the mill, calling out, "Cerryl got the boards. I was coming this way, so I thought I'd bring 'em for you."

"Good."

"Good day, master Hesduff," said Brental.

"Good day, young Brental. Hard to believe I'm a-looking up to you."

As the three talked inside the mill door, Cerryl looked at the fresh blood welling across his bruised and blistered feet, then squared his shoulders.

"Good boards for rough cut . . . Pick them out, Brental?"

"No, master Hesduff. Young Cerryl did. Has an eye for wood, I'd say."

"Does indeed . . . Would you load those on the cart? Now . . . about the timbers, Dylert?"

Brental slipped back out of the mill, pushing the handcart.

Cerryl stood and walked over to the back of the mule cart. "I can load these." He took the top pair of floorboards.

"We can get it done twice as fast together," Brental said mildly.

Cerryl didn't object. His feet still hurt, if not so much as before. Neither spoke while they stacked the boards.

"Brental! Bring that cart back."

Brental nodded and wheeled the cart back into the mill, returning shortly with eight six-cubit timbers laid across it.

Again, Cerryl helped Brental load the timbers into the mule cart. Brental tied them in place with two lengths of hemp as Hesduff and Dylert strolled out of the mill.

"We'll be seeing how these work out, and I'll be back before long." The crafter nodded to the millmaster.

"And we'll be here, Hesduff." Dylert smiled politely.

"Sure you will be. A pleasure, Dylert. Always a pleasure." Hesduff untied the mule and climbed onto the cart seat, then flicked the reins.

As the cart creaked away and down the road, Brental slipped up beside Dylert and began to speak to his father in a low voice. Cerryl might have been able to hear them if he strained, but he just sat on the wall dumbly, fearing the worst. If only he'd had some coppers before he started at the mill . . . if only his feet hadn't grown so fast . . . He wanted to shake his head but didn't. What good would it have done?

Once the mule cart left, Dylert walked over to Cerryl. He shook his head. "Cerryl?"

"Yes, ser?"

"Have I been cruel to you? Have I beat you? Or failed to feed you? Or clothe you?"

Cerryl looked at the stones of the causeway. "No, ser. Never, ser."

"Boy . . . you ask for little. I know that. But there's a time for brains and a time for pride. What if Brental hadn't seen? How long afore you'd never walk again?"

"I'm sorry, ser. I did not think."

"No, you didn't. You've had a hard life, but I'd not make it harder. Don't you, either. Take care of your body, boy. Be the only one you have." Dylert nodded at Brental. "You say those old boots of yours will fit?"

"Be better if he didn't work in the mill for a day or two. Ought to go barefoot."

"Place be clean enough to do without for a day or two." Dylert laughed. "Viental always be taking off." He looked at Cerryl. "You can help Dyella round the house. No boots. Understand?"

"Yes, ser." Cerryl looked up. "Thank you, ser." He swallowed. "Thank you." He had to look down, afraid Dylert would see how close to tears he was.

"That be all right, Cerryl. Just get those feet well."

"Yes, ser."

"Now . . . up to the house and tell Dyella you'll be doing chores for her. Darkness knows, she could use the help with all the wool coming in." He snorted. "And Erhana could spend more time on her lessons. Always looking for a way out, that child."

"Yes, ser." Cerryl nodded.

"Put the boots in your cubby first," said Brental. "You need to clean the old ones sometime. Might be someone else could use them later."

Cerryl nodded again, forcing his eyes up to meet Dylert's. "Thank you, ser."

"Off with you, boy."

Cerryl could tell that Dylert didn't feel as gruff as he sounded, but he answered politely, "Yes, ser."

IX

The white mages, powerful in the paths of peace and wary of war, girded their robes and invoked the hopes of peace . . . but all were doomed.

For Nylan, the dark angel, again lifted his hands, and he unbound the Accursed Forest of Naclos, and the forest rewarded him, and rendered back unto him the fires of Heaven and the rains of death. And Nylan laughed and cast those fires and rain across the west of Candar. And Ayrlyn sang songs that wrenched soul from soul and heart from body.

The Mirror Lancers found their light lances turned upon them, and the very earth rose and smote them, and the righteousness of the white mages was for naught as their glasses exploded before them, and death rained upon all . . .

The very ground heaved, and . . . the Grass Hills were seared into the Stone Hills, so dry that nothing lives there to this day . . .

The few white mages who remained, they slipped away to the east, far across the Westhorns, and even beyond the Easthorns, fearing that the west of Candar was no place for the goodness of white.

Indeed, they were sore justified in their fears, for the demon women of Tower Black, the heart of the evil kingdom of Westwind, grasped the Westhorns as a constricting snake seizes its prey. Their metalled roads pinioned the very peaks, and all trade bowed to their black blades.

The dark forests of Naclos swelled back over their former domain, those lands that the ancient white mages had freed, and the forests once again swallowed the lands in darkness. Therein dwelt the evil druid Nylan and the songmage Ayrlyn, and their offspring made Naclos their own, and the shadows of their power shaded all of Candar from the Westhorns to the Great Western Ocean.

. . . and in the fullness of time came the white mages to Fairhaven, to begin again the struggle to reclaim all of Candar from the grip of darkness . . .

> *Colors of White*
> (Manual of the Guild at Fairhaven)
> Preface

X

After stepping out onto the porch, the bean soup that had been dinner filling his stomach comfortably, Cerryl looked out from under the eaves. A line of rain splattered on the stones of the causeway that linked the lumber barns and the mill.

"Won't be stopping any time soon," offered Viental, standing by the railing. "Either sit and wait, or run. Me . . . I stopped running a long time ago." The stocky laborer turned, walked to the empty bench against the house wall, and sat down heavily.

"You get wet about the same if you run or you walk." Rinfur shook his head. "You walk to your room and hang up your clothes, and they got time to dry."

"While you shiver in your blankets," answered Viental. "Not for me, thank you."

Cerryl sat cross-legged on the planks of the porch floor, his eyes on the darker clouds to the southwest, over the mines, over the old house where he had lived as long as he could remember until he'd come to the mill. Was Syodor out in the rain, using it to uncover new gleanings? Or were his aunt and uncle sitting before a warm hearth? He rubbed his forehead, aware of a dull throbbing growing above and behind his eyes.

"Be raining for a long time," Rinfur said with a shrug, stepping out from the porch and striding toward his room in the first lumber barn. "Might as well get wet so as I can get dry soonest."

"I can always get wet," answered Viental with a deep laugh. "Better to stay dry, I say."

The rain dripped off the edge of the eaves steadily, in a pattern that seemed to pound into Cerryl's skull. Abruptly, he stood.

"Going to get wet, are you?" asked Viental.

"It will happen sooner or later," the youth answered, starting down the stone steps.

"Not for me," called Viental.

Cerryl walked through the rain and the growing twilight back to the barn. Once inside his room, he pulled off the damp canvas jacket and hung it on the peg by the door.

At least inside his room, the pounding of the rain wasn't quite so pronounced. Still, for a time Cerryl sat on the edge of his pallet, trying to ignore the splatting of the rain and the throbbing in his skull that almost kept rhythm to the patter of the rain on the side of the barn.

Tap! Tap!

Cerryl frowned, then went to the narrow door, opening it.

A broad-shouldered figure stood there, patch over one eye.

"Unc—"

"Hush!" Syodor's hand covered Cerryl's mouth. "Not a word. Follow me."

"In the rain?" asked Cerryl, inadvertently massaging his forehead again, trying to relieve the dull pressure behind his eyes.

"Only safe way," said Syodor, the water dripping off his oiled leathers, turning and slogging across the meadow grass away from the lumber barn.

Cerryl threw on his too-small canvas jacket and followed his uncle toward the line of oaks across the hill.

Crack!

A line of lightning flashed, followed by the drumroll of thunder.

Cerryl winced. The lightning—or the thunder—kept thrumming through his skull, but Syodor plunged onward, toward the ancient oaks.

"Couldn't do this, lad, except when I knew the rain'd last. Had to do this afore long."

Do what? Cerryl wondered but did not ask, just stepped up beside his uncle and kept walking, his boots squishing on the wet grass and soggy ground. His hair was soaked again, and rain began to ooze down his neck. He shivered, more from his headache than from the chill of the cold water seeping down his spine.

"Wish you were older, but there be a time for aught and all, and that be now . . ." The gnarled miner's voice died away as he came to a stop under the dark oak, the last one in the line leading from Dylert's house across the hill and overlooking the lower meadow. Syodor reached inside his oiled leathers and handed Cerryl a small oblong package—something wrapped in old mine canvas. "Brought these for you, young fellow. Don't you be opening 'em here. Rain be spoiling them."

"What . . . are they?" Cerryl could sense the faintest of white glows, even beneath the canvas.

"Books, your da's books. Wish I could have taught you letters." Syodor shrugged. "Best no one knew you lived, and we feared anyone knew letters'd tell the mages. They might have come for you."

Even as he wiped water away from his eyes, Cerryl kept his face calm, ignoring the headache as well. Finally, he asked, "Uncle, you never told me. What happened to my da? And mother?"

"The white mages killed your da . . . with their magic. They sent the lancers after your ma. She finally went to 'em. That was after you were safe with us." Syodor peered out from under the oiled leather hood. "Figured they knew about her, she did, but not about you. You were but a mite then, fit in my hand."

"But why?" Cerryl swallowed. "What did he do?"

"Your da . . . I don't know . . .'cept your ma, she told Nall that he took some books 'cause no one would teach him. That he wanted to learn how to be a real mage, not a rock mage nor a hedge mage. He learned his letters somewhere. Never did say where." The miner looked away from Cerryl and downhill toward the damp clay of the road from the mines.

After a moment, Syodor pointed to the canvas-wrapped books that Cerryl held. "Them . . . might be them. I thought about destroyin' 'em . . ." He shook his head. "Your da died for 'em. Mighta been crazy, thinking he could have been a great mage, if he'd been born to coins, but we don't choose our folk. Even so, don't seem right that way. Seen you with your scraps of glass." He laughed. "Didn't think as we knew, did you, lad? Someday . . . anyway, seeing as you be what you be . . . time you have 'em." His jaw squared. "Don't tell a one aught about 'em. No one. Mages might think they be lost forever . . . 'less they hear, and they listen on the wind. 'Cept in the rain." A rough smile crossed his lips. "You be like them. Your head, it aches in the rain, does it not?"

Cerryl nodded.

"Their glasses . . . their magery, the falling water makes it hard for them to see. Hard, too, for 'em to see into caves or small rooms . . . that's what your ma said, anyhow. Like your da, she saw more than most folks . . ."

Cerryl wanted to shake his head, or yell, or something. There was so much more he wanted to ask, and his head ached, and he didn't even know where to start. "But . . . why . . . why . . . did the white mages kill her?"

"Couldn't say for sure. . . . She never told either Nall nor me. Said the less we knew . . . safer you'd be."

"She had to leave? Why?"

"They had lancers a-looking for her most places. . . . Shandreth asked me once if I'd seen her. Had to tell him no, even when she was eating and sleeping not a hundred cubits from the hearth."

"Looking for her?"

"Don't know as who else. White lancers . . . they be mean men, Cerryl. You stay clear of them, no matter what it be taking."

Cerryl shivered, thinking about the day he'd seen the white lancers in Howlett. They'd looked mean then.

"The mages . . . they be mages, but the lancers are killers, without souls, no better than the old black demons of the Westhorns." Syodor fingered his chin. "Could be a mite worse, from what I hear." He shrugged. "Well, boy . . . got to be going, be well away from here afore the rain lifts. Wouldn't want my image showing in the glass, not with the power of them books showing, too." Syodor extended a big hand and clapped Cerryl on the shoulder. "We'll be seeing you as we can. You know that, lad, do you not?"

"I know." Cerryl swallowed. "I know."

"Be off now."

Cerryl stood under the dark oak, watching until Syodor vanished into the rain and mist. Then he walked slowly back to the lumber barn.

In the dimness of the room, Cerryl eased open the canvas, glad that he could see better than most in the dark. There were two slender books, bound in age-darkened leather. His eyes watered as he glanced at them.

Then he frowned. Between them was a white-bronze circlet. He turned it over. Two rough patches in the metal on the back indicated brackets or something had once been attached.

Except for a thicker rim, the circlet, a half-span across, was of uniform thickness and smooth to the touch. Yet . . . Cerryl studied it for a long time in the darkness.

Finally, he nodded. Somehow, the pin or ornament was made of two separate metals that met in an undulating edge, put together so smoothly that he could not feel the joins, only sense them with the sight that was not sight.

The books went behind the board with the book fragment he already had cached there, but the circlet—that he kept, his fingers around it even when he lay back on his pallet and drifted into an uneasy sleep.

XI

A soft breeze brushed across the porch, carrying the scent of late apple blossoms, the turned earth of the garden to the southwest of the house, and the less welcome odor of the horse manure Cerryl had spent the day cleaning out of the stable.

Cerryl sat on the edge of the porch, his boots on the top stone step, looking eastward, supposedly toward Lydiar. The more distant hills were fading into the early twilight.

"What do you do at the mill, Cerryl?" asked Erhana from the bench behind him.

"Whatever they need me to do. You saw me with the shovel and manure." Cerryl's hair was still damp, plastered against his skull, and his forearms itched, despite his washing in cold water before dinner. Without the nightly washing before dinner, he had discovered, his arms became covered with an ugly red rash, and after dealing with the stable, he'd definitely needed to wash up, almost all over.

"Da—Father—Siglinda says that I should say 'Father.' Father doesn't let me in the mill. He let Brental in there when he was smaller than I am."

"Brental will have to run the mill."

"I wouldn't want to." Erhana lifted her head slightly—Cerryl could tell that without turning. "I'm going to have a wealthy consort and live in a fine house in Lydiar." Her voice dropped slightly. "You didn't say what you really do in the mill."

"I sweep floors, stack the timbers, move things, clean the sawpit. Brental's beginning to teach me about the oxen." He paused, then asked, turning finally to look at the dark-haired girl, "What do you do with that lady in the parlor?"

"She be—she is not a lady. She's Siglinda, and she gives me my lessons." Erhana cocked her head and offered a superior smile. "I'm learning my letters."

"Oh?"

"Letters are important for a lady."

"I'd wager you don't know them well enough to teach me."

"Why would you want to know letters? You're always going to be working in the mill."

"See?" Cerryl said with a grin. "You can't do it."

"I can, too."

"You'll have to prove it." Cerryl looked disbelieving.

"I don't have to prove anything to you." Erhana sniffed.

"You don't. That be right," Cerryl said, grinning again.

"You couldn't learn letters, anyway."

"You don't know that, not until you try and I can't learn." Cerryl smiled. "Of course, that might mean you couldn't teach me, either. Your da, he says . . ." Cerryl let the words trail off.

"He says what?" Erhana's voice sharpened.

"Nothing . . . nothing."

"You're . . . nothing but a mill rat, Cerryl."

Cerryl forced a shrug, intent on keeping any concern from his face. "If you really knew your letters, you could teach them to a mill rat. You're just calling me names 'cause you can't."

"Cerryl . . . you are . . ." Erhana paused. "You are . . ."

He stood. "If you're that good, you can teach me letters. I be here every night after supper."

"I don't have to teach you anything."

Cerryl forced a smile, then grinned before turning and walking down toward his cubby room.

"Cerryl . . ."

He forced himself to keep walking.

XII

Cerryl rubbed his forehead again, trying to massage away the dull ache from somewhere deep within his skull. The massage didn't help, and he resumed restacking the flooring planks, ensuring that there were indeed ten in each pile, as Brental had instructed him—a dozen stacks of ten.

He paused, his eyes going to the half-open mill door and to the steady rain beyond, rain that had fallen from gray skies for the past two days. He looked back at the span-wide planks, his eyes watering. With a sigh, he counted the last stack again. Ten.

Why did the steady rain give him such a headache? Syodor had said it affected all the white mages. He could use his mirror fragments to pull up images—places like Fairhaven, the white city, and even the cows in the lower pasture. Did those things mean he was a mage—or could be? Or that the mages would kill him, as they had his father, if they discovered him?

He'd only been able to have a few sessions with Erhana and her copybooks, but already he could pick out some of the letters in his books, although the script was curved and more elaborate than that in hers. He could make out a handful of words, not enough to read any-thing . . . not yet.

His fingers went to his belt pouch and tightened around the talis-man—was that what it was?—that Syodor had given him. Had it been his father's? Or had his father picked it up somewhere?

"... afore midsummer, Dorban will be here for the seasoned oak—the big timbers for the shipyard ..." A good thirty cubits away, Dylert's voice trailed off.

"He always complains," said Brental, "but he comes back."

Cerryl did not turn his head. He'd learned years earlier that his hearing was sharper than that of most folks. He'd also learned that he gained more information by not letting on.

"He hopes that we'll lower the price if he complains enough ..."

Cerryl kept listening as he started in on the third pile.

"Oooo." He stopped and carefully eased out the splinter. Although he tried to be careful, wood had splinters, some of them sharp enough to cut deeply if he were careless or if his mind wandered—as it just had.

Cerryl shook his head. Was Erhana right? That he'd spend the rest of his life in the mill, the way Rinfur was?

His lips tightened, but his eyes and attention went back to the hardwood planks.

Standing closer to the big blade of the saw itself, Dylert and Brental continued talking, but Cerryl shut out their words.

Outside the mill, the rain continued to fall, beating on the roof, on the stones, and inside Cerryl's skull.

XIII

Cerryl hurried out of the mill and along the causeway, noting the bean plants in the garden on the hill, already calf-high in the midmorning light. He found it hard to believe that summer had slipped into Hrisbarg, almost without his knowledge.

The gray-haired Siglinda's voice drifted down from the house porch toward the mill, clearly audible with the wheel and the saw silent. "No! He *is* going to the market. Read what is on the page. In any case, 'be' is not a verb cultured people use, except with the subjunctive."

Cerryl half wondered what she meant, what the subjunctive was. He tried to hold on to the idea that he should use "is" instead of "be." Still, he needed to find Dylert.

He slipped into the first lumber barn, then froze as he saw the two figures by the racks. He waited, listening, so still that he could feel himself blend into the white oak stacked on his left. In the racks across the narrow side aisle of the second lumber barn were the various-sized planks and timbers of first-quality black oak.

"I am most certain that the duke would confer his best wishes upon you for providing what I need at a most reasonable price," said the small stocky man in the gray tunic. "His best wishes . . ."

Dylert stood at the edge of the center aisle, gesturing toward the racked black oak cuts. "Fine talk, master cabinet maker," said the millmaster with a gentle laugh, "but cutting lorken or black oak means sharpening the blade for darkness-near every log. Best wishes don't pay for the work or the time. Nor the wear on the blade."

"I'm not asking you to deliver, Dylert. I'm the one paying a wagon to carry it all back to Lydiar."

"You haven't much choice, Erastus. There's no one in eastern Lydiar who's taken care to preserve black oak and lorken. You want good lorken, you'll come to me, or go a fair piece west of here."

Erastus offered a shrug. "The duke has insisted on a black-oak-and-lorken chest. I had thought you might understand."

"Let the duke pay for it, then," answered Dylert.

"I'm already paying for the wagon. Three golds for the wood," suggested the crafter.

In the shadows of the wood racks, Cerryl frowned. Erastus's words felt wrong. Was that because he bargained?

"Erastus, it's four golds for that much lorken. That doesn't include the oak you need for bracing."

"You're a brigand, Dylert, a black-bearded brigand with the smile of a streetwalker and the heart of a mage."

Dylert laughed. "You know better than that. Six golds for the lot, and I'll even throw in some of the pine planks for your apprentices to work with."

Erastus sighed. "You don't bargain much. How about a few lengths of golden oak as well?"

"A few," conceded Dylert.

"Be generous," suggested Erastus. "If the duke isn't grateful, then I will be."

"I'd count on your gratitude far more than the duke's," answered Dylert. "Far more."

"Six golds," Erastus agreed. "Once the wagon's loaded, and I've seen the wood."

"Fair enough. You'll get the best."

"I'll bring the wagon to the door here." Erastus gestured.

The millmaster nodded, then watched as the crafter walked out, passing within a half-dozen cubits of Cerryl.

Once Erastus was out of the mill, Dylert beckoned toward Cerryl. "What do you want, lad?"

"Brental sent me. There's a crack in the second big blade. He said you should know. He and Viental are changing it now." Cerryl waited.

"Darkness and demons! First, Erastus and now a cracked blade. That's a good ten golds for a blade like that." He shook his head, then fingered his trimmed black-and-silver beard. "Ten golds . . . where . . ." His eyes focused on the youth. "You move like a serpent, young fellow. Never saw you until Erastus was leaving. How much did you hear?"

"Just the part about the duke wanting a black-oak-and-lorken chest, ser. And after that." Cerryl met the millmaster's eyes.

"Well . . . let it be a lesson to you. Folks always expect that you'll do more for less if a duke or a great man wants something. Sometimes, it's like as true. Most times, the great man never heard. Old Erastus there, he was trying to get me to charge him less. You think that he'd be asking a copper less from the duke had I even *given* him the lorken? Ha!" Dylert snorted. "Now . . . another blade to be reforged and tempered and cut and sharpened . . . They don't think of that when they want the wood cheap. No, they don't."

Cerryl nodded.

"And another thing, lad. Don't think I don't know you been sweet-talking Erhana into teaching you the letters after dinner." Dylert grinned. "Or any other time."

"I don't do it when I'm supposed to work, ser." Cerryl looked down at the clean-swept floor stones.

"That you don't, and you work hard. Harder than any boy I had here." Dylert frowned. "Why the letters?"

"My da, he could read. Least I could do is learn my letters," said Cerryl, knowing he was not telling the entire truth, and hoping Dylert did not press him.

"Trying to match your da." Dylert nodded. "Folks don't talk much of your father. You know why?"

"They said he was a wizard."

"He tried to be a wizard, lad. There be a difference." Dylert paused, then added, "The white mages, they choose you . . . if they think you might be one of them. No one be making them do what they do not wish to do. No one be crossing them. And trying to be a mage without their blessing . . . that be a mighty crossing." Dylert cleared his throat. "You understand that, lad?"

"Yes, ser."

A creaking issued from the door to the barn.

"Dylert! Wagon's here. I got a long trip back," called Erastus.

"Then, we be loading right now," returned the millmaster before looking down at Cerryl, if not so far down as the fall before. "You can use the handcart. Get the best ten gold oak planks from the second barn. You got a good eye. He gets good seconds. Understood."

"Yes, ser."

"Better run back and tell Brental that I'll be there soon as we get Erastus off. Then get the oak."

"Yes, ser."

"Good." Dylert smiled. "Off with you."

Cerryl scurried out of the barn and toward the mill, half-sighing in relief as he ran to give Brental the message. Dylert hadn't said he couldn't keep learning his letters, and he hadn't forced Cerryl into an actual lie.

XIV

In the background, Cerryl could hear both wheels rumbling and thumping, and the water roiled down the millrace behind where he sat in the shade, brush in hand. Neither the intermittent light breeze nor the shade was enough to keep him from sweating in the hot afternoon, nor to keep away the flies that buzzed back and forth, seemingly always at the back of his neck. He absently brushed one away, only to feel it circling back.

Whhhrannnnnn . . .

Cerryl looked up from where he sat on the low stone wall, not letting go of the stiff brush he used to clean the oxen's yoke. Scrubbing the yoke was a slow and tedious process, working the dirt and grime out without scarring the wood.

Inside the mill, at the far end of the center aisle, Brental, Viental, and Dylert worked a big pine log through the beginning of a series of cuts. On one side Brental checked the guides through which the log fed, drawn by the cradle wound from the upper and smaller waterwheel. One the other side, Dylert watched, one hand on the cradle release, the other on the drop gear. Viental reset the log after each pass, edging the cradle a quarter span more toward the blade.

Cerryl blinked. The reddish white glow surrounding the blackness of the blade—had he seen that? Right through the heavy log? He thought he had before, but on this afternoon, the glow seemed brighter. He squinted, leaning toward the mill, his fingers tightening around the broom handle.

Why could he sense something he couldn't see? Not see properly anyway. The reddish white glow was there—the same glow he'd felt in the mines that even Syodor had avoided—and the same glow that, in a much lesser degree, permeated the books from his father.

He frowned. Another question, one he pondered, time and time again. Why had his uncle never mentioned that he had been the master-miner? Cerryl hadn't learned that until Dylert had said so.

He studied the yoke, then nodded. Even Brental would be pleased. He looked back at the blade. It seemed brighter, yet with an angry reddish tint, one he hadn't seen before.

He bent down to lift the yoke to carry it back up to the stables, but his eyes went back to the mill, where the reddish white of the blade, that color no one else seemed to see, loomed over the massive log and the mill blade, almost as though it were ready to lash out at Brental and Dylert. He took a step down the causeway, then stopped and glanced back again.

His lips tightened before he set down the brush and yoke and scurried into the mill, almost running down the center aisle, the clomping of his heavy boots drowned in the screech of the saw and the thumping of the waterwheels.

Dylert, standing on the platform above and to the right of the saw, waved him back.

Cerryl shook his head and pointed toward the blade.

Dylert gestured again, impatiently.

"Please, ser! Stop the blade," Cerryl shouted, but his words were lost in the whining of the blade. He pointed to the blade again, gesturing, trying to make Dylert understand. Then he glanced toward the drop gear on the small platform below Dylert.

Before Cerryl had taken more than a pair of steps, the millmaster had dropped down to the drop gear lever and yanked it.

Cerryl took a deep breath as the whining screech of the blade died down, and a dull *clunk* reverberated through the mill.

Dylert turned away from the drop gear, clambered back to the water gates and closed them, and set both wheel brakes.

Brental looked from Cerryl to the saw platform, where the blade was still hidden, locked in the big pine log.

Viental just scowled.

The millmaster climbed down and walked toward Cerryl. "Now . . . never seen you run like that, lad. Hope this be worth it. Best be worth it, indeed." His face was streaked with sweat, with sawdust plastered across his cheeks and imbedded in his beard. His jaw was set, waiting.

Cerryl swallowed. "Ser . . . the blade . . . something be—something is wrong with it."

After a moment, Dylert frowned. "You be seeing that from without?"

"Hearing, ser," Cerryl lied. "It . . . sounded wrong. I know . . . you are the millmaster . . . but I had to tell you."

"Hpphhmmm. Sounds he hears," grumbled Viental.

Brental glared at the stocky laborer.

"Well . . . we be shut down. Might be looking afore anything else." Dylert frowned. "If there be a crack or flaw," he shrugged, "then we stand lucky. If not," he looked at Cerryl, "a lot of work you'll have to do, young fellow. A darkness lot to make up for this."

"Yes, ser."

Dylert glanced at the other two. "Got to clear the blade anyway. Let's be at it."

Cerryl stepped back and watched as the three men wrestled the log off the blade. Sweat continued to ooze down his back.

"Now . . . he has to hear it . . ." mumbled Viental, with a look at the youth.

"Time enough to complain when we find he be wrong," answered Dylert. "If he be wrong. Cerryl's not a flighty chap, like some."

A last shove by Viental, and the log slipped away from the blade. Brental looked at the drop gear and then at the water gates before taking a cloth and brushing away the sawdust that had swirled around the circular toothed blade.

The color drained from the redhead's face. "There's a crack here . . . might not a held another pass." His eyes went to Cerryl.

Then Dylert glanced at Cerryl, frowned, then grinned. "Guess you might yet make a mill man, boy. Anyone hear a blade off-true like that . . ." He shook his head. "My da, he claimed he could. I never could. That be why . . . I check the blade so often. Thought he was a-tellin' tales."

Cerryl looked down for a moment, his eyes on the sawdust-covered stones around the saw platform. "I wasn't sure, not all the way, but . . . I didn't want anyone hurt, and you talked about how a broken blade . . ."

"He listens, too," said Brental. "Glad I am that he does."

Viental shook his head ruefully. "Know why my mother said to wait afore talking."

"Well . . . good thing Henkar got the new blade forged and tempered . . . This rate we'll never survive . . . two blades this season. Best we get to it," Dylert said. "Can't be cutting with a cracked blade."

While the three men wrestled to replace the blade, Cerryl stepped back and slipped out of the mill, trying to keep from shaking as he did. Again, he'd barely managed to avoid revealing what he had really seen.

Outside, in the hot but slightly cooler shade by the now-silent mill-race, he swallowed.

Finally, he lifted the heavy yoke and walked slowly uphill toward the stables.

XV

Cerryl looked at the handcart, upside down on the flooring stones just inside the mill door, then at the dark-stained and battered half bucket filled with grease.

With a slow and silent deep breath, Cerryl reached into the bucket and dipped out a globule of the dark substance with his right hand and methodically began to grease the cart wheels and axle, using a thin stripped fir branch, barely more than a twig, to push the grease where his fingers couldn't reach.

Behind him, at the other side of the mill, Dylert directed Brental and Viental as the three continued cutting a half-dozen oak logs from the upper woods, logs that Dylert had marked and felled a season before. Cerryl's eyes went to the saw platform, but his senses only saw the normal whitish red of the cutting, not the angry red of a stressed or cracked blade. He nodded and looked back down at the dark gray grease.

After another repressed sigh, he dipped out more grease.

"Some folk here to see you, Cerryl." Erhana stood in the door to the mill, her voice barely audible over the whine of the big blade and the *thump, thump* of the wheels.

"Me?" Cerryl finished daubing grease on the top exposed part of the cart's axle. "To see me?"

Erhana smiled, then added, "Your aunt and uncle, I think."

Cerryl looked around for the grease rag, then saw it under the side of the upended left cart wheel, where he'd placed it to keep any extra grease from falling on the floor stones. He picked it up and wiped his hand as clean as he could, then straightened, and walked out the door into the sunlight.

Overhead, the summer sky was filled with white puffy clouds scudding westward, clouds that cast fast-moving shadows across the hills of western Lydiar and the forests to the north of the mill.

Cerryl glanced from Erhana to his aunt and uncle and then back to the brown-haired girl. "Thank you."

Erhana nodded and slipped uphill toward the house where Dyella was carding wool in the shade of the porch.

"How are you?" Cerryl asked after a moment.

Syodor carried a small pack. Nall stood beside him, empty-handed. Both looked downcast, somehow smaller than Cerryl recalled them.

"You've grown." Nall licked her lips nervously.

"My feet have, anyway." Cerryl offered a smile.

Neither Syodor nor Nall returned the smile.

"What . . . what is the matter?" Cerryl felt uncomfortable with the proper use of "is," at least in speaking to his aunt and uncle, but he remained determined to speak properly. He looked steadily at his uncle.

"Things have been better, lad. Aye, they have been." Syodor looked at the ground, not speaking for a time. "The duke . . . my patent . . . said no longer could grub the mines."

"I'm sorry." Cerryl nodded gravely, feeling that his words offered little comfort. "I really am. I wish I could do something." Even as he spoke, sensing the discomfort of his aunt and uncle, he found himself wondering why Syodor's words felt so wrong, even though his uncle had often worried about the patent.

"Best you can do, child," said Nall, "be to take care of yourself."

"You got a place, Cerryl. Better than we could give you now." Syodor again looked down at the stones of the causeway. "Dylert be a good man."

"I know, uncle . . . but what about you? Where will you go?" Cerryl swallowed. He'd never expected Syodor or Nall to be anywhere but at the house by the ancient mines.

"Don't you be worrying about us," admonished Nall. "Not like as we got that much longer to worry, child. 'Sides, we got a place."

Cerryl looked back at his uncle.

"Got a cousin in Vergren," said Syodor, his voice flat. "Sheep country there. He's got an extra cot. Small, and it needs some work. Even managed to borrow his mule cart. Take most of our things."

"Isn't there anything . . . any place else?"

"What else we need, lad? The mines are over for me. Have been for a long time. Just didn't want to admit it."

Syodor's voice was rough, Cerryl realized belatedly. "I'm sorry. Can you tell me where you'll be?"

"Tomorrow we set out," said Nall. "Like as dawn. Gerhar be Syodor's cousin. His place be on the old north road, past the second hill. In Vergren, that be."

"Tomorrow?"

"The Duke's man gave us but four eight-days, and it was most of that finding Gerhar." Syodor forced a wry smile, one that did not touch his remaining good eye. "Lucky we be that Gerhar has but one young daughter and can use the extra hands."

Cerryl shook his head. "Perhaps I should come . . ."

"No." Syodor's voice was as firm as Cerryl had ever heard it. "Better you remain here with Dylert. Leastwise you have a trade. If anyone asks, best you tell them you be an orphan, but that your folk come from Montgren, Vergren way." He laughed once. "That be true enough, now."

Cerryl moistened his lips.

"Brought you some things," said Nall, after another moment of silence.

Syodor opened the pack. "Pack be yours, too, Cerryl. Sooner or later, like as you be needing it." He took out something, something that glowed white beneath his hand with the light that was like that of the sun, and yet not. "This, it be your da's," the miner added gruffly, extending a small knife in a sheath. The knife and sheath were nearly toy-sized, small enough to fit within Cerryl's palm. "This, too," Syodor added, placing a silver-framed mirror—a screeing glass—beside the knife.

Cerryl glanced down at the items in his hands, then at Nall.

She met his glance. "There be no denying what a man be. Your da, he couldn't ha' been other than he was. Nor you, Cerryl. He was a-fiddling with the light afore he could talk, or so your mother said. Too young, she said." Nall shrugged. "You be a mite older. I seen you with the glasses and the white fire. Tried to keep you from a-burnin' yourself too young."

Syodor nodded. "Anyways, we thought . . . we wanted you to have them, not when you be too young, though. I kept them away from the house," the miner added. "Knew as you'd feel them somehow."

"There be a warm winter coat there. You da's . . . saved it for you, and a scarf, your ma's best scarf . . ." Nall sniffed. "Know as you can't use a scarf . . . but felt you ought to have something that was hers." She stepped forward and abruptly hugged Cerryl. "Did the best we could for you . . . and for your ma." Tears streaked her face.

Cerryl could sense the absolute certainty of her words, and, swallowing hard, he had to fight to keep his own eyes from watering. "I know you did. Always be thankful . . . always." He swallowed again and hugged her back, realizing how thin and frail she had become.

As suddenly as she had hugged him, Nall backed away in two swift steps, sniffed, and blotted her eyes. "Had to come with Syodor. Wouldn't ha' been right, otherwise."

Syodor grasped Cerryl's forearm with both hands and squeezed, and gnarled and bent as the one-eyed miner was, Cerryl could still feel the strength. "You be not a burly man, young Cerryl, but strong you be in ways not of the eye. If you be careful, you be doing well for yourself." Syodor released the grip and stepped back quickly. "We be right proud of you." After a moment, he added, "Best we be going, now. A long trip tomorrow."

"Take care...please..." Cerryl stammered, feeling somehow numb, as though he should say more, do more, but not knowing what else he could say or do.

"Best as we can, lad," said Syodor, "and you the same."

Nall sniffed again and nodded. The two turned and began to walk down the lane.

Cerryl wanted to run after them. Instead, still holding the canvas pack, in which he had carefully replaced the mirror and the knife, Cerryl watched as his aunt and uncle walked slowly down the lane, back to the main road, and the mines—and Vergren.

"Cerryl? What you doing—" Dylert stopped talking as he saw the two figures walking quickly toward the main road. "That Syodor?"

"They came to say good-bye," Cerryl said slowly. "The duke canceled his patent, and they have to leave the mines. After all those years..."

"Where are they going?" Dylert's voice was softer.

"Uncle has a cousin in Vergren. He's going to tend sheep, he said."

"Sad thing it be," offered Dylert. "The masterminer of Lydiar, and a shepherd he must end his days."

"I offered to help them." Cerryl looked down at the causeway. "Uncle Syodor—he insisted I stay here." He looked at the millmaster. "That's all right?"

Dylert laughed sadly and shook his head. "Cerryl, you be worth more than I pay you. Would that I could pay more, but stay you can, young fellow." His gaze went to the distant figures. "Darkness if I can figure the ways of the world. Older I get, the stranger it seems. Masterminer, best there ever was, and a shepherd he must be." The millmaster shook his head again.

Cerryl swallowed and continued to watch, long after Dylert had left, until Syodor and Nall vanished on the dusty road, amid the fast-moving shadows of the clouds.

XVI

Unto the generations stood the black tower on the heights of the West-horns, and from it issued forth the demon warriors and their blades, controlling trade and using the very blood of those who displeased them to create the mortar that bound their stone roads.

Nor did they suffer any man grown to survive upon their heights, discarding him like an empty husk of maize once they had wrested his seed from him . . .

For all this wickedness, Westwind survived and prospered, until the day when the Guild at Fairhaven sent a hero to Westwind, a stranger who beguiled the Marshal of the heights with song. Yet once she had borne son and daughter, the Marshal laughed and sent away that hero. In her evilness, she had her guards slay him in the depths of the West-horns.

That son, who was called Creslin, grew strong, and cunning as his mother the Marshal, and before he was grown to the age of death or exile, he sneaked away from the heights, taking the talismans of darkness that had held the forces of white and right at bay for long generations.

In time, he came to Fairhaven, pretending to be but a poor soldier, but the brethren were not deceived, and they discovered his deception and captured him and bound him to be a stoneworker on the great highway, far from Fairhaven.

The powers of darkness, in their sinuous way, corrupted a young woman and a white mage from the far west, deceiving her into thinking that she was but escaping from the captivity of darkness, and enticed this mage Megaera into freeing the black demon that Creslin had be-come . . .

Colors of White
(Manual of the Guild at Fairhaven)
Preface

XVII

In the continuing diffuse light of the summer evening, Cerryl glanced around his room, scarcely bigger than a closet. He glanced at the door, then took the small silver-rimmed mirror from its hiding place behind the wall board under his cubby. His own reflection glimmered back at him—dark brown hair, a face almost triangular with a broad forehead, wide-spaced gray eyes, and a narrow not-quite-pointed chin.

He felt his chin—still no signs of a beard, and near-on fourteen years. Finally, he set the mirror on the seat of the stool. After that came the miniature knife and sheath.

He slipped the knife from the sheath and studied it, with eyes and senses. Too small even for an eating knife, the blade was not iron or anything like it, but a whitish gold or white bronze that shimmered like polished silver or almost like a mirror. The metal held an inner light, a white radiance with the faintest touch of red, but a radiance Cerryl knew that only he—or the mages of Candar—could sense.

He wasn't a mage, not yet, perhaps not ever. Yet he could sense some things that he thought only mages could sense. Was that the way his father had felt?

With a last look at the shimmering blade, he slipped the knife into the sheath and replaced both knife and sheath behind the board. Straightening, he sat on the edge of his pallet—little more than a sack filled with straw lying on a plank platform, and covered with a tattered gray blanket.

So much there was that he needed to know, and dared not ask, not with what had happened to his father. Yet . . . a mill hand for life? He was beginning to understand what had driven his father—even as he understood how unlikely it was for his father, or himself—or any poor child—to have the chance to become a mage.

He shook his head, almost violently. *Why does it have to be this way? A mill hand? Why?*

Later, after calming himself with deep breaths and the thoughts of a quiet hillside spring, he squared himself on the edge of the pallet and looked down, concentrating, staring at the silver-rimmed screeing glass until the familiar white mist covered the silver. He continued to push his thoughts at the mists, seeking, asking, searching. "Somewhere . . ."

A face filled the center of the glass, sweeping back the silver mists, the face of a girl with blond curls, curls bearing a hit of red, and green eyes that seemed to look out of the mirror at Cerryl, eyes that looked within him and found him wanting.

"No . . ." The word was half-gasped, half-grunted as his head felt almost jerked back by the force of her gaze, an expression that swept aside the distance and the mists of the screeing mirror as if neither existed.

When he looked down at the glass again, it was but a mirror, blank, reflecting but his own sweat-wreathed face back at him.

Who was she? How could a girl so young have such power? Was she the daughter of a white mage? Or had what he'd seen been just an illusion? Cerryl shivered, then slipped the glass back into its hiding place.

Who was she? The question remained unanswered, even in his mind. He stood and walked to the door, his hand on the door latch. Then he shook his head and opened the window door to let the cooler evening air ease into the room, hoping the breeze wouldn't bring too many mosquitoes with it.

Turning back toward the pallet, his eyes were drawn to three books lying there—*Olma's Copybook, The Naturale Historie of Candar*, and the battered one on the end, *Colors of White*. If he understood the few pages of *Colors of White* he had puzzled and labored through, the book had two parts, but the second part had been ripped off. The first part told how the white mages had come to build Fairhaven, and the second part was supposed to be about how chaos and order worked, and that was the part he needed to have and to learn about.

What good was history? Some parts of history might be interesting—like the fall of Lornth and the rise of Sarronnyn or the stories about ancient Cyador—but most of it seemed useless for what Cerryl needed—an understanding of what a white mage was, what skills and talents were needed, and how to train and develop those talents.

Besides, the history book was hard to read, even slowly, with so many words he could not recognize. He took a deep breath, and his eyes turned back to the middle book, the one Erhana had lent him—*Olma's Copybook*. It was a little child's book of letters, but Cerryl had forced himself to work his way through the pages, struggling with and learning everything on each page before going to the next.

With a sigh of resignation, he opened the copybook.

At least in the summer, there was some light after he finished at the mill and supper, although even without lighting his stub of a candle, he could see perfectly well. As he'd gotten older his night vision, or sense of things, had continued to sharpen. In pitch darkness, he had trouble reading, but it would be a while before that occurred, and long before that he would be too tired to continue his self-taught lessons in letters.

XVIII

Cerryl stepped out of the warmth of the kitchen into the comparative cool of the porch, his stomach almost feeling distended from the amount of mutton stew he had eaten. His arms and legs and back all ached. He'd spent most of the past eight-day up in the higher woods with Viental and Brental, learning how to judge when a tree could be felled and whether it should be. That part had come easily. Not so easy had been working with the ax and the two-man saw.

The ax bothered him, in the same way the mill blade did—the darkness of the honed iron feeling both like fire and ice at the same time. The oiled and honest iron of the ax even felt hot to his touch, nearly hot enough to burn his fingers, calloused or not.

Perhaps Erhana would come out on the porch after she helped her mother clean up after dinner. Cerryl hoped so. He walked to the north end of the porch and looked toward the higher hills, where he'd spent most of his time lately. The low buzz of insects and the scattered chirps of crickets rose out of the growing dusk.

"Dylert's got lots of woods up there," said Rinfur from behind him. "They say the family patent goes back to his great-grandsire."

"Too many woods," puffed Viental, standing on the top porch step. "Too long a day. Too much logging. I need to lie down."

"That's not because of your logging," laughed Rinfur. "It's your eating. You swallowed enough stew for three of you. And one of you is more than enough."

"Most funny," said Viental. "We should make you saw the trees. Your horses do all the hard work."

Rinfur laughed, a good-natured tone in the sound. "That's 'cause I'm smarter than they are."

"Not much," answered the stocky laborer as he started down the porch steps.

"Just enough," admitted Rinfur, stepping up beside Cerryl and standing there silently for a time. Behind them, in the kitchen, the sounds of voices and crockery and pans continued.

To the north, the sun that had dropped behind the hills backlit a low cloud into a line of fiery pink.

"Like this time of day," said Rinfur. "Quiet . . . not too hot, not too cold, and the work's done, the belly full."

Cerryl nodded.

"Think I'll walk over to the stable, see how the gray is doing. Worry about that hoof still." With a nod, Rinfur turned and crossed the porch, leaving Cerryl alone at the railing.

The youth ran his hand through hair still slightly damp from a quick rinse before dinner. He watched as the cloud slowly faded into gray.

The door from the kitchen opened, and he turned.

"Oh . . . I didn't know you were out here, Cerryl," blurted Erhana, her hands around a book.

"I was waiting for my lesson," he answered with a careful smile.

"This is the more advanced grammar."

"I can try."

Erhana shrugged and sat on the bench. Cerryl sat beside her, careful not to let his leg touch hers. She opened the book, and Cerryl followed her as she slowly read aloud.

". . . the cooper fashions barrels from staves of wood. Barrels are used to store flour and grains. Some barrels hold water and wine . . ."

Cerryl wondered if all grammar books said things that people already knew, but he said nothing and tried to match what Erhana read with the letters on the page.

"It's getting dark," Erhana said after a while. "Can you even see the book?"

"I can still see it," answered Cerryl. "What's an 'acolyte'?"

"That's not in the copybook."

"I know, but I wondered."

"I can't help you if you ask me about things that aren't in the books."

"I'm sorry."

"Why do you want to learn your letters?" Erhana asked abruptly, closing the grammar book and letting it rest on her trousered legs.

"I need to learn things," Cerryl answered, shifting his weight on the hard surface of the bench.

"They don't write about sawmills in books, silly boy." Erhana laughed. "Not about how the mill works, anyway."

"They should," Cerryl offered. "Everyone knows about coopers and fullers and smiths."

"Of course. You begin to read by learning how the words you know are written."

Cerryl refrained from wincing at Erhana's self-satisfied tone.

"Isn't there a book that has all the words you don't know?"

"That's a dictionary. Siglinda has one. They have lots and lots of words and how to spell them and what they mean."

Cerryl fingered his chin. Where could he find one? "A dictionary?"

"That's right." Erhana sighed.

In the momentary silence, Cerryl could hear voices in the kitchen. He strained to pick out the words.

". . . no sense in telling him now . . . good thing he was up in the woods when Wreasohn came . . ."

"Have to tell him sooner or later, Dylert . . ."

"Can't stay here, not forever . . ."

"Hush . . . he's still on the porch. We'll talk about it later."

"Best let Erhana help him with his letters, then. Poor lad."

In the growing darkness, Cerryl swallowed. Something awful had happened to Syodor and Nall . . . but what? And why? Who would harm a partly crippled old miner and his consort who were helping a cousin raise sheep?

"You're quiet, Cerryl," ventured Erhana.

"Oh, I was still thinking about dictionaries," he lied quietly. "They must be hard to come by."

"I guess so. Siglinda always says hers is worth its weight in gold." Erhana shrugged. "I don't know as they're worth that much."

"Books aren't cheap," he pointed out. "They have to be copied page by page."

"Siglinda says there are lots of scriveners in Lydiar. When I'm rich, I'll hire one and have him copy all the books I want."

The porch door opened, and Dyella peered out. "Are you still out here, Erhana?"

"Yes, Mother." Erhana stood, clutching the grammar. "I'm coming."

"Best you be. Canning the early peaches we are tomorrow." Dyella glanced toward Cerryl. "And more logging for you as well, Cerryl."

"Another side slope." Dylert's voice rumbled out from the kitchen.

"Yes, ser," said Cerryl, easing his way toward the steps. "I'll be ready."

"Till the morn," said Dylert just before Dyella closed the door behind Erhana.

Cerryl's boots clumped on the planks of the porch, noisy because he was too tired to move silently. He walked slowly down the steps and the path to his room. His legs and back still ached. He glanced back at the house, looming up like a black blot in the late twilight. What had happened to his aunt and uncle? Had they died in a plague? Of the bloody flux? In an accident?

Around him, the chorus of insects rose and fell, rose and fell as he meandered slowly down toward the finish lumber barn.

Why didn't Dylert want to tell him? How could he find out?

He almost stumbled as he opened the door to his cubby room. The screeing glass? That he could try.

After closing the door, and the window door as well, he eased the silver-rimmed mirror from its hiding place and set it on the stool. Then he sat on the edge of the pallet and began to concentrate, trying to visualize Syodor's weathered face, strong hands, and leather eyepatch, Nall's gray hair and probing eyes.

The mists swirled . . . finally revealing a burned-out cot. The roof timbers were black, the mud-brick walls cracked. The windows, ringed in black, gaped like a skull's eye sockets. Lines of blackness seared the grass around the walls.

"No . . ." Cerryl tightened his lips, refusing the tears that welled up inside him. "No."

He sat, rigid, on the edge of the pallet, well into the full darkness of night, the blank mirror on the stool before him showing nothing.

XIX

The gray and the dun plodded slowly across the hill, dragging the log harness. Rinfur guided the big horses, his eyes watching them, the log they dragged toward the wagon ramp, and the road ahead.

Dylert, Viental, and Brental stood waiting until the last log was dragged up the ramp. Then they rolled it sideways onto the wagon.

While the four men loaded the cut logs onto the wagon, Cerryl had continued sawing the smaller lengths of pole pine branches into sections a cubit long, wood for cooking and heat, stacking each length neatly in the pile.

Despite the leather gloves Dylert had given him, Cerryl's hands were blistered, and his fingers ached—along with his arms, legs, and back. He kept sawing, stopping only to blot back the sweat that continually threatened to run into his eyes. His shirt was soaked, and his feet felt like they rested in pooled sweat inside the heavy boots.

"Cerryl, lad," called Dylert as Viental and Brental wedged the last log in place on the wagon bed, "rack that saw back on the side of the wagon and take a breather."

"Yes, ser."

"Looks to be dry for a day or so. Rinfur and you can come up tomorrow and pile all the hearth wood in the small wagon." Dylert grinned at the teamster. "A little lifting would not harm you, Rinfur."

"So long as Cerryl does most of it." Rinfur grinned and continued unhitching the two horses he had used for dragging the logs so that he could reharness them to the full team to bring the log wagon down to the mill.

Brental picked up the log harness and slipped it into the panel under the wagon seats.

Dylert looked at Cerryl, who had just racked the handsaw. "Takes more than just a strong back."

The brown-haired youth nodded.

"Have to gauge the trees." Dylert wiped his sweating forehead in the late afternoon sun as Rinfur switched the horses' harnesses from the log-dragging rig to the wagon. "Watch 'em year by year. Cut them too soon, and you lose coins. Wait too long, and the heartwood gets too brittle and tough. You can break a blade and get nothing but firewood and kindling. We got the widest blade this end of Candar, but it be good but for two cubits and a span on a single pass . . ."

Cerryl nodded. That explained why Dylert's woods had few trees more than three cubits thick.

". . . need some of the old trees, so as to anchor the woods," the millmaster continued. "No matter what they ask in Lydiar, I cut but what be ready to cut." He shrugged and wiped his forehead again. "If the trees go, then what will Brental's children have?

"Course, that's one reason for the pole pines. They grow faster, and some folk don't care how long their timbers last, so long as they don't have to lay out much in coins."

"Some figure they'd not be living when the roof or the flooring fails," added Brental sardonically.

"Master miller, the team be ready when you are," said Rinfur.

"Time to go, then." Dylert hopped onto the wagon seat beside the teamster. Viental clambered onto the pile of logs on the wagon bed.

Brental looked at Cerryl and shook his head. "Fools and madmen ride the logs."

"The fools be those who walk when they could ride," quipped Viental.

"Until the log rider never walks again," murmured Brental under his breath.

Cerryl studied the logs but could see no sign of the reddish white that had warned him when something was stressed and ready to break. Still, the wagon bed seemed bowed under the weight of the pine logs.

"Only take less than half that were it oak," commented Brental, stretching his legs and hurrying to catch up to the wagon. "An' less than that for black oak or lorken."

Cerryl had to scurry to match the readhead's pace.

"You be mighty silent, young Cerryl," said Brental, glancing sideways at the youth as the two walked downhill behind the wagon. Dylert talked in a low voice to Rinfur, and Viental continued to perch on top of the logs, laughing with each sway of the wagon on the rutted road.

"I am tired," Cerryl said carefully.

"You sound like Erhana, with her fancy language," Brental said with a chuckle.

The youth stiffened inside but did not answer.

"Cerryl . . . I meant no harm, young fellow."

Ahead of them the log wagon slowed and groaned as Rinfur eased it through a depression in the logging road.

"I beg your pardon," Cerryl replied softly. "I know you did not."

"You know, Cerryl, that folk reckon Da as more prosperous than most of the merchants in Lydiar? He doesn't talk fancy. Never had a velvet cloak nor even a fine linen suit . . ." Brental let the words trail off. "He also reckoned—Da does, I mean—your uncle as a good man. Means a lot from Da. He not be saying that 'bout many."

"I know. He has been good to me, and I'm most grateful."

"You be grateful from the first, and we all know that, but it not be what I meant." Brental shook his head. "Fancy words be just fancy words, not the man. You work hard, and that makes you, not the words."

Cerryl nodded. "That's true here, but uncle . . . Syodor . . . he always said that away from the mines, people judged on how one dressed and spoke."

"You be thinking of leaving?"

"I have nowhere to go." Cerryl blotted more sweat to keep it from his eyes and tried not to limp from the strained muscles in his legs.

Brental frowned slightly.

Ahead, the wagon creaked going around a wide turn in the road through a space of oaks and maples not much taller than the horses' ears.

"Can it hurt to listen to Erhana and try to speak better?" asked Cerryl.

"No . . ." answered Brental with a laugh, "not so long as you keep working hard. Da nor I, we watch the work, not the words."

Cerryl offered a faint smile.

XX

The handcart squealed as Cerryl pushed the load of gold oak planks toward the green-painted wagon drawn up before the mill door. He wanted to groan because the squeaking meant that he needed to grease the wheels and axle again, and he hated getting into the grease. Rather, he hated the time and effort it took him to get clean afterward. Somehow, he didn't have that deft a touch with matters mechanical and always ended up a mess, unlike Dylert or Brental, who always made everything around the mill look so effortless.

The handcart kept squealing, the sound drowning out the low rumble of the wheels on the stones of the causeway.

Under the high and hazy clouds of late summer, sweat streamed down his face and down the back of his neck. The meadow grasses below the causeway and to the east of the lower lane hung limply, already browning well before harvest. Not the faintest hint of a breeze had appeared for most of the past eight-day.

Cerryl pushed and sweated, and the cart squeaked and rumbled along the causeway toward the mill. Just outside the big south door, Dylert stood by the wagon talking to a narrow-shouldered man with a wispy ginger goatee in a sleeveless leather vest.

The youth's eyes passed over the emblem on the side of the wagon, then stopped. He squinted against the glare of the sun from the shiny paint and read to himself—"Enfoss and Sons, Master Builders"—half-wondering exactly what Enfoss built.

He slowed the cart as he neared the wagon.

"Here you be, master Enfoss," said Dylert, putting out a hand to help slow the cart. "The best of the golden oak."

"And at a pretty price, too, master Dylert." Enfoss grinned at the mill master, showing yellowed teeth that peered from his face like a rat's. "I paid for more than one puny cartload."

"You paid for three, and three you'll get." Dylert smiled back at Enfoss; then he moved to help Cerryl reload the wood onto the big green wagon. "Just set it on the tailboard, lad, and get the next load. I'll stack it right in the wagon."

"Yes, ser." Cerryl began to lift the planks, two at a time.

"You picking up more on the way back?"

"With what you charge, Dylert? Now, that be hardly likely." Enfoss guffawed.

"You could go to Howlett and pay twice as much for less," suggested the millmaster, lifting four of the heavy planks as though they were feathers.

Before long, Cerryl was pushing the empty cart back to the first lumber barn, glad it only squeaked when laden and not all the time.

Cerryl's shirt was totally soaked by the time the high green wagon rolled down the lane. Enfoss never looked back. For a brief time, both Dylert and Cerryl watched, until the wagon turned eastward on the main road that, Cerryl had been told, eventually joined the wide, stone-paved, wizards' road between Fairhaven and Lydiar.

Dylert nodded, as though he had been assured that Enfoss was indeed on his way back to Lydiar, and then turned. "Cerryl?"

"Yes, ser? I know the cart needs grease again, but it didn't start making noise until I had a load on it."

Dylert shook his head. "Would that all fellows were as worried about their tools. I was going to tell you that you do a good job of picking woods. Nice not to have to worry, it be. As for the grease, tomorrow be fine for that. Put the cart back in the first barn and go wash up and spend some time on yourself 'fore dinner."

"Thank you, ser." Cerryl grinned.

At the sound of a distant horn, both turned toward the lane that led down to the main road. A horse walked slowly up the last section of the road, turning onto the lane up to the mill, each step labored, hardly moving, carrying a bare-headed blond man in dark leathers. Cerryl could see the lather. He could also hear the drumbeat hoofs of many other horses and see the dust rising beyond the hillcrest on the road from Lydiar—a good two kays east of the mill.

Another series of notes rose across the afternoon, and a company of lancers rode over the hill, moving at what seemed to Cerryl to be a fast trot. But he wouldn't have known one gait from another, except a walk from a full gallop.

His eyes went back to the single horse and rider.

The rider gestured toward them. "You two. One of you—you have it—you must help!" He spurred his mount, and the horse took another dozen steps, and then his leg seemed to give way. The rider half-fell, half-flung himself clear and staggered into a heap in the dusty road.

"Cerryl—there be trouble," murmured Dylert. "Help me close the mill door, quick-like."

Cerryl turned and ran to the door, pushing while Dylert pulled. When the long sliding door had but a cubit left to close, Dylert gestured to Cerryl. "Cerryl! Hurry and close the door on the finish barn, and stay inside! Be making sure you stay there. Understand?"

"Yes, ser." Cerryl nodded and ran down the causeway to the finish lumber barn. He glanced over his shoulder.

The rider was rising to his feet, glancing back at the oncoming lancers.

Cerryl tugged the finish barn door, smaller than the one at the mill, until it was nearly closed, before slipping inside. His eyes went to the mill, its door closed, and then back to what he could see of the road, but all he could see was the rider, turning back toward the mill, drawing a blade.

The youth's lips tightened, and he pulled on the door, sliding it closed—almost. He left a sliver of space between the massive doorpost timber and the door itself, so little that no one could have seen without being right at the door. Then he watched, squinting through his peephole.

The dusty rider half-walked, half-staggered uphill, moving determinedly toward the mill, carrying a shimmering blade. His eyes flicked uphill, and Cerryl almost felt as though the rider sought him.

The man drew closer to the mill, less than two hundred cubits from where Cerryl hunched behind the door. He wore a belt scabbard, not a shoulder harness the way the demon women had or the way mercenaries supposedly did. His sleeveless tunic was stained and streaked with dust and dirt, as was the once-fine silk shirt beneath it, and even at a distance, Cerryl could see—or sense—that the fugitive's face was flushed and that a faint white glow surrounded him—like it cloaked the books from Cerryl's father.

The fugitive's eyes raked across the buildings and fixed on the finish barn. Abruptly, he turned as the drumming of hoofs rose again, nearer, and a score of lancers appeared, but a hundred cubits or so downhill from the single man.

All the lancers wore the cyan livery of Lydiar, except for the man riding beside the lancer officer who led the troop. The exception was a figure dressed entirely in white—a white mage.

Cerryl shivered but kept watching.

The lancer officer gestured, and the lancers reined up. Three lancers, bearing bows already strung, rode to the front of the column and drew arrows from their quivers with a fluidity that bespoke long practice.

The fugitive squared himself to face the archers. He raised a hand, and a small ball of fire arched from his fingertips toward the lancers.

Cerryl held his breath as the fire flared toward the Lydian lancers, yet none moved.

The white mage nodded, and simultaneously the fireball splattered into fragments that fell short of the riders. A tuft of brown grass burst into flame, and then ashes.

For a moment, the shoulders of the blond man in the travel-stained clothes slumped; then he straightened and drew his blade, raising it to the late afternoon sun. The metal glistened as though it held the fires of the sun, even after he had lowered it to chest height. He faced the lancers, neither stepping back nor forward.

The lancer officer snapped an order, and the archers released their nocked arrows.

The fugitive's blade seemed to flash, and he stood untouched, two broken arrows lying by his feet, both somehow charred and snapped.

The lancer officer glanced at the white wizard. This time, the wizard raised his hand, and a larger fireball flared toward the blond man.

Once more the golden-fired blade flashed, and fragments of fire spewed around the fugitive. Cerryl could see a black slash across the back of the man's left arm. The man was breathing heavily but continued to hold his strange blade in the guard position.

Another firebolt flashed from the white wizard, parried by the blond man, and yet another firebolt. After the third firebolt, the fugitive barely could raise the sword.

Cerryl missed the order from the lancer officer, but arrows flew toward the blond man. The first arrow took the fugitive in the arm. A second missed, as did a third as he threw himself to the side, but his leg slipped on the gravel of the road.

As he fell, the man hurled the blade. It flashed white and gold as it spun hilt over point and into the low brush at the end of the meadow by the road.

Two firebolts flashed from the hands of the white wizard in succession, exploding over the body of the fallen man and rising into a pillar of flame.

When the fires receded, all that remained was an irregular star of blackened ground—no body, no ashes, just an odd-shaped star of soot. Soot and the odor of burned meat.

Cerryl leaned against the doorpost and swallowed hard to keep from gagging. By the time he had regained full control, the drumming of hoofbeats had died away, and the lane was empty. Even the dust over the road to Lydiar had begun to settle.

He slowly pushed the barn door open enough to slip out. Then he studied the lane and the road. The lancers—and the white mage—had indeed left on their return to Lydiar.

Slowly, Cerryl walked down the lane, avoiding the star-shaped patch of soot, until he reached the area where the dead man had thrown the blade. A faint glint of something tugged at his eyes, except that tug urged him to look away.

He fought the feeling and followed it to a deeper patch of grass. Gingerly, he picked up the blade by the hilt, a hilt of bronze, apparently wrapped in something like silk.

Cerryl studied the blade, noting that it was not iron or steel or anything like it, but more like the metal of the knife that had been his father's.

The sound of boots on the road alerted him, and he slipped the blade behind him as he turned.

Brental smiled. "You need not hide that blade, Cerryl. I see we had the same thought. You found it, and it be yours. Might I see it?"

After a moment, Cerryl extended the blade sideways, looking over Brental's shoulder as Dylert walked down the lane from the barn.

Brental took it, then squinted. "I can hardly see it. It twists your eyes right well away from it." He shivered and quickly handed the blade back to Cerryl. "It be yours, if you wish it."

Cerryl took the blade back.

Dylert nodded, as if to agree that the blade was Cerryl's.

Brental glanced past Cerryl, toward the Lydiar road, before speaking. "You saw the firebolt? The flame the poor fellow cast? Pity-poor chaos flame, too, it was."

"Chaos flame?" blurted Cerryl.

"Aye," answered Dylert. "The fellow with that blade there, he'd a been a renegade white—one who'd not follow their rules. Strict they be, about chaos and its use." He looked hard at Cerryl. "Seen a handful over my years. A man has the talent and not be under their rules and protection, the white mages, they like as not kill or ruin a fellow . . . and them's the lucky ones." He shook his head slowly. "In their own way, they be fair, fairer than most dukes and the like. But a man should walk a fair piece to stay on their good side. Aye, and he should."

Their good side? Had they one? Cerryl wondered.

"Glad I be as just a mill man," said Brental, following his words with a nervous laugh.

Cerryl forced himself not to look down at the blade in his hands, a blade that felt strangely comfortable and simultaneously uncomfortable as he held it loosely.

"Well . . ." Dylert added into the silence, glancing to the west where the sun hung low over the house. "Day's done. Be time soon for dinner." He turned and walked briskly back uphill.

After a moment, Brental nodded and followed his father.

With the near-setting sun warming his face, Cerryl looked down at the blade, the same white bronze as the knife from his father, recalling how the dead man had knocked down arrows and firebolts . . . and how his efforts had been in vain.

And how he had sought Cerryl. The youth shivered.

XXI

Cerryl reread the passage in *Colors of White,* trying to keep the sounds and images in his head, as he'd overheard Siglinda tell Erhana during one of the tutoring sessions when he'd been stacking hearth wood outside the millmaster's house.

"... all that is under the sun can only be because of the chaos of the sun. Even the wisest of mages cannot perceive any portion of all that exists on and under the earth itself except through the operation of chaos."

He wanted to shake his head. He understood the words, but there was something about the meaning that eluded him.

Brental had said that the man who had fled the lancers of Lydiar— and the white wizard—had flung chaos fire against the wizard. Cerryl had seen that, and how the wizard had turned it back with little more than a glance. Or so it had seemed. Still, the fugitive had held his own for a time against outlandish odds.

Cerryl wasn't sure if he wished the blond man had won or not, but he wouldn't soon forget the cold and impartial attitude of the white wizard, acting as if the fugitive were little more than vermin to be destroyed.

He cleared his throat, realizing he had been murmuring the words, and clamped his lips shut as he studied the page again, then flipped to another page, farther along.

Still nothing about chaos fire.

He tried another page, and then another.

He glanced down at *Colors of White* again. Why didn't he have the second part, instead of a worthless history? The second part would have explained everything, like how to create chaos fire.

He frowned, touching his chin, a chin that remained beardless and smooth. Could he create chaos fire?

In the dimness, he held up his left hand, concentrated on somehow making fire appear at his fingertips, the way the fugitive had.

Was there a glow there? He squinted through the gloom at the faintest spark at the tip of his index finger. Then the point of light vanished. He could feel the sweat beading on his forehead. A deeper and ugly red glow lingered in the air for several moments.

Cerryl took a deep breath, then another.

XXII

In the light drizzle that drifted from the low-hanging gray clouds, Cerryl used the dark brown laundry soap and washed his hands and face at the well, the one uphill of the south end of the porch. He shook his hands as dry as he could in the damp air, then began to walk toward the porch of the mill master's house, noticing that Rinfur was already stepping into the kitchen. Viental had gone—again—to visit his "sister."

Dylert was waiting on the porch just back of the top step, his face somber.

"Yes, ser?" Cerryl could feel his stomach tightening, but kept his expression pleasant.

"You've learned the letters, haven't you, boy?" Dylert asked, stepping back and gesturing for Cerryl to take a seat on the porch bench.

"Ser?" Meeting the millmaster's eyes squarely, Cerryl managed a blank expression. He did not sit down.

Dylert laughed. "Young fellow, from your look I'd not know, but my daughter I can see through like she was fine timber."

"Yes, ser. I asked her to teach me. But only when I was not working, ser." Cerryl's gray eyes continued to hold those of the millmaster. "Most times, after dinner."

"I've no complaints with your work or anything else you have done, young Cerryl." Dylert fingered his beard, then cleared his throat. "That'd not be the problem."

Cerryl waited.

"That fellow—the one the white mage got the other day? Something like that . . . well, it happened to your da. You know that, do you not?" Dylert's eyes flicked downhill, toward the spot on the edge of the road where the rocks and clay remained blackened.

"I know that something happened. Uncle Syodor and Aunt Nall—they didn't say much about it."

"Syodor . . . he was . . . he be not the type to speak of it." Dylert fingered his beard again.

A pattering of heavier rain swept across the porch roof, followed by a light gust of wind that ruffled Cerryl's hair. Water began to drip from the eaves.

"Speaking or not, though, fact is, be a dangerous time to stay here for a young fellow with a da like yours."

"Did the white mages kill Uncle Syodor, too?" Cerryl asked softly. "You would only tell me that he and Nall were dead."

"Too sharp for your own eyes, you be, young fellow." Dylert frowned. "Like as they died in a fire, that be what Wreasohn said. How that fire got started, I'd not be guessing. Nor you, either."

Cerryl nodded. *But why? What had they done to anger the white mages?* If the mages knew Cerryl existed, wouldn't they have come after him?

"I've a wagon of white oak a-heading to Fairhaven the day after next. To Fasse, the cabinet-maker there." The millmaster cleared his throat. "I've a scroll here—Siglinda, she helped me with it—and it says that you're a hardworking young fellow better suited to finer things. It also says you're a tattered britches relative of mine, of a distant cousin." Dylert frowned. "Don't be making me a liar, now."

"I won't, ser." Cerryl could feel the ache in his guts growing, but kept his eyes on Dylert.

"It's like this, Cerryl. Your da and your uncle, they did things that, well . . . they did not . . . I mean . . . the white mages can be jealous . . . of anything much . . . much close . . . to what . . . what they do." The millmaster wiped his forehead. "You be their son and nephew, and Hrisbarg . . . well, small it is. All the folk know all the folk." He shrugged. "In Fairhaven . . . none care . . . not that ways, anyway."

What had Uncle Syodor done? His uncle had stayed away from anything like the white mages had done, and Aunt Nall—she'd had a fit when she'd even seen a fragment of a mirror or glass around Cerryl.

"I thought of Tellis. Been owing me a long time, ever since I sent him the best gold oak timbers for his shop . . . and a few other things." Dylert's face clouded.

Cerryl wondered what favor was so bad that the genial Dylert had a bad memory about it.

"Now, Tellis, he's a cousin of Dyella, and he's a scrivener. You know what a scrivener is?"

Cerryl didn't have to feign puzzlement. Why was Dylert talking about scriveners?

"Scriveners write things for others," Dylert said slowly, "and in Fairhaven they make books, like the ones Erhana let you read."

"Yes, ser."

"Well, you be liking books, and Tellis owing me, and sure as he could use a young fellow works hard as you . . . and Fairhaven being a better place for you . . . and . . . well . . . being a place where someone with . . . the kind of talent mayhap you have . . . seeing as if you didn't use it . . . it wouldn't be so unexpected . . . and Tellis, he knows how that land lies, if you see the line I'm laying . . ." Dylert cleared his throat.

Cerryl did see the line Dylert laid. The millmaster was worried that any passing white wizard might stumble on Cerryl and hold Dylert responsible. He was also suggesting that Cerryl would be safer in Fairhaven, especially if he did not use his talents openly—or perhaps at all. "Yes, ser."

"You understand, young fellow . . . it's not just you . . ."

"I understand, ser. You've been fair and good to me."

"Dinner be ready," Dylert said. "We'll talk more after we eat. You be needing some clothes, and a pair of good boots."

"Thank you."

"After we eat," Dylert repeated, opening the door to the kitchen.

XXIII

Under the spells and songs of Creslin, who descended from the black Nylan and the dark songmage Ayrlyn, Megaera persuaded her cousin, the Duke of Montgren, to give both herself and Creslin refuge, for the white brethren had pursued the two and sought to bind them before they brought yet more darkness unto all of Candar.

In his weakness, the duke brought his cousin and her dark liege Creslin under his protection, and Creslin used the refuge at Vergren to build his powers, until darkness infested every stone of that ancient keep, until the very sun was kept at bay.

In the depths of that keep, Creslin took Megaera for consort, and bound her to him with the dark tie that meant, should he die, so, too, would she. Such blasphemy of light and goodness was too great even for the duke, and he fell into a stupor.

Fearing that, without the duke's protection, the keep would be opened to the forces of light, Creslin and Megaera fled over the northern hills.

As he knew what the evil pair might bring upon Candar, the Viscount of Certis sent forth a host, but Creslin seized the winds of the north and pummeled that force with spears of ice and hammers of frost, and he slew from the depths of a magic fog the fair young wizard that advised the lancers of Certis, and only a handful of those lancers ever returned to Jellico.

When Creslin and Megaera reached the port of Tyrhavven, there they seized a ship of the duke's, binding the crew with darkness and forcing them to carry the two dark mages across the gulf to the desert isle of Recluce . . .

Colors of White
(Manual of the Guild at Fairhaven)
Preface

XXIV

After washing at the well and coming back to his room to finish dressing, Cerryl took out the silver-rimmed mirror and studied himself. The pale gray shirt and trousers were not new but almost could have passed for such, and the thick-soled boots Brental had given him seemed barely worn. In his pack, besides his books, were his old work clothes and an older sheepskin jacket, the fleece to the inside and barely matted.

His hair was shorter—Dyella had trimmed it for him the day before—but the shorter length seemed to emphasize the narrow triangular shape of his face. He fingered his chin, feeling the first hints of what might be a beard. Somehow, he doubted that any beard he grew would match the thick splendor of those of his uncle or of Dylert, or even the red bush sported by Brental.

The mirror went back in the pack, wrapped inside his spare small-clothes but on top of the heavier books. Then he slipped the scroll to Tellis on the very top and laced the pack shut.

He looked around the room, bare as ever, the blankets folded on the foot of the pallet, the board where he'd hidden his few valuables securely back in place, the white-bronze sword left there as well, the only possession he had left behind, but it was too big to conceal in anything he owned.

Thrap! Cerryl turned at the knock.

"You coming, Cerryl?" asked Rinfur. "Be a long day even leaving now."

"I'm coming." Cerryl lifted the pack off the stool and opened the door. Outside, standing at the back of the finish lumber barn, he paused and looked across the hillside. The oaks loomed across the field like ancient guardians of night, and the predawn gray was beginning to lighten. Cerryl closed the door and swallowed. A single *terwhit* echoed from the oaks to the west, and the night hum of insects had long since died away.

He turned toward the mill and lifted his pack. After receiving all the clothes from Dylert, Cerryl had been more than hesitant to ask the millmaster for his pay, and had kept putting off asking. Now he wished he hadn't. What would he do in Fairhaven with only two coppers to his name—the same two coppers he'd brought to the mill? Should he have taken the short blade from the fugitive? His lips tightened. Not with the aura of chaos around it. He knew enough to know the blade alone would bring him trouble, much as he disliked leaving it behind.

His eyes went uphill to the empty porch of the millmaster's house. Erhana was doubtless still sleeping, though the thin trail of smoke from the kitchen chimney indicated that Dyella was up and at work.

Dylert was inspecting the wood that had been loaded the afternoon before, and Rinfur was rechecking the harnesses as Cerryl hurried toward the wagon.

"Put your pack under the seat," Rinfur called without looking up or toward Cerryl.

The brown-haired youth eased the pack under the seat.

By the time he had straightened, Dylert had vaulted off the wagon. "Here's what I owe you, young fellow, and a bit to spare." Dylert pulled a cloth purse from his belt and extended it to Cerryl. "You be just like your uncle, not one to ask or press. Sometimes, mayhap, you must." The millmaster grinned. "For all that, young fellow, we be missing you here. You got that scroll?"

"Yes, ser." Cerryl wanted to feel the purse but didn't, instead fastening it to his belt. "I thank you."

"No thanks be due. You worked hard, and you deserve the coin. And the recommendation to Tellis." Dylert grinned. "He can be gruff. Don't let it fool you. Understand?"

Cerryl nodded. He cleared his throat.

"Yes, lad?"

"Ser? In . . . my room . . . I mean . . . it was my room . . . there's a board under the cubby . . . behind it . . . there's a bronze blade . . . Brental might want it."

Dylert nodded solemnly. "He might. Whether I let him . . . that be between us. I thank you for saying such . . . and you be a wise lad not to carry it."

"You . . . best know." The words were hard for Cerryl to get out.

Dylert smiled and clapped Cerryl on the shoulder. "Keep that head in place, lad, and you be doing fine."

Rinfur walked toward them.

"The provisions Dyella set up be under your seat, Rinfur. Extra this time." Dylert nodded toward Cerryl. "Still growing, I'd wager."

"Don't know as growing," answered the teamster, climbing up onto the seat, "but he eats like he be. Best be up here, lad. A long road ahead we got."

Cerryl followed Rinfur's example, except that, with his shorter legs, he had to pull himself up onto the seat. He looked at Dylert, knowing he should say something but not knowing what. Finally, as Rinfur flicked the long leads to the team, he said, "Thank you, ser. Thank you again."

"Be nothing, young fellow. Take care, and give Tellis my best."

"Yes, ser."

Cerryl swallowed as the wagon lurched off the causeway and onto the lane heading down to the road. He wanted to look back but didn't, instead fixing his eyes on the stream to the left of the lane, his eyes skipping over the patch of blackened soil and rock that remained even after a handful of eight-days of sun and rain.

Until Rinfur had the team on the straightaway toward the road, the wagon moved at the slowest of walks. At the end of the lane, Rinfur turned the team right—left on the road away from Hrisbarg proper.

"Hrisbarg is that way," said Cerryl, pointing to the right and the uphill road.

"Aye, but the wizards' road be this way, lad, and that road be smoother and far swifter than the way through Hrisbarg and Howlett." Rinfur smiled, showing brown teeth. "Trust me. The roads I know, and master Dylert'd not give over this wagon to one he'd not trust."

That was something about which Cerryl had few doubts at all.

"You ever been on a wizards' road?" asked Rinfur.

"No. Never been on a wagon before, except around the mill," Cerryl admitted, shifting his weight on the hard seat.

"A lot you be seeing, then."

"What's Fairhaven like?"

The teamster laughed. "A poor driver like me be not the one to tell. The buildings, most like be made of stone so white it glitters. All the ways and byways be paved with white stone like the wizards' road. Peaceable, too. A girl could walk stark naked, they say, and not a man dare touch her." Rinfur grinned. "Never seen such, but some say the white mages send out female lancers like that to tempt the wild."

Cerryl moistened his lips. He wasn't sure whether they were already dry from the dust or from what he was hearing.

"Those try to molest 'em, well, they end up working on the great highway on the far side of the Easthorns. Working till they die, some folks say."

The wagon slowed as it climbed the low hill to the east of the mill.

"Do you know why master Dylert sends a wagon to Fairhaven?" Cerryl asked, wanting to say something.

"Don't know as I understand," said Rinfur, "Fairhaven being half again as far as Lydiar, and master Dylert not sending wagons to the port." He shrugged. "Near on twice a year, I take a wagon to Fasse. Always white oak. The good oak. He's from Kyphros, says there's no white oak there."

Cerryl looked over his shoulder at the planks and small timbers neatly secured in the wagon bed. "It must be worth a lot."

Rinfur shrugged again. "Can't say as I know. The coins go by messenger."

By messenger? Dylert had charged Erastus something like six golds for a quarter of a wagon half the size of the mill wagon—or less. That had been black oak, but even if Dylert charged half that.... Cerryl shook his head. At least fifteen golds of wood lay stacked in the wagon.

At the thought of coins, Cerryl felt those in the purse and frowned. From what he'd figured, Dylert owed him about twenty coppers, or two silvers. The purse held more than two silvers—that he could tell.

Three silvers and ten coppers. Why? Dylert had been generous enough in giving him clothes and better boots. Because the millmaster wanted Cerryl away from the mill? Because he felt he owed something to Syodor?

The wagon slowed as it reached the hillcrest, then picked up speed slowly.

"Easy . . . easy now," murmured Rinfur.

Cerryl put out a hand to the end of the wooden wagon seat to steady himself.

As the wagon came down the low hill, Cerryl squinted. Ahead was a line of sparkling white—white despite the orange light of the rising sun, a line of white that arrowed to the right through the hills as though the hills had been cleaved to allow the road passage.

On each side of the wizards' road was a low stone wall, and to the south that wall separated the road from a small river.

"Something, be it not?" asked Rinfur. "Ah . . . here we go. Be a relief to get on the main road to Fairhaven." Rinfur slowed the team with a slight pressure on the leads as he guided them past an empty stone booth, no more than four cubits by four. "Sometimes, they have a guard here, check if you paid the road taxes."

"And if you haven't?" asked Cerryl. "How can you tell?"

"Don't let you on. There's a medal on the side of the wagon, driver's side. Bound with magic, some ways."

The wheels rumbled on the flat stones, and Cerryl recalled Syodor's statement about the road having been paved with souls. He tightened his lips, then forced himself to relax—as much as he could as the wagon picked up speed on the flat and white stones of the main road, now heading due west. West toward Fairhaven.

XXV

Cerryl wiped his forehead. Despite the gentle dry breeze out of the west, he still found himself sweating in the midday sun. His eyes went from the team to the road, so straight that he could see the gentle crown of the road more than two hundred cubits ahead.

After half a day, the road still amazed him—so level that Dylert's causeway seemed rough by comparison, stretching for kays, the entire length with low walls on each side. On the inside of the wall on both sides was a half-cubit-wide drainage way formed of the same smooth stone blocks, with large stone drains no more than every fifty cubits. Not a blade of grass nor a single weed marred the space between the walls.

His eyes drifted to the left, the south side of the road, where the pinkish white stone wall dropped almost fifteen cubits to the nearly dry stream below.

"What else do you know about the wizards' roads?" he finally asked Rinfur.

"What be there to know?" countered Rinfur, not taking his eyes off the team. "My grandda, he drove the roads, and it be said that his grandda drove them as well."

"They don't look that old." Cerryl looked at the low stone wall to the left. His eyes said that the even edges and slightly rounded corners looked as though they had been quarried and set within the past few years, yet there was a sense of darkness and age about the stone, a sense that he could feel rather than see.

"They be old." Rinfur laughed. "Some folk say that the black demon

Creslin—the whites forced him to build half the road afore he escaped, and that be why he created the black isle, so as to build a land that would bring down Fairhaven. Been generations, and it hasn't happened. Don't look as it will, either."

Cerryl shivered, looking at the road, so straight, so ordered, so perfect. Ahead was a faint mistlike cloud of dust, partly shrouding a wagon rumbling toward them.

"Over now . . . now . . . Ge-ahh!" called Rinfur. The team edged to the right.

The brown-haired youth watched as the other wagon neared. Two men sat on the seat of that wagon, drawn by a matched team of four grays. Both men wore cyan livery. The driver flicked the reins, almost imperceptibly, and the wagon, larger even than Dylert's wood wagon, edged toward the wall on the south side of the road.

The brasswork of the oncoming wagon glistened in the midday sun like spun gold, and the cyan paint shimmered metallically, and a brown canvas was strapped over the wagon bed, hiding whatever the cargo might be.

Behind the wagon rode four lancers in the same cyan livery as those who had followed the white wizard to the mill in pursuit of the renegade wizard. Cerryl forced himself to sit erect, to look casually at the wagon as it passed.

White dust drifted up from the wheels of the cyan wagon as it passed on the left, headed toward Lydiar, Cerryl supposed. Neither the driver, nor the soldier beside him, gave Cerryl or Rinfur more than the briefest glance. Nor did the lancers who trailed the wagon.

"Do you know whose wagon that was?" Cerryl asked.

"Mayhap the duke's—having his colors and his guards," answered Rinfur, "a-coming back from Fairhaven. If you can't get it in Lydiar or Fairhaven, folks say you be not getting it anywhere." Rinfur gave a low chuckle. " 'Cept on Recluce, and it not be healthy to say that too loud."

"Why doesn't anyone talk about Recluce?" asked Cerryl.

" 'Cause it be not exactly healthy, especially in Fairhaven. The whites have no love of the blacks. Never have, and never will, not since the days of the ancients when the black demon Nylan overthrew ancient Cyador and brought darkness back to Candar." Rinfur shook his head and glanced over his shoulder. "Enough said, lad. Dylert says you know your letters, and you be going to apprentice with Tellis, the scrivener. Well . . . I'd be expecting Tellis has books that be saying more than this poor teamster ever knew . . . and reading be safer, too."

Cerryl glanced back, but the road was clear.

Rinfur flicked the reins. "Now . . . the traders' square in Fairhaven, that be something the like I never saw before . . . spices, and blades of metals of all colors, and . . ." He shook his head. "That be something you need see . . ."

Cerryl nodded and listened as the wagon rumbled westward.

XXVI

With the rumbling of the big wheels on the smooth wizards' road and the hot afternoon, Cerryl found his eyelids getting heavier and heavier. The late afternoon sun, shining directly at his face, offered another incentive to let his eyes close.

"Darkness!"

At Rinfur's expletive, the team swerved, and Cerryl found himself grasping for the sideboard with one hand and the wagon seat with the other. His eyes popped open.

"Demon-cursed messenger! Think they own the road," mumbled Rinfur as he guided the team back from nearly scraping the right-hand wall.

Cerryl glanced over his shoulder, but all he could see was a mist of white road dust.

"Course they do. You don't give them the road, and the wizards have you whipped."

"Even if it happens on the part of the road in Lydiar, or Certis?" asked Cerryl, shifting his weight on the hard wagon seat.

"Don't be wagering on that. The wizards rule their roads. And a lot more besides that."

Cerryl waited.

"Dylert, he was telling me. Years ago, it was. The old line of dukes, the ones in Lydiar I be meaning, they told their traders not to be paying the road tariffs to the wizards. Three days later, there were two-hundred-score lancers on the road outside Lydiar and a score of white wizards. Never said a word, did they. Just marched into Lydiar and cast fire down on the duke's palace. He was in it, a course. Ruins stood for nigh-on forty years 'fore anyone dared rebuild it—even the new duke the wizards named."

"If the white mages are so powerful, why aren't they the dukes of Lydiar and Certis and . . ."

Rinfur raised his free hand.

"Used to be a Duke of Montgren, once upon a time. He befriended that black demon—Creslin, I think. The whites killed him and all those in the keep. Then they leveled the keep. Montgren still belongs to Fairhaven."

"But you said they did that to Lydiar. Leveled the duke's place, I mean, but there's still a Duke of Lydiar."

"Got me," said Rinfur. "All I know be that no duke or viscount or whatever in his mind be crossing the white mages. No teamster not give way to a white messenger." He shrugged. "That be enough."

Cerryl glanced ahead. The almost mountainous hills the road had bored through after they had left Hrisbarg had already dwindled into low rolling hills, half topped with trees, half with meadows, and each line of hills seemed lower than the previous set.

"Won't be long. Hills about to end," confirmed the driver.

Cerryl nodded and watched.

Fairhaven rested in a gentle valley, and the road descended ever so gradually toward the mixture of white structures, white road, and green grass. The trees were mainly evergreens barely again as tall as the roofs they shaded. Cerryl saw no leaf-bearing trees, none. Was that why Dylert could send white oak to Fairhaven?

The paving stones of the road, somewhere along the way, had turned from pinkish granite to slightly off-white gray granite, as had the stones of the walls. As the wagon cleared the last low hill, the road walls ended, replaced with a long curb slightly more than a span high. Beyond the curb was green grass, green still despite the nearing of harvest.

Cerryl had trouble seeing the city ahead against all the whiteness, a white that seemed somehow brighter than it should have been even with the clear sky and the glare of the late afternoon sun in his face. The glare seemed to intensify as the lumber wagon rolled closer.

"Ahead be the gates," explained Rinfur, gesturing almost directly in front of the wagon, down the avenue of white stone wide enough for at least four wagons abreast.

Cerryl tried to see where Rinfur pointed, but the sun hung just above the horizon, and looking westward only left Cerryl with a headache and an image of blinding whiteness from the sun off the white of the road.

Rinfur began to rein in the team, slowing the wagon gradually until it creaked to a stop behind a mule cart piled with pottery. In front of the mule cart was another wagon, a small one drawn by a single bony horse and filled with gourds or squashes. The squash wagon stood just short of a small white stone building outside the gates. The stone gates did not seem that tall to Cerryl, not more than ten or twelve cubits high, not particularly impressive for a city that ruled, in one form or another, much of Candar.

The two white-clad soldiers or guards stepped up to the driver of the squash wagon, inspected the wagon, poked desultorily at the squashes, and motioned the farmer past the gates. The mule wagon creaked up to the gates, and Rinfur eased the lumber wagon forward but had to touch the brake to ensure the wagon stopped completely.

A squealing continued after the lumber wagon slowed. Cerryl turned. A coach and a wagon had lined up behind them. The coach, dark gray with a pair of grays, was driven by a teamster in gray as well. The driver avoided Cerryl's eyes. Behind the coach was another wagon, but the coach blocked Cerryl's view, and he looked back toward the gates.

The two guards had stepped up to the driver of the mule cart. One gestured at the medallion. The driver gestured, shrugging as if he did not understand.

Cerryl strained to hear the words.

"... your pass is two years old ..."

"I did not know, ser." The cart driver shrugged, looking at the soldiers helplessly.

"You knew. Don't lie to us." The taller soldier took the driver by the arm and pulled him off the cart.

"Handlers!" called the second guard. At his word, two men jumped from somewhere and unhitched the mule, leading it away down a lane to the east toward a low structure. A stable? Cerryl wondered, still looking at the unattended cart of wood and pottery.

Whhsttt! Whhhstt! Two firebolts flared from the top of the guard tower, enveloping the cart. When Cerryl's eyes cleared and the flames had died away, all that remained before the gates was a calf-high pile of white dust, sifting back and forth in the light breeze.

Cerryl managed to keep from swallowing as he could half-see, half-feel the currents of red-tinged white energy that swirled around the gates, energies apparently unseen by anyone save the mages who had employed them—and Cerryl.

Two men in chains appeared from the gate, one bearing a broom, the other a scoop and two large buckets. Almost before Cerryl could swallow, the ashes and the men in chains were gone, and the soldier was motioning for Rinfur to pull up the lumber wagon.

Cerryl turned to Rinfur.

"It happens, young fellow. See why you not be crossing the white mages?" Rinfur chucked the reins gently, just enough to get the team to take a dozen steps or so and bring the wagon up to the white guard building.

The two white-clad soldiers stepped away from the white stone curb, just as they had with the wagon and the cart, almost as if nothing had happened. One inspected the medal on the wagon side. The other looked at Rinfur. "Goods? Destination?"

"White oak from Dylert, the millmaster of Hrisbarg. The wood be going to Fasse, the cabinet-maker off the artisans' square." Rinfur's words were polite, even, and practiced.

How often had the teamster carried white oak to Fairhaven?

The second soldier's eyes lingered on Cerryl for a moment, then passed on, dismissing him as scarcely worthy of scrutiny, before lifting the canvas in the rear and studying the stacked woods. Then he nodded to the other soldier in white. "Wood."

The first soldier stepped back and nodded. "You can go."

"Thank you," answered Rinfur politely.

Cerryl managed to keep from swallowing until the wagon was rolling again, past the gates and down the avenue. Shops and dwellings were set back from the avenue, and the avenue itself was divided so that on the side taken by Rinfur, all the carts and wagons and riders traveled toward the center of Fairhaven.

From what Cerryl could see, though, more wagons, empty wagons, were departing, heading for the gates through which he and Rinfur had just passed, their wheels rumbling on the whitened granite paving stones.

Scattered individuals walked briskly along the stone-paved walks flanking the avenue, their steps firm and quick. Only one looked toward the lumber wagon, and that was a young mother in a pale blue tunic and trousers, burping a child on her shoulder.

Cerryl smiled but received no response as she turned and resumed walking in the same direction as the wagon. He watched for several moments, but the wagon slowly extended the distance between the woman and Cerryl, and he looked ahead again. To each side of the avenue were houses, large but low houses of a single story, each surrounded by a low wall with a wooden gate. Trees with dark green leaves rose from the courtyards created by the walls, the dark leaves contrasting with the white roofs and walls.

"It's quiet," said Cerryl.

"A lot quieter than Lydiar, I dare say. More peaceable, too."

"Coins . . . too," ventured Cerryl.

"Coins, aye. Always be coins where you find power. Still, can't say as I exactly like Fairhaven," Rinfur said with a lowered voice. "Sort of gets on your nerves after a time." The teamster shrugged, not taking his eyes off the avenue, although he had kept the wagon to a slow walk. "Safe place. Safest city in all Candar. Say you could leave your purse on a wall and come back a day later and find it. Me . . . I wouldn't be trying that, but it be what they say."

Cerryl's eyes, slowly adjusting to the glare, looked westward toward the single white tower that rose out of a square that had to have been more than a kay away down the avenue. He could see—or feel—waves of the unseen red-tinged whiteness emanating from the tower, almost like flames and heat from a fire, except that whatever the tower radiated wasn't hot, not like a fire, anyway. "What's that?"

"That's the wizards' square—their tower. You not be wanting to go there." Rinfur shivered. "No, ser."

Cerryl nodded.

The two halves of the avenue split apart into half-circles around a space of green grass, white stone paths, and low spread-leafed trees. A low fountain gurgled in the center of the circle. The outside of the avenue was dotted with shops—a cooper's, then a coppersmith's, several shops whose symbols were unfamiliar to Cerryl, then an inn, and a stable.

"This be the artisans' square, here. You can go round the circle and drive back the way we came. Down that side way we go." Rinfur eased the team down a street to the right, a side way almost as wide as the main and only street of Hrisbarg. "Fasse's be the second shop there. Can't put a wagon before a shop. Have to use the rear courts."

Cerryl nodded. After what he'd seen at the gates, he had no doubts that the laws of Fairhaven were followed. He glanced back at the grass of the square, vacant except for two toddlers tended by a girl barely older than Cerryl and a white-haired man sitting on a stone bench. Cerryl felt something was missing, yet he hadn't any idea what that might have been.

As the wagon turned down an alleyway and then rolled into the back courtyard of a shop, a thin man hurried out. Everything about him was thin, Cerryl decided—the twiglike and wispy mustache above narrow lips, the angular face, the skinny shoulders, and the pointed brown boots.

"Greetings, master Fasse."

"Greetings, ah . . . teamster." Fasse's eyes flicked from Rinfur to the wagon and then to Cerryl. "Who's the young fellow? I don't need another apprentice, you know? Haven't needed an apprentice for years, thank you."

"Cerryl knows the woods right well," drawled Rinfur, a glint in his eye. As Fasse opened his mouth, the driver added, "He be headed to master Tellis in the morn."

Fasse closed his mouth and nodded abruptly.

"I shouldn't be telling master Dylert you be needing an apprentice, should I?" asked Rinfur almost belatedly.

"No apprentices," confirmed Fasse. "Not now. Not ever."

Rinfur ensured the wagon brake was locked, then inclined his head to Cerryl, who began to loosen the ties on the canvas covering the wood.

"Careful there, young fellow. Don't let the canvas cut the oak. Even oak can be scarred." Fasse hurried to the tailboard and unfastened one side as Rinfur loosened the other.

Cerryl folded the canvas and laid it across the wagon seat, then slipped down to the ground and joined the other two at the rear of the wagon.

"Which first, master Fasse?" asked Rinfur.

"The heavy ones, of course, for the big racks on the wall. Would I put light planks there? The very thought of it!"

"Just two planks," Rinfur said to Cerryl, there not being much room to work with.

Cerryl nodded and walked his way back along the planks as Rinfur slid them gently out of the wagon. The two carried the set inside through a narrow door that opened out. The cabinetry shop was small, no more than a dozen and a half cubits square, and half of that was taken with racks for wood. The youth's nose itched with the faintest trace of sawdust, and he wished he could scratch it, but carrying the wood took both hands. He sniffed instead, and his nose itched even more.

"Gentle, gentle with that oak. Not a scar, not a scratch. The whites, they can sense if but a bruise there be." Fasse scurried around Rinfur and Cerryl as they carried in the wider planks. "On the first rack there, the one padded with the rags. Do be gentle."

The two eased the planks onto the padded rack, then walked back to the wagon for another load. Cerryl rubbed his nose. What was it about sawdust?

The sun was touching the tops of the shops to the west by the time, following Fasse's directions, they had unloaded and stored all the white oak.

Rinfur stretched. "We need to stable the horses. We can leave the wagon in the courtyard," Rinfur explained.

"The stable by the inn?" Cerryl glanced around the courtyard that barely held the wagon.

"Aye. If you sweep out the wagon and cover it . . ."

"I can do that."

"Master Fasse?" called Rinfur.

"Yes, teamster?"

"A broom, perhaps, so that Cerryl can clean up the wagon and the courtyard while I stable the horses?"

"There be an old one here somewhere."

By the time Fasse had reappeared with a ragged-edged straw broom bound in cloth strips, Rinfur had long since departed with the team.

"The dust and scraps . . . in the pail in the corner. Piddling chunks, too. Don't be leaving any signs of sawdust or dirt. The patrol won't be having that."

"Yes, ser." The patrol? Cerryl merely nodded as he wondered. Patrols inside the city? For what? Then he wanted to shake his head. If the courtyard had to be spotless, why was Fasse so reluctant to come up with a broom?

By the time Rinfur returned, Cerryl had finished sweeping the courtyard and was pushing the wagon, a span at a time, into the corner where it blocked neither the shop door nor access to the alley itself. The teamster added his shoulder to Cerryl's efforts, and they eased the wagon into place. Cerryl covered the wagon with the canvas and reclaimed his pack.

By then, Fasse had reappeared and stood in the doorway. "Not much to offer you this eve," he suggested, not looking toward either of the two from Hrisbarg.

"Whatever you have, master crafter, that will serve fine," answered Rinfur with a smile. "We're just poor mill workers."

"Ah . . . yes . . . let me check with the consort." Fasse turned and went through the door and vanished down a narrow hall.

"Always does that," said Rinfur. "He has to feed us, but he never wants to admit it. Folks from Kyphros, they say, be like that."

His pack half-dangling from his shoulder, Cerryl stifled a yawn. It had been a long day, a very long day.

"Not that we be having much this eve, saving a mutton stew that be mostly carrots and onions, but you be welcome," said Fasse, reappearing suddenly.

"Thank you, master crafter," offered Cerryl.

"Thank you," added Rinfur.

Fasse gestured toward the door, and the two entered. The door closed behind the three with a *snick* of the latch.

"All the way to the end, and the door on the right," Fasse suggested.

Cerryl followed Rinfur down the narrow corridor and stepped through the door from the gloom into a surprisingly bright room, the walls a spotless white plaster, the floor a polished golden oak.

The odor of stew filled the room, coming from the stew pot that sat on the oblong waist-high black metal structure that Cerryl realized, after a moment, must be a stove. A scuttle of coal sat beside the stove, which was set in an alcove with windows on each side. The windows and shutters were open wide. Cerryl nodded almost to himself, sensing the flow of chaos-tinged heat from the hot stove out the window on the right side.

"This be my consort, Weylenya." Fasse jerked his head toward the gray-haired, round-faced woman in brown who stood before the stove, then gestured to the benches flanking the trestle table. There was a place set on each side and at each end. Backed stools faced the ends of the tables.

"I am honored to meet you," Cerryl said after an awkward moment.

"Good it be to see you, again, lady," added Rinfur.

"A poor stew it be, but filling." Weylenya inclined her head. "Company we had not expected."

After waiting his turn to use the washstand in the corner, Cerryl stood back until Rinfur picked the bench where he would sit. Then Cerryl stood behind the bench on the other side.

"Sit," said Weylenya with a laugh, carrying the stew pot toward the table. As the men sat, she ladled stew into the four brown earthenware bowls. "Bread be coming."

Soon, the aroma of dark bread mixed with that of the stew as Weylenya set a wicker basket in the center of the polished walnut table.

"Brew in the gray pitcher, watered wine in the brown," Fasse explained.

Following Rinfur's example, Cerryl poured the amber beer from the gray pitcher into a brown mug with a chipped handle. With a chunk of the brown bread in one hand, he sipped the beer. Despite the slight bitterness, he enjoyed the taste.

"Good brew," affirmed Rinfur. "Always have a good brew here."

"Get it from Herlot out in Weevett. Keep it in the coldest corner of the shop. The woods help, but I don't know why." Fasse took a swallow from his own mug. Weylenya drank the watered wine between small bites of bread and stew.

Cerryl found himself looking down at an empty bowl.

"Growing lad, I see." The crafter's consort stood and returned with the stew pot, refilling both the teamster's bowl and Cerryl's.

"Thank you." Cerryl offered a grateful smile with the words.

"A polite young fellow you are." Fasse nodded. "Polite indeed. Why you be coming to Fairhaven, young fellow? Aim to make your fortune?" Fasse laughed. "Seen lots of young fellows. Either want to pile up the coins or become mages. One or the other."

Cerryl finished chewing a mouthful of the hot bread. "I have to learn to become a scrivener."

"What? No coins?" asked the cabinet maker. "No great dreams?"

Cerryl forced a gentle smile but said nothing.

"Know your letters?"

"Yes, ser."

"Knowing your letters, and not having dreams, you might yet make a good scrivener." Fasse shook his head. "Too many folk these days, wanting to be rich or powerful. Not like the old times, when a man took pride in his work. That was when the work counted, not the coins."

A half smile crossed Weylenya's lips, as if she had heard the words more than a few times before.

"Now . . . the young 'uns, they want the coins afore the first join is set, afore the barrel holds water, afore the . . . ah, what's the use? An old crafter railing 'gainst a world that doesn't know where it's going, doesn't recall where it came from." The crafter lifted his mug and drained it, then looked at Rinfur. "You be sleeping in the loft, the two of you. You know where, teamster."

"Yes, master crafter."

Cerryl finished his stew and the last corner of the dark of bread, trying not to yawn while he ate. The day had been long, and his buttocks were sore.

Yet, even after he straggled up the short ladder to the loft and the narrow pallet alone, not caring that Rinfur had said he was taking a walk, he could not sleep, tired as he was. Though he lay on the narrow pallet, thinner and harder than the one at Dylert's, his eyes remained open, resting on the thick beams of the workroom ceiling.

Around him, beyond the stone walls of the shop, he could sense the flows of red-tinged white. The energies he'd felt in the mines, or even with the white mages who had fought at the mill, were insignificant compared to those which suffused Fairhaven. He shivered.

Careful . . . he would have to be most careful. Already he had seen enough to know that Fairhaven was a dangerous place for him—for anyone. With those thoughts, his eyes finally closed.

XXVII

After helping Rinfur move the wagon and harness the team, Cerryl waved as the teamster eased the wagon out of the courtyard. Then he swallowed as Rinfur and the team disappeared behind the buildings of the side street leading to the square.

Finally, after a deep breath, he hoisted his pack and slipped into Fasse's shop. The crafter stood to one side of the front door, surveying the street outside and the handful of passersby.

"Ser? Could you tell me the way to Tellis the scrivener?"

"What? Oh . . ." Fasse half-turned. "That be right. Dylert be sending you there." The crafter fingered his narrow ginger mustache, then lifted and dropped his angular shoulders. "Tellis? His place be across the square and four long blocks up the lesser artisans' way."

Cerryl wanted to ask Fasse who or what the lesser artisans were, but the cabinet-maker's continued glances toward the square were enough to discourage questions. "Thank you, ser. I appreciated the bed and the food. Very much."

"Be nothing, young fellow. You be doing the same for another some day." Fasse glanced toward the main avenue again. "Best you be off. I be awaitin' a mage." The crafter gestured toward the polished white oak chest that stood to his left.

Cerryl's eyes took in the chest, waist high, and finished with something that glistened like fresh oil but was just as clearly not.

"Have to be varnished for them. All they touch . . . they destroy in time. The varnish helps." Fasse looked down the avenue to his right again.

"Thank you." Cerryl nodded and shouldered his pack.

"High price for managing chaos . . ." murmured the crafter.

Cerryl concealed a frown as he stepped through the open door and onto the raised stone sidewalk, still marveling at the very idea. In Hrisbarg, sometimes the shopkeepers put down boards during the rains, but pedestrians and horses shared the streets, and Cerryl knew to watch where he put his feet.

He waited for a two-horse wagon piled with baskets of potatoes to pass, and crossed the western part of the avenue. The farmer on the seat had never even glanced in his direction.

The sun was barely above the roofs to the east of the square, and long shadows lay across the white stone avenue and the sidewalk stones and curbings, and darkened the emerald grass. The slight coolness of the evening before had vanished, and neither grass nor stone bore the slightest trace of dew. Although the air was already warm, the oval shape of what Rinfur and Fasse had called a square was empty. A handful of people walked the sidewalks, mostly from the gates toward the center of Fairhaven, and the creaking of wagons and the clop of hoofs on the stones were the loudest sounds.

Cerryl almost felt as though his breathing were too loud in the hushed city. He straightened his shoulders and followed the white stone walk across the center of the empty square to the far side. There was a single street there—without a name or symbol. Was it the way of the lesser artisans?

With the slightest of shrugs, he crossed the empty eastern half of the avenue and started up the unnamed street. Cerryl glanced into the first shop, peering between vivid blue shutters drawn back open against bright white-plastered outside walls. A potter sat cross-legged, throwing a pot on a wheel powered by a foot pedal. Behind him was a low wooden shelf displaying an array of pots and crockery. The gray-haired man did not look up as Cerryl studied him.

Cerryl walked slowly eastward, along the lesser artisans' way that was but the eastern side street away from the square—exactly across the square opposite the side street that adjoined the alley leading to the rear courtyard of Fasse's shop.

The next shop was that of a weaver. Two girls, each younger than Cerryl, one brown haired, one redheaded, sat on the floor working back-strap looms. Behind them a man flicked the shuttle on a floor loom that filled half the small room. Skeins of colored yarn—all colors of yarn, except black—hung from pegs set into the wall just below the roof beams. The round-faced brown-haired girl grinned shyly at Cerryl, even while her fingers slipped the yarn wound on the hand shuttle through the spread woolen yarn.

Cerryl offered a grin in return.

"Mind the loom, Pattera," came the comment from the weaver.

"Yes, ser," murmured the girl, dropping her eyes from Cerryl.

Cerryl nodded and continued along the street. Pattera had been pretty enough, yet nothing to compare to the golden-haired girl he had seen but once in his screeing glass. Would he ever meet her? Or was she the daughter of some white mage who would treat him like the other whites had dealt with his father—or the fugitive at Dylert's mill? He repressed a shiver. "Careful . . . Cerryl," he whispered to himself.

On the inside wall of the next shop were rows of small shelves filled with small wooden boxes and a large chest of many drawers, and a scent—many scents—that Cerryl didn't recognize. Spices? Why so many? The heavy man who looked up from a wooden mortar and pestle on a polished table offered an enigmatic smile before looking back at the dried herbs before him.

So silent was the lesser artisans' way that Cerryl could hear his own footsteps. Somehow, he had expected that Fairhaven would have been busier, even so early in the day.

The line of shops ended at another cross street, rather than at the alleyway he had expected. On the far corner was another shop, but this one sported a sign over the open door bearing an open book and a quill poised above it. Hoping that the sign referred to the scrivener's, Cerryl crossed the street and eased into the shop, pausing just inside the open door to let his eyes adjust.

The front of the shop was a small area, less than four cubits square, with white-plastered walls and empty except for two stools and with a golden oak cabinet that was made up of a two-drawer chest with three attached bookshelves above the chest. The top shelf held a silver pitcher, and the second two were each largely filled with leather-bound volumes.

Even from the door, Cerryl could smell the tanned leather. He took another step into the front room and paused, scanning the two dozen or so books on the shelves before him, but aside from the different colors of leather, there were no identifying marks on the spines. Nor did any of the books bear the unseen but sensed whitish red of chaos that the three books in his own pack bore.

Two doors led from the front room—one on the right side, which was closed, and one on the left. After another moment, Cerryl stepped toward the door behind the left side of the chest, stopping in the doorway.

A single man bent over a table in the workroom, a space not much bigger than the front room. The far wall was filled, half with a huge doorless cabinet that contained shelves transformed into cubbies filled with rolled leathers, parchments, palimpsests, real glass jars, stoppered crockery vials, and other manner of items unfamiliar to Cerryl. On each side of the cabinet were racks, the one on the left holding an array of hand tools; the one on the right, green leathers cut into long strips perhaps two spans wide and more than two cubits in length. A writing desk was flush against the left wall, the worktable against the right. The scrivener was stitching something with a long needle that flashed in his fingers.

Cerryl waited until the man paused before speaking. "Master Tellis?"

Tellis straightened and turned, revealing a spare and surprisingly thin face above a more rotund frame. "Yes, young fellow? Are you here on an errand for your master?" The scrivener seemed to squint as he surveyed Cerryl.

"No, ser." Cerryl stepped forward and extended the scroll. "Master Dylert sent me, ser."

The briefest of frowns crossed Tellis's face as the scrivener took the scroll. Cerryl waited, his eyes not leaving the scrivener, much as he wished to study the workroom.

Tellis read through the scroll, licking his lips, once, twice, as he neared the end. "Dylert says you're a shirttail relative."

"Yes, ser."

"He also says you work hard, and that'd not be something he'd offer easily." Tellis scratched the back of his head, absently disarraying the thick, brown-flecked hair. "Tell me about master Dylert. What does he look like, and what does he favor?"

"Master Dylert . . ." Cerryl managed not to frown. "He is a fraction of a span taller than you are, ser, but tall as he is, he is a wiry man. His beard is black but shows silver. His eyes are brown. He always wanted the mill clean, and the planks and timbers stacked in the barns by their size and quality." Cerryl shrugged. "His speech is hard, but he is fair."

"And his household?"

"His consort, Dyella, she is warmer." Cerryl smiled. "She often gave me extra food."

"Spoken like a young fellow, thinking of the food. Go on."

"She has brown hair. It's thinner. Erhana favors her mother, excepting her face, and Brental—I don't know. He is the sole one with red hair, so far as I know, but . . . he was good to me as well."

"Where are your people?"

"None are living . . . now. My uncle . . . he lived in Montgren." Cerryl swallowed, fighting the burning in his eyes, wondering why the question had upset him.

"You lived with your uncle, then?"

"Yes, ser. Until I went to work for master Dylert."

"You miss him, your uncle, I mean?"

Cerryl nodded, swallowing again. "My aunt, too."

"Dylert . . . a good judge of men, but far too good for his own good." Tellis shook his head. "Ah . . . well . . . we have you to deal with. Not so as I really need an apprentice, you understand, but an extra pair of working hands . . . that we can manage."

"Yes, ser." Cerryl kept his eyes on Tellis, his voice polite.

"A few matters, young fellow . . ."

"Cerryl."

"Important matters, if you intend to remain here."

Cerryl nodded again, waiting, trying not to shift his weight from one leg to the other as the scrivener studied him again, trying to appear serious and attentive.

"Well, Cerryl . . . you'll learn as the days pass. But there are some things that don't change. You'll be pumping the water for all, and we'll be getting to that. Water's close here in Fairhaven, and this is a clean house. You look neat, but clean is better. I expect you to bathe leastwise every third day, and wash your hands and face every time before you work in the shop here. That's after breakfast and after supper. Dirty hands, dirty sweat—they've ruined more books than fires or bugs. And you'll need another set of clothes. I'll provide that, but you wash them."

Cerryl nodded. "Yes, ser."

"Another matter. You'll be spending some time with Arkos the tanner. You won't be touching the binding till you understand the leather. That clear?"

Cerryl gave another nod.

"And the parchment, as well."

"Yes, ser." The youth just stood there, afraid that another nod would show him as agreeably dull.

"Your wages are a half copper an eight-day for the first five eight-days. If we're both satisfied after that, a copper an eight-day for the rest of the first year. Then we'll talk." Tellis fingered his not-quite-pointed and clean-shaven chin, then pulled his hand away, almost disgustedly. "And after all my talk . . ." His eyes went to the washstand in the corner. "You'll have your own towel . . . Cerryl, is it?"

"Cerryl . . . yes . . . ser."

"And don't wipe your face with your hands. Your sleeves, a clean rag, but not your hands."

Cerryl found himself nodding again, against his better judgment.

"Now . . . let's see how well you listen. Tell me what I told you."

Cerryl continued to meet the scrivener's eyes as he responded. "You want my hands and face clean any time before I go to work. I'm not to wipe my face with my hands. I'm to bathe at least every third day. I must spend time with the tanner to learn about leather and parchment, and I'm the one who will pump water for the house and shop. And I start at a half-copper an eight-day."

"A good memory, leastwise." A slight smile flickered across the scrivener's lips. "Follow me." Tellis led the way back into the front room and then through the other door.

Behind the showroom was a narrow kitchen—with a small iron stove, half built into the wall, presided over by a slender woman whose back remained turned from the scrivener and Cerryl—and to the right of the kitchen, through an archway, Cerryl glimpsed a common room, with a trestle table, and a wall bench piled with pillows.

Tellis gestured to the thin, almost frayed-looking woman whose blonde-and-gray hair was square cut in a thick thatch just below the bottom of her ears. "This is Beryal. She runs the household, she and her daughter Benthann."

"No. I run the household. Benthann runs you." As she turned slowly, Beryal's pale blue eyes appraised Cerryl, and he felt as though she had looked right through him. "A new apprentice? About time. You need someone who listens to you "

"That's true enough." Tellis laughed. "Beryal and Benthann are better at directing than listening."

Cerryl nodded, wondering what sort of household Tellis really had.

"You need directing, master scrivener, at anything but scrivening." Beryal's cool eyes flicked back to Cerryl. "I ring the bell once for meals. Just once. Supper is true midday. Be noodles and quagroot today . . . and dark bread. You get brew with dinner, water any other time, unless you want to buy something and share it." After a quick nod, she turned back to the stove and the heavy iron skillet in which something simmered.

Tellis gave a rueful smile and motioned for Cerryl to follow him through the kitchen, past Beryal, who did not look up. Cerryl could smell warming butter, a spice he couldn't identify, and something that smelled good but unfamiliar.

Beyond the spare common room, Tellis stepped through the rear door and into a small stone-paved courtyard, empty except for the hand pump and catch basin in the right-hand corner. "We don't use this much. It's too hot in the summer, and too cool in the winter." He gestured. There was a wooden gate in the middle of the back wall, between what looked to be two small rooms. "The supply storeroom—that's the door on the left. The space on the right is yours. You can come and go as you please through the back gate. Works better that way."

Cerryl glanced around the courtyard again. There was a third door on the right wall, and a narrow door near the common room door on the left.

Tellis followed his eyes. "Those are our rooms."

The youth didn't ask who "ours" included, or what room was whose, but nodded.

"Put your things in your room. Arrange it how you like and then come back to the workroom."

"Yes, ser."

Tellis nodded and left Cerryl standing in the empty courtyard, his pack on his shoulders. Cerryl crossed the courtyard, perhaps ten cubits square, and gingerly lifted the latch and opened the door.

He let his breath out slowly. The space was perhaps four cubits by five and contained a pallet bed—wider than the one he had used at Dylert's—a washstand with pitcher and basin, and a narrow doorless wardrobe of plain and battered pine, plus a stool. The floor was stone, and the faintest film of white dust covered everything.

His nose itched, and he rubbed it, then set his pack on the foot of the pallet. He took another deep breath before opening the canvas flap and lifting out his jacket. He left his battered half-copy of *Colors of White* inside the pack—and his medallion from his father. He would need to find a hiding place for them, and soon.

XXVIII

As soon as Cerryl had arranged his things and returned to the work-room, Tellis stopped his work. "Might as well freshen the water. Empty the basins in the house first. Then fill the pitchers."

Another figure appeared behind Cerryl. Beryal tapped Cerryl on the shoulder. "Be more than that. Use the polished bucket on the peg. The rough bucket's for scrubbing. Always pump a bucket first and empty it. No telling what be in the pump. Empty the basins into the sewer catch before you start pumping water, and don't be using the bucket for dirtied wash water. Sewer catch be outside the courtyard gate. If there's dirt in the basins, wash them under the pump. That's before you bring water into the house. Understand?"

Cerryl nodded and headed for the courtyard, carrying the empty basin. After emptying it and the one on the kitchen washstand, he rinsed them and replaced them. Then, heeding what Beryal had said, he began pumping, letting a bucket's worth of water spill over the polished wash stones before rinsing the bucket itself and filling it. He carted the water back to the workroom to refill the pitcher.

"When you finish with the water, Cerryl . . ." Tellis did not complete the sentence, preoccupied as he was with the nipping press in the corner.

"I'll come back."

Tellis grunted without looking up.

Cerryl trudged back out to the kitchen, where Beryal was kneading bread. The faint odor of yeast filled the room, and he took a deep breath.

"You can refill the pitchers on the corner table."

"They're next," Cerryl said, knowing that was what she wanted.

"Good."

He slipped past her and carried the bucket through the common room and out into the courtyard, back to the long-handled pump. He lifted the pump handle. While it still amazed him that clean water flowed beneath the streets, he was happy enough not to be lifting buckets from a deep well. With the bucket three-quarters full, as much water as he dared carry, he turned and started back across the courtyard. A cool breeze, foreshadowing winter, ruffled his hair.

"Hello . . ." A girl's face peered over the whitened wood of the rear gate. "Are you Tellis's new apprentice?" She giggled, then offered a shy grin before brushing a strand of brown hair back off her forehead. "You must be. Only apprentices carry water."

Cerryl set down the bucket and walked toward the gate, stopping several cubits back and studying her, knowing he'd seen her. Then he nodded. "You're Pattera, the weaver. I'm Cerryl."

Pattera's smile vanished. "How did you know my name?"

"I was walking by the shop, and your father told you to mind the loom." Cerryl offered his own grin. "That was when I was looking for Tellis's place."

"Oh . . . you were the boy in the window."

Cerryl wasn't sure he liked being called a boy, but he nodded and kept smiling.

"Father doesn't like it when I look at boys." She glanced over her shoulder and down the alleyway. "I'd better go. I'm supposed to be at the market." Another shy smile, and she was gone.

Cerryl picked up the bucket and reentered the house.

"Those weaver girls are nothing but trouble, Cerryl. Mind that," said Beryal. After a moment when he didn't answer, she added, "Cerryl? Did you pump one pail and empty it out first? I didn't see that."

"I rinsed the bucket."

"Like I told you? Just like I told you?"

"No, ser."

"Go do it, and be thankful I'm asking. Benthann would have emptied the pitcher over you." Beryal had covered the bread dough with a gauzelike cloth and was slicing pale green roots into a skillet. "Then she would have made you mop the floor."

Without speaking, he turned and went out and through the courtyard and the gate and lifted the access stone to the sewer, pouring out the bucket. It was easier to comply with Beryal's whims than to argue that he'd cleaned the bucket before he'd started and run the pump through several cycles, letting the water flow over the wash stones.

Cerryl replaced the stone and straightened, feeling eyes upon him, then looked toward the end of the alleyway. Pattera waved at him from where alley and street met. With his free hand he returned the gesture. Carrying two long cylindrical loaves of bread in her left arm, the brown-haired girl slipped from sight down the lesser artisans' way.

Back in the courtyard, Cerryl refilled the bucket and returned to the kitchen, where he first refilled the pitchers on the table in the corner.

"Do it right first, next time."

"Yes, Beryal."

Beryal turned and slipped the skillet onto the hot stove.

Cerryl stepped away from the heat of the kitchen, wiping his forehead on his sleeve, and out into the courtyard, where he replaced the bucket on the peg over the pump. After washing his hands and face, and feeling the chill of the breeze on his damp skin, he hurried back to the workroom.

No sooner had he stepped through the door from the kitchen into the showroom than Tellis called out, "Cerryl?"

"Yes, ser."

"At the desk."

Cerryl cautiously approached the empty writing desk against the wall.

"Just sit down." The scrivener set the wood-framed and oblong slate on the writing desk. Beside it was the sheet of parchment that contained the practice sentences—one for Temple script and one for the old tongue. Each sentence contained every letter character. Tellis handed Cerryl an oblong of chalk. "You need more practice. Look at the models. Every letter you write should be identical to every other one—of the same letter, I mean."

Cerryl understood. Each letter *alir* should be the same as every other *alir*. The tedium bothered him, not the ideal Tellis espoused. "How do you know whether to write a book in Temple or old tongue?"

Tellis cleared his throat. "Mostly old tongue here in Fairhaven. In Lydiar, were I scribing there, most would be in Temple. The blacks were stronger there after the fall of Cyador and Lornth, and Relyn is still revered on the coast."

"Relyn?" The name wasn't familiar to Cerryl, and he wondered if Relyn had been a duke or something.

"The founder of the Temples." Tellis shook his head. "You must read more. I'll give you an old history . . . but wash your hands each time before you open it."

"I will," Cerryl promised, even as he wondered what good history would do him. Still, scribing promised a better life than millworking, and if Tellis thought he should read a history, it might not hurt too much.

"The Temple tongue is easier, and it is used more every year." Tellis shrugged. "The white mages prefer the old tongue, though, like as I can see, the two are not that dissimilar. Now . . . practice."

Cerryl looked at the chalk between his fingers, then looked at the practice lines of old tongue, even if he really didn't need to do so to know the words. He already knew the sentence by heart. Still . . . he'd better concentrate on replicating the shapes of the letters.

At the sound of footsteps in the front showroom, when Cerryl had written but a dozen lines on the slate, Tellis straightened from his repairs to the recalcitrant nipping press.

Cerryl did not turn. He could sense that the customer was a white mage; the telltale red-tinged white energies suffused the shop. He forced himself to copy another sentence, concentrating on the form and shape of the letters, almost drawing them, his fingers trembling.

"Yes, honored ser?" offered Tellis smoothly.

"Do you have *The Founding of Fyrad and the White Lands*? Sterol had said that you had recopied versions of some of the old tales."

"Yes, ser. In the burgundy on the end . . . would you like me to show you?"

"Please." The voice was bored.

"Here. You see, this was copied from the master version—"

"That's clear enough. Show me the end pages."

Cerryl forced himself to begin another sentence in old tongue. The chalk squeaked, but neither Tellis nor the mage spoke. Cerryl stopped and used the small bronze scraping knife to whittle off the imperfection in the chalk stick.

". . . not interested in . . . *Red Shield of Rohrn* . . . what about *The Legend of Fornal*?"

"I am still copying that, honored mage. Another two eight-days, perhaps."

"Here is a silver. That should hold the *Fornal* volume, should it not?"

"Yes, ser."

"I see you have *Histories of Cyador* . . . both volumes, yet. For what are you offering them?"

"They are hand-copied with light brimstone iron ink, ser. A gold and two silvers each."

"Two golds for the set, and another gold for the *Fornal* when it is ready. That's beyond the silver I gave you . . . if . . . if it is ready within three eight-days."

Cerryl swallowed. Three golds and a silver for three volumes? He'd never seen a gold himself. At his wages . . . earning a gold would take years.

"Yes, ser. It will be ready."

"Good."

"Do you want me to deliver the histories?"

"I'll take them . . . if you have something for me to carry them in."

"A book carry bag. I have one here for you, ser." A drawer of the showroom chest rumbled slightly. "Fine wool, it is."

"Put the histories in it. Gently, scrivener. Gently."

Cerryl found himself looking blankly at what he had written when Tellis stepped back into the workroom.

"That's better, young fellow. Keep looking at the models." Tellis stepped toward the workbench.

He had not quite filled the slate when Tellis reappeared at his shoulder.

"A fine hand you have, young Cerryl, but it takes more than pretty characters to make a scrivener." Tellis shook his head. "You can work. That I know, for you work without praise or punishment, and Dylert can judge that better than any man I ever met."

Cerryl waited. Usually waiting attentively would encourage people to say more—that he had learned.

"Even a fine hand and hard work will not make a scrivener," Tellis went on. "Nor will colored leather bindings and the finest folio stitching." He paused and looked at Cerryl.

"What will, master scrivener?" asked the apprentice, taking his cue from Tellis's pause.

"That . . . that takes a love of the words, of what they say. A scrivener is not just a bookbinder. He is not just a scribe. Not just a recopier of ancient tales and histories . . ."

"So . . . you're filling another poor lad's ear with dreams and drivel?" Cerryl looked up at the acid tones.

The young woman who stood in the doorway from the showroom was blond, trim but muscular. The dark blue eyes seemed to flash, even though the light from outside made her face appear veiled in shadow. "Tell me this one's name. If he stays, I might remember it."

"Cerryl, lady," offered the apprentice.

"He's polite, too. You always pick the polite ones. They don't tell you how empty your words are." The eyes flicked to Cerryl. "Oh, I'm Benthann. I'm the one who makes poor Tellis's days miserable and his nights glorious."

"Benthann . . ." The scrivener's voice was calm, unstressed. "Did you get the vellum?"

"Arkos will deliver it this afternoon. I couldn't be bothered to carry it." Benthann smiled. "Besides, I got it for less than you wanted to pay. Four silvers for the lot. Last time it cost you eight, and this is better." She paused.

Cerryl forced himself not to turn to see Tellis's reaction.

"Coins are all that count, Tellis. Did anyone buy anything today?" Benthann glanced at Cerryl. "They usually don't, you know. They look and make pleasant noises, and then they leave." She glanced from Cerryl to Tellis.

The scrivener offered a faint smile but did not answer her question.

"He doesn't really need the shop at all," continued Benthann. "They offer more coins for him to be a scribe."

"They wouldn't do that," responded Tellis mildly, "if I were not a reputable scrivener with a shop. You know that, Benthann."

"You need not spend so much coin and time on those presses and the colored leathers..."

Cerryl wondered why Tellis didn't just say that someone had bought two books for three golds and ordered a third. He looked at the scrivener.

"The leather protects the words, and the whites value that protection." The spare face remained calm, almost disinterested.

"You have a word for everything." Benthann's voice carried a tone between a sneer and a laugh. "I will see you later. Good day to you, young Cerryl."

Cerryl blinked, and the young woman was gone.

"She has not learned that there is a truth beyond coins." Tellis gave a headshake and looked at Cerryl, then at the slate. "Wipe it clean and copy again, this time all in old tongue."

"Yes, ser."

With a smile, Tellis produced a thick woolen rag. "Use this. At the end of the day wash it out and hang it on the end of the rack here." He pointed.

Cerryl took the rag and began to wipe the slate clean. What sort of a shop did Tellis run, and who was Benthann?

He kept his face expressionless as he cleaned the chalk from the practice slate.

XXIX

Cerryl struggled to sweep the sawdust away from the mill pit, but the cold wind coming through the east door kept blowing the sawdust and wood chips back toward the pit from which he had just shoveled them. His arms burned from the resins, and his gloves were worn through.

Behind him, the big blade rang like a chime. *Clannnngggggg!!!*

"Up . . . up, you lazy apprentice!"

He glanced around the room in bewilderment. Where was his cubby? The open wardrobe wasn't his. And his books? He sat up in the bed, shivering from the chill. What about the other blankets? One wasn't enough.

"Breakfast is almost ready, and you need to bathe."

Bathe? Cerryl shook his head, trying to climb out of the white fog and dream that seemed to hold him.

Clannnggg!!

"You awake in there?" demanded the voice. Beryal's voice, he realized finally.

"I'm awake," he croaked.

"Heard dead frogs more alive than you. Best be moving." Beryal's voice faded.

Slowly, he put his feet down on the chill stone floor, wincing. Then he stood and, in his drawers, pulled the threadbare towel over his shoulder and padded to the door, carrying his battered wash bucket. The courtyard was gray and gloomy before sunrise, and heavy clouds swirled overhead. A chill wind whipped across his bare chest as he filled the wash bucket and plodded back to his room.

Once clean—and shivering—he dressed and then left his room, opened the gate, and emptied the wash water into the sewer catch. He looked down the alleyway to the lesser artisans' way but saw not a soul. Despite the swirling breeze, there was but a hint of the white street dust, and not a scrap of litter or rubbish in the alley. And not a single rodent.

From what Cerryl could tell, Fairhaven had few rodents—he'd never seen one—and streets cleaner than the floors of many houses in Hrisbarg. Nor did the air smell, except with a faint bitterness that reminded him of the mill blade after Dylert had cleaned, sharpened, and oiled it.

He closed the circular catch basin cover, not too much more than half a cubit across. From the sound of the wastes, the sewer beneath was large. He looked at the stone cover again. Why was it so small? Another minor mystery, and one probably not worth worrying over.

He walked back to his room, closing the gate and then replacing the wash bucket on the peg on the wall by the door. After deciding not to wear his jacket to cross the small courtyard, he hurried to the common room—warmed by the stove. The warmth felt good as he slid onto the empty bench.

"Took you long enough." Beryal dumped two slabs of bread fried in something onto his plate.

He looked at the strangely fried bread blankly.

"Never seen egg toast before?"

"No, ser."

"Beryal does it well," said Tellis, taking the chair at the end of the table. "Best egg toast in Fairhaven."

"You must be feeling good this morn," observed Beryal from the stove where she fried more of the heavy bread.

"A good morning it is, if a bit chill, but the winter here is mild, compared to the plains of Jellicor." Tellis yawned.

"Men." Beryal smirked and walked back to the stove.

Cerryl looked around the common room. Benthann? Now that he thought about it, he'd never seen her at breakfast.

"Don't be looking for her mightiness," said Beryal. "Not afore mid-morning, leastwise."

Cerryl held back a cough. For a mother, Beryal wasn't exactly warm and supportive of her daughter. Neither Nall nor Syodor had ever been that cutting, and he hadn't even been their son. Nor had Dylert been that cross, even when Brental had nearly ruined the big blade on a lorken log with knotted heartwood.

Tellis coughed, loudly.

"Don't you be coughing and snorting at me, master Tellis. I cook, and I clean and do as you order for the household, but my words be my own." The sizzle of the frying bread emphasized Beryal's statement. More emphasis followed when she slammed the crockery platter and the browned egg toast before Tellis.

Cerryl kept his eyes on his plate, except when he reached for his mug of cool water.

"Don't know why I keep you two around," murmured Tellis.

"We all know that, and there'd be no reason to talk more about it," answered Beryal, back at the stove fixing her own egg toast. "Cerryl, would you want more toast?"

"If I could have another piece . . . please."

"That you can, and you ask, unlike some who sleep forever." Beryal carried the skillet over and slipped a third chunk of the browned egg-battered toast onto his plate.

"That was yours . . ."

"There is more where that came from. Not be starving myself, not in this household." Beryal grinned. "And I thank you for caring."

As she turned her back, Tellis grinned at Cerryl.

Not knowing quite what the grin meant, Cerryl offered a faint smile in return. "Good toast it is, ser."

"It is indeed," said Tellis. "Enjoy it as you can."

Beryal sat down across from Cerryl and began to eat her egg toast. The three ate silently. Before he realized it, Cerryl glanced at his suddenly empty plate. He repressed a burp, took a last swallow of water, and then looked toward Tellis.

"You best start to work, Cerryl. I'll be there in a moment. You set up to keep copying the *Sciences* book, but don't you be starting yet."

"Yes, ser." Cerryl eased off the bench and went to the washstand, cleaning and drying his hands before heading to the workroom. He put the book on the copy stand but did not open it to the marked page. Then he took the penknife and put a fresh edge on his quill, laying it beside the inkwell.

He used a whittled twig to stir the ink and check its consistency. More water? He decided against that and took the top parchment sheet from the cabinet, getting out the bone buffer to ready it for copying. After polishing the sheet, he arranged his stool.

"Good," said Tellis as he bustled into the workroom. The scrivener rummaged in the bottom of the supply chest before lifting out an oblong section of parchment that he carried and set on the writing table.

"Practice parchment. Not for writing, but for scraping." He covered his mouth and coughed. "You've seen me scrape away your errors." Tellis lifted the sharp-edged knife. "It's time you became better, and practice is the only way. The blade must be sharp, yet absolutely clean. A blade with oil along the edge—the oil will mix with the old ink and leave flecks or dots that you'll have to scrape even deeper to remove."

"Yes, ser." That made sense to Cerryl.

"And you must scrape at an angle, firmly and delicately enough to separate the ink from the parchment. Like this. Watch." Tellis wiped the knife on a clean white cloth, then rehung this cloth on a peg. His fingers nearly concealed the knife as he slipped the blade against the top line of writing on the practice parchment. "See?"

Cerryl blinked. Where three words had been, the parchment was clean, as though nothing had been written there.

"No substitute for good parchment. Paper, even the woven split-reed paper, a few years and it's dust, specially here in Fairhaven. A parchment volume will last forever, cared for as it should be." Tellis paused. "I'll do it once more. Now watch."

Cerryl watched as another set of words vanished.

"You try it."

Cerryl took the knife and the cloth, and wiped the blade as he had seen Tellis do.

"Good. Don't put any pressure on the edge. Dulls it too soon."

Then the apprentice eased the edge across the next word on the line, all too conscious of the *scritching* his scraping produced.

"No . . . no . . ." Tellis's voice took on an exasperated edge. "Angle the blade just so, the way I showed you. You want to scrape off but the slightest of the parchment, just to clean it. You must feel the grain and the nap of the parchment, polished smooth as it may be."

Feeling his fingers were like fat thumbs, Cerryl angled the knife against the nearly worn out palimpsest and tried to follow the example Tellis had demonstrated.

"Better . . . better . . ." Tellis straightened. "After you copy another two pages, practice on that worn shred, just like that. A good palimpsest—a good one—it should be smooth enough and clean enough that none but the best of scriveners can distinguish it from a fair parchment."

"Yes, ser."

"If I'm not back before then, copy another set of pages, and then practice with the palimpsest some more. I need to talk to Nivor about the latest oak galls. They don't steep right." Tellis shook his head. "And the iron brimstone has too much of the brimstone. In time, the ink made from it will burn the pages, and I'd never want that said of any of my books."

"How long will that take?" asked Cerryl.

"Years, Cerryl lad, but books must last forever, not a mere handful of years. What be the point of a book that turns to dust before its scrivener?"

Cerryl nodded, though he wasn't certain he agreed totally with his master. Many people produced goods that didn't outlive their maker yet were valued, and most of what he had copied or read seemed to be either common sense that didn't need to be written down, or things of little use to most folk.

Once Tellis had slipped out into the chilly late morning and up the lesser artisans' way, Cerryl glanced at the book on the copy stand—*The Sciences of the Heavens*, then read the lines carefully, half aloud.

   . . . not always understood that all the stars were not studded
   on a distant and concave surface, but are scattered at immense

distances from one another in space so limitless as to be inconceivable . . .

So limitless as to be inconceivable? The words seemed to roll through Cerryl's thoughts. So limitless that one could not understand or comprehend the distance? He shook his head. Why did the white mages write about such matters? Where were the books that told about how to handle chaos? Or order? The stars might be distant, so distant that the ancient angels had traveled forever, but how would such stuff help him understand about mastering chaos?

He took one slow easy breath, then another, before dipping the quill once more into the iron-gall ink and slowly copying the next line of the manuscript . . . and the next.

He finished one set of pages, then scraped clean two lines off the practice palimpsest and started copying the next set of pages from *The Sciences of the Heavens.*

. . . stars, established and scattered as they are at vast distances from the sun, cannot receive the fires of chaos from the sun, and thus, must contain their own founts of chaos, which appear as points of light in the night sky . . .

"How can you even see?" Benthann peered into the workroom. "The day is dark. It's like a cave in here, and you haven't even lit the candle."

Cerryl glanced up, realizing that the workroom was dark. Somehow, he hadn't even noticed the growing dimness. "I didn't realize . . ."

"Such a hardworking apprentice. You even save him the costs of candles and lamp oil. Do you know where Tellis might be?"

Cerryl eased the quill away from the parchment. "He said he was going to Nivor the apothecary's."

"A course, he'd think of that just before it snows. More of the formulations for ink?"

"He did not say, Benthann." Cerryl used her name because she wasn't that much older than he was, yet she slept with Tellis but wasn't his consort. He wondered if Tellis had ever had a consort.

"Light be praised that he's not over at Arkos's place. Should it cross his mind to ask, I'm off to the traders' market. Before it snows." With a toss of her head and a flip of the short blonde hair, she stepped out of the doorway from the showroom, then into the street, leaving the door ajar.

Cerryl set the quill on the holder and eased away from the desk and out to close the door. He paused at the outside door, his hand on the brass lever, and watched as snowflakes danced in the gray day, soaring desperately on the swirling breezes as though they did not want to touch the bleached granite stones of the street.

Benthann had already vanished, and he shivered as the wind gusted. He shut the door and walked back to the desk. He paused before using the striker to get the candle lit. No sense in calling attention to his ability to see in the darkness.

Before he reseated himself, he wiped the quill on the cleaning rag, gently and with the angle of the nib's cut, then dipped it into the ink, trying to sense as well as see the amount of ink drawn up into the shaft.

The iron-gall ink felt similar—in a faint way—to the big sawmill blade. He nodded. Both were iron, and, to him, iron felt different, not menacing but definitely something to be wary of, even if he didn't quite understand why. He wasn't a mage, not even close to being one.

XXX

Cerryl wiped up the last of the stew with the dark bread, then took a sip of water from the battered brown earthenware mug that was his. In the cool of late winter, the hot midday meal warmed him all the way through. He was in no hurry to go back to copying in a workroom heated only indirectly by the kitchen stove, not until his fingers warmed up more, anyway.

"Ah, a good stew," said Tellis, stretching.

"Everything I cook is good, master Tellis." Beryal smiled from where she sat across the table from Cerryl. "But the next one won't be so tasty."

"It is," confirmed Benthann. "I never complained about your cooking, Mother." She raised her left eyebrow, arched so high that Cerryl wanted to laugh.

"Let us not get into that," Tellis interjected hurriedly, then added, "Why won't the next one be so tasty?"

"Spices—what few peppercorns I have would not season a mugful, and we have no saffron, no cumin, no—"

"Enough! I understand." Tellis covered his mouth and coughed.

"Have you ever been to the traders' square?" asked Beryal, looking directly at Cerryl and ignoring Benthann's second raised eyebrow, this time the right.

"No. I'd never been to Fairhaven before I came here," Cerryl admitted. "I've only been out around the square here, and to the farmers' market."

"There's no place like Fairhaven anywhere," said Tellis. "Lydiar is damp and rotting away, and they talk of Jellico and its walls, but inside the walls are crooked streets and hovels and beggars." The scrivener snorted. "Fenard has a great and glorious history, but outside of history and walls, it's a pigsty."

"The white mages don't need walls," pointed out Beryal. "Who would dare attack Fairhaven?"

Cerryl didn't voice an answer, but it struck him that there were probably people who would like to . . . or someone who would sooner or later.

"You keep Cerryl inside the shop too much," said Beryal.

"Apprentice has to earn his keep."

"You can spare Cerryl for a bit," noted Beryal. "He needs to see more of Fairhaven than the artisans' way. What if you want him to run something for you?"

"Not too long, then," answered Tellis with a theatrical sigh.

"I need four silvers, too." Beryal said, her eyes straying toward the untended stove. "Spices do not buy themselves."

"Four?" Tellis counterfeited an incredulous look, then winked at Cerryl, smoothing his face as Beryal looked up.

"Five'd be better," countered Beryal. "Spices are dear this time of year, and will be getting more so."

"Coins . . . you'd think that this poor scrivener is made of coins."

"Coins—not at all. Excuses, yes." Beryal turned her eyes to Cerryl. "Well . . . you best be getting ready, since you gulped down all there was to swallow."

Cerryl slipped off the bench and headed for the washstand.

"After you wash, best you change to that new tunic," Beryal said. "What you're wearing is frayed at the elbows. And wear your jacket. I'll wait, but be quick about it." She turned to her daughter. "Today, you can do the dishes."

"If I must." Benthann raised her hands and dropped her shoulders in an overdone shrug. "A burden to bear."

"Only if you wish to eat," answered her mother.

Cerryl scurried back to his room and pulled off the brown-splotched work shirt and slipped on the pale blue tunic that Tellis had left one day on his pallet without a word.

"Better," said Beryal when he reappeared in the common room holding the leather jacket from Dylert that still fit tolerably well. Tellis had left, presumably for the workroom.

"You look like a real apprentice," added Benthann from the kitchen worktable where she sloshed dishes in the washtub.

"I don't like to wear it around the inks and dyes and the glues," confessed Cerryl.

"The boy thinks about his clothes," said Beryal, "unlike some. Considering how they might be dirtied . . . imagine that." With a twisted smile, her eyes went to Benthann.

"Oooo . . . I might drop one of these." The younger blonde juggled an earthenware platter, then caught it.

"Trust that you don't," suggested her mother, adjusting the short gray-and-blue woolen wrap that was too heavy for a shawl and too short for a cape. "Master Tellis may offer coin for clothes, but platters be another matter."

Cerryl looked at the recently washed floor stones.

"We need be going," said Beryal, touching his shoulder. "Out the front way."

"Yes, Beryal." Cerryl glanced through the open door from the showroom into the workroom, where Tellis was hunched over the stretching frame. The scrivener did not look up as they stepped out onto the street. Cerryl closed the door gently.

The sun shone through high hazy clouds, imparting little warmth to either Fairhaven or Cerryl. He fumbled the top bottom on his jacket closed and slipped his hands up under the bottom edge to keep them warm.

"It's another five long blocks down toward the wizards' square, not so far as the white tower, say three blocks shy of that." Beryal shifted her basket to her left arm and started down the lesser artisans' way toward the artisans' square.

Cerryl shivered as they stepped back into the shadows of the narrow street. The shutters of all the shops were closed against the chill, and the light and fitful breeze occasionally carried the smell of burning ash to him. He thought he heard the click of the big loom as they passed the weavers, but it could have been the shutters rattling or the sound of the cooper's wooden mallets.

"Are we getting anything else?" he asked when they stepped out of the shadows at the edge of the artisans' square. The square was empty except for a man hunched on a white stone bench under a blanket.

"Besides spices? Not unless it be a true bargain." Beryal laughed as she turned left and continued her brisk pace. "Like as I have to run out of things before Tellis opens his purse—for spices and stuff for the kitchen, anyway." Her eyes went to the man under the blanket. "On the crew for the Great White Road, he'll be afore long." She shook her head. "Some folk never learn. Anything be better than that."

Cerryl wondered at the slightly bitter undertone, suspecting he knew all too well to what Beryal referred.

"The history Tellis made me read, it says that the black mage—the one who founded Recluce—he worked on the white road and escaped, and that he was the only one who ever did."

"If he did . . ." Beryal laughed and lowered her voice to almost a whisper, "no wonder that he cared little for the white mages."

"Is it that bad?"

"It is nothing to talk about." Beryal shook her head. "Especially not where others can hear. Or Tellis."

"Tellis?"

"Aye, Tellis." Beryal lowered her voice. "His father was a white mage, save he knows not whom."

"What?" blurted Cerryl, wondering why Dylert had sent him to Tellis, repressing a shiver.

"The mages, they cannot love a mage woman." Beryal shrugged. "She would not survive the birth. Most times, anyway, they say. The children of the mages, for they have women but not honest consorts, they are raised in the pink house off the wizards' square. They call it a creche. Some become mages. Some do not. Those who have not the talent, they are apprenticed into the better trades. Tellis is a scrivener."

Cerryl forced a nod. "That . . . I did not know."

"I had thought not. Best you do, and say little." Beryal seemed to walk a shade faster.

Cerryl stretched his own legs to keep up.

The artisans' shops around the square gave way to a line of larger structures—an ostlery, then a long building without a sign of any sort, although two carriages waited by the mounting blocks outside the arched doorway.

Cerryl glanced across the avenue at the building, his view blocked for a moment by a wagon laden with long bundles wrapped in cloth that was headed in the same direction as he and Beryal. The rumble of the ironbound wheels on the whitened granite of the paving stones sounded almost like distant thunder.

"The grain factors' exchange," Beryal explained, lifting her voice above the sound of the wagons. A second wagon—its high sides painted bright blue and drawn by a single horse—followed the first.

What did grain factors do? Cerryl wondered. "How do they exchange grain there? There aren't any wagons or silos."

Beryal laughed. "They exchange pieces of parchment. Each piece of parchment has on it a statement of how much grain the factor will sell—something like that. Tellis explained it once."

Cerryl nodded, understanding that such trading made more sense than carting grain from place to place. "Are there other exchanges? For other things?"

"I'm sure there are. Tellis has talked of them, but I've forgotten where most of them are. There's an exchange for cattle somewhere on a square south of the wizards' tower. I remember that because it's near where they sell flowers from Hydlen."

Beryal stepped off the stone sidewalk and into the avenue around a squat woman balancing a basket of folded laundry on her head. Cerryl followed, glancing down the avenue ahead. Another wagon was headed their way, but a good hundred paces away. He stepped back onto the sidewalk beside Beryal, still marveling at how many wagons rolled up and down the avenue.

Tellis, the son of a mage? He pushed the thought away.

The next block, past a cross street narrower than the way of the lesser artisans, held small stores—none seemingly more than ten cubits wide, and all with iron-banded doors left open. Cerryl peered around Beryal at one of the doors, getting a glimpse of a man working at a battered desk or table, and a sense of metals glittering.

"The jewelers' row," Beryal said. "Silversmiths, goldsmiths, those who cut and polish gems."

A whole row of such? Cerryl shook his head.

"Nearly ten eight-days, and you've not been here?"

"I've been along the avenue, but always in the evening when the doors were bolted, and I wondered why."

"Now you know. Even in Fairhaven, cold iron is the best protection for gold and silver and gems." Beryal chuckled. "Though fewer try to break that iron here."

"What happens to those they catch?"

"The road." The woman shrugged. "It's almost always the road, except for those that offend the mages. Most of them don't get that far, they say. I wouldn't know . . . don't want to know." A shiver followed the shrug.

Beryal didn't say more, and Cerryl didn't ask, but he understood the shiver, especially after what he'd already seen . . . and heard.

After the jewelry row came the houses behind low whitened granite walls, each with a gate for pedestrians and one for horses and carriages. All the horse gates were open.

The avenue widened, forming another circle around a bare, stone-paved expanse. Every peddler and merchant in the square hawked from a cart—red carts, green carts, blue carts, green-and-gold carts.

"No dawdling." Beryal walked briskly past the pair of white-uniformed guards who surveyed the paved stone expanse and the circle of carts drawn up upon it. Cerryl forced himself not to look at the guards but to keep his eyes on the carts and the handfuls of people surrounding them.

"Ser, would you have sea emeralds . . . or the flame rubies from Southwind?"

Cerryl shook his head, wrinkling his nose at the oppressive scent of the cloth thrust practically under his nose and stepping back, bumping into a square-faced woman, who glared at him.

"My pardon," he said quickly and turning.

"Oil soaps, smooth as a bairn's cheek . . ."

"Elixirs! Get your elixirs here . . . the best in tinctures of the sea . . ."

The apprentice dodged two thin women who bustled toward Beryal and him as if to separate them, then eased closer to Beryal.

"Where . . . ?" murmured Beryal to herself, rather than to Cerryl, as she strode past a blue-and-cream cart piled high with baskets and into a clearer space in the middle of the circular square.

Cerryl followed, glad to get an uncrowded breath.

A flash of golden-red hair by a green cart caught Cerryl's eye, and he forced himself to turn slowly, so slowly he felt as though he were barely moving. The golden-red hair belonged to an older woman—one a good decade older than the girl Cerryl had seen but once in the screeing glass and never dared to seek again. The reddish blonde–haired woman walked briskly away from a cart where roasted fowl turned on a spit, fowl placed there so recently that the skin was still dun and far from golden, and no savory odor filled the square.

Cerryl glanced sideways at Beryal, who seemed not to have noticed his momentary interest.

"There." Beryal walked swiftly toward the red cart and a white-haired woman wrapped in a blue woolen shawl.

"Spices, the finest spices . . . spices from Austra, fennelseed and seristar from far Hamor . . ." The seller stopped as Beryal stepped up to the cart. "Your pleasure, lady? Perhaps some seristar? Or sweetmint leaves?"

"I might be thinking of peppercorns," began Beryal. "Were they not too dear."

"The best in peppercorns are those from Sarronnyn, and you are most fortunate, for those I have."

"I cannot taste the difference. Have you any from Hydlen?"

"They are poorer. See." The white-haired woman fumbled with the pouches on the cart shelf, then extended both hands. "The dark and round ones—those are from Sarronnyn. The wizened ones . . . from Hy-dlen."

"Plump peppercorns oft be soft."

"These are round and firm. See." The seller placed one in Beryal's palm.

Cerryl eased away from the two and toward the gold-and-green cart adjoining the spice peddler's space. Several knives and daggers were laid out on a cheap cotton velvet cloth of green.

"Be wanting a short blade, young ser?" The man by the cart was built like a barrel and wore only a tunic in the chill sunlight. Blackened teeth marked his too-friendly smile.

Cerryl pretended to study the blades, then shook his head.

"Bronze blades, white-metal blades, iron blades, steel blades—what-ever please you," persisted the seller.

"They look good," Cerryl said politely, "too good for a poor ap-prentice."

"This one"—the big man pointed to a dark iron blade less than a span long—"good for eating, cutting in the shop, takes an edge with ease. Only a silver, just a silver."

Cerryl shook his head sadly, not that he wanted any sort of iron blade. The darkness within the metal bothered him, for reasons he couldn't even explain to himself.

"As you wish, young fellow." The peddler turned to a brown-bearded man in faded blue trousers and a sheepskin jacket. "You, ser? A skinning knife? The finest in the eastern lands right here . . ."

Cerryl slipped back toward Beryal, his eyes traversing the square—no sign of golden-red hair. Why did he keep thinking of the girl in the glass? It had been more than a year—more than two—since he had seen her, and only in a glass yet. He shook his head, but he kept studying the traders' square while Beryal continued her haggling.

"You call that cumin? Looks and smells like water-soaked oris seeds."

"Alas, my lady, a dry year it was in Delapra." The seller shrugged. "This is what I have. Five coppers a palm, and a bargain at that."

"One, and you do well at that," countered Beryal.

Cerryl let a faint smile cross his face as he slowly surveyed the square and waited.

XXXI

Cerryl walked slowly down the lesser artisans' way. His breath puffed from his lips in white clouds, and he found himself hunching into his battered leather jacket, his hands up under the bottom edge to keep them warm. He should have worn his gloves, but Tellis had been so insistent that Cerryl hurry that he hadn't dared to go back to his room for them.

He saw that the weavers' shutters were ajar, and he paused, peering through the narrow opening to see Pattera and her sister working away, Pattera at the big loom, her sister Serai at one of the backstrap looms. As he watched, Pattera tucked the shuttle into a leather bracket on the loom frame and, wrapping a brown shawl around her, scurried toward the door.

With a faint smile, Cerryl stepped back from the window and turned to wait before continuing toward the tanner's. The latch clicked, and the door opened.

"Cerryl . . . wait, I can spare a moment. Father's gone to Vergren for some more wool."

"Pattera . . . now that he's come, would you close the shutters all the way?" called Serai from inside the weaver's.

"It wasn't like that." The brown-haired girl flushed and looked away from Cerryl, even as she latched the shutters. "I mean . . . leaving the shutters ajar. I just like to see people go by. Serai doesn't."

"People are different," Cerryl agreed. "Even sisters."

"Especially sisters." Pattera paused. "Where are you going?"

"Out to Arkos's. He's finished some more of the good vellum that Tellis needs for something." Cerryl smiled crookedly. "Tellis won't say for what, but I'd bet he's going to copy something for the mages. That's always what they ask for."

Pattera nodded. "They want virgin wool, too."

"Why? Do you know?" Cerryl had his own suspicions, but he wanted to hear what Pattera had to say.

"I can walk a little ways with you. Is that all right?" she asked shyly.

"Of course."

"About the wool," Cerryl prompted, resuming his walk down toward the square, since Arkos's place was a good ways beyond Fasse's cabinet shop, well to the south and east.

"Oh . . . Father says it's because the virgin wool is stronger and re-sists chaos better. There has to be chaos around the mages and what they wear, with all the chaos some of them must handle." Pattera paused, then added, "Don't you think so?"

Cerryl offered a shrug as he walked. "I would guess so. I certainly wouldn't be the one to say." His eyes flicked across the bright blue shutters of the potter's shop, firmly closed against the chill, and to the empty square ahead, where the wind blew a small white dust spout across the white granite stones of the thoroughfare.

"The sheep in Montgren have the best wool—except for the black wool of Recluce, but we couldn't ever scrape up the coins for that." Pattera shook her head. "They say it lasts forever."

"Tellis says that a good book should last for generations." Cerryl frowned. "Then he says that the ones used by the white mages never do. When they look at books in the shop, they never touch them."

"That's strange."

"I thought so, too," Cerryl lied.

"How do you know?" Pattera asked.

"I'm guessing, in a way," he admitted. "I've never seen them touch one. They ask Tellis or me to show them the book or open it to a page, and if they buy anything, we wrap it so that they don't touch it." After a moment, he added, "They must touch them sometimes, but I haven't seen any one of them do so."

"That is strange."

Cerryl stopped at the edge of the avenue and looked at the brown-haired weaver. "Do you want to come with me?"

"I'd like to, but Serai would get mad and tell father." Pattera grinned. "Sisters are like that."

"I wouldn't know," Cerryl admitted. "I grew up alone."

"Father said you were an orphan."

"I was raised by my aunt and uncle, and then they died in a fire." *A mage fire, and I don't know why.*

"Oh . . . Cerryl, I'm sorry. At least we have father." Pattera glanced back up the way. "I'd better be going." With a quick smile, she turned and scurried back toward the shop.

Cerryl watched for a moment, then waited for a canvas-covered wagon heading out of Fairhaven to pass before crossing the square. He put his hands back under his jacket and began to walk more quickly. At least it wasn't raining.

XXXII

After settling into his jacket and wrapping his blanket around him, Cerryl opened the book—*Great Historie of Candar*—to the strip of leather that served as his place mark. The worn binding testified to its age, but Tellis had insisted it was the most accurate of the histories. The scrivener had also insisted that Cerryl read the book.

The apprentice scrivener yawned, but forced himself to look at the pages, clear enough to his night vision in the dimness that he didn't bother with the candle.

> . . . yet Relyn was skilled with words and his blade, for the black demon Nylan had given him a mystic blade and an iron hand in return for his own good right hand, which Ryba the evil had sliced off to place Relyn in bondage to Nylan . . .
>
> After the battles for the Westhorns, Relyn made his way eastward, beguiling all who would listen with song-gifted words and honeyed phrases.
>
> . . . Relyn, traitor as he was to the great heritage of Cyador, not only built the first black Temple east of the Westhorns, but spent his years preaching against the truth of the old Empire.
>
> Where the first Temple rose is uncertain, for it was rightly burned by Fenardre the Great as an abomination . . .
>
> Later, Relyn fled from Gallos through ancient Axalt and came to Montgren and spent many hours with the shepherds who lived there . . . with him came the teachings of the black demon Nylan and the forbidden songs of Ayrlyn . . .
>
> . . . and Relyn brought them the way of forging the iron that burns chaos and cannot be broken, and the shepherds turned their forests into charcoal and their hills into gaping pits and charnel heaps and wrought the blades that severed souls . . . and bloody Montgren came into being . . .

Cerryl half shook his head and yawned. Montgren bloody? The peaceful land of shepherds and rolling meadows, of fine wool and stillness?

He rubbed his forehead. He still didn't understand all the words, but more and more were familiar, and many he could puzzle out from how they were used.

> . . . in the time after the rebuilding of Jellico, many of those writings were put to the torch, accursed as they were . . .

Cerryl rubbed his forehead again. How could writings about what had happened or what someone believed be accursed? He could see how a history could be wrong. Or how what someone believed might upset others, but were people really such fools as to think that words on a page carried a power beyond their meaning?

Or were they fools? He closed the book gently. If Fenardre the Great had killed all those whose beliefs he opposed and burned their writings, who would know? Especially if he had scriveners write down what he wanted.

Cerryl shivered. How could he know whether what he read was truth . . . or what the writer wanted the reader to believe was truth? He was just an apprentice scrivener who had seen very little of the world. He knew about the mines, the sawmill, the trees, something about plants and gardens, and he was learning about books and letters, and a little bit about Fairhaven.

Had Relyn been an evil man or just someone Fenardre and the whites didn't like? How could Cerryl ever tell?

He set the book aside and lay back on his pallet, eyes wide open for a long time before they finally slipped shut.

XXXIII

Cerryl set the quill in the holder, then yawned.

Tellis glanced from his worktable and away from the thin green leather volume on which he was completing the last steps of binding— something Cerryl had seen only intermittently, as though Tellis were keeping it from him. The scrivener looked at his apprentice and the copying desk. "I trust that your yawn is because you were awake late and reading the *Great Historie,* not because you find the trade book so boring."

"I have been reading the *Historie,*" Cerryl answered, trying not to reveal just how boring he found copying *Rules, Laws, and Accompaniments of Trade.*

"And what has it taught you about the founding of Fairhaven?" asked Tellis, straightening, and sweeping a scrap of old velvet over the thin volume.

"Ser . . . I've not read that far. I've just finished reading about Relyn and how he brought iron forging to Montgren . . ."

Tellis brought his hand down in a chopping motion. "And that does not tell you about Fairhaven? Cerryl . . . Cerryl . . . you must read what is written and what is not written."

Cerryl let his face reflect the puzzlement he felt.

"You have read, then, about how the black demons brought down ancient Cyador and seized all of Candar beyond the mighty West-horns?"

"Yes, ser."

"And how this Relyn started spreading their teachings to the east?"

"Yes, ser."

"Then . . . where did the white mages go? Does that not suggest something to you?" Tellis snorted in exasperation.

"They must have come east and built Fairhaven?"

"What does the very name Fairhaven suggest?"

Cerryl nodded, feeling stupid as he realized that Fairhaven effectively meant white haven, or the equivalent.

"Well?"

"A place of refuge for the whites," Cerryl supplied.

"Oh, young fellow, I'm not angry at you. No one has taught you to think, and a scrivener must learn to think, especially about words and what they mean and where they came from." Tellis shook his head slowly and sadly. "Words say so much more than anyone supposes. So much more."

"Master Tellis?" Cerryl ventured after a moment of silence.

"Yes?" Tellis's tone was patient.

"How can you tell whether what is written in a book is true? I mean, if it's about something you don't know?"

Tellis smiled. "There may yet be hope for you. A good question that is, a very good one, and one for which there exists no simple answer. Still . . . I will try." The scrivener fingered his bare chin for a moment. "First . . . nothing which is written tells all the truth, even if every word be true, because the scrivener chooses which parts of the truth to include and which to exclude."

Cerryl nodded. That made sense, but it didn't help much.

"So you must always keep in mind that some of the truth is absent. Then, you must ask if the words that the writer used are in accord with each other. That is why I have my doubts about many parts of *The Naturale Historie of Candar*. The book is written pleasantly enough, if that be the only guide, but," Tellis frowned, "there are sections that do not agree. It records that the first druids slew all the armies of Cyador at the Battle of Lornth. How could that be when the historian earlier wrote that Nylan forsook the way of the blade and when he went bare-handed into the forest of Naclos after the battle? Or that Ayrlyn slew scores, yet was a healer? There hasn't ever been a healer who could lift a blade." The scrivener snorted. As the snort passed, a wistful look flitted across his face and vanished.

"Could things have been different then?" asked Cerryl.

"It is possible, but," emphasized Tellis, "but . . . people and their traits change seldom, and it is more likely that the historian erred than that people changed in great measure."

Cerryl concealed a frown, attempting to look as though he were considering the master scrivener's words. At the same time, questions raced through his mind. The white mages were jealous of their pow-ers—did that mean they always had been? If people truly didn't change . . . was that why Candar was little different from in the days of Cyador—with one white empire replacing another, one black power replacing another?

"How do you tell a truly good ruler?" he blurted, as much to cover his confusion as to seek an answer.

"That is another good question." A crooked smile crossed Tellis's lips. "And one even more difficult to answer. A good ruler may not be loved by his people, for all people have appetites greater than their abilities and must be restrained. That is one task of a ruler. He must also ensure that the roads are good, and that enough grain is stored away for times of famine and pestilence. Both tasks require taking from the people, and seldom do we like those who take from us." Tellis picked up a thin wisp of leather or vellum, possibly a trimming from the binding frame, and tossed it in the direction of the waste bin. The scrivener missed, and Cerryl knew he'd have to pick it up later.

"Your words say that no one likes a good ruler," ventured Cerryl, wondering at the slight bitterness in Tellis's last few words about those who took from others.

"People are what they are," answered Tellis. "Enough. Your eyes grow wide and like a mirror. I fear I have said too much, and I must return to binding." Tellis stretched and shook out his fingers, as if to loosen any tightness in them. "And you to copying."

Cerryl picked up the quill and looked across the workroom at the green leather, evenly shaded all the way through, already stretched and shaped and ready for the binding. "You have not shown me much of binding."

"You wonder why, young Cerryl, I have taught you little, except by observation, about binding?"

"I have had much to learn," Cerryl temporized, carefully setting the quill back in its holder. He sat up straight on the stool, wondering about the volume Tellis had covered.

Tellis laughed gently, pointing toward the page that the young man had copied earlier in the day. "Your hand, it is already better than mine. I should take you from that?"

"You flatter me, ser."

"Not by much, young fellow. Not by much." The scrivener shook his head. "Why do you worry about the binding? A binding is there to protect the words within—no more, no less. I do my poor best to make that protection beautiful, but what good is a fine binding that will last for generations if the ink you have copied onto the pages fades into faint shadows on the parchment?"

"None, ser. Not after the ink fades."

"That is another matter, young Cerryl. Those who do not know books assume that any copyist can do what a true scrivener does. Do they think about what ink might be? Ink . . . you must know how to mix the ink, the proportions and the bases." Tellis peered intently at his apprentice.

Cerryl nodded, wondering if it would be a day where Tellis declaimed for all too long and then bemoaned the fact that Cerryl had copied too little.

"Now . . . that is the formula for common ink?"

"The distillate of galls," began the young man, "the darkest of acorn seepings, boiled to nearly a syrup, the finest of soot powders, with just a hint of sweetsap . . ."

"And only a hint," interrupted Tellis. "And the stronger ink?"

"Black oak bark, iron brimstone . . ." Cerryl paused. "You've never given me the amounts exactly."

Tellis shrugged. "How could I? The strength of the galls, the acorns, and the black oak bark are never the same. You must sense the ink, as I do, if you wish to be a master scrivener. Of everything in life be that true."

"What?"

"Is the avenue the same each time you go to the square? Or a stream? It appears the same . . . but is it?"

"That old argument!" A brassy laugh echoed through the workroom from the doorway where Benthann stood. "He has fine words, young Cerryl, but they are only words." She stepped into the room and toward Tellis. "I need some silvers for the market."

Tellis stepped away from the worktable. "Get on with the copying, Cerryl. I'll be but a moment."

"Yes, ser."

As the scrivener followed Benthann back toward the kitchen and common roam, Cerryl cleaned the quill's nib, then took the penknife and sharpened it before dipping it into the ink.

Oxen didn't change—or Dylert's hadn't—and Tellis was saying that most people didn't either.

His eyes fixed on a faint ink splot on the plastered wall. He wouldn't be most people. He wouldn't.

XXXIV

In the gray before dawn, Cerryl stood looking at the bucket of water, ice already forming on the edge. How long would winter go on? He shuddered at the thought of washing in the freezing water. The trees hadn't new-budded, and the old leaves remained gray, and that meant spring was more than a few eight-days away. Yet he hated both the freezing water and the way he smelled without washing.

Too bad he couldn't use the stove to warm his wash water the way Benthann did—or even Tellis. They expected him to be clean with water that froze on his skin. It wasn't fair.

He shook his head. Life wasn't fair. The only question was what anyone could do about it, and he didn't have a stove to heat his wash water. He shivered again as a gust of wind rattled through the courtyard.

He frowned. A stove contained fire. So did chaos. He knew. He'd seen and felt the heat.

He studied the bucket and the frost rime on the edge, looking at it as though it were a screeing glass. He frowned, trying to replicate the sense of white fire he could feel in the books—and had seen thrown by the fugitive.

Then he stopped and picked up the bucket, walking to his room. If he did manage to warm his water, he wouldn't do himself any good by showing the world—or Tellis, skittish as his master was about the white wizards. The son of a white? In some ways, that was hard to believe, and in others . . . all too easy.

Once inside, Cerryl concentrated on the water in the bucket. He could get the sense of flame—a pinpoint of white fire appeared *over* the bucket—but when he tried to lower it to the water, it just vanished. Did water have too much of something? Order?

Cerryl shook his head. Real fire held chaos, but it heated water.

"Stupid," he murmured to himself. "You can't put a brand in a stream." Or the burning splinter used to light tinder in a pitcher of water. So how would he heat the water? If he moved the fire under the bucket, he'd just burn the wood. Applying chaos-fire to the bucket would do exactly the same thing, and the burn marks would have Beryal, and especially Tellis, asking questions.

He looked around the small room, his eyes finally lighting on the plain brass candlestick. Taking his own penknife, he cut a short length from the cord he usually carried in his pocket, then soaked the cord in the cold water, leaving it draped over the side of the bucket, half in the water, half out. He removed the candle from the holder and set it on the pallet, then placed the brass holder on the floor stones beside the wooden bucket.

Cerryl swallowed. Would what he planned work?

He *enfolded* the brass in the white of chaos until he could feel the heat almost blistering off the brass. Then he looped the wet cord around the metal and lifted its holder quickly, then lowered it into the water. With a hiss, a gout of steam erupted from the bucket.

His head ached . . . even heating water took effort, just to warm it so that it was lukewarm. He coughed to clear his throat. He'd been so tense that he'd almost forgotten to breathe, and his throat was raw.

He dipped the washrag into the warmish water and began to wash. With even half-warm water, it wasn't bad, and practice would certainly help, as it had with his copying.

Practice . . . but did he dare?

He swallowed and looked at the bucket and the faint steam of the warm water in the cold room. Slowly, he lifted the now-tarnished candleholder out of the bottom of the bucket and set it back on the table.

He had to think of a better way. The brass wouldn't hold up for long. He massaged his forehead. Neither would his head.

With a sign, he began to dress quickly, knowing that if he didn't get to the common room quickly, Beryal or Tellis would be knocking on his door.

He left his room with the door ajar, hoping the cool breeze would help remove the faint odor of hot metal and the slightest hint of chaos, and walked quickly across the courtyard.

Still . . . even lukewarm water had felt better than freezing—much better.

XXXV

. . . and when they had come to the desert isle that was Recluce, Creslin the black slew all those of the duke's garrison as who would not swear unyielding loyalty to him, and the remainder he bound with the chains of dark order.

Once this evil deed was accomplished, more of the dark mages appeared, as if from the shadows, and stood behind Creslin, and gloom darkened the very sun.

A handful of stalwart blades, seeing the power of Creslin and the darkness that cloaked him and the faceless dark mages, swore such a powerful oath, yet resolved to stand firm against the evil, seeking a means by which they could return Recluce to the white fold, and peace and prosperity.

Megaera the wily, putting on perfumes and essences, enchanted them, and then, once under her spell, when they revealed their stalwart nature and fidelity to the Duke of Montgren and to the White Way of Truth, she laughed.

She turned her powers upon them and burned them, saying to all that such stalwarts had attempted to force themselves upon her, and that she had but defended her virtue.

Creslin and the dark mages declared that it was so, and so it was recorded, save in the true records of the Guild . . .

Colors of White
(Manual of the Guild at Fairhaven)
Preface

XXXVI

Cerryl checked the ink, then laid out the quills, and finally took down the thin and worn brown leather volume Tellis had given him two days earlier. While far shorter than the *Trade* volume he and Tellis had finally finished for some merchant at the grain exchange, *The Science of Mea-*

surement and Reckoning almost made reading the histories of Candar a pleasure.

He glanced toward the showroom, wondering where Tellis might be, and whether he should open the front door—or at least the shutters. The master scrivener had not been at the table when Cerryl had eaten his gruel, and Beryal had said nothing, just urged Cerryl to eat and get on with his business.

"Open the front shutters! You'd think . . ." Tellis's voice rasped from the front showroom.

Cerryl set the *Measurement* volume on the copy stand and hurried to comply.

Tellis dragged himself over to the workroom table and slumped onto the stool. After a moment, acting as though each movement caused great pain, he stood and shuffled to the chest, unlocking it and extracting something. Then he shuffled back to the table and looked morosely down at the faded green velvet wrapped around what appeared to be a thin volume.

"Is there anything I can do, ser?"

"Suppose you have to. Promised this . . . I'd be doing this myself, but this flux . . ." Tellis coughed, then held his forehead and closed his eyes for a moment.

"I can do it, ser," Cerryl said, glancing at the green velvet.

"I know. Dependable, you are." Tellis massaged his forehead once more, then looked up. "Master Muneat wanted this as soon as I finished it." Cerryl stepped over to the worktable. A slim volume bound in green leather lay on a square of green velvet. He knew vaguely that Tellis had been working on the book, but it was one of those the scrivener kept to himself.

"Do not be opening it."

"But what is it . . . if I might ask, ser?"

"It is . . . verse . . . of a particular sort." Tellis flushed.

"Oh . . ."

"It's called *The Wondrous Tales of the Green Angel*. And I don't know why." Tellis coughed, almost retching, drawing himself erect after a moment. "But Muneat, he wanted it . . . and matters have been slower than I would have liked . . . don't turn down a pair of golds for a volume of less than fourscore sheets . . ."

Two golds?

"I promised, and it needs be delivered." Tellis looked at Cerryl. "You can deliver a volume, can you not?"

"Yes, ser . . . ah . . . where am I going?"

"Master Muneat's. You know the houses past the exchange? Past the jewelers' row?" Tellis tried to clear his throat.

"Yes, ser, just past the market square?"

"His is the first house on the far side, the very first one. There is a fountain with two birds in the courtyard before the front door. You go to the front door." Tellis paused, then swallowed hard. "This must go only to the hand of master Muneat himself. He is short, not much taller than you are, and he has a wide white mustache, and he is mostly bald."

"What—"

"You just tell whoever opens the door that you must deliver it to his hand, and his alone, and that you will wait—or return whenever he deems fit. You be most polite, but only to his hand—or return."

"Yes, ser."

"And wear your good tunic. Go get it on and return."

When Cerryl returned, Tellis had wrapped the volume in the velvet, then tied the cloth with thin strips of vellum, so that none could see the volume. Cerryl picked it up, wishing he'd known of it . . . just to see what such wondrous tales were. Green angels? He'd heard of the black angels of Westwind, but not green angels.

"You go straight there, and come straight back. You hear?"

"Yes, ser. Straight to master Muneat's. The first house past the market square on the far side. A fountain with two birds."

"Good . . ."

Cerryl bowed again, then gingerly picked up the wrapped volume. Tellis did not move, and the apprentice slipped away and out through the showroom door.

The air on the street was cold, but the bright sun helped warm Cerryl as he walked down the way of lesser artisans toward the square. The shutters were still closed at the weaver's, though he could hear the shuttling of the big loom when he passed.

Across the market square, Fasse's door was ajar, and a wagon stood at the curb of the avenue, with a driver beside it. Some cabinet being picked up by whoever had commissioned it? Who had the coins for such—besides people like dukes and viscounts?

Cerryl turned down the avenue, past the inn, and the smell of fresh-baked bread, and past the ostlery beside it, and the faint scent of hay brought in from somewhere and stacked in bales beside the stable door. Hay? In very early spring? Or had it been stored somewhere all winter?

Three carriages were lined up by the grain exchange, with the drivers standing by the middle carriage.

"Morning, boy!" called the older driver at one side.

"Good morning, ser." The sun felt good on Cerryl's face, and he smiled as he hurried down the walk past the jewelers' row—the iron-bound doors yet closed. He did catch the odor of hot metal from the last shop before the market square. In the square itself, the many-colored carts filled the pavement, but only a handful of those interested in their wares had appeared.

Cerryl's steps slowed as he passed the square. The first dwelling on the far side . . . He paused at the open wrought-iron gate, looking into the open expanse of dark green grass, bordered by bushes that lined the inside of the wall, and split by the polished granite walk that led straight to a fountain—a fountain with a bird on each side of the jet of water that splashed into the basin. Two birds, Tellis had said.

Cerryl just looked at the front of the dwelling for a moment longer. The walk circled the fountain and led to a stone-columned and roofed portico that sheltered a huge polished red oak door—bound in iron. He'd thought that the houses along the avenue had been little more than one level. He'd been wrong, but that had been because they were larger, far larger in breadth, than he had thought. While the dwelling before him appeared to be but one level, that one level was twice the height of most of the shops along the way of the lesser artisans.

The shutters were open to reveal real glass windows—at least a half score on each side of the entry portico, each window composed of dozens of diamond-shaped glass panes that glittered in the morning sun, casting a silvered reflection across the deep green grass that filled the space before the house—or small palace.

Beside the smooth stones of the granite walk were rectangular and raised flower beds, filled with dark green plants bearing delicate white flowers. The scents of flowers—different kinds, scents he'd never smelled—drifted around him in the still air of morning, yet he could see no flowers.

Finally, he squared his shoulders and stepped through the gate, walking slowly but firmly up the walk. Tellis had told him the front door, and that was where he was headed.

Several drops of water flecked his face as he passed the fountain, and he shifted the book to his left hand, away from the fountain.

Standing in the shadows of the portico, a tall space that made him feel very small, he lifted the heavy and brightly polished brass knocker, then let it drop.

Thrap! The hard impact on the knocker plate seemed to echo through the stillness. Cerryl waited.

A gray-haired man in a blue tunic and trousers opened the door. "Trade is at the side door."

"Master Tellis told me to deliver this to master Muneat, to his own hand."

"I'll take it for him, boy." The servitor smiled pleasantly.

"No, ser. Only to his hand. I can wait, if he would like. Or I can come back again."

The man in green frowned. "Wait." The door closed.

Cerryl shifted his weight from one foot to the other. The sun seemed to beat on his back, even the back of his legs.

Finally, the door reopened, and the green-clad servitor looked at Cerryl. "Master Tellis, you said?"

"Yes, ser. The scrivener."

A faint smile cracked the thin lips. "I'm Shallis, and I'm not a ser. I'm the house seneschal." He opened the door and stepped back. "You are to come in and wait here in the foyer."

Cerryl eased inside. The foyer ceiling was high, twice as high as the showroom's in Tellis's shop, and polished dark wood planks stretched between the arching granite supports. The base of each pillar was a polished rose-tinged stone, so smooth that it shimmered in the light from the open door.

"You may sit on the bench there." Shallis closed the door and pointed to a white oak bench with a low back, set slightly away from the waist-high polished rose marble wainscotting. His eyes went to Cerryl's boots. Then he nodded. "Master Muneat will be here when it suits him."

"Thank you." Cerryl didn't know what else to say. He sat on the front edge of the bench as Shallis stepped through the archway into the house proper.

Cerryl's eyes followed the seneschal, taking in what he could see of the hallway beyond the foyer, a hallway that was larger than the large common room in Tellis's house, even larger than the kitchen and eating area in Dylert's house.

The sole archway he could see from the bench was draped in blue, a fabric that dropped in fine folds that shimmered in the indirect light from the windows Cerryl could not see. The hallway floor beyond the foyer arch was polished marble, set in interlocking squares, so smooth and so clean that Cerryl would have feared to walk on it.

A gilt-framed portrait hung on the wall, but Cerryl could not see much except that the figure was a white-haired man in a white shirt, and with a blue short jacket of some sort and dark trousers. The portrait was flanked by two lamps set in bronze wall sconces, polished to a fine sheen. Even the lamp mantels glistened.

The scent of flowers was stronger inside the foyer, reminding Cerryl of Dyella's gardens above the mill. He shifted his weight on the bench again, looking down at the velvet-wrapped book.

The faintest of rustlings caught his ear, and his eyes went back to the hallway, where a woman, impossibly slender, crossed the marble floor and entered through the archway the room on the left side of the hall, past the shimmering hangings. Her gown—not tunic and trousers but a form-fitting dress or gown—was a deep red that also shimmered in the indirect light. Cerryl thought she had worn silver combs in dark hair, but she had moved so gracefully and silently that he was not sure.

A different scent, one like fruit and roses together, slipped past him, then seemed to vanish.

Cerryl swallowed as he heard a clicking on the marble. A short figure in deep blue—even in deep blue leather boots—was walking toward the foyer. He wore a shimmering white silk shirt, and a dress jacket and matching trousers of a deep blue velvet. The bald forehead, the silver hair, and the white-silver mustache told Cerryl that master Muneat approached, and the apprentice jumped to his feet, waiting. Behind Muneat walked the seneschal, his face blank.

"Young fellow . . . Shallis said you were from master Tellis." A surprisingly shy smile crossed the broad and jowled face.

"Yes, ser. Master Tellis sent me to deliver this." Cerryl extended the velvet-wrapped book. "He said it could only go to your own hand."

"To my own hand, ha!" Muneat laughed again, taking the book. "My own hand. Would that others respected my hand so much."

Ceryl didn't know what to say. So he waited for the older man to stop laughing.

"And you would not be budged, not if you're from Tellis. Verial was like that, too. Two golds I promised your master, and two golds it shall be. And a silver for you, and two for him."

Cerryl managed to keep his mouth shut as Muneat handed him a small leather pouch and then a silver. "Your master's coins are in the purse. The silver is yours."

"I thank you, ser." Cerryl bowed. "And Master Tellis thanks you."

"Always a pleasure dealing with Tellis. Always a pleasure." Muneat smiled broadly. "And it is good to meet you, lad. Your name?"

"Cerryl, ser."

"Cerryl. A good name. And a good day to you." Muneat laughed again, a gentle sound, and turned to the seneschal.

Shallis stepped around his master and forward to open the door.

"Thank you, ser," Cerryl said again.

"And a very good day to you and your master. Tell him I have another, perhaps in an eight-day or so."

"Yes, ser."

Cerryl stood on the granite paving stones before the fountain for a long moment, then slipped the pouch inside his shirt, and the silver into the slots on the inside of his belt—far safer for him than a wallet— though he'd never heard of a cutpurse in Fairhaven. But he didn't wish to discover such existed the hard way.

Back on the avenue, Cerryl glanced back at the house—or palace—

then down the avenue, past the half-dozen or more similar dwellings. He shook his head. He'd had no idea, no idea at all, of what wealth really was. Dylert he'd reckoned as a wealthy man. He shook his head once more before turning back up the avenue, thinking he could yet smell all the scents of flowers that had filled master Muneat's home.

And the red gown—how many coins must one have to wear such gowns for no reason at all? He forced himself to walk briskly past the market square, past the jewelers, past the artisans' square and up the street to Tellis's, ignoring the silver in his belt. Silver he could always spend. Getting it was harder. He shook his head—except for those like master Muneat.

Back at the shop, Cerryl went straight through the showroom to the workroom. Tellis sat slumped at the worktable.

"Are you all right, ser?"

Tellis slowly straightened. "Was he in? Did you give it to him?"

"Yes, ser." Cerryl extended the pouch. "He gave me this. Said there were two golds and two silvers in it for you."

Tellis's eyes brightened as his trembling hands took the pouch and fumbled it open.

Coins spilled on the table.

"There are three silvers here, as well as the golds. Did you not count?"

"Ser . . . he handed me the pouch. That was what he said. I thought it better not to question his word."

"Muneat plays his tricks, but he is generous, unlike some." A ragged smile crossed Tellis's lips. "He gave you something?"

"Yes, ser. He gave me a silver."

"Good. Keep it safe." The smile faded. "Do not be thinking that you'll see its like again soon."

"No, ser. I know that." Cerryl paused. "Master Muneat said he would have another in an eight-day or so."

"Did he open it while you were there?"

"No, ser."

Tellis nodded slowly.

"Ser . . . what is it that . . . I mean . . . I sat in the foyer . . . polished marble . . ."

"He has more coins than most," Tellis said dryly, massaging his forehead and not looking at Cerryl. "He is one of the largest grain factors in Candar. I believe he even has several ships that sail out of Lydiar."

Cerryl glanced around the suddenly very cramped workroom, a room that would have fit even inside the front foyer of Muneat's small palace.

"He is not alone in his riches in Fairhaven, Cerryl. Far from it."

The apprentice wondered what the dwellings of the other rich folk looked like inside.

"Get me some of the yellow tea Beryal said she'd brew."

"Yes, ser." Cerryl turned and headed toward the kitchen.

"Yellow tea . . . yellow tea . . ." mumbled Tellis behind Cerryl. "Darkness . . . hate the stuff . . ."

Beryal looked up from the kitchen worktable, where she poured a hot liquid from the kettle into a mug. "You're back so soon?"

"They didn't make me wait. Tellis sent me for the tea." His eyes traversed the common room, clean and plain—and very small. Very plain.

"He's stubborn," said Beryal, lifting one of the smaller mugs and extending it to Cerryl. "Wouldn't stay in bed. No . . . has to get up and make the rest of us feel his pain."

"He doesn't look well."

"Anyone who drank all that double mead at the Pillion last night should look like that. Benthann, she cannot lift her head." Beryal frowned. "Take the master his yellow tea."

Cerryl slipped back to the workroom and extended the mug.

Tellis took it wordlessly.

Cerryl sharpened the quill, then stirred the ink, and set *The Science of Measurement and Reckoning* on the copy stand, opening it to the bookmark. He could almost see the polished marble and the shimmering hangings, and the dark red dress . . . even the dark blue velvet and flawless silk worn by Muneat. Cerryl knew, from what he'd learned in talking with Pattera, that the silk shirt alone probably cost a gold. He'd never seen half that in his entire life.

He took a slow breath. He couldn't change what was. Not yet, perhaps not ever. He dipped the quill in the ink. *But you can do more than be a scrivener . . . you can!*

At the worktable, Tellis sipped bitter yellow tea.

XXXVII

Cerryl dipped the pen into the inkwell, then resumed copying the page before him, trying to concentrate on the words and the shape of his letters, knowing that no matter how closely his efforts resembled those on the scrivener's master sheet, Tellis would still find some way to suggest improvement. One moment, the scrivener was praising his hand; the next, he was complaining about the way Cerryl copied one type of letter or another, or that he didn't fully appreciate the complexities of being a scrivener.

The apprentice scrivener held in a sigh. Too many sighs, he'd discovered, elicited unwelcome questions. His eyes went to the book on the copy stand.

> ... the inner lining of the bark of the river willow should be scraped, then dried until it is firm and stiff. Then it must be ground into the finest of powders with a polished hardwood mortar and pestle ...

Why did powdered willow bark hold down chaos fever? Who had discovered that? For all the volumes that Tellis pushed on him to read, Cerryl felt that he almost knew less than when he had come to Fairhaven more than a season before, since each new book opened far more questions than it answered.

Scritttchhh ... With the sound of the street door opening, Tellis backed up, nearly into the waist-high waste container, and then stepped around his worktable, leaving the stretching frame, and slipped past Cerryl and into the showroom.

"You keep at that herbal copying," the master scrivener added over his shoulder as he hurried toward the showroom.

Use of plants and herbs for healing might be of some interest, certainly more than words about measuring that meant little, reflected Cerryl, but herbs didn't seem to help with controlling chaos. Then he frowned, thinking about how he felt when he tried to warm his wash water. Would the powdered willow bark help reduce the warming in his body and the headache his using chaos caused?

With the flash of white he saw through the open door, Cerryl stiffened, listening intently.

"... how might I be of service, honored ser? Perhaps a volume of one of the histories ... ?"

The response was muted enough that Cerryl could not make out the words.

"Ah, yes ... that would take several eight-days, perhaps longer ... you understand?"

"... understand ... the heavy binding ... virgin vellum ... how much ... ?"

"Three golds, honored ser."

"That is dear."

"The vellum and the leather alone—"

"No more than five eight-days, scrivener, or not a gold to you. And all by your hand. Not another soul but you to handle the original. Do you understand?"

Cerryl could feel the chill and power of the mage's reply, even from the workroom copy desk.

"Yes, ser. Before five eight-days, with the heavy binding and the best of virgin vellum."

"No one else but you."

"Yes, ser."

Cerryl abruptly moved the quill, just in time to keep the ink from splattering on the page he was working on. He wiped the splot off the wood, cleaned the nib, then resumed his laborious effort to copy the page from *Herbes and Their Selfsame Remedies,* trying to look busy when Tellis reentered the workroom.

"Don't know where as I'll even be getting the time. Yet three golds, that is not a commission I can turn down." Tellis frowned, then coughed, and looked down at the worn volume in his hands. "Dealing with mages—every gold you earn. And earn again."

"I can copy it, ser," offered Cerryl.

"This one I'll be copying," Tellis announced.

"If things are hard, ser, I can do it."

The master scrivener shook his head. "Some volumes, the whites say that only the master may copy."

"Why? How can they do that?"

"Cerryl . . ." This time, Tellis provided the sigh, and not quietly. "Have you heard nothing? The White Council must approve any craft master in Fairhaven. You know the star with the circle above the door? Must I remind you what that master symbol means? Without that star, I'd get no copying or scribing from the Council . . . or any of the mages."

"But you're the best in Fairhaven. Everyone on the square says so," Cerryl said quickly.

"You are loyal—I will say that," answered Tellis. "The mages look for more than ability, Cerryl. They also demand loyalty. Without White Council approval, a tradesman or a crafter can never be more than a journeyman here. Journeymen get no Council business." Tellis snorted. "And little else, either."

"Even able ones?"

"What merchant or tradesman dare deal with a scrivener not in the Council's favor? Even Muneat would turn away his little pleasures."

"He has coins . . ."

"Coins are not power, Cerryl. Sometimes, those with coins can purchase power. Now . . . best I start. Set the herbal volume on the high shelf. You'll have time to copy when I rest. You can go and get the oak bark and the vellum this will take.''

Cerryl cleaned the quill, then wiped his hands, stood, and lifted *Herbes and Their Selfsame Remedies* from the copy stand.

Tellis set the book he carried on the copy stand and opened the blank cover to the flyleaf.

Cerryl's eyes went to the words there, and he froze for a moment that seemed all too long as he read the title—*Colors of White*. Tellis had the entire book there, not just the first part but the whole book. The entire volume he'd wished to lay his hands on for so long—and he couldn't touch it.

''Don't be standing there. Be off with you. First to Nivor's for the black oak bark. You know the kind. Then when you bring that back, I'll need more of the virgin vellum. But come back and set the bark to steep first, before you go to Arkos's.''

That meant twice as much walking, but Cerryl nodded politely. ''Ah, ser . . . won't I need some coin for Nivor?''

''Pestilence . . . yes. Arkos will trust me for the vellum, but Nivor trusts no one.'' Tellis fumbled in his purse. ''Not more than a silver and five coppers for a tenth stone of the bark, either, no matter what that thief Nivor says. If he won't give it to you for that . . . then come home without it.''

''Yes, ser.'' Cerryl took the coins and put them in his own purse with the three coppers that were his.

''You can tell him I said so, too.'' Tellis shifted his weight on the stool. ''Man's more brigand than apothecary . . . but don't tell him that. Now, be off with you.''

''Yes, ser.''

In moments, Cerryl had pulled on his better tunic—used for errands and holiday meals—and stepped out into the spring afternoon, warm, but with the hint of a winter chill that had not yet vanished, and gray, with the promise of rain before evening. He hoped the rain wasn't too long or too heavy; he could do without the attendant headache.

He stretched, then started for the lesser artisans' way. After a dozen steps or more, he glanced toward Pattera's window—ajar as usual. Only her father worked at the big loom. His eyes went toward the square.

''You!''

The voice was peremptory and high-pitched, the words coming from behind Cerryl, and he almost stopped. But who would want anything from him? Were they talking to the master weaver?

''In the blue . . . I mean you.''

Cerryl turned ... and swallowed as he saw the white tunic, shirt, and trousers. He bowed immediately. "I did not realize ... I'm sorry, ser ..."

"No, you didn't ... did you?" A musical laugh followed—a laugh with a hard tone that made Cerryl want to shiver, even as he realized that the mage was a woman, an attractive figure with flame red hair and eyes that went through him, eyes that seemed to contain all colors and yet none at all. A faint scent of something—sandalwood, perhaps, drifted toward him.

He bowed again, saying nothing.

"Do you live here, young fellow?"

"Yes, ser. I'm an apprentice to Tellis."

"The scrivener?" Another laugh followed. "Most interesting. Do you know your letters?"

"Yes, ser." How could an apprentice scrivener not know the letters? Still, Cerryl kept his tongue.

"Both tongues?"

"I do not know Temple as well as the old true tongue," he admitted.

"The old true tongue," she mused. "And you mean what you say. Better and better. What is your name?"

"Cerryl, ser." Cerryl had to work at keeping his voice level, feeling as though he faced some sort of examination, a dangerous examination, even though he could not explain exactly what or why.

"Cerryl the apprentice scrivener ..." She laughed more musically than before. "Keep learning your letters and all that you can. It might be enough." She paused, and her voice turned harder. "You may go on whatever errand your master sent you."

Cerryl tried to gather himself together as he bowed.

"Go."

"Yes, ser." He bowed again, turned, and hastened down toward the square and toward Nivor the apothecary's.

The woman in white—she was certainly a mage, and not all that much older than Cerryl. He shivered, recalling the cold eyes that had changed color with every word and the cruel laugh. He wasn't sure he wanted to know what she had meant about his learning more might be enough. Enough for what?

He shivered, though he tried not to do so. So much went on in Fairhaven that few saw. His brief experience with master Muneat had shown him one side of it, but that wasn't all. Though he *saw* little of the power of chaos that lay hidden, that power he could feel, unlike that of the golds of the factors. And the hidden chaos made him shiver, unlike the golds.

XXXVIII

Cerryl lay on his back, under both the thin blanket and his leather jacket, not quite shivering but not exactly warm, either. His eyes looked generally in the direction of the ceiling beams, but his thoughts were well beyond his room.

Tellis had the complete volume of *Colors of White*, the whole thing, with the sections missing from the volume Syodar had given Cerryl. The apprentice scrivener turned on his side, drawing his legs up so that he was curled into a ball, trying not to think about the volume locked inside the chest in the copy room, and trying even harder not to think about the key in the hidden niche by the door.

"It's not as though . . ." he murmured. As though? As though he would be stealing? He wouldn't hurt the book. He'd read it in the work-room in the dark. Stealing knowledge? But did knowledge belong to anyone? Or was that how the mages stayed in power—by keeping their knowledge to themselves?

Cerryl turned over once more and looked through the darkness at the ceiling beams again. He wanted to sigh, but what good would that have done? He could almost feel the white-dusted volume calling him.

Tellis hadn't said no one else could read it, but that no one else was supposed to copy the book. Cerryl winced at the self-deception. No one else was supposed to handle it because the white mages didn't want anyone besides a craftmaster they trusted to read it. A craftmaster who was the son of a mage?

Sooner or later, they'll find out that you can handle chaos a little . . . if they don't know already. Wouldn't it be better to learn what you can now? Momentarily ignoring the thought, he turned over on the pallet. Then he turned back. Some moments later, he found himself looking at the ceiling beams once more.

Finally, he sat up and swung his feet over the side of his bed, not letting them touch the cold stone of the floor for a moment. Then he stood. He eased open his own door and surveyed the dark and silent courtyard. The sole sounds were those of the breeze and the clopping hoofs and creaking of a wagon somewhere down on the avenue.

Cerryl took a deep and silent breath. Wearing only the jacket and his smallclothes, he padded noiselessly across the courtyard. The door to the common room scraped, but only slightly, as he closed it behind him and eased around the table and through the kitchen.

Cerryl slipped into the workroom, not lighting a candle, and trusting his own night vision. The key slid from its recess beside the door into his fingers, and the cabinet lock barely *snicked* as he turned the key and opened the door. The book itself lay in the first drawer, half-illuminated to Cerryl's senses by the traces of chaos power dusting it. For the moment, he left it there untouched.

None of the white mages would be able to tell that Cerryl had read it, because his own faint chaos power traces would be obscured by their far vaster power. Still, he rinsed his hands in the cool water remaining in the pitcher, wanting to reduce further the faintest residue of the chaos energy that seemed to flow within him and out through his bare fingers. After drying them on his own towel—still damp from when he had washed before dinner—he turned back and lifted the book from the drawer and carried it to the copy stand, setting it down and opening it roughly halfway through, toward where he thought the second section might begin.

In the dimness, even with his night vision, he had to strain to read the words on the page to which he had turned.

A mage must use order to channel chaos, for nothing else can contain the pure flame of chaos, yet he must not be constrained by that order, lest his power to use chaos for good be turned to naught . . .

Cerryl flipped through more pages. He wanted answers, not philosophy.

. . . there be two types of healing, the use of order to strengthen the flesh and the use of chaos to destroy all manner of illnesses arising from whence the elements of the world mortify the flesh . . . in the second, the mage must ascertain the very source of the mortification . . . his energies must but destroy that source and none other, for any other destruction will most assuredly destroy also the patient . . .

Cerryl wanted to beat his forehead. *How* was he supposed to concentrate chaos energies inside someone? He understood the ideas, even those he hadn't known about. Technique was the question, not philosophizing about the technique. He flipped through several more pages.

> . . . those marshaling the fires of the air must understand that the aether itself acts as though it were a function of order, pressing in upon the energies of chaos focused by the mage . . .

That didn't tell him anything, either. At least he didn't think it did. His forehead was damp, despite the chill night air in the workroom, but he read on.

> . . . so that even a line of chaos fire will reassemble itself into a globe of such fundamental fire when hurled through its own power over even the shortest of distances . . .

Cerryl forced himself to keep reading. Maybe he just didn't know enough. Maybe.

How long he read—that he had no idea, except that his head felt as though it were twirling on his shoulders and filled with burning sawdust when he replaced the book in the cabinet and relocked it. The key went back into its recess, and he retraced his silent steps back to his room.

He closed the door and looked through the darkness at his pallet, frowning. He felt as though someone were observing him, yet nothing moved. nothing offered the slightest of sounds, except the wind.

Finally, with a shiver, he slipped under the blanket, realizing that his feet were like blocks of ice. He shivered again, and might have once more, except his eyes were too heavy.

XXXIX

From his makeshift copy post at the end of the worktable, Cerryl looked away from the propped-up copy of *Herbes and Their Selfsame Remedies* and stifled a yawn. The nighttime reading was taking its toll, particularly late in the day, and yet he dared not yawn around Tellis. Not too much, anyway.

"Sleepy again, I see," observed the master scrivener from the copy desk where he labored over *Colors of White*. "You mayhap spending time with the *Historie*?"

"I have been reading," answered Cerryl. "There is much I don't understand." His nose wrinkled at the faint smell of some substance that had worked its way into the worn surface of the worktable—or was it the discarded oak galls festering in the bottom of the waste bin?

"Then you should ask," ventured Tellis, his eyes back on *Colors of White,* his fingers steady as he replicated the letters on the virgin vellum. "What do you find hard to understand?"

Cerryl dipped his own quill and copied for a moment before replying. "There is so much." He paused, ensuring the quill was well clear of the vellum before he spoke. "There are mentions of iron birds that brought the white way to Candar, but little is said of the time before Cyador."

"I thought you had questions about matters difficult to understand." Tellis continued to copy, his eyes on the book, the quill nearly a blur under fingers swift and sure.

"Those as well, master Tellis." Cerryl nodded, then copied another few words, his thoughts jumbled as he tried to recall something he could claim was confusing.

"Such as?" prompted Tellis.

"Well, there are so many things, but I do not understand about Westwind. How could anyone live on the Roof of the World? No one lives there today, but the histories say it was even colder then, yet Westwind prospered until it got warmer." Cerryl wanted to smile to himself at coming up with the question. Instead, he dipped the quill and resumed copying.

"Oh, Cerryl." Tellis actually sighed. "You read, and you understand the words, and yet you do not see what is before you. When the winters were colder, then only the angels could bear the Roof of the World for much of the year, and they did not have to spend so much gold and effort to defend themselves. Few could reach their citadel. After the great change, when the years got warmer, then the western lands thought about what had once been theirs, and they sought to reclaim those domains, for the warmer weather made the summers in the lowlands harder on the flocks and herds and the green grasses of the highlands more attractive. The Roof of the World was easier to reach for more of the year, and the guards were stretched thinner. Do you not see?"

"When you put it that way, master Tellis, it is clear enough, but that is not the way the *Historie* reads." Cerryl frowned as he noted the fractional widening of his letters. He wiped the quill's nib clean and took out the penknife to sharpen the point.

"The *Historie* is written for men who think, not for those who wish every word explained."

Although Tellis's voice was mild, Cerryl winced. He supposed he deserved the reprimand. He tried the reshaped nib on his palimpsest, then nodded at the letter width.

"You are younger than your years in your thoughts and far older in your heart," Tellis added. "I can do little for your heart, but for Dylert's sake I will press you to think. Another puzzling question—a better one?"

Cerryl did not answer immediately, stifling a yawn once more.

"No matter how tired you are, Cerryl, you must always keep your thoughts and wits about you." After a moment, the scrivener added, "In Fairhaven, especially."

Cerryl looked down, trying to dredge up another question, a better one. After what seemed far too long, he spoke. "Nowhere does it say why the black mages can control the winds. The white mages can create fire, and I know fire creates drafts, but . . ." He let the question hang.

"That is a better question," said Tellis.

Cerryl had hoped so. He covered his mouth with the back of his free hand. Was it the bitter odor seeping around the writing board he had laid over the battered surface? Or just his own tiredness?

"The great winds are spawned, we are told, in the cold places of the world, above the Roof of the World and in the far north. Leastwise, that is where the great winds seem to come from. The black mages, as their ancestors the black angels, are creatures of the cold and, hence, are closer to the chill and the wind, while the white mages come from the warmth of the sun and hold to mastery of flame and prosperity." Tellis nodded at his explanation.

"But it takes fire to forge iron, and the white mages cannot bear its touch," countered Cerryl.

"Touch cold iron sometime, and feel it suck all heat out of you." Tellis smiled. "Remember, nothing is as it seems, and though I do my best to instruct you, there is much beyond what even a master scrivener knows, even one raised with the education I was fortunate to receive."

Cerryl covered his mouth again, wishing he did not have to yawn so much.

"A good thing it is we are near finished for the day." Tellis glanced at Cerryl and shook his head. "You go. A quick nap will do you good. Beryal or Benthann will knock on your door. No reading—a nap, dinner, and a good night's slumber. Tomorrow I'll be at the tower, for they want a copyist, and you must speed copying the *Herbes* book. Nivor asked about our progress yesterday."

"Yes, ser." Cerryl nodded politely. The herbal book wasn't totally boring, but he did not find it nearly so interesting as even the *Historie*, which he read periodically in order to answer Tellis's questions.

"Off with you."

Cerryl closed the *Herbes* book, cleaned the quill, and stoppered the ink, then washed his hands. Tellis did not look up from his copying of *The Colors of White*.

"Dinner won't be that long," Beryal announced from the kitchen as Cerryl passed through the common room and stepped out the back door into the courtyard.

"Thank you, Beryal." He wiped his forehead with the back of his sleeve as he stood for a moment in the light and cooling breeze, a breeze that carried the scent of wet wool from the alleyway.

Cerryl took a step, then another, and stopped, looking around from the middle of the courtyard. He glanced toward the rear gate, confident he would see Pattera there. The space was empty. He frowned, certain that someone had been watching him.

After a moment, he turned back toward the main part of the house, but no one stood in the doorway to the common room. He glanced back at the gate, and then at the side door to the room Tellis and Benthann shared. The doors were closed, and the gateway empty.

Slowly, he walked to his room, but the feeling of being watched continued as he opened his door. The room was empty.

Abruptly as it had come, the feeling of being watched vanished. Cerryl shuddered as he closed the door.

With the chill in his bones, all thought of sleep vanished. He checked the shutters—closed tightly. Then, almost furtively, Cerryl eased the screeing glass from behind the wooden panel he had loosened, leaving his books there.

Could he? He looked down at the silver-rimmed glass, seeing the thin-faced reflection of a youth with barely a hint of a beard—if that. Not even a man yet, and why was he even thinking about using the glass? His eyes went to the closed shutters. Yet he had to do *something*. More and more, he felt that everyone else pushed him, directed him, that everyone else had the answers and that he would have fewer and fewer choices, especially if he waited until he got older.

He glanced back down at the glass, then frowned. Did he dare? Did he not dare? Was it the girl with the red-blond hair? Or the redhead?

He should have given up on the girl in green, yet he kept thinking about her. Why? How could a scrivener's apprentice aspire to any consort?

"Consort?" He barely murmured the word. What an idiotic notion! He couldn't rightly aspire to being a white mage, for all his talent and his secret study. He couldn't even aspire to great wealth, such as that shown by Muneat.

He pushed back those thoughts, swallowed, and looked down at the mirror. As he concentrated, surprisingly the white mists formed and cleared.

The young woman sat at a writing desk, a golden oak desk in a small room. The walls were hung with green silks, and behind her was a high bed covered with blue-green silks and pillows. The oiled gold oak window shutters were closed.

Quill pen in her hand, she looked down at whatever she wrote. Then she set the quill in the holder. Abruptly, she frowned.

She was older, Cerryl could tell. Then, so was he. Her face crinkled into a frown, and she glanced up from the writing desk, her eyes going in one direction, then another.

She stood and walked to the window, then turned, her eyes going to the glass on the wall.

Abruptly, Cerryl released his hold on the glass. She'd known she was being watched, but how?

Even so, he could feel heat radiating from his glass, as though someone had thrown chaos-fire at it just as he had broken off his viewing. He wiped his forehead, suddenly feeling even more tired.

Quickly, as though he feared he were being observed by some other scrier, he slipped the silver-rimmed mirror back into its hiding place. After a moment, he took a deep breath, relieved that the feeling of being watched had not returned. He'd gotten away with using the glass.

This time, a small voice in his head reminded him. *This time*.

With a brief smile, he pulled off his boots and lay down on the pallet, his eyes closing almost as soon as he stretched out.

Almost immediately, he found himself walking across a high-vaulted room, a hall really, where the ceiling was supported by fluted white stone columns. The room was empty, yet it was not.

"You . . . you don't belong here, scrivener's apprentice. He will turn you to ashes if you stay."

The voice was sultry, but Cerryl couldn't make out the face. He turned, but there was no one beside him.

"I won't be seen, not if I don't wish to be. We whites control the light, you know. If you were worth anything, you could, too. In little ways, anyway." The unseen laugh was cruel, as he remembered from somewhere.

Thrap!

"Come on, you sleepy apprentice. Dinner be awaiting!"

Cerryl struggled out of the whitish fog. Had the redheaded white mage really been in his dreams? He hadn't seen her, but the voice had belonged to her. How could he forget that voice? He shivered.

"Cerryl!"

"I'm coming," he rasped. "I'm coming." His head felt as though it were being squeezed in the nipping press.

"Good thing you are." Benthann's voice faded away as he struggled into a sitting position and pulled on his boots.

After a moment, Cerryl stood, almost staggering as the pain of the headache came and went. He gathered himself together and made his way from his room, across the courtyard, and inside into the common room.

"Did you get a nap?" Tellis looked up from the burkha steaming on his platter.

"Yes, ser. You were right. I was tired." Cerryl slid onto his end of the bench, careful not to get too close to Beryal. He broke off a chunk of the dark bread and set it on the edge of his platter, then used the ladle to serve himself a portion of the hot-mint brown stew. "This smells good."

"Always does, and you always say it does." Beryal laughed.

The apprentice shrugged and scooped up a mouthful of stew with the bread, trying not to gulp it down.

"Be summer before too long, real summer." Tellis grunted, then served himself more of the burkha.

"It was hot today," Cerryl said, taking a long swallow of water, still half amazed that the water in Fairhaven was fit to drink.

"Be hotter yet in an eight-day or so. Then people be out in the streets all the time." Beryal snorted. "Too hot to stay inside."

"I was standing in the courtyard this afternoon, and I *know* someone was looking at me." Benthann turned to Beryal. "Tellis and Cerryl were both in the workroom, and you were at the market. When I looked up and down the alley, no one was there." She frowned. "Hasn't been the first time in the last eight-day, either."

"Swore I could have heard someone in the back alley last night." Beryal's eyes lifted from the crockery to Cerryl. "Did you hear anything?"

"I fell asleep trying to read the *Historie*." Cerryl managed a sheepish expression and dropped his eyes. He had fallen asleep over the *Historie* more than once.

"Lad . . ." Tellis cleared his throat.

"Even your dutiful apprentice can't always stay awake over those musty books." Benthann laughed. "Proves he's a normal young fellow after all."

"He's normal, all right." A faint smile crossed Beryal's lips.

Cerryl flushed.

Benthann laughed.

"A scrivener can't fall asleep over books," announced Tellis, "normal or not."

"You're a spoilsport." Benthann offered an overfull pout.

"Eat," ordered Beryal.

Cerryl followed her orders, partly because it was easier, especially with his headache, and partly because he was still hungry.

After dinner, Tellis and Benthann vanished into their room, and after he helped Beryal—silently, his thoughts still on the girl in green and the power she had almost thrown through the glass at him—Cerryl crossed the courtyard to the rear gate, then walked toward the street. The girl—except she was a woman now—or her family had coins, but not so many, he suspected, as Muneat. Did anyone really *need* all those coins, all those silks?

Does anyone really need to master chaos? He laughed at his own question, softly, as he turned the corner onto the way of the lesser artisans.

In the twilight, he continued slowly down the way toward the square, feeling that another pair of eyes followed him. He did not look back, knowing that he would see no one, trying to ignore the prickling on the back of his neck and the continuing throbbing in his skull.

"Cerryl!" Pattera bounded out of the weaver's door. "Where have you been these last eight-days?"

"Master Tellis has had a large commission from . . . a large commission, and I've had to do much of the regular copying as well as the chores." Cerryl shrugged. "And he wants me to read the histories as well." The apprentice didn't have to counterfeit the yawn.

"You have dark pouches under your eyes. Oh, Cerryl . . ." Pattera glanced back at the light from the doorway. "I can walk down to the square with you. Where are you going?"

"I was just walking," he admitted. "I have a headache." Cerryl took a step toward the square.

"Your master makes you squint over those books too much." Pattera began to match his steps.

"You have to study books if you want to be a scrivener."

"Not all the time."

"Most of the time." He paused at the avenue while a small donkey cart plodded past. The woman on the seat, reeking of roast fowl, did not turn her head.

As he crossed the white pavement, Cerryl massaged his temples with his left hand, trying to loosen the tightness he felt.

"Not that way," said Pattera. "Just stop. Sit on the bench there."

He sat on the second stone bench in the square, the empty one, and let her strong fingers work through his shoulder blades and up into his neck, letting her loosen the tension there. The faint odor of damp wool clung to her arms, and he wondered if the acridness of iron-gall ink clung to him.

How could someone who smelled of ink even think about a woman with silk hangings and dresses?

Yet he did, and he knew he would, even as he felt guilty accepting Pattera's ministrations while thinking of the blonde in green.

XL

Now . . . keep your mind on the copying at hand," said Tellis from the doorway. "No thoughts about your young friend the weaver. Not while you have a quill in your hand." The master scrivener grinned.

Cerryl flushed. "Yes, ser."

"When you become a true journeyman . . ." Tellis paused. "By then, you won't listen. I didn't, either, but I was lucky, and then unlucky. Elynnya was special." He shook his head. "Just appreciate what you have while you have it, and don't ask too many questions." His voice turned more cheerful. "After I beat some sense into Arkos, I'll do the same to Nivor, and then I'll be at the tower for most of the rest of the day. The honored Sterol wants something copied that cannot leave there." The scrivener lifted his hand and pointed at his apprentice. "I expect continued good progress on the copying—and keep the letter width the same."

"Yes, ser."

Tellis nodded and turned away.

His young friend the weaver? Pattera was nice enough, and attractive in a dusky fashion, and certainly enamored of Cerryl. That wasn't enough. But what was? A girl with red-blond hair whose father would scorn a mere scrivener's apprentice? And there was the redhead who kept turning up in his dreams—unwanted. She was certainly some type of mage; attractive as she was physically, she made his skin creep. He hadn't ever thought of a woman that way before.

A moment later, Cerryl heard the front door open, and the off-key bells of the refuse wagon, before Tellis closed the door behind him.

Cerryl scurried to the waste bin by the worktable. He lifted the heavy wooden container and lugged it outside, following Beryal, who had the kitchen bin in her arms.

They stood as the square-sided wagon rumbled along the way, at a pace not much faster than a walk. Two young guards in white uniforms flanked the hauler, their bored eyes flicking from the wagon bed to Beryal and then to Cerryl, dismissing each in turn.

Cerryl lifted the bin and dumped the contents—leather trimmings too small for anything, palimpsest scrapings, squeezed oak galls—over the side of the wagon, then stepped back.

"Tellis isn't ever here when the wagon comes. You notice that?" Beryal held the door to the shop for Cerryl.

"He is the master scrivener."

"He would be the master of more than that." Beryal shook her head, then started to close the door. "But he never will be. Those with coins keep them close."

Benthann pushed by them and through the door, not even looking at her mother or Cerryl, and ran down the street to catch the wagon, a smaller waste box in her hands.

"Then there be some who think that the waste wagon waits for them." Beryal grinned and closed the door before she turned back toward the kitchen.

Cerryl used the cleaning rag to wipe off the sides and the rim of the waste bin, before easing it back into place. He seated himself at the copy desk and started to clean the quill he had abandoned when he had heard the wagon bells.

Benthann glanced in the workroom door. "You could have called me."

"I didn't hear the wagon until it was almost here, and the big bin was full." He looked up, but Benthann hadn't stayed to hear what he said. He shrugged to himself, realizing he probably wouldn't ever understand the young woman. Then, there were a lot of things he didn't understand, undercurrents that kept tugging at him—like Tellis's gloom when he mentioned his consort. He wanted to know more but dared not ask. There was so much he dared not ask.

After he finished sharpening the nib, he smoothed the vellum and dipped the pen into the ink. Tellis was right; he needed to make good progress on the *Herbes* book, boring as it might be.

He frowned as he recalled Tellis's words—something copied that could not leave the mages' tower. Did that mean that the books that really said something about how to handle the chaos forces always remained guarded by the mages? If that were so, how could he ever learn? Except by experimenting, and that was clearly dangerous.

He forced his eyes to the book on the copy stand and began to replicate the letters on the new vellum.

. . . if the leaves be brown, and dried, and powdered, then they
may be used as to purge the bowels . . . save that never more

than a thimble be used for a full-grown man . . . and never be offered to a child or anyone of less than four stones . . .

Another face appeared in the doorway from the front room.

"Cerryl, I be off to the market," announced Beryal. "Benthann left for darkness knows where a time back. There's a pair of coppers on the table in the common room, should Shanandra ever bring the herbs she promised. Two coppers for the lot, no more. You understand?"

"How big a lot? And what?"

"Ah . . . some brains you have, unlike my daughter. Enough to fill the basket by the table without crushing the leaves. There should be sage and tarragon, fennel . . . Dried, they should be, but not so dry as to powder if put under your thumb." Beryal nodded, then left.

Cerryl cleaned the nib gently, afraid that the ink might have congealed or built up, then redipped the pen and tried a line on the practice palimpsest. "Good."

His eyes went back to the copy stand and the *Herbes* book there.

XLI

In the dim light of predawn, Cerryl carried the chamber pot through the rear gateway and out to the sewer catch. He set the pot on the white-dusted stones, opened the stone lid, and, in a quick motion, lifted the pot and emptied it, holding his breath as the fetid fumes swirled up before he could close the lid. Sometimes the fumes were overpowering, and at times there seemed to be none at all.

He carried the pot back into the courtyard, where he half filled it with water, which he swished around to rinse away any of the residue. Then he went back to the sewer dump and emptied the pot again. He sniffed the pot gingerly. It smelled clean enough to return to his room.

He turned in the direction of a scraping sound from the alley, near where it joined the way of the lesser artisans. Kotwin the potter was closing his own sewer dump, chamber pot in hand.

The faint and acrid smell of stove coal drifted into the alleyway as Cerryl turned. He smiled then, after closing the gate behind him, and stepped into the courtyard and back to his room, where the bucket of wash water he had already drawn waited.

With a quick glance at the closed door and shutters, he looked at the water in the bucket, concentrating on it, and on his vision of chaos fire in the shape of a poker into the bucket.

Hsssttt . . . The steam rose from the bucket, and Cerryl smiled. Warm water was much better than the ice-chill liquid from the pump. He pulled off the ragged handed-down nightshirt and stretched.

A chill mistlike sense filled the small room, and there was the feeling of being inspected somehow, but a cold inspection, as though he were a side of beef or a gutted river trout. He forced himself to finish washing and dressing as methodically as normal, somehow knowing that reacting to the unseen inspection would only make his situation in Fairhaven worse, and hoping that the unseen observer had not caught his little use of chaos.

He never tried to call the chaos forces when he felt watched, but it was clear someone, somehow, was using something to look for chaos use. Should he go back to cold water? He had to fight a wince at that thought.

He couldn't help wondering, as he pulled on his tunic, what he had done to have a white mage using a glass to follow his actions. Had it been the red-haired mage?

Tomorrow, he told himself, *no warm water.* Then, he'd said that the day before as well. He sat on his pallet and pulled on his boots. He carried the wash water back out to the sewer dump before returning the bucket to its peg on the wall and heading across the courtyard to the common room and breakfast.

"Saw you a-coming." Beryal slid a crockery platter with a slab of egg toast on it in front of him even before he sat down.

"Thank you." He poured a small portion of the bitter yellow tea, knowing it would cut some of the greasiness of the toast.

"Cerryl?" rumbled Tellis.

"Yes, ser?"

"I checked the herbal book when I got back last night." Tellis mumbled his words. "You are doing well, and you've kept the letter width about the same. A little variation, but not at all bad."

"Thank you." Cerryl popped a large mouthful of the heavy toast into his mouth and followed it with a sip of the tea.

"You'll have to keep it up. The High Wizard wants me back again today, and it could be late most nights for an eight-day or two. They have a great deal of copying."

"No one else can do it?" asked Beryal. "You'd think as they'd have their own copyists."

Cerryl kept a straight face and took another mouthful of egg toast, letting the master scrivener address the question.

"Like as they do, but not for works that should last. Those who handle the stuff of chaos—I've told you this, Beryal; why don't you listen?—if they were to copy those volumes, the life of both the originals and the copies would be far shorter." Tellis moistened his lips before taking another swig from his mug and then the last morsel of his egg toast. "Another piece, if you please. A long day ahead."

Beryal slipped away from the bench and walked back to the hot stove, scooping a dollop of tallow into the heavy iron skillet.

"What else do you want of me, master Tellis?" Cerryl finished his own egg toast.

"You need to keep working on the herbal book. Almost nearing the end, are you not?"

"Yes, ser. Within the next few days, or sooner."

"I'll be needing another batch of the dark iron-gall ink, too. And so will you. I'm taking the big jar."

"Egg toast." Beryal dropped another slab of the egg-battered bread into the skillet, and then a second. "And one for the apprentice, too."

"Thank you." Cerryl smiled and poured more of the tea.

"Don't forget to clean the jars before you mix new."

"No, ser." Cerryl gathered himself together, then asked casually, "What sort of books do you copy there?"

"Whatever they wish," answered Tellis with an enigmatic smile.

"I was not asking about what was within the books, ser. I only wondered . . ."

"There's little enough in them I understand—or would want to, my dear apprentice." Tellis's face grew stern. "Nor should you, when you are called by one of the great ones. It is a challenge and an honor."

"Better than that," interposed Beryal. "It pays good coins."

Tellis ignored her comment and stood. "It would not do to be late, not for the mages. I'd not like to have their glasses spying on me."

"Spying on you? Why would they do that?" Cerryl asked innocently.

"Who knows?" Tellis shrugged. "I've little enough to hide these days, but in Fairhaven even the blank walls have eyes. Best remember that, young Cerryl. Even with your weaver friend." A broad grin crossed the scrivener's face before he gave a quick nod and stepped to the washstand.

"Aye," agreed Beryal. "Little enough that they don't see, there is."

Cerryl gulped the last mouthful of egg toast.

"And keep those hands clean," Tellis added before he stepped out of the common room and into the front room to gather supplies from the workroom.

Cerryl nodded. Clean hands and another long day of copying . . . and worrying about whether he had already doomed himself—like his father.

He thought of the amulet that lay hidden in his room. Would he end like that? A memory to a few people and a piece of jewelry the only remnants?

He forced himself to finish the bitter yellow tea, knowing he would need the warmth within him.

XLII

In the early afternoon, Cerryl sat at the trestle table, chewing on the fresh-baked bread that Beryal had left. He had sliced several small chunks of cheese from the yellow brick.

"Tellis won't be home until well after the taverns are shuttered," Beryal had said with a snort right after Tellis had left in the early morning. "As for my daughter, she can cook, if she wishes. The bread and cheese are for you. I'm off to see Assurala—my mother's sister's daughter. She lives in Ghuarl—that's this side of Weevett." With that, Beryal had marched out the front door, even before Cerryl had been able to ask how she was getting there.

So he had kept copying until his fingers were numb before returning to the common room for something to eat . . . and drink. With a good afternoon's work, he might finish the remainder of the herbal text yet before evening.

A slight breeze drifted in from the courtyard, through the door and shutters he'd opened before he sat down. On the barely moving air came the scent of roses and other flowers, though there were none in the courtyard. Tellis didn't believe in such fripperies.

The courtyard was quiet, and the door to the bedroom Tellis and Benthann shared was closed, although the shutters beside the door were open.

Cerryl used his left hand to rub his stiff neck. If only Tellis hadn't taken *Colors of White* with him. He tried to shrug the stiffness out of his neck and shoulders. With more time, maybe he could have made more sense out of the book.

Finally, he stood and put the cheese into the cool chest and the bread in the big bread box on top of the pantry cabinet in the kitchen. Then he walked out into the courtyard to wash at the pump. The day was warm enough, and that way he wouldn't have to empty the basin and refill the pitcher in the common room.

As Cerryl stepped into the sun, he realized that the day had become hot, not just warm, as the light seemed to cascade around him like a rain of warmth, of fire. He paused and tried to sense the light, to feel it.

After a long moment, he swallowed. The light was so much like chaos fire . . . and yet different. For a time, he just bathed in the light, letting his perceptions weave with it.

Then he shook his head and walked to the pump. He washed quickly and straightened up as he heard a door open, looking to the rear gate first. No one was there.

"You were almost glowing—when you stood in the middle of the stones there." Benthann stood in the shade by the door to her—and Tellis's room.

Cerryl shook his hands dry and tried to avoid looking at the blonde, who leaned against the wall by the door.

"You did, you know? A golden youth." Her face clouded for an instant. "And you don't even know. Neither does your little weaver girl."

Cerryl waited, not certain what to say.

"You're the only one here," observed the blonde. "Mother went off to prattle on with cousin Assurala." Her voice rose from a husky purr into a shriller parody. "Life was so much better, Assurala, oh, yes, it was, back when the young folk listened." Benthann grinned, more girlishly than Cerryl had ever seen.

He nodded, trying not to look directly at Benthann and the thin shirt that left little to the imagination. "I need to get back to work."

"I suppose you feel that need." She smiled again and turned toward the common room door, walking in front of Cerryl. As she stepped from the shade of the eaves and into the sunlight, Cerryl swallowed. Her shirt was like mist in the full sun, and she wore nothing under it. Nothing.

Cerryl let her go into the main part of the house and waited several moments before he followed and opened the door.

Benthann stood by the table, her back to him, when she spoke. "I wondered if you'd come in."

"I have to finish the copying."

"I'm a true bitch," said Benthann, turning and stretching so that the mist-thin fabric outlined every curve. "I know it. Tellis knows it. My mother certainly does."

"You . . . you've been . . . fair to me."

"You mean I've mocked you less than I've mocked the others?" A crooked smile crossed her lips. "You must wonder."

"Wonder?" Cerryl felt stupid, as though each word were less intelligent than the last.

"Wonder why Tellis puts up with me. Would you like to see why Tellis puts up with me?" The blonde unfastened two of the buttons on the thin shirt that left little to the imagination.

Much as he would have, Cerryl shook his head with a slow smile. "You're far too rich for me, Benthann."

"You're like the others. You're a coward." Yet her words were not biting, and her tongue ran across the full lips, sensuously.

"It's not always bad to be a coward," observed Cerryl, stifling the urge to swallow and managing somehow to maintain an even tone. "Especially if you recognize those times and what you are."

"You don't have to be a coward." She stepped toward him.

Cerryl could smell the roses, and something else, something that beckoned. He just stood there, barely able to keep from lurching toward her, just as he had wanted to lurch back into Muneat's small palace, or summon the image of the woman in green again and again.

"There's no one else here."

"I'm here," he finally said, all too hoarsely.

Surprisingly, Benthann smiled. "You're smarter than they were." She stepped back.

Cerryl shook his head. "I'm not that smart. I just watch and learn from others." He wondered if he'd been all that wise to back away. He swallowed again.

"Hard, isn't it?" Benthann smiled more gently. "I mean, when a woman says she wants you—a pretty woman."

"You are pretty." That was true and safe.

"I am. I know that, for what it's worth. Pretty and good at selling my body. You wonder why my mother puts up with me?" Benthann laughed. "I saved us both. I climbed into Tellis's bed, and I don't regret it. He was grieving, and he needed something."

"His consort?" ventured Cerryl.

"And his son. Barely older than you, and he fled to the black isle." Benthann smiled crookedly. "I knew Vieral; that's how I found Tellis. It was better that than working off your debts and dying on the white road because your father gambled and drank his tavern away."

Cerryl wanted to shake his head . . . or something, but he listened, and his eyes strayed back to the thin shirt, and the curved figure beneath.

"Sex is the only power a woman has in Fairhaven. Remember that. Even if she has a strong room full of coins, or, light forbid, she's a mage, sex is the only real power a woman has." She smiled brightly. "But I like you, Cerryl. You look at me like I'm real."

"You are real." His voice was hoarse.

His words brought a headshake. "I'm not. Everything is a pantomime. Oh, I'm mostly honest with myself, but no matter what I try or see, it's all the same. Sex is all a woman really has."

Cerryl struggled for words before he spoke. "What about those women devils, the ones who used twin blades?"

"Westwind? They're all dead, aren't they?" Benthann stretched again.

Cerryl could see her nipples through the thin white fabric of her shirt, and he forced himself to think about the differences in the shape of the letter lok in Temple and old tongue.

"A woman who has to defend herself with a blade doesn't know her real power." Her fingers played with the shirt again, and Cerryl caught a glimpse of a darker nipple against creamy skin. "Nor one who has to use coins to buy her men."

He swallowed silently.

"Let me show you." She leaned toward him, and her lips brushed his cheek. "I could . . . and I like you. You haven't grinned that awful smile or panted all over place."

He could feel his trousers tightening. "I believe you. You don't have to show me anything."

Benthann fingered the fourth button on the thin shirt, and leaned toward him.

This time Cerryl did swallow.

"I'm much prettier than that weaver girl."

"Yes," Cerryl said hoarsely. "Yes, you are."

He couldn't move as she took one last step and brushed his lips with hers, his chest with hers. She stepped back quickly. "Like all of them, you're a liar. But you're a sweet liar, and you try to do what's right." She offered a too-bright smile. "I won't make both of us liars."

Cerryl swallowed, still swimming in the fog of roses and unknown flowers that ebbed and flowed around him.

Benthann half-slumped against the trestle table. "I am a bitch. I told you that."

He shook his head.

"The white mages are the same, you know?"

Cerryl could feel the look of bewilderment cross his face before he could control it.

"They're men. They like sex. No matter what they say, that's all a woman offers them."

"Women offer more than that," protested Cerryl.

"You're young, Cerryl. See if you feel that way ten years from now. Even five." Benthann gave a hard short laugh. "It works the other way, too. The only thing a man offers a woman, really, is power. Coins are power. Don't forget that. Sex for power, power for sex, that's the way the world works. Tellis had the power to save us, and I give him sex for that, and sometimes he's gentle."

Cerryl let the appalled expression fill his face.

"I could love you just for that look. Tellis is pretty good to me, but he's still randy beneath that proper exterior. Who would think it of the most proper scrivener?"

His apprentice would have, especially after thinking of the green angel book, but he didn't think voicing such an opinion would have been exactly wise—not at that moment. "We don't see everything, no matter how hard we look."

"Some folks don't want to see things."

"I can see that." Cerryl took a half-step toward the kitchen.

Benthann smiled lazily. "Still worried?"

"Yes." Cerryl took another step.

"You should be." She paused, then added, "You know, Cerryl, I could have gotten you between the blankets, if I'd really wanted to."

"I know," Cerryl admitted, slipping slowly toward the door to the front room. "I know."

"You're too nice. You didn't pretend to listen. You really listened."

"Next time, I might not be so nice," he answered, his hand on the doorway to the showroom.

"I'll remember that."

Cerryl smiled, almost sadly, knowing there wouldn't be a next time, knowing Benthann knew that as well. Neither could afford a next time.

XLIII

In the hot and still air of the workroom, Cerryl set the jar of ink on the worktable.

"Let's see." Tellis poured a small amount of the fluid into the ink-stand, then lifted one of the older quills from the holder before him and dipped it into the ink. "It looks right."

The master scrivener wrote three words on his working palimpsest, with a quick fluidity that Cerryl envied. Then Tellis set aside the quill and studied what he had written. Finally, he nodded. "You can't tell for certain for years, but I'd say you did a good job. It feels right, and you do get a feel for these sorts of things in time."

"Thank you, ser." Cerryl didn't know what else to say.

"You listen, Cerryl. I wasn't sure at first, you know. You always are so polite. Some folks are polite and never hear a thing." Tellis cleared his throat. "Enough praise. You need to get to work on the new job." He looked toward the volume by the copy stand—*An Alchemical Manual.*

Cerryl nodded. He'd already looked through the first pages, and the manual was even more boring than the herbal book had been, even more boring than the measurements book had been.

"After you finish cleaning up," Tellis added.

Clunk! With the sound of the opening door to the front room came a hot and light breeze, more of the fine white dust from the street—and voices.

"Is this the place?"

"Trust me, Fydel."

"Not so much as others, dear Anya."

Tellis glanced at Cerryl. "You stay here. You can fill the inkstands and then put away the ink." The scrivener hurried around the worktable and into the front room. "Could I help you, sers?"

"Do you have *The Book of Ayrlyn?*" The voice was feminine, if hard, and Cerryl thought he'd heard her before. The white mage in the street? What was she doing at the scrivener's? His heart beat faster. Why would she enter the shop?

"I'm afraid I don't know that book, ser."

Cerryl frowned as he filled the inkstand on the worktable and moved to the copy desk. Even he could tell Tellis was lying.

"You have not heard of it?"

"There's not a scrivener alive who has not *heard* of it. None of us would dare touch it, much less copy it."

Cerryl could sense the absolute truth in the scrivener's words. He forced himself to concentrate, then filled his own inkstand.

"Ah ..." A musical laugh followed. "That is more truthful, scrivener. Have you ever seen the book?"

"Many years ago, in Lydiar, the duke had a copy, and his personal scrivener showed it to me. I did not touch it or read it."

"My ... you do respect us. That is good. What about *Colors of White?*"

Cerryl put the ink jar on the proper shelf, then walked to the washstand and basin.

"... copied that for the honored Sterol."

A young-faced and stocky man in white—although he had a dark and heavy beard—peered through the doorway into the workroom. He stared for a moment at Cerryl.

Cerryl got the same feeling as when he felt he was being watched through a screening glass. "Might I help you, ser?"

"No. I was just looking." A lazy smile followed. "Are you the scrivener's apprentice?"

"Yes, ser."

"The only one?"

Cerryl nodded.

"I suppose you do things like mix inks and scrub the place?" The mage's voice was pleasant but held a condescending tone.

"Yes, ser." Cerryl wanted to meet the man's eyes but looked down instead, afraid the other would see the anger and fear within him. "I also do some copying and run whatever errands master Tellis wishes."

"You know your letters?" The mage stepped to the copy desk and opened the cover of the book, then closed it, half contemptuously.

"Yes, ser."

"Both tongues?"

"Yes, ser."

"I suppose you know Temple better?"

"I'm better with the old tongue," Cerryl admitted.

"Thank you." The mage nodded and turned out of the doorway and toward Tellis.

Cerryl listened.

"Was there anything back there?" asked the woman mage.

"Just the apprentice, and an alchemist's book to be copied." A deep laugh followed. "I think we can go, Anya."

"Thank you, master scrivener."

The front door closed, and Tellis stepped back into the workroom. His forehead was glazed with sweat. Cerryl knew his own forehead was damp as well.

"The bearded one. What did he want?" asked Tellis.

"He wanted to know if I were your only apprentice. I said I was."

"What have you done, Cerryl?" Tellis's voice sharpened. "What have you done?"

"Nothing." The apprentice looked helplessly at the scrivener. "I can't think of anything out of the ordinary. I've read the books, run errands, and copied things. I've never even been close to their tower."

"Do you know any black mages?" The bushy eyebrows seemed to stand out as the scrivener peered at his apprentice.

Cerryl looked directly at Tellis, meeting his eyes squarely. "Ser, I wouldn't know a black mage if he appeared in the front room."

"I don't understand. I've been so careful." Tellis fingered his bare chin. "Why would they be here?" He looked at Cerryl again. "Are you sure you don't know anything about this?"

"Ser," Cerryl said carefully, "we've all felt we've been watched. Beryal said something about that. I've felt people were looking from the alleyway." He shrugged again. "I haven't done anything any different. I haven't stolen anything. I haven't insulted anyone. I haven't gone any-place I wasn't supposed to go."

"Then why did the white mages come in here? They didn't want a book. They asked me about a forbidden book."

"They asked about *The Book of Ayrlyn*. You've never said anything about it. What is it?" Cerryl glanced at Tellis. "Why would they ask about that? You only copy the books they want."

"That's just it." The scrivener fingered his chin once more, frowning. "I don't know why they asked that."

"I don't know what the book is," Cerryl suggested obliquely, hop-ing Tellis would offer a clue.

"Oh . . . one of the old forgeries. It's supposed to be the story of one of the ancient black angels. It couldn't be. There's nothing from that time. They didn't have scriveners. The Guild would know."

"So they're looking for a forgery? They should know you better than that."

"They should," Tellis agreed. "You haven't been copying anything else, have you?"

"No, ser. I haven't copied a line you haven't told me to. Not one."

"I believe you." Tellis frowned again. "But it doesn't make sense. What could they possibly be looking for?"

Me, Cerryl wanted to answer. *But why? It can't because of Uncle Syo-dor and Aunt Nall. They'd already have turned chaos on me.* "They act like they're looking for something, but maybe they're asking all the scriv-eners or people who might have books. They didn't seem upset when they left."

"That's true." Tellis's face brightened slightly. "They just take peo-ple away for the road if they've done something wrong." A furrow crossed his forehead. "It is troubling, though."

"Yes." Cerryl had to cough to clear his throat. "I could barely answer when he stood there."

"You see why you don't ever want to cross them? They know almost everything."

"Yes, ser." Cerryl only hoped they didn't know absolutely every-thing. His stomach remained clenched in knots, and every word felt like an effort. He knew there would be no more warm water, and no more reading of forbidden books—not for a long, long time.

He swallowed.

"Well . . . white mages or not . . . you've copying to do." Tellis's voice sounded forced, and he wiped his forehead.

"Yes, ser." Cerryl feared his own voice sounded equally false.

"Take out that ink and get to it, then."

"I filled the stands already." Cerryl stepped toward the copy desk.

"Good. I need to go over to Nivor's. It won't be more than a moment or two. You see what you can do. Skip the illustrations on the overleaf. I'll do those. You start on the main text."

Cerryl took out his penknife, hoping his hands would not shake too much, hoping Tellis would leave and that he could gather himself together.

"Keep the letter width thin." Tellis stood by the workroom door for a moment, then jerked his head away. The door closed firmly, almost as though it had been slammed.

Cerryl just sat on the stool for a time before his hands stopped shaking, and before he dared to sharpen the quill.

XLIV

Cerryl rubbed his eyes, then picked up the chamber pot and trudged out through the courtyard and through the gate to the sewer catch, still in his tattered nightshirt and half-wondering why he bothered.

Because some white mage probably tracks all the sewer dumps. He frowned, then lifted the lid and held his breath as he dumped out the odoriferous contents into the even more concentrated and noxious wastes that flowed through what seemed to be a large tunnel of fired and glazed brick. How many kays of such tunnels ran beneath Fairhaven . . . and why? So that the city smelled a little better?

When the chamber pot was empty, he lowered the dump lid and retreated to the courtyard pump, where he rinsed the battered crockery chamber pot. Then he returned to the sewer dump. Once was enough, especially since he wasn't looking forward to bathing in chill water, not that he had dared to do otherwise for the last eight-day. Not after the visit from the pair of mages, and not with Tellis looking sideways at him and grumping at everything he did, as if he'd suddenly been declared a thief—or worse.

"Cerryl . . ."

He looked up. Pattera was flattened against the whitened bricks of the alleyway—gray in the dawn—less than a dozen cubits from the sewer dump and the back gate.

"Don't say anything," she whispered. "They say that the mages are coming for you—that you're a . . . renegade. That's what they say."

"Who says?" Cerryl hissed back, turning.

"They do."

"Who?"

"Just . . . I have to go. You have to get away before they come. Just go . . . please."

She turned, and Cerryl watched blankly as Pattera scurried back down the alley, the shawl over her nightdress flapping as her bare feet padded on the stones.

A renegade? Him? For heating some water? They couldn't have known about his reading *Colors of White*. Besides, the book really hadn't said anything, not anything that wasn't common sense, except for the history part. He'd read the same things in the histories that Tellis had given him, and those weren't forbidden. Tellis didn't dare to have anything like that around.

With a last look down the now-empty alley, he lifted the chamber pot and reentered the courtyard, closing the gate. He glanced down the alley again from the gate. The way was empty, without a sign that Pattera had ever even been there.

His bare feet carried him back to his room. Why had she come to warn him, and how had she known? Did the weavers' guild know? Or had her father overheard something?

Cerryl moistened his lips and opened his door.

When he had replaced the chamber pot in the corner of his room, he returned to the pump again, this time with his wash-water bucket. The cold water spilled across his hands as he filled the bucket.

Cold water? For how long? For the rest of his life? Or until someone showed up to claim he was a renegade?

He walked slowly back into his room.

Should he run?

He shook his head. Running would only tell them he had done wrong—and they'd kill him like his father and the fugitive at Dylert's.

They might anyway, but he hadn't done anything *that* wrong, of that he was convinced. But . . . did they care?

Should he get rid of the books and his father's amulet? No . . . if they came for him, those wouldn't matter, one way or another, and he wasn't going to give up what little he had of his father out of fear.

Still . . . he shuddered as he dipped the washrag into the bucket of too-chill water. For all his hopes, for all his dreams, he had nowhere to run and no way to escape.

The cold water on his face helped . . . for a moment.

XLV

Tellis cleared his throat. "I continue to wonder about those mages. No one at the tower has said so much as a word, and yesterday Sterol requested that I come again the day after tomorrow to act as a copyist." The scrivener scratched the back of his head, then fingered his chin.

Cerryl continued to sweep the floor stones of the workroom, bending to ease the dirt and tiny leather and vellum scraps and bits of dried glue into the wooden dust holder. For days, Tellis had been muttering about the mages, for days, always half-questioning Cerryl, not quite insisting that Cerryl was the reason.

"What do you think, Cerryl?"

The apprentice finished sweeping the dirt and leavings into the holder and straightened, carefully emptying the holder into the waste bin before replying. "I don't know, ser."

"They were here. How can you not think something?"

"I was afraid," Cerryl admitted. *I still am.* "I'd never seen more than one white mage before I came to Fairhaven."

"The one even questioned you." Tellis's voice bore the faintest tone of reproach.

"All he asked was what I did and whether I was the only apprentice." Cerryl slipped the empty dust holder onto its peg and leaned the broom in the corner. He stepped over to the washstand to clean his hands. "He stared at me for a moment, and then he left."

"That's all he did?"

"Yes, ser." How many times had Cerryl told Tellis that?

"But why would they ask about that book?" Tellis fingered his chin again. "They have to know I wouldn't ever cross them."

"Neither would I," Cerryl added. *Not openly. It's too dangerous.* "I didn't even know that there was such a book."

Tellis coughed. "Can't get my throat clear. Not for anything." He coughed again. "I just don't understand. I've always followed the guidelines. Always." His voice cracked slightly.

"They are mages," Cerryl said evenly, drying his hands and stepping toward the copy desk and the waiting volume—*An Alchemical Manual*.

"That is just it," insisted Tellis. "They must have a reason; they must have."

"They must have." Cerryl leaned forward and inspected the quill in the holder, forcing his voice to remain even, trying to keep his hands from shaking. "They are mages." He paused. "Do you want me to keep working on this, ser?"

"That?" Tellis's head twitched. "Oh, the manual for Nivor? If you can keep the letter width thin enough. That last page is barely passable. For a journeyman, yes, but not from Tellis the scrivener." He frowned. "You aren't listening to me these days, not enough."

"I try, ser. I'm cutting the nibs the way you showed me yesterday, and I am comparing the letters to the gauge."

"You shouldn't have to compare. You should know."

"Yes, ser." Cerryl lifted the quill.

"See that you do."

The apprentice nodded.

"I still don't understand about the mages . . . Sterol trusts me with all of his books. Why would he send lesser mages into my shop? Why?"

Cerryl kept breathing evenly and took out his penknife to resharpen the quill. After working on it, he stood by the copy desk, waiting, hoping he could either get on with the copying or go on an errand.

"My shop," Tellis repeated. "Why would any mage come to my shop? My shop, of all others."

"Stop moaning, Tellis," interrupted Beryal from the doorway. "If they'd a wanted you on the road, you'd be pounding rocks already. Your high and mighty Sterol would a squashed you like a ground lizard under his shiny white boots. Same's for your apprentice there. They were looking for something. They didn't find it here. Count yourself lucky, and stop moaning. If they were after you, you wouldn't be getting copy work."

Cerryl wanted to sigh in relief, or smile. He didn't.

"Beryal . . . you are not the one to lecture me." Tellis turned and glared at the older woman.

"I be telling you I'm on my way to the market, ser." Beryal inclined her head. "Deria said there were some tender chickens a-coming from Howlett. Some roast fowl would do us all good. Course, I'd need a half silver or so, for that and all else you'd be needing."

Tellis sighed, then looked at Cerryl. "You can do what you can with Nivor's book. Keep the letters slender. When I get back, you can scrub the floor in the front room."

"Yes, ser."

"After that, you can scrub down the courtyard."

"Yes, ser."

"The market, ser?" prompted Beryal. "You'd not be wanting me to be the last one in line for a fowl, you know?"

Tellis gave another sigh and marched out of the workroom, Beryal trailing him.

Cerryl felt like sighing, and did, if silently.

XLVI

Cerryl was only halfway through the workroom door when Tellis barked, "Cerryl, the letters on this sheet are too wide. It's near worthless. Nivor won't pay for such sloppy work. I'll have to redo this page and the one before it." Tellis lifted the sheets of vellum. "All these are good for is palimpsests—for low-coin copy work."

"Yes, ser. If you like, I can copy them over with narrower letters." Cerryl kept his voice even, standing just inside the doorway.

"Why didn't you do it that way to begin with?" Tellis's voice took on a tone that almost verged on whining. "I've showed you time and time again."

"I thought I was doing it the way you wanted, ser." Cerryl struggled to keep his voice even and subservient.

"It is not the way I taught you. Can't you get anything right?" Tellis waved the vellum.

Cerryl did not answer.

"Can't you? I have spent seasons instructing you, and you still make your letters too wide." The scrivener's eyes flicked to Cerryl and then toward the doorway to the front room. "I never had white mages in the shop, except to purchase books. Now . . . we are watched and questioned. What do you say to that?"

"Ser, I have done nothing wrong." Clearly, any answer would be useless, but not answering would be worse.

"The only thing you do right is run errands and scrub the floor. Even your ink will fade before its time."

"Yes, ser." Cerryl understood. For some reason, Tellis did not want to throw Cerryl out on the street, but he was going to make life impossible for his apprentice . . . so impossible that Cerryl would not stay. Yet, at the moment, he dared not leave, not if his feelings were accurate, and they were all he had to guide him.

"All your wages—what I owe you—would not pay for the vellum you have ruined."

"You may have my wages, ser. I would not displease you."

"You have displeased me." Tellis sniffed. "Go empty the chamber pots."

"Yes, ser."

"And wash them."

"Yes, ser."

"Wash them well."

Cerryl bowed and turned.

"Then you can go to the renderer's for hoofs. I need to make binding glue."

"Yes, ser."

As he stepped out of the workroom, the apprentice could still hear Tellis muttering.

"A favor for Dylert . . . and where does it get me? Because he helped my son . . . and still, where, light forbid, is the justice in it? This may right the balance, if I can but survive."

Cerryl stepped into the kitchen, wondering what he could do, and how he could stay, at least until the white mages lost interest in him.

"Where you be going?" asked Beryal.

"Tellis told me to empty the chamber pots and wash them."

Beryal smiled. "You cannot be doing that. Your own is clean, for I saw you do that, and so is mine, and my daughter would have your head faster than would Tellis were you to wake her so early."

"What can I do?" Cerryl glanced back toward the workroom.

"The courtyard could use a sweeping, and Tellis could use some time by himself, and I will tell him that I told you to do that after you cleaned the two chamber pots." Beryal looked at Cerryl. "He is fearful. He has seen what the mages do to those who displease them. He has seen such too many times."

"But he has done nothing, and surely the mages know that." Cerryl glanced over his shoulder again.

"His son . . ." whispered Beryal, looking toward the front room. "We all carry black angels, and fear is Tellis's. Later . . ." Her voice resumed its normal timbre. "Go sweep the courtyard."

Cerryl picked up the broom and walked through the common room and into the courtyard, wondering if Tellis would complain about his sweeping as well. Beryal had started to say something about Tellis's son. Had that been the Verial that Benthann had mentioned?

Cerryl wanted to scream and cry all at the same time. No one *said* anything, and he was in no position to ask, and yet the answers affected him somehow. Would life always be like that?

With a silent sigh, he started sweeping in the corner by the door, making sure that the broom straws flicked each join in the stone tiles clean. He supposed he could scrub the tiles once more after he finished sweeping.

"Cerryl!"

He looked up from the broom. Tellis stood in the doorway, paler than the white granite of the avenue. "Yes, ser."

"The mages want you."

Cerryl forced his eyes away from the rear gate, the only possible escape, except that escape was a trap. Perhaps all life was a trap. He turned toward Tellis, still holding the broom. "Me, ser?"

Tellis gestured.

Cerryl walked toward the door, only slowing to lean the broom against the wall.

"In the front," rasped Tellis, pushing his apprentice in front of him and toward the front room with the bookcases and copied volumes.

Cerryl walked through the common room and kitchen, knowing that Beryal was there, yet not really seeing her. He also ignored the murmured words of the scrivener, who followed.

"This is what I get for doing a favor for Dylert . . . the white guards at my shop door." Tellis sniffed self-sympathetically.

In the showroom stood a single mage in white, a tall and rugged blond man with a purple blotch on one cheek, a mage whom Cerryl had never seen. "You are the scrivener's apprentice?"

Cerryl bowed. "Yes, ser."

"Your name is Cerryl?"

"Yes, ser."

"You are to come with me. Now. You need nothing. You bring nothing."

"Yes, ser."

The mage turned to Tellis. "You owe him nothing, and you are free to find another apprentice. Good day, scrivener." The gray eyes, over-laid with a sheen of gold, fixed on Cerryl. "Outside."

"Yes, ser." Cerryl understood he had no chance if he ran. His only hope was to stand firm and admit nothing more than the mages already knew about him, and to be unfailingly polite. He bowed and turned, opening the door.

Outside the shop were six guards in white, and before them two others in white tunics and trousers like the mage, except that their tunics bore a thin red stripe across each sleeve.

Already the day was hot, and white dust sifted through the air on the lightest of breezes. Cerryl wanted to rub his nose but didn't, wrinkling it slightly to try to stop the itching.

"Walk beside me." The mage smiled, an expression without warmth, and absently brushed something darkish from the white tunic.

The mage nodded to the guards and the two others in white.

All the shutters flanking the way of the lesser artisans between the scrivener's and the artisans' square were shut. So were the doors, despite the bright sunlight and the warmth of the morning.

Once on the main avenue, walking briskly toward the mages' square and the white tower that loomed over it, Cerryl took more notice of his surroundings.

They passed the last of the artisans' shops and left the square behind. An ostler led a saddled chestnut out of the stable toward a tall man dressed in blue, standing before the small inn. The saddlebags on the horse bulged, indicating a traveler. Past the ostlery was the long grain exchange building. No carriages stood by the vacant mounting blocks, though the windows and the shutters of the exchange were open, and two men in maroon tunics talked in the arched doorway.

At the grinding of ironbound wagon wheels, Cerryl could feel the white guards move closer. Did they think he would try to jump on a wagon—or under the wheels? The ubiquitous fine white dust rose from the avenue as the brown-stained wagon, behind two horses, rolled past. In the wagon bed were a half-dozen huge barrels, each nearly man-high, roped together. Who needed barrels that large?

Feeling the dampness on his forehead, Cerryl stepped across the narrow side way and back onto the stone walk of the jewelers' block. Perhaps half the iron-banded doors were open, and the air held the acrid odor of oil, hot metal, and other burned substances. Cerryl glanced sideways at the white mage, but the man's oval face remained impassive.

Beyond the goldsmiths' and silversmiths' shops was the long stretch of large houses, each behind low white-granite walls. In one garden, in the house beyond Muneat's, two small children gamboled, a slender young woman watching from the shade of a tree trimmed into the shape of a sphere. In the next, two gardeners worked on pruning and shaping vines around an arbor.

Yet the only sounds Cerryl heard were the delighted cries of the children, and he wondered how long children in Fairhaven showed such joy. As their cries died away, the murmur of voices from around the colored carts that filled the market square rose. The muted hubbub from the peddlers and the buyers gently drowned out the sound of the guards' boots on the hard granite.

Yet not a head turned as Cerryl and his small procession passed the market square and continued down the avenue, past another section of large houses with well-kept walls and gardens.

Cerryl began to squint in the warm morning sun as he neared the wizards' square. The wizards' tower itself reared perhaps sixty cubits over the other lower buildings in the square, a blot of white stone that cast a shadow along the avenue.

The glare from the tower, and from the lower white stone buildings around the square, seemed to pulse, as if each stone cast arrows of brilliance at him so that the shadow from the tower offered little relief from a sun that had gotten hotter with every step from Tellis's shop.

Cerryl could sense the unseen whiteness of chaos, curling around the tower itself like invisible smoke. With the glare and the chaos, he found it harder to make out the structures around the circular square, save all were of a granite even whiter than that which paved the avenue, and none except the tower exceeded two levels.

The square itself held a pedestal, with a statue, surrounded by an expanse of grass, grass so dark green that it appeared almost black in the late morning sun. Rather than being in the center of a building or standing alone, the wizard's tower rose from the south side of a building that otherwise appeared to contain two stories. There was no entrance to the tower from the avenue.

The mage gestured to the squared archway above three steps nearly twenty cubits side to side. "There."

Although the last and smallest of the successive joined square stone arches that framed the entry to the building was more than eight cubits high, there were no carvings on the smooth stone, and no windows flanking the entry. Cerryl found the featureless white stone unsettling. Even more of the fine white dust swirled up from his boots as he stepped through the entryway into a high-ceilinged foyer. Another framed entryway was to his right, and a hallway continued straight ahead.

"The stairs." The mage pointed to the stone-railed staircase to the left.

Cerryl followed directions and started up the steps, realizing as he did that the white guards and the other two mages had remained in the foyer and that he and the mage climbed the stairs alone. At the top was another stone doorway—without a door—and a pair of guards.

The guards nodded at the mage, who gestured for Cerryl to keep going. Cerryl stepped through the entryway to find another set of steps to his right.

"Up the stairs," ordered the mage. "To the third level."

Although the apprentice found himself panting halfway up the second set of stairs, the mage climbed silently, without straining. Cerryl noted that, despite the size of the building and the polished flat granite and fitted joins, there was no ornamentation anywhere—only smooth and featureless walls that seemed to go on and on. The fine white dust also seemed to catch in his throat and lungs and to make breathing even more difficult.

When the mage stopped at a landing outside a blank white oak door, with a single guard, Cerryl tried to catch his breath, and the mage stood silently beside him.

"Come on in, Kinowin," grated a voice from the other side of the door, "and bring in the young man as well."

The stone-faced Kinowin opened the door and gestured for Cerryl to enter first, then followed him inside the tower apartment. Kinowin turned to the single mage in the room. "This is the scrivener's apprentice, as you wished, honored Sterol."

"Good." The white-clad mage who stood in the tower room was broad-shouldered, a head taller than Cerryl, but not so tall as the big mage who had escorted Cerryl. His hair was iron gray, and his neatly trimmed beard matched his thick and short-cut iron hair. His face was ruddy, almost as if sunburned. A golden amulet hung around his neck, and on his collar was a pin that resembled a golden starburst. "You may go, Kinowin. Wait outside until I summon you."

Kinowin bowed. The heavy white oak door clunked shut.

Brown eyes that appeared red-flecked studied Cerryl for a time.

Cerryl stood, waiting, conscious that the mage had not mustered any power to concentrate chaos—not that Cerryl could sense, in any case. The room was a personal chamber—a large personal chamber that contained a desk and matching chair, several white wooden bookcases filled with leather-bound volumes, a table in the center of which was a circular screeing glass, and four chairs around the table. At the far end of the chamber, behind the mage, was an alcove, bigger than Cerryl's room at Tellis's, which contained a double-width bed and a washstand. Against the stone wall at the mage's left hand was another small table holding but a large bronze handbell.

"You will answer my questions."

"Yes, ser."

"Where were you born?"

"I don't know, ser." That was true. Cerryl had no idea where he had been born.

"Didn't your parents tell you?" The mage glared at Cerryl as if the young man were an idiot.

"They died when I was very young. My aunt and uncle said I was born while my parents were traveling back to Hrisbarg."

"Do you have any idea of your birthplace?"

"It had to be within several days' journey of Hrisbarg or Lydiar, and my uncle and aunt were from Montgren."

The mage sighed. "Kinowin says you can work the stuff of chaos. Is that true?"

"I don't know, ser. I once looked in a glass, and someone in white broke it." That was almost true, close enough.

The gray-haired man's forehead furrowed, and the fingers of his right hand strayed to the amulet around his neck. "You expect me to believe that?"

"It felt like the glass broke," Cerryl corrected, "but it didn't. My head hurt for a long time afterward." That *was* true.

"You see . . . don't bother to lie. It's not worth the effort for either of us."

"Yes, ser."

"You know your letters, I suppose?"

"Yes, ser," Cerryl repeated.

"Temple better than old tongue?"

"No, ser. I know the old tongue better."

"It's good you admit to something, though I would expect that of Tellis's apprentice," snorted the white mage. "You know that none but the white brethren may mold the white fires?"

"Yes, ser. That was why I didn't want to try the glass again."

"You didn't know that was using chaos?" The mage's tone was unbelieving, scornful.

"I wasn't sure until after I did that one time," Cerryl admitted. "I thought it might have been, but I was afraid to ask anyone. How could I?"

"That was wise of you." Sterol nodded. "And what else have you not revealed?"

Cerryl flushed.

The gray-haired mage waited.

"I think . . . think . . . I can sometimes see something white, except that it's not seeing, that might be chaos force." Cerryl looked down.

"Why think you that it is chaos force?"

"I don't know, except the glass was coated with it that one time, and the mage who brought me here had some of it around him for a moment."

Sterol gave a short barking laugh.

Cerryl waited once more.

"You are lucky, young fellow. It pleases me to allow you the opportunity to learn." Sterol laughed. "Besides, having an orphaned scrivener's apprentice will teach them that they are not so mighty as they think." The penetrating eyes fixed on Cerryl. "You will watch and remember everything and tell no one?"

"Yes, your mightiness."

"Honored Sterol will do. One day I may ask you . . . about how you find the halls. Until then, keep your observations to yourself, *all* to yourself. Is that clear?"

"Yes, honored Sterol."

"I would have you remember one maxim, young fellow."

"Yes, honored Sterol."

"There are old white mages, and there are bold white mages, but none will you find who are old and bold." Sterol laughed again and reached for the bronze bell on the small wall table, ringing it twice.

The door opened, and Kinowin reentered, bowing, looking toward Sterol.

"Our young friend here has remained well enough within the rules that he is suitable to be considered for instruction." Sterol smiled, showing white teeth. "You may take him to Jeslek for instruction, and tell the mighty Jeslek that he may not administer more than minor discipline. *Minor* discipline."

"Yes, Sterol." Kinowin bowed.

Sterol glanced at Cerryl. "You may go."

"Yes, honored Sterol." Cerryl bowed again, waiting for a nod or a sign.

"Go."

Cerryl turned and stepped through the door that Kinowin had opened.

"You are very lucky, young Cerryl," said Kinowin as they headed down the steps.

"Yes, ser. I know, ser."

"What did you say to Sterol?" A note of curiosity entered Kinowin's rough voice.

"I told him the truth, ser." *As much as I dared.*

Kinowin laughed, an almost jolly note that echoed up and down the stone enclosed steps, incongruous between the stark white walls. "You might grow up to be dangerous, Cerryl. The truth! Ha!" He laughed again.

Cerryl shivered within his tunic but continued down the steps to where the two armsmen in white guarded the entrance to the tower. Beside them, on a stool, sat a boy in a red tunic. Neither the guards nor the boy seemed to pay that much attention to Cerryl or the mage.

"Jeslek could have quarters within the tower but prefers to live in the older building behind the main hall." Kinowin walked quickly down the wide steps from the tower entrance into the foyer, turning left and down the hallway they had not taken when they had first entered the building. "He is very knowledgeable and very powerful."

Cerryl got the hint behind the words—Jeslek was dangerous and a rival of Sterol's. "All mages seem powerful to me."

"Some are far more powerful than others."

From the end of the hallway, Kinowin led Cerryl through another squared series of arches and then crossed an open courtyard with a fountain. The fountain was a simple jet of water spraying from an oval-shaped stone in the middle of a circular pool.

Jeslek's quarters were on the second level at the rear of the older building—also of stone, even whiter than that of the tower itself, and about as far as possible from those of Sterol, Cerryl calculated.

A single guard in white stood by the door. "The honorable Jeslek has requested he not be disturbed."

"I am here from the High Wizard," said Kinowin. "We will wait." He motioned to the bench across the hall from the white oak doorway, then sat.

After a moment, so did Cerryl.

"Do you have any questions?" asked Kinowin, in a gentler tone seemingly at odds with his rugged appearance.

"This has been sudden..." Cerryl shook his head. "It's hard to believe I'm here."

"That's what happens to most students," said the mage, a warmer tone in his voice. "The talent often comes suddenly, about your age, and we try to find it before it turns dangerous." After a moment of silence, he added, "If you don't learn how to use it properly, it can destroy you and everyone around you. Some people think that we're too harsh." He faced Cerryl, and the purple blotch was more pronounced. "Have you ever seen a renegade white?"

"Once. He threw firebolts. Another white mage was chasing him."

Kinowin nodded. "That's what many people see. Others see us destroy some young man who was their neighbor. What they do not see is the twisted destruction within the man—or the deaths that follow uncontrolled use of the power." He gave a quick dismissive headshake.

Cerryl found himself surprised at the concern in the man's voice and the momentary bleakness in Kinowin's eyes.

"To survive your talent, Cerryl, you must be absolutely obedient until you fully understand both your powers and your limits. Otherwise..." Kinowin coughed and cleared his throat. "Otherwise, you will destroy yourself, if the Guild does not destroy you first."

Cerryl was the one to shiver.

Abruptly, the door opened, and a white-haired mage stood there, gazing past the guard toward the two on the bench. "You might as well come in, Kinowin. How can I concentrate with you smoldering outside my chambers? Come on in." He turned and walked into the single room.

Kinowin stood, and Cerryl scrambled erect as quickly as he could, following the blond mage. The guard closed the door behind them.

"Your guard said you did not wish to be disturbed, yet Sterol insisted that I come and await your pleasure to deliver my charge." Kinowin bowed and gestured to Cerryl.

Jeslek's white tunic and trousers and boots shimmered. Cerryl swallowed, then quickly closed his mouth. The mage bore the face of a young man, but his hair was white and glistened. Like Sterol, Jeslek wore a golden sunburst on his collar. Unlike Sterol, he wore no amulet. Sun-gold eyes turned from Kinowin to Cerryl and then back to the rugged blond mage. "You come from the honorable Sterol today?"

Another figure in white, with the red slash across the tunic sleeves, stood silently by the table bearing the screeing glass.

Kinowin bowed yet again. "Honored Jeslek, the High Wizard bade me to convey young Cerryl here to you. You are to instruct him." Kinowin smiled blandly.

"And . . . what else? You have more to say, Kinowin?" asked Jeslek. "You act as dutiful aide only when it suits you."

"I was bidden to inform you that you are limited to minor discipline." The words were flat and bland.

A broad and false smile crossed Jeslek's face. Cerryl wanted to climb under the stone floor tiles on which he stood. "Ah . . . I see. The honored Sterol is too engrossed to instruct his own apprentices." After a pause, another smile followed. "You may tell the High Wizard, when his onerous and laborious duties permit him to receive you again, that I will give his apprentice every advantage that I allow my own students, and that I will treat this young man as any other."

"I will tell him, honored Jeslek." Kinowin bowed once more before he turned and walked quickly from the chamber.

Jeslek waited until the door opened and closed. Then the sun-gold eyes fixed on the former scrivener's apprentice. "Cerryl. Is that your name?"

"Yes, ser."

"What did you do before you were brought to the tower?"

"I was an apprentice to Tellis the scrivener."

"Then you know your letters?"

"Yes, ser.

"And the old tongue?"

"Yes, ser."

"Do you have any other skills?"

"I know something about woods, ser. I once worked for a sawmill master."

"Good. You have worked with your hands." A fainter smile crossed Jeslek's face. "Now you are a student mage, an apprentice mage, if you will. No matter what you may have done, or not done, you are not to attempt to work with chaos, or order, unless you are instructed to do so. If you disobey—and are caught—your mind will be bound, and you will work until you die on the white road. Do you understand?"

"Yes, ser."

"By the way, I can tell if you have used chaos within the last eight-day, and longer. You have been careful, I can see, but the traces are there." All hints of a smile vanished.

"Ser?" Cerryl swallowed.

"Yes?" Jeslek's voice was cold.

"Sometimes I can see when chaos has been used. Does trying to see that count as using it?"

"No. Merely looking does not leave traces, either. I do encourage all my students to watch and study. But only watch and study, except when I tell you otherwise."

"Yes, ser." Cerryl bowed, waiting.

"No other questions?"

"Ser . . . outside of what I asked . . . I don't know enough to ask more," Cerryl admitted, knowing he was running a slight risk but feeling it was necessary.

"Ha! I see one reason why Sterol accepted you." Jeslek turned to the youth who stood by the table, wearing the white tunic with the red-slashed sleeves. "Kesrik, you make sure Cerryl here gets quarters with the other students, a set of the proper tunics and trousers and white boots. His look sturdy; see if you can change them. Just once. And make sure he gets his own copy of *Colors* in the next eight-day."

Kesrik bowed, his square face impassive, his blue eyes cold.

"Go with Kesrik." Jeslek's sun-gold eyes glittered cold.

"Follow me." Kesrik turned and left. Cerryl found himself scrambling to follow.

XLVII

Outside the window, the sudden warm rain pelted down on Fairhaven, the first in the handful of days since Cerryl had arrived in the halls of the mages. The rain hissed as it struck sun-warmed stone, and moister air seeped through the louvers of the closed shutters. Inside, Cerryl sat on the edge of the chair across the table from Jeslek, aware of the growing pounding inside his skull, a sensation that had not been there before the storm had fallen across the city.

Jeslek studied Cerryl for a time, and Cerryl had the feeling that the mage used more than his eyes.

Finally, Jeslek gave a crooked smile. "What do you think being a mage is all about?"

"I don't really know what mages do, ser."

"Tell me what you *think* we do."

Cerryl moistened his lips. "Mages rule Fairhaven. They can use chaos powers. They study many things."

"How do you know we study—" Jeslek laughed and broke off the question. "You were a scrivener's apprentice. I forgot. Well, you'll be studying more than you ever thought possible. And there will be tests along the way. Some you may not even recognize as such." The white-haired mage with the golden eyes paused. "Why do you think mages study so many things?"

"To rule better?" guessed Cerryl.

"That's a guess, young Cerryl, but it's partly right. We study the better to govern. Governing is not ruling. Governing is more like guiding or counseling. Someone like the Emperor of Hamor, or the Duke of Lydiar or the Viscount of Certis—they rule. The Guild governs. Yes, we make rules, but most of the rules are more of a code of common sense. Waste breeds a sort of scattered chaos that leads to sickness. So we make sure waste stays out of the city. Beggars and other parasites bring sickness and theft. We keep them from Fairhaven. If coins alone rule, then the city will fall to those with more coins. For that reason, we check those who think of little but coins. Clean water keeps sickness away, and we make sure the water for the city is clean. There's nothing magical about any of that." Jeslek smiled brightly—and emptily.

Cerryl waited, not knowing what he could say.

"Every great once in a while, someone sees a mage cast chaos-fire, and then everyone thinks that's all a mage does. If that happened to be all the Guild were—a group of wizards throwing fire—Fairhaven would have fallen generations and generations ago."

"Yes, ser."

"I know you want to be respectful, but you don't have to say that every time I pause. A polite silence will do." Jeslek stood. "You need to understand more about what the Guild is and why it is necessary." The white mage lifted the volume on the table and extended it to Cerryl. The cover was worn and scratched, and infused with the unseen white of chaos. "Read this. You can read?"

"Yes, ser. There are some words I probably don't know." Cerryl followed his instructor's lead and stood quickly, his eyes still on the white-haired and sun-eyed wizard.

"Ask Kesrik or one of the other students. Ask me if you can't find anyone who does know."

"Yes, ser." Cerryl wouldn't have asked Jeslek in any case, and definitely not after that statement.

"You have two eight-days to finish the first half of the manual. But start today, and I'll question you on what you've read at your next lesson." Jeslek gestured toward the door. "Kesrik is waiting. I will see you tomorrow."

Cerryl bowed and turned.

As Jeslek had said, Kesrik stood waiting outside by the guard.

"Good day, Kesrik." Cerryl offered a head bow as he passed.

"It's raining." Kesrik inclined his head infinitesimally as he stepped by Cerryl and through the door, closing it behind him.

Cerryl paused, wondering again about the strangeness of the Halls of the Mages, where so little was really said, and where his instruction seemed so minimal—where he spent more time waiting for Jeslek than listening or learning. Or had that just been to give him some time to adjust? If so, what was next?

He looked down at the leather-bound volume in his hands, then back at the closed white oak door. Before he headed down to the common, or the library, or his room—he wasn't sure where he should start reading—he opened the cover to the title page—*Colors of White: the Manual of the Guild at Fairhaven.*

He almost wanted to laugh. After hiding a copy of half the book for years, and stealing time to read parts of the one that Tellis had been engaged to copy, he had his own copy—and was *ordered* to read it.

He shook his head, thinking about the books still hidden in Tellis's house—and the broken amulet. He missed the amulet most.

Cerryl closed the cover of *Colors of White* and started down the steps.

Once downstairs, he glanced into the library, looking for Faltar, but the room was empty except for two mages at the table in the far corner—Fydel and Esaak. The brown-haired and square-bearded Fydel was gesturing, almost drawing something in the air. Apparently impassive, Esaak sat with his back to Cerryl.

Cerryl tiptoed toward the common. That way, if Faltar appeared, he could ask him what, if anything, he should look out for in the book. His steps were silent as he walked down the corridor, wondering if he would discover any new truths in the book he had found difficult and boring when he had read it before.

He hoped so, but his lips pursed as he thought about what he had read before in *Colors of White*.

XLVIII

Despite the breeze from the open windows of the study common, sweat beaded in his hair, even cut as short as it was, and oozed onto his forehead and down the back of his neck. Cerryl ignored it and flipped to the next page of *Colors of White*, forcing himself to read each word and to fit the thoughts together, wondering how any of them related to the histories Tellis had forced on him, the mill work he had done for Dylert, or the reality that was Fairhaven, which included both chaos-fire and the vast golds of those like Muneat . . . or even why his father had been hunted and he had been spared.

So much made so little sense.

"You read that so quickly." On the other side of the study table, Faltar shifted his weight, his eyes lifting from his own book, his blond hair almost white with the late afternoon sun through the tall study windows backlighting it.

"Big surprise . . . he was a scrivener. That's what they do." The low murmur came from the only other occupied table, the one at which Bealtur sat.

Cerryl kept his eyes on the page of *Colors of White* that lay open before him, ignoring the low-voiced and snide tone of the goateed student.

"Reading is one thing . . . scriveners don't understand. That's why they're scriveners."

The thin-faced Cerryl licked his lips and kept reading.

". . . not enough behind the eyes to do more than copy . . ." Bealtur stretched and smiled at Cerryl.

Cerryl smiled back.

His back to Bealtur, Faltar frowned.

Cerryl closed the book, gently, and stood, walking from the open common down the narrow white-stone hallway to his cell. There, he opened his door and stepped inside, into a space even smaller than what he had occupied in the back of the mill barn at Dylert's. The bed was softer and the room without drafts, though he had to stand on the end of the bed to open and close the ancient oak shutters.

He also had a stool and a small desktop built into the wall, with a bookshelf above it. Two sets of whites, four sets of smallclothes, two blankets, and his boots—that was all. That was the total of what any of the student mages had, except for the books on their shelves, and those varied according to their mentors. There was no mirror. None of the cells had mirrors. Once he would have considered his cell almost rich— before he had seen Muneat's dwelling or the bedchamber of the woman in green through his glass.

Cerryl placed the worn copy of *Colors of White* on the shelf, next to *The Founding of Fyrad and the White Lands*, which had arrived in a package from the High Wizard. Beside them was *Great Historie of Candar*. On the desk lay a thinner volume—*Naturale Mathematicks*.

His eyes crossed the mathematicks book. He'd scarcely even looked at that. It had been left for him; he didn't even know who might be his tutor there. His stomach growled. He glanced at the door, knowing he needed to head to the meal hall.

Thrap.

"Are you coming to eat?" Faltar's voice was clear through the door.

Cerryl took a deep breath. "Yes. I'm coming." He stepped into the corridor and closed the door. None of the cells had bolts, just simple latches.

"You felt like smashing Bealtur, didn't you?" asked Faltar, running a hand through his thin blond hair and pushing it off his forehead.

"I wasn't that angry." *Almost, but not quite,* came the correcting voice in his thoughts as Cerryl matched steps with Faltar.

"It's Kesrik. He's trying to get you angry. He's using Bealtur." Faltar glanced back along the hall. "That's what he did to Yullur. Yullur tried to throw fire at him, and . . ." The words trailed off.

"Sterol or Jeslek or someone found out, and put him on the road?"

"No . . ." Faltar glanced back down the empty hallway again. "Yullar tried it when Sterol was just outside the study. Kesrik knew it and ran at Sterol for protection. Yullar was so angry, he didn't really see the High Wizard when he threw the chaos-fire at Kesrik." Faltar gave a twisted smile. "The High Wizard didn't have a choice then. He turned Yullar into ash and put Kesrik on sewer duty and the refuse wagons for nearly a season. It didn't matter. When he came back, Kesrik had a big smile on his face for a couple of eight-days, and none of us could do anything about it."

Cerryl nodded. "What did the honored Jeslek say?"

"Who knows? He stays away from the High Wizard. He travels a lot, all the way to Gallos at times. He's taken Kesrik, but not always."

The two walked slowly into the small meal hall, a hall containing but a dozen circular tables and a table that held platters and dishes of food.

Two mages in white sat at a corner table. Cerryl knew one.

"The bald one with jowls—that's Esaak."

Cerryl had seen the other mage, a burly and rugged-looking man with trimmed ginger whiskers, come to Jeslek's quarters once, but Jeslek had dismissed Cerryl on an errand immediately. "Eliasar . . ." he murmured, dredging up the name. "It is, isn't it?"

"I think so."

"What do you know about him?" Cerryl kept his voice low.

"He's in charge of the white lancers. He doesn't like Sterol much. That's what Lyasa told me."

Did anyone? Cerryl wondered, even as he stepped toward the momentarily empty serving table. His twitching nose told him that the burkha was even more heavily seasoned than normal, and he took just a small dipping of the sauce, beside the large heap of heavy egg noodles. Dark bread, cold and nearly stale, and a pearapple also went on his platter. The light ale was almost drinkable, and he was tired of water all the time. So he carried the mug of ale and the platter to a wall table as far from the older mages as possible.

One of the serving boys in red quickly refilled the pitcher after Faltar had poured a mug.

Faltar slipped onto the stool across from Cerryl, glancing back at the dark-haired serving boy. "When I did that, I always wanted to be a student mage."

"You came from the creche?"

"Most of us do, except the few who come from coins—like Kesrik. Or Anya—you know, the red-haired mage?"

Cerryl nodded.

"Kesrik's father is a trader. He has more teams and wagons than the Duke of Lydiar." Faltar grimaced. "That's what he says."

"I know. He's told me." Cerryl bit into the chewy bread, twisting off a corner with his teeth and eating slowly.

"He's also told everyone else." Faltar laughed gently. "But he's no better than any of us."

"He's better at getting others into trouble," Cerryl pointed out.

"You put things so well, Cerryl."

Cerryl was certain he didn't. Otherwise, why would Kesrik be trying to force him into doing something stupid?

Faltar frowned, then covered it with a smile. "How are you finding all the histories?"

Cerryl felt the eyes on his back and framed the name "Kesrik" without speaking.

Faltar nodded, nearly imperceptibly.

"A lot of it's new to me," the thin-faced student answered quietly, but not quietly enough.

"Sleeping in a bed is new to some. And bathing." Kesrik's tone was light as he passed on his way to the serving table. Bealtur walked beside the older student mage.

"It is good not to have to draw ice-cold water every morning to bathe." Cerryl smiled brightly at Kesrik. "I appreciate the advantages."

Faltar swallowed.

"It's good you do," answered Kesrik blandly, turning away.

"I told you," whispered Faltar.

"He's not the problem," Cerryl said quietly. "Let him think he is. It's safer that way." He took a mouthful of barely sauced noodles, followed by a sip of the ale. At least he could eat all he needed.

XLIX

Cerryl watched as another gold oak carriage rolled through the shadow of the white tower and up to the front of the Hall of Mages. He turned and walked toward the back of the foyer, near the doorway to the fountain courtyard.

Faltar and Bealtur stepped through the doorway, Faltar's blond hair shimmering in the indirect light, Bealtur's wispy goatee looking more like iron-gall ink dripping off his chin.

"Why are they gathering?" asked Cerryl.

Bealtur offered a smile, one underlaid with a sneer. "All the mages—or most of them anyway—have a meeting twice a year. That doesn't count the special meetings, Broka says." Bealtur squared his shoulders.

"What do they do at the meetings?" pursued Cerryl.

Faltar rolled his eyes, then looked at the white stone floor tiles.

"Mage stuff. This time there's something about trade. The black ones on Recluce are causing problems. They always do." Bealtur added, after a pause, "The meetings are where students become real mages. Next year, it'll be my turn—and Kesrik's."

Cerryl wasn't sure he wanted to be anywhere near when Kesrik became a full mage, not that he'd have any great choice.

A thin and gray-haired wizard walked briskly up the steps and through the open double doors on the right side of the foyer, into the Great Hall, or Council Chamber.

"Sverlik! All the way from Fenard . . ."

"How goes it with the young prefect . . ."

The voices died away. Another mage walked past where Cerryl, Faltar, and Bealtur stood at the side of the corridor, then stopped and studied the three. His hair was an impossible shade of gold, but deep lines ran from the corners of his eyes and mouth.

Cerryl waited, feeling as though he'd somehow been caught doing something he should not.

"Ah, yes, I can remember standing just about there, and thinking I really wanted to know what went on in the Great Hall." Under a yellow cast to his face, the man grinned through equally yellowed teeth. "Then you become a mage, and it's not nearly so exciting." He laughed gently and continued on toward the hall.

"It'll still be exciting," murmured Bealtur, his eyes following the white wizard until he vanished into the Hall.

A heavier step—and a sense of power—fell across the three.

Cerryl recognized Jeslek even before turning.

"You won't learn how to be mages by watching people enter the hall." Jeslek's sunburst collar pin seemed to radiate light, as did the sun gold eyes that surveyed the three students.

Cerryl inclined his head, remembering Jeslek's statement about respectful silence.

"Good. You all understand, I see. I suggest the common is more appropriate for you." The familiar bright and perfunctory smile followed the words.

Cerryl bowed slightly, as did the others.

"Off with you."

"Yes, ser."

Jeslek continued to survey the three until they turned and began to walk through the archway into the courtyard.

As the students crossed the courtyard, past the fountain, Bealtur looked back toward the foyer and the Great Hall for a long moment.

Cerryl kept his eyes on the doorway to the rear building, once more having the feeling that he was being watched through a glass. But by whom, with the mages gathering?

He stopped by his cell and opened the door, frowning as he stepped inside and lowered the latch, because the feeling of being watched dropped away abruptly. On his desk was a earthenware mug, and beside it a bottle, a true glass bottle.

He picked up the mug—empty, then set it aside and lifted the bottle toward the window. He couldn't tell what the liquid was. So he lowered the bottle and uncorked it. The aroma of cider seeped from the bottle, almost too strong.

Why would anyone leave him cider?

He looked at the bottle and sniffed it, then poured a bit of the liquid into the mug. He looked at the liquid and sniffed again. It certainly smelled like cider.

He looked at the liquid, then tried to study it with his chaos senses. Abruptly he stepped back, as the ugly white-red of chaos seemed to swirl from both bottle and the liquid in the cup.

Poison? Did the sense of chaos in food and drink mean poison? Cerryl glanced around but could not sense anyone screeing him. He slipped the mug and bottle under his tunic, then went to the door, listening until the corridor seemed empty.

He left his room and strolled down the corridor, easing into the jakes, glad that the halls had jakes and not chamber pots, and slipped into the stall in the corner, where he eased out the bottle and poured the cider down into the darkness. He glanced around, then wiped the bottle with his tunic. He hoped that would blur or wipe away any tint of his chaos—if there were such a thing. He set the bottle and mug against the wall in the corner, then walked to the adjoining washroom— also empty, breathing a little more easily.

Jeslek had said there would be tests, not all that he would recognize. Had the poisoned cider been a test? Or did someone really want him dead? And why? He was almost unlearned, untutored.

He shook his head. Did he have to sense all the food and drink in the halls? Should he have already been doing that? He swallowed, then headed for the commons.

L

Why are you here, young Cerryl? Jeslek and Sterol sent you." The slender older mage answered his own question and smiled broadly. "They sent you to me, and I will teach what I know of anatomie, which is considerable."

From where he sat on the hard bench against the wall, Cerryl bowed his head and waited.

"But the question remains. Why? Why study anatomie?" Broka paused but did not look at Cerryl as he walked by the student as if Cerryl were not there. "Many are the reasons for the study of the anatomies . . . many, indeed . . ."

The mage turned abruptly, and his long fingers brushed Cerryl's arm as he passed, and Cerryl wanted to cringe. He remained sitting straight up, instead, his eyes intent on the slender wizard.

"From chaos unto chaos—that is the rule of anatomie—and of life. Life is that brief moment when chaos seizes order and creates living form, and death is when chaos abandons order. It ceases to animate form, and the form ceases to live, if you will." Broka offered a toothy grin, then turned and walked toward the window in a gliding, swaying stride that reminded Cerryl of a lizard—or a viper.

Cerryl looked at the skeleton on the wooden stand in the corner away from the window. Had the man or woman been a criminal or just a poor unfortunate?

"We know food supplies chaos energy to the body, and with that energy, the body grows and changes. Any individual living body is not only constantly changing its substance but its size. When such changes cease, we have death." Broka fixed Cerryl with his deep-set eyes. "Do you understand that, young Cerryl? When the body loses its chaos energy in one way or another, it dies."

"Yes, ser."

"Pure chaos is formless, but man is not. In fact, all land creatures with bones share a generality of structure. The hand and arm of a man, the foreleg of a dog, the wing of a bird—indeed all manifest the same type of construction."

Broka sidled toward the skeleton on its frame, pointing toward it. "Now we shall begin with the skeleton—precisely . . . precisely two hundred distinct bones." He gestured toward Cerryl. "Come here. You do not just listen. You must touch, and feel. Feel . . . especially. For feel is essential to a chaos master." A soft but guttural chuckle followed.

Cerryl rose and walked gingerly toward the skeleton, trying to position himself so that the array of bones stood between him and Broka.

"All bones are of one of four types—lengthy bones, short bones, plank or flat bones, and irregular bones." Broka pointed to one of the arm bones. "Feel that."

Cerryl complied, letting his fingers trace the length of the off-white member, feeling white dust slip away under his fingertips.

"Real living bones are not so smooth, not so cool and inviting, but this will start you on learning."

In the oppressive warmth of the small chamber, Cerryl wanted to yawn and step back from Broka simultaneously.

"*Prestad's* will give you all the details. That's the book I will give you. Jeslek says you can read, and read you will." Broke pushed a lock of long graying sandy hair back off his forehead, offering another broad smile.

"Yes, ser," answered Cerryl, uncertain what to say or do.

"Why should you study anatomie? There are two reasons. You should learn anatomie so that you can use chaos to heal effectively or kill effectively. The other reason is that the Guild says you should learn anatomie." Broka shrugged. "If I do not think you have learned your anatomie, then you will not become a full mage." He looked at the skeleton. "You may indeed serve the Guild in other ways." Yet another smile followed. "Do you understand?"

"Yes, ser."

"Good." Broka thrust forward a book Cerryl had not seen him pick up. "This is *Prestad's Anatomical Explications.* You will read section one until you think you understand it. We will meet in an eight-day."

Cerryl took the book.

Broka glided toward the door, toothy smile in place, opening it and stepping back, his smile almost mocking.

LI

Jeslek's quarters were warm—as were all the quarters in the late summer days before harvest. The mage turned from the glass, a glass that had momentarily filled with white mists before returning to being a simple mirror once more. He glanced at Kesrik, then studied Cerryl before resuming the examination.

Cerryl remained perfectly still, his back to the stone wall.

"You have read *all* of the first half of *Colors of White*?" Jeslek glanced from Cerryl to Kesrik.

"Yes, ser." Cerryl had read every page of the first part at least twice in the eight-days since he had been accepted as a student mage, and more than that before, not that he would ever admit such.

"I see." Jeslek frowned. "Explain this. 'Even the wisest of mages cannot perceive any portion of all that exists on and under the earth itself except through the operation of chaos.' " He looked at Cerryl. "You recognize that?"

"Yes, ser."

"Tell me what you *think* it means."

Cerryl ignored Kesrik's barely concealed smirk and began to speak slowly but deliberately. "Light is formed of chaos by the sun, and we see through light. Without light, without chaos, we cannot see. The book also says that a trained mage can use that part of chaos light that the eyes cannot see to sense even more."

"You have read that part. What about this? 'Order is limited, and chaos without bounds. Yet the use of chaos is bounded by order.' " Jeslek offered another hard smile.

Cerryl swallowed. While he recognized the words, he'd never thought about exactly what they meant. Still, he had to try. "Chaos has no bounds, but for a mage to make use of its power requires that it be bent to the mage's will. Will is a form of order."

Jeslek's sun-gold eyes glittered. "Are you saying that a white mage must soil himself with black order?"

"No, ser. As I understand it, a mage uses his will to harness the power of chaos. If his will is attuned to chaos, then order serves chaos."

Cerryl could sense disappointment in Kesrik and a glittering sort of elation in Jeslek, an elation that bothered him.

" 'Although chaos itself is all-powerful and knows neither rules nor bounds, the world obeys rules that do not change.' How does *Colors* explain that?"

Cerryl couldn't stop his puzzled expression. "Ser . . . I must have missed something. I am sorry. I do not recall any words like that."

"I am glad you do not. Those words are not in the *Colors of White*." Jeslek nodded. "Until tomorrow. You may go. I will expect you to know the entire book in another pair of eight-days."

"Yes, ser."

"Then we will begin your practical training."

"Yes, ser."

"You won't like it. None of the students do. I didn't. Go."

Cerryl bowed, then turned, catching a few words before the guard shut the door behind him.

"Kesrik . . . where did young Cerryl make things too simple?"

Too simple? Where had he made things too simple? Cerryl walked down the corridor to the steps and down toward the meal hall, where he hoped he might find some leftover bread—or something.

Jeslek had not changed expression when he had spoken the last phrase. Where had that come from? Some forbidden book? Or had Jeslek just invented the words? Either way, it had been some sort of trap.

The student mage forced a long and slow breath. How many other traps lay before him? Had the poison been a trap? He still didn't know. The bottle and mug had vanished, but whether one of the skulls or cleaners had merely taken it or someone else, he couldn't have said.

Then there was the continued reference to light. Even in the scary dream he had had at Tellis's where Anya, the red-haired mage, had been invisible, she had mentioned the power of light. But what *was* the power of light? How could he find out? So far, *Colors of White* hadn't said much directly, and he was almost through the second half—the first time.

He thought about Jeslek's questions. No . . . he definitely wasn't through studying the book—not if he wanted to survive. His stomach gurgled and growled, probably because he'd not been able to eat that much in the morning, knowing that he was to be examined by Jeslek, and also because he'd had a headache from the heavy rain.

He decided to go by the meal hall. There might be something left.

"You look famished, young mage," called one of the serving boys, looking up from a broom and dust holder. The blond youth in the red tunic of the creche flashed a smile. "There's still some bread there, and I'll just have to throw it out."

"Thank you." With a grateful smile, Cerryl took the crusty end section left in the basket, letting his senses check it quickly before picking it up. It held no chaos he could detect, and he broke off a piece and chewed carefully, his thoughts still on light. He couldn't *do* anything with chaos, but that didn't mean he couldn't think about it.

After finishing the bread and quieting the growling in his stomach, Cerryl walked down the corridor to his cell, where he paused to reclaim *Colors of White*. He paused a moment longer, certain that someone else had been in the room, although none of his meager possessions—or his books—were missing.

He smiled. Nothing would be missing, not that he would miss the loss of most of what he had—except for the difficulty it would cause. With his abrupt removal from Tellis's house, he had lost the only possession he really missed having—the old amulet that Syodor had said was his father's.

Theft wasn't tolerated in the Halls of the Mages, and the higher mages could tell when someone lied. So if Cerryl said something had been stolen, and told the truth, someone else would be in great difficulty. Cerryl didn't even want to consider the situation he'd be in if he lied.

He tucked the ancient tome under his arm and continued on down the corridor to the study.

Faltar and Lyasa were the only students there. Lyasa was buried in a huge volume Cerryl had never seen, though he couldn't make out the title. He slid onto the stool at one of the empty tables and opened *Colors of White*. The study wasn't that warm, perhaps because of the earlier rain, and the late summer sky was still cloudy. But the study chamber was close, almost warmly clammy, and Cerryl could feel the dampness gathered in his tunic.

"Cerryl?" Faltar had moved to the stool opposite him. "How did it go?"

"He asked me a lot of questions. The worst was the one about chaos being all-powerful, yet being limited by order." Cerryl opened *Colors* but did not look down, his eyes still on the slender Faltar.

"He asked you that?" Faltar shook his head. "I've been studying *Colors* for over half a year, and Derka hasn't been that hard on me. The High Wizard must want you to suffer."

Did Sterol? Or was he after something else?

"I don't know." Cerryl smiled faintly. "It doesn't matter. I still have to know what he wants me to learn. There's no choice, is there, really?"

"Sometimes . . . sometimes, Cerryl, you're scarier than the High Wizard."

"Me?"

"The way you accept things. I'd have trouble."

"No. You wouldn't. Because you wouldn't, they don't try." That was clear enough to Cerryl. He was being tested in more ways than one, and he had no choices. None at all.

LII

As the door opened, Cerryl and Kesrik stepped back to the wall out of deference and habit.

The ruddy-faced and rugged-looking mage with the purple blotch on his cheek smiled at Jeslek. "Greetings." His eyes fixed on Jeslek, who seemed slender by comparison, and ignored the two student mages.

"How might I be of service?" Jeslek's low voice was smooth, almost resonant, as he glanced at the taller mage who had just entered his chambers.

Kinowin bowed to Jeslek. His white collar bore the same golden sunburst as did Jeslek's. Cerryl didn't remember it from when Kinowin had brought him to the tower. Had it been granted at the last meeting of the white mages?

"With the road tariffs and the trade problems with the accursed isle, the High Wizard has asked how far the Great White Road can be used."

"It's somewhere beyond Tellura," answered Jeslek. "If you will wait but a moment, I will offer a more precise reply. Not that such precision will be of great use to His Mightiness."

"As you see fit."

Cerryl could sense the tension between the two but didn't fully understand it, since, according to student gossip, both shared a dislike of Sterol. Then, he'd come to understand early that people always made their lives more difficult than necessary.

"I do," answered Jeslek. "One should be as precise as possible when serving the High Wizard, even when precision is meaningless."

Cerryl watched, with both eyes and senses, as Jeslek stood before the table and concentrated on his screeing. Standing beside Cerryl, Kesrik looked—and felt—totally bored, as though he'd seen the process over and over.

Cerryl still watched, trying to sense how Jeslek marshaled the white of chaos and the darkness of order and focused both upon the glass. Even though he could not see the shimmering surface clearly, he could sense the image forming—the image of a stone-paved highway.

Abruptly, the image shifted, to one where swarming figures milled in a shallow gully that ended suddenly just beyond them. Then the glass blanked. Cerryl moistened his lips, trying to assimilate how the mage had gathered the images so quickly.

Jeslek lifted his eyes from the glass with a satisfied smile. "The Great White Road is well past Tellura, two days, perhaps, and the preliminary ditching is complete to a point northwest of Quessa."

A ghost of a frown passed across Kesrik's face.

Jeslek's eyes flicked to Kesrik and then to Cerryl before returning to Kinowin. "Will that suffice?"

"I will tell the High Wizard."

"Perhaps you could speed the construction," suggested Jeslek, "with your carefully protected use of chaos."

"Perhaps, but not so well as you," countered Kinowin. "You are master of the earth forces."

A faint breeze drifted through the window, bearing the faintly acrid scent of graying leaves and of fall, then vanished before cooling the room at all.

Cerryl felt sweaty within the red-tipped whites of a student mage but stood as impassively as he could.

"We go where we are called," said Jeslek.

"True." Kinowin bowed and departed.

As the door closed, Jeslek turned to his students, his eyes going to Kesrik. "You don't know anything about Quessa, do you?"

"No, ser," admitted the stocky blond.

"You have my leave to use a screeing glass and the library. The day after tomorrow, you will know everything there is to be found about Quessa." Without pausing, the white wizard turned to Cerryl. "You don't know where either Tellura or Quessa are, do you?"

"No, ser."

"You were a scrivener's apprentice?"

"Yes, ser."

Jeslek nodded. "Good. We could use another map of Candar—a good map. You have two eight-days to draw a detailed map of eastern Candar. It will show the location of Tellura, Quessa, and all the main cities east of the Westhorns. You may obtain vellum from wherever you choose." He fumbled at his purse and then tossed two golds at Cerryl. "If you need more, see me. If you have spare coins, return them. You might as well leave and start now. A white mage who does not know geography is useless."

Cerryl quickly placed the golds in his purse.

"Go." Jeslek paused. "You do *not* have leave to use a glass. Nor to ask any full mage."

"Yes, ser."

"Two eight-days, and do not stint your other studies." His sun gold eyes glittered.

Cerryl bowed, ignoring the glint in Kesrik's eyes, leaving quickly. He nodded to the guard outside. "Good day."

"Good day, young ser."

Cerryl found his feet carrying him down the stairs and toward the library, where all the books and maps were stored, though he knew already no map would show Quessa. Jeslek wouldn't have asked for such a map were it available.

Jeslek hadn't really had to task Cerryl with a more onerous task than Kesrik, had he? Why had he insisted on a full map? Was it another test? Was it just to get Cerryl out of the way?

That didn't feel right, although Cerryl didn't know why, as with so many things. He clamped his lips together and kept walking. It didn't matter. He had a map to draw.

LIII

The hazy fall afternoon light gave the workroom an almost misty appearance. Cerryl blotted his forehead with the back of his forearm, just below the rolled-up sleeves, and took a deep breath. He looked at the map on the table and then at his hand. It was shaking.

Carefully, he set the quill in the holder and shook his hand, then rubbed it with his left, studying his work.

The outlines of the land were there, and the boundaries of each land, and the Easthorns and the Westhorns and the rivers and the coastlines. A few tiny dots marked some of the towns and cities, but most remained to be placed, and he had less than an eight-day remaining.

"Still working on that map?" Faltar stood in the doorway of the small room adjoining the library, a room Cerryl hadn't even known existed until he had to search for a worktable on which to create his map. "Derka made me do one of Lydiar and Hydlen."

Cerryl looked up. "Is it somewhere that I could study it?"

"It's on the racks."

"The new one, with the purple ink?"

Faltar nodded.

"It's a good map."

"Derka said so."

Cerryl grinned. "I've already copied that part. Mostly, anyway. Except for naming the towns." He corked the ink bottle and straightened and stretched, trying to loosen muscles in his back that he hadn't even realized were stiff.

"You're using black ink?" Faltar peered at Cerryl's vellum.

"It's what I know how to make."

"I wish I'd known that. I used an old formula in the alchemical scrolls. Black would have looked better." Faltar's eyes went to the doorway, then to Cerryl.

"If you have to make more for something, I'll show you." Cerryl kept massaging his hand.

"Have you managed to locate those towns?" Faltar looked back down at the map.

"I'm fairly sure about Tellura. I don't know where Quessa is. No one I could ask knows, and I wouldn't ask Kesrik."

"I cannot imagine why." Faltar offered a grim smile. "Nor could you trust his reply."

The younger student mage gave a short nod, then looked at the map. "There is so much left undone on this, and I'm supposed to do some anatomie drawings for Broka, too, and tomorrow I have to meet Esaak, and I know I haven't read enough of that book he left for me."

"He's a crusty sort," said Faltar. "Just listen as much as you can. He'll eventually get around to telling you what he wants—after he's told you how worthless all of us are, and how we appreciate little or nothing about mathematicks."

Cerryl sighed.

"I came to ask if you wanted to take a walk up to the market square." Faltar offered a smile. "It sounds like you need a walk or something."

"With this hanging on me?"

"A trip to the market will do you good," insisted the older student. "Besides, you can scarcely hold that quill. You need some air. You can struggle over your map this evening, with a fresh head, after the peddlers have gone."

Cerryl flexed his hand. "I'll walk with you. You can do the buying."

"Don't you have any coppers?"

"A few. Now and then, Sterol sends a small purse," Cerryl grudged, not wanting to admit that Sterol had been more than moderately generous, at least not where Kesrik or his friends might overhear.

"Ah . . ." Faltar nodded, eyes traveling back to the door. "Well, he should, High Wizard or not. You're his responsibility."

Was he? Cerryl felt more like an orphan than ever. He got the coins but never saw Sterol. *Stop feeling sorry for yourself. It doesn't help.* "Just for a short walk, that's all."

"We have to be back for the evening meal," Faltar pointed out. "Even if I find something more tasty in the square."

"All right." Cerryl replaced the ink in the cubby that Derka had granted him, along with the quills and the holder and the inkwell. He could clean the inkwell later. The vellum went onto one of the library's drying racks.

"You'll feel better."

"I'm sure." Cerryl washed his hands quickly, glad he wasn't the one who had to clean the basins anymore, and joined Faltar in the corridor.

They nodded to Lyasa as she passed, and the black-haired student nodded back, but her olive brown eyes were focused elsewhere.

The courtyard was empty, and the light wind threw spray from the fountain across the two. The dampness felt good on Cerryl's forehead. He touched his brow, but it didn't feel warm, or any warmer than usual.

The main corridor of the front building was empty, until they reached the foyer, where Cerryl's eyes were drawn to a slender red-headed figure in white, who hurried up the steps from the foyer proper toward the tower entrance. Behind her remained a faint fragrance, one similar to sandalwood but more floral.

"You know Anya?" asked Faltar.

"Not exactly. She stopped me once on the street and then came to Tellis's shop once."

"She probably sensed you had the power. That's one of the things Sterol uses her for. I'd prefer some of the others." Faltar grinned. "One especially."

Cerryl repressed a shiver. "Isn't that dangerous? For her, I mean? A child of two whites?"

"I'm certain Anya's powers are enough to ensure she has no child. Of course, I wouldn't mind trying."

"You have a one-rut mind."

"I wouldn't mind having her in that rut."

"Enough . . ." Cerryl shook his head as he stepped through the front archway and down the steps to the avenue.

"I really wouldn't. You should see—"

"Enough!" Cerryl's exclamation was half-gruff, half-laughing.

"What about Lyasa?"

Cerryl rolled his eyes.

"I told you I'd get your thoughts off that darkness-filled map."

"You have. You have. I promise you that you have."

Cerryl glanced back at the tower and the Halls of the Mages that adjoined it. Just a set of white stone buildings, with no ornamentation, with more buildings stretching out behind them—kitchens, stables, an armory, barracks for some of the white guards and lancers, and, nearly a half kay north, the creche where the children of white mages were raised.

Almost two seasons, and he still couldn't believe that he was in the Halls of the Mages.

On the far side of the avenue, a team of four black horses drew a high-sided maroon wagon away from the square.

"Sarronnese carpet merchants. They don't like Fairhaven much, just our coins." Faltar laughed.

"How do you know?"

"I've seen their wagons before. Derka told me. I think most of his family were traders."

"Do you know about yours?"

Faltar shrugged. "No. My father was a mage. I wonder if Derka . . . but I don't know. That's something they never say."

"I'm sorry. I wasn't thinking."

"You were a scrivener's apprentice . . ." Faltar said gently.

"I told you, didn't I?" Cerryl wasn't sure what he'd told to whom anymore, but he thought he'd told Faltar.

"Yes. When you first came to the halls." The blond student mage glanced up the avenue, toward the line of clouds to the east. "We'd better hurry. That looks like rain."

"It won't get here for a while, and the wind feels good." Cerryl walked faster, enjoying stretching his legs.

"Sometimes . . . I wonder what it would have been like. To have a trade, I mean."

"It's different. I don't miss the sawmill."

"Sawmill?"

"Oh, I was a mill boy before I was apprenticed to Tellis. The winters were cold, and I never seemed to get warm. Dylert was fair, but the work only got harder as I got bigger."

Faltar's steps slowed as he looked sideways. "No one would ever guess. You're not that big. You look more like a scrivener."

"Thin and scrawny?"

Faltar flushed.

Cerryl laughed softly. "I do. I know it."

Two girls, probably not much older than Pattera, saw the white tunics and slipped down the side way in the middle of the row of the grand houses with their now-gray trees and gardens.

"They weren't that pretty," said Faltar.

"Who?"

"The girls. Don't you like girls?"

"I like girls. I wasn't looking."

"Ever had a girl? You could, any time, if you wanted."

"No. I could have, but . . ." Cerryl wondered how Benthann might be doing. Somehow, he'd felt it would have been wrong to go back to Tellis's, even if he couldn't quite say why.

"And you didn't?" Faltar's voice rose slightly.

"It could have caused a lot of trouble."

"Well . . . it's different here. If you find a girl who's willing, and most will give you a tumble."

"Why? Because they'll get a dowry settlement from the Guild?" Cerryl struggled to keep the edge from his voice.

"Well . . . it's better that way."

"I suppose."

"Oh." After a moment, Faltar asked, "You've been through a lot of hard times, haven't you?"

"Why do you say that?"

"I don't know. Except you don't see things the same way. And you're so quiet. Sometimes, when you're in a place, it's as though you're almost invisible."

"Sometimes, I wish I could be. Especially now."

"Derka says that some of them can do that. They bend light around themselves. There's another way to do it, but he won't tell me what it is. He says it's not a good thing to do."

Light again—always light. Cerryl nodded.

"Why do you want to be invisible?"

"I am already. Kesrik, Bealtur, they wish I didn't exist. I'm not a mage's son, and I don't come from coins."

"Kinowin didn't, either."

"And he looks like he had to beat them into accepting him. He's a head taller than even Jeslek."

"They say that Creslin was small."

"But he was a black mage."

"Power is power," said Faltar.

Was it? Cerryl glanced past the last house on the left—Muneat's, the only one he knew, with the bird fountain—and to the square, where only a handful of shoppers still remained around the colored carts. "They say coins are power, too."

"It's not the same. Coins aren't. Kesrik comes from coins, and Sterol doesn't give a copper."

"Maybe that's why Sterol is High Wizard."

"It's not just chaos power. Jeslek can hold more chaos than anyone." Faltar glanced around nervously.

"It's what you can do with it. I know that. And Sterol and Jeslek aren't the best of friends. They wouldn't have quarters as far apart as they do if they were."

"That's true. None of the mages talk about it, though."

"What good would it do?" Cerryl stepped off the curb and started across the empty avenue to the square. "They'd risk making either Sterol or Jeslek angry."

A wisp of thin smoke, bearing the smell of roast fowl, drifted by the two students.

"Smells better than anything in the halls."

Cerryl had to admit that it did.

"Split a half fowl?"

"How much, do you think?" asked Cerryl.

"Two coppers, maybe, for a half. One for you and one for me."

"Since it's not often . . ." The younger student grinned, trying not to think how many days' pay that would have been once.

Faltar walked over to the blue wagon and the hefty woman in gray at the spit over the charcoal in the metal firepit. "How much for a half?"

"Three coppers, ser."

"Two," insisted Faltar. "I'm hungry enough that I don't want to haggle."

The woman shrugged. "Two, I can live with. It's late." She pulled the spit off its holder and deftly lifted a thick black knife—more like a cleaver.

Cerryl found his mouth watering as Faltar handed him the browned and dripping quarter fowl, and he bent forward so that none of the drippings would touch his tunic.

"Better than in the halls," confirmed Faltar, his mouth nearly full.

"Yes," mumbled Cerryl, finding himself nearly ravenous.

They ate silently and quickly.

Cerryl had to lick his fingers clean, and they still felt sticky.

"I'm going to look around." Faltar inclined his head and then slipped toward a green-and-blue cart—or the slender girl holding up a woven basket.

The younger mage smiled to himself and turned the other way, passing a cart filled with long yellow gourds and thin green ones. He paused after several vegetable carts at another kind of cart painted gold and silver. Three blades lay on a display board covered with blue velvet. One was short and dark—and he could feel the chill of ordered iron. The second was of fired white bronze, like a white lancer's sabre, although it wasn't. The third was a huge iron broadsword, one that Cerryl doubted he could have lifted, with a wound-copper hilt.

"You like the sabre? For you, a mere gold," insisted the pallid man by the cart, limping forward from where he had been talking to a darker swarthy fellow.

"No . . . no thank, you." Cerryl smiled and stepped back.

"As you wish, ser."

He could sense the anger and disapproval and turned. "I'm not a weapons mage." He wasn't sure there were any weapons mages, but the blades felt wrong for him.

The man bowed, almost as if puzzled.

Cerryl nodded and passed to the next cart, where colored scarves were wound loosely around polished wooden pegs on a display board and fluttered in a breeze that barely ruffled his hair.

"Scarves of silksheen, real silksheen from Naclos."

Cerryl had never heard of anything from Naclos, and he reached to touch a silver scarf. As his fingers touched the fabric, smoother than anything he had ever felt, the color darkened almost into gray. He let go of the edge of the scarf and watched as it flashed silver.

"Only two silvers for you, young ser. Just two silvers."

Two silvers for a scarf barely a cubit and a half long and half that in width? Two silvers? Cerryl had never had a whole silver at one time. He smiled politely and stepped away.

The sound of the first bells of late afternoon echoed up the avenue and across the square. The vendor at the next cart began to unroll the canvas to cover the cart bed and the three baskets of potatoes that remained.

"Best we head back." Faltar appeared at Cerryl's elbow.

"Did you find anything?"

"No. One pretty girl, but not that pretty."

"That wasn't what I meant." Cerryl turned toward the Halls of the Mages.

"Oh . . . things? What would I do with anything except books? Derka would only ask me what value it had."

"We can't hold property, can we?"

"No. Didn't Jeslek tell you that?"

"Not in so many words. He never says anything directly."

"Derka doesn't much, either."

"I wonder why."

"We're supposed to figure it out, and if we can't, well, then . . ." Faltar left the sentence unfinished.

Cerryl knew well enough what the other meant—all too well.

LIV

Cerryl sat at the table, looking blankly at the slate and the wedge of chalk beside it. The whole room smelled of chalk, unlike any of the other mages' chambers he had been inside.

Standing at the other side of the ancient table was the heavyset Esaak, wearing flowing white robes of the older style, rather than the white tunic and trousers used by Sterol and Jeslek and all of the younger mages.

"Master scholar Cerryl . . . might I have your attention?" Esaak's jowls wobbled as he spoke, and his voice rumbled.

"Ser?"

"Have you read any of the book I left for you? *Naturale Mathematicks*, it is called, if you do not remember."

"Only a few pages, ser."

"Why not more, might I ask? Is the ancient and honored study of mathematicks beneath you?" Esaak half-turned, walking a few paces across the dusty floor.

"No, ser. I fear I am beneath it."

"Such refreshing honesty." The older mage's words dripped irony. "You seek to disarm me with false modesty." He coughed several times, with a rumbling deeper than even his bass voice.

Cerryl felt tongue-tied, feeling he was off on the wrong foot.

"Well?"

"No, ser. I can read and write, but my education has been limited to history mostly. The honored Jeslek has insisted that I read all of *Colors of White* and complete a large map within a short period of time. I have to do some anatomie drawings for the mage Broka. I read the first section of the *Mathematicks*, but much of it was so unfamiliar . . ."

"Tell me what you thought you read . . ."

Cerryl wanted to sigh.

"Go on. What was the first section about? Surely, surely, you can tell me what the words said?"

Why did *all* the mages ask questions rather than tell anything? It seemed to Cerryl almost as though he were being asked to teach them. He moistened his lips. "Ser . . . the very beginning I understood. That was about the history of reckoning, where the first use of numbers were words like 'yoke' and 'pair' or 'couple'—two things because we have two hands. Then, as people gathered more goods or crops, or lived in larger settlements, larger numbers were needed, and they came up with terms to count larger groups of things, like 'score' and 'stone' . . ."

"What is similar about the two?"

Cerryl looked as blank as he felt.

"They're each a pair multiplied by ten," snapped Esaak. "A stone is a pair of fists ten times over. A score is a couple of hunters ten times over. Go on."

"Then the book started talking about something called partition enumeration . . ."

"And when it got a little difficult . . . you stopped reading?"

"No, ser. I kept reading. I understood the idea of dividing groups of things into groups of the same size and using symbols to represent larger numbers, like ten score, but when it started on how to scrive such numbers, and that you had to have a symbol for nothing . . ."

"Why shouldn't there be a number for nothing? Isn't not having something as important to know as having something?"

That wasn't exactly what Cerryl had meant. At least, it wasn't what he thought he'd meant. "It is, ser. I meant . . ."

"What did you mean? Mathematicks is precision, not vague statements about a few stone or score. How would you like it if a lancer scout told you that the force you faced was a bunch of scores of armsmen?"

"I'd want to know more."

"And you should." Esaak gave an even louder and more dramatic sigh, readjusting his robes as he did. "You know . . . you're all alike. All of you seem to think that what we teach you is because we owe you something.

"Oh . . . the days, the years I have spent pounding and prying knowledge into empty-ordered heads. For what? So that you can go off and dash your brains out against some evil-hearted order magician from the black isle? So you can overload a ship and sink it in the sight of rough water?" Esaak exhaled noisily.

Cerryl waited, not knowing what to say, or even if he should attempt to say a word.

"You all can see the value of even learning to fire-scrub sewers, or to memorize every bone in the body the better to destroy it, or to make maps for the day when you will direct lancers in battle . . . But what is behind it all? Mathematicks! Calculations! Numbers!"

Cerryl felt like slinking out by the time Esaak was through, although the older mage had said enough—eventually—that Cerryl could grasp the idea of a symbol of nothing as a place holder for calculations. It made sense, but, like too many things, no one had ever explained it.

There was one question that Esaak had raised and not really answered—what did all the mages do besides make life difficult for student mages? If Jeslek happened to be any example, they didn't spend all that much time with students, just enough to set them on projects and complain about the results. They came and went, and so did many carriages and wagons, and Cerryl had overheard talk about various rulers, and soldiers, and even sewers. Jeslek had talked about governing but said that it wasn't ruling but guiding, without ever defining what he meant.

Cerryl felt dazed. He had learned much already, but none of it really answered the question of what exactly the white mages did. Everyone talked around everything without describing it.

Slowly, he walked back to the common, then began to hurry as he realized he was due to meet Eliasar. He dropped the book on his cell desk and practically ran to the common.

The blocky mage rose from the corner table and looked toward the flustered Cerryl. "You can slow down. Where were you?"

"Esaak was tutoring me on mathematicks . . ."

"Is he still using that stupid example about 'a bunch of scores of lancers'?"

"He did use a phrase like that, ser."

"Let's get you out to the armory, boy, and I'll tell you why it's a stupid phrase." Eliasar turned and marched toward the rear corridor.

Cerryl found himself nearly running to keep up with the quick steps of the battered-looking Eliasar.

"Old Esaak is right about one thing. Numbers and calculations are important, but in battle—ha! Who knows?" Eliasar stepped into the rear courtyard, striding past six mounted lancers without even looking at them.

Cerryl gave the mounts and their riders a slightly wider berth than the mage.

"Look—I need to know exactly how many horses I'm taking on an expedition to say, Spidlar. Spidlar's as good an example as any. We'll be fighting there before long, anyway, unless I miss my guess. How much feed does a mount require? How many mounts? How many days? So how much grain do I need? How many lancers? How many levies that we have to feed? How much can I count on from foraging? That's the sort of things you need numbers for. Darkness, half the time in a fight, you can't see how many, or where, or know if what you've got is even where it should be. And you don't have time to use a glass, and even if you did, you probably couldn't figure out what you saw quick enough to use it before it changed."

Eliasar marched through an open doorway and into a long room filled, it seemed to Cerryl, with racks and racks of weapons. The white mage passed the line of white bronze lances, shimmering in their racks, and stopped in the rear before another set of racks, yanking out what appeared to be a padded shirt. "Put that on. Right over your tunic. Won't be wearing it that long anyways."

Cerryl pulled on the padded shirt.

"Now this." Eliasar extended what appeared to be bronze body armor of some sort, a combination of breastplate and back plates and shoulder gauntlets or whatever they were called. "Over your head."

The student mage struggled into the heavy bronze half-armor.

"Remember this is white-bronze. Good steel is heavier."

Heavier? Cerryl wasn't sure he could have carried heavier armor.

"And this is only partial armor." Eliasar picked up a long heavy blade and a pair of gauntlets and marched out, as if expecting Cerryl to follow. "You won't wear this, probably not ever, but you'll wear it today."

The youth followed the older mage back out and across another courtyard, along yet another corridor and out into an empty practice yard where a heavy wooden post, more like a heavy slashed tree trunk, stood. Eliasar stopped a half-dozen cubits short of the post. "How do you feel?"

"It's heavy," admitted Cerryl.

Eliasar handed Cerryl a pair of bronze gauntlets. "Put them on."

Cerryl pulled on the gauntlets, flexing his fingers. Surprisingly, the fingers of the metal gloves moved easily.

"Take this." Eliasar extended the blade, then pointed to the wooden post. "Go ahead. Take a whack at it."

Cerryl just looked. "I don't know how."

"Just lift the blade and chop." Eliasar stepped back several paces.

Awkwardly, Cerryl lifted the blade and swung it. The white bronze bounced off the wood, and Cerryl staggered back a step, trying to keep his balance.

"Strike again."

Cerryl levered the blade around, and his whole arm ached as the blade struck the post and rebounded.

"Do it again."

With both hands on the big hilt, Cerryl forced another thudding blow to the post, followed by yet another, further numbing Cerryl's arms.

"Keep at it!" demanded Eliasar.

When the arms mage finally allowed Cerryl to stop, the youth was drenched with sweat, and he could barely lift the blade to hand it back to Eliasar.

"It's not so easy, is it?" asked the blocky mage, taking the gauntlets back as well.

"No, ser."

"You barely swung that blade for a tenth part of a morn, and some battles last all day. Best remember that when you order armsmen to fight." Eliasar turned, clearly expecting Cerryl to follow, leading him to yet another courtyard that Cerryl had no idea existed.

A line of straw dummies was set up before canvas hangings.

"Archery. There's three sets of hangings. Easier on the shafts and heads that way." Eliasar picked up a curved stave from somewhere, or so Cerryl thought. "Now . . . here's a bow. Here's how you string it." In a fluid motion that Cerryl could barely follow, the arms mage had the bow strung. "You try it." As quickly as he had strung the weapon, Eliasar unstrung it and handed it to Cerryl.

Cerryl had to use his knee and most of his weight to even bend the bow, and scraped skin off the sides of two fingers in somehow stringing the weapon.

Eliasar took the bow, inspected it without words, then nocked an arrow and put a shaft through the left arm of the center straw figure. "Little off there." A second shaft went through the middle of the figure's chest. "Here you go."

The first shaft popped off the string on the draw because Cerryl's sweaty fingers lost their grip. He wiped them on his trousers and tried again. That shaft skidded along the sand in front of the targets. It took five attempts before a shaft even hit the hangings.

By then blood streaked the fingers of his right hand.

"That's enough. Clear you've had no training in arms." Eliasar took back the bow, unstrung it, and wiped it down with a cloth he produced from somewhere.

"You'll never raise a blade—or a bow. So why do you suppose I made you do all this?" Eliasar grinned. "And you'll do it a score or more times before you ever ride with the lancers."

"So that I understand what lancers do?"

Eliasar smiled coldly. "So you don't do something that kills them or you because you don't understand. You don't understand. You haven't even started to understand." The grin returned. "Least you can wear armor and move. Might be some hope for you." Eliasar turned. "Let's get that off you and get you back to the common."

Cerryl forced his steps to match those of the older mage, although he found himself practically panting to keep up.

"Be another eight-day or two. Mayhap longer, if you get sewer duty, but I'll see you again. Then we'll be showing you how to ride proper-like. That's something you will do, and we'll make sure you know that."

Cerryl had the feeling that Eliasar would, and that the mage enjoyed making life difficult for students.

LV

Cerryl looked down at the map outline lightly penned on the vellum spread across the table before him. He almost felt like jamming the quill into the smooth wood of the table or banging his head against the wall—or better yet, picking up Kesrik or Bealtur and pummeling either into a pulp, or tying them to a log and running through Dylert's big saw.

Already one eight-day and two days had passed, and all he had was an outline on vellum. His fingers still ached from his morning with Eliasar, and that hadn't made copying any easier or quicker. He'd had to develop a real scale of distances, one that fit on the size vellum he'd been able to get from Arkos, and that had taken almost two days because none of the maps in the books or the bigger ones in the mages' library really agreed, not that well.

Not only were all the sizes and scales different, but often the names weren't even the same. Some had Fenard spelled as Fenardre—after the ancient lord of Gallos, Cerryl guessed—and Jellico as Jellicor. The West-horns were the Ouesthorns on some maps. One town in Certis had four names: Yytrel, Rellos, Estalcor, and Rytel. Cerryl figured, from the ages of the various histories and places, that the current name was Rytel—unless it had changed again.

West of the Westhorns was worse, but he didn't have to worry about that, darkness forbid.

Because one of the places that Jeslek had mentioned—Quessa—wasn't on any map anywhere, Cerryl had asked the few students he trusted, like Faltar and Lyasa and the diffident Heralt. None of them knew.

While he would have been reluctant to approach any full mage he didn't study with—effectively Jeslek, Broka, and occasionally Derka—he had to ask himself why Jeslek had forbidden such questions. To force Cerryl to search the library and all the histories? To make the task harder? Another of Jeslek's endless tests?

He looked at the map, then lifted it and reattached it to the working rack in the corner.

Questions would have to wait.

After washing up, Cerryl found himself marching up the avenue toward Fasse's shop. Jeslek hadn't forbidden him to talk to others who might know, and he thought he recalled that Fasse had come from Gallos. He hoped his recollections were correct.

In the midafternoon, a line of wagons rumbled along the white stones of the avenue. A series of bells rang, and Cerryl smiled as he saw, trailing the cooper's wagon, a white-sided refuse wagon.

Once past the market square, filled mainly with women, he reached the jewelers' row, where in the cool afternoon most doors were closed, except for one. As he passed the green-lacquered open door, he glanced inside, where a goldsmith held a glittering choker to the light of the door for a woman dressed in pale blue. Cerryl couldn't have guessed how much gold was in the necklace, only that it was far more than he would likely ever see, even if he did become a full mage. For all of the strangeness in the Halls of the Mages, love of gold did not seem a magely fault.

One guard in pale blue livery stood by the door, and another almost between her and the goldsmith. Cerryl nodded to the guard, who did not nod back, and kept walking, past the rest of the fine metalsmiths', past the grain exchange, and finally to the artisans' square.

The door to Fasse's shop was ajar, and Cerryl edged inside. Fasse stood, polishing cloth in hand, by a gold oak chest.

"Yes, young ser?" The twiglike and wispy mustache twitched as the cabinet-maker turned to Cerryl.

Cerryl found the setting strange. A craftmaster—one whose loft he had slept in back at a time when he had barely a handful of coppers to his name—was calling him "ser."

"Fasse, my name is Cerryl, and once I slept in your loft. I am working on a project for the higher mages . . ." What else could he call Jeslek? ". . . and I thought you might be able to help."

"Young ser, you did look familiar." Fasse's brow furrowed as he stepped back from the gold oak chest he polished. "Yet, how could I be helping you?"

"I am making a map, and there are some towns in Gallos . . . Might you know where Quessa is?"

Fasse scratched the back of his head, his eyes going sidelong at Cerryl for a moment. "Hmmm . . . aye . . . I was there once, as a boy, but how . . . how would I say . . . explain . . . that be many years ago."

Cerryl waited.

"Best as I recall, it be three days' ride to the west of Hierna, only two days east of the Westhorns, the first hills, that be."

Cerryl swallowed. "Ah . . . I know where Tellura is, but not Hierna."

Fasse twisted one end of the thin mustache. "Tellura . . . I never went there, though all said it was to the south and east of Linspros and somewhere south and east of Hierna." Then he hung the polishing cloth on a wooden peg next to one of the smaller wood racks. "And never having been there, I'd not know how to say to get from one to the other. Or how long one might have to travel."

"Do you know anyone in Fairhaven who might know?"

Fasse twisted the other end of his mustache, scratching his head with the other hand. Then he pursed his lips. "Lwelter the potter—he might, seeing as his consort, she was Analerian, and they travel all Kyphros . . . might be that Hierna be too far north for herders." Fasse shrugged. "Best I could do."

"Lwelter . . . where could I find him?"

"You know Arkos the tanner? You must . . . ah . . ." Fasse swallowed.

Cerryl ignored the audible gulp. "I know Arkos. Is Lwelter near there?"

"Two shops toward the square. Leastwise, I think it's two. You'll find it, young ser."

"Thank you, Fasse." Cerryl nodded and left, repeating as he walked toward the tanner's what Fasse had said until he was sure he had the information firmly in mind.

From what Cerryl could tell, the potter's shop, the one with the outsized pitcher over the doorway, was three shops toward the square from the tanner's. He opened the door gently and stepped inside.

A young man, not that much older than Cerryl himself, sat on a stool, one foot pumping the treadle that powered the wheel. Cerryl watched as the base of a pot or a pitcher rose from the clay under the stubby fingers of the young potter.

The potter never glanced at Cerryl.

Finally, Cerryl cleared his throat. "I'm looking for Lwelter, the potter."

The slender man looked up from the wheel, then stiffened as he saw the white tunic and trousers. "Lwelter, ser?"

"He might know something," Cerryl said.

"Lwelter?"

Cerryl nodded.

"As you wish, ser." He turned on the stool. "Da! Mage here to see you." Then he turned back to the wheel. "If you don't mind, ser . . ."

"Go ahead."

Shortly, a stooped man shuffled out from the back room. Lwelter's sightless eyes looked past Cerryl. "Ser . . . ?" The cracked voice wavered.

"Lwelter?"

"That's me. Always been me, even when I could see."

"I was talking with Fasse, and he said you might be able to help me. You once spent time in Gallos and Kyphros, he said."

"Been a long time back, a long time, when Deorca was younger than Flait here."

"What can you tell me about Quessa or Hierna?"

"Hierna, ah, yes, that was the next town but one from Zrenca, and Zrenca, that was where I found Deorca." A smile creased the thin and pale lips. "A long time back."

"How far is Hierna from Tellura?"

"Not too far a piece. There's a day, a short day between Hierna and Zrenca, but Zrenca is but a hamlet, not a proper town at all, you know."

"And how far is Tellura from Zrenca?" Cerryl asked politely.

"I'd say, if there were a road, straight that is, it might take two days by horse, but the hills and the streams they don't flow straight, and the roads wind more than the streams."

"Zrenca is two days straight west from Tellura?" pursued Cerryl.

"Mostly, but I'd be guessing . . ."

"And Hierna is another day west from Zrenca?"

"Ah . . . no. Hierna . . . you go as much north as west from Zrenca, and a short day, a half day hard riding."

"Have you ever heard of a town called Quessa?"

Lwelter shrugged. "Knew it be west of Hierna, more than a few days . . . two, mayhap three."

"How big is Hierna?"

"You been to Weevett, young fellow?"

In the background, the stubby-fingered young potter winced ever so slightly.

"Well, Hierna's half again as big as Weevett, lessen one's growed more than the other in the last ten years." Lwelter laughed.

"Do you know anything about Quessa?"

"Some said it was a hamlet like Zrenca. Never went there. Deorca had a cousin consorted with a miller there."

"Did you ever go to the Westhorns from Zrenca?" asked Cerryl.

"Me? I was a potter, not a herder. 'Sides, even then, folks worried about the black she-angels. Folks say they're all dead. Don't you believe it." Lwelter cackled, shaking his head. "Don't like the lowlands, the angels don't."

"Da." The word was firm. "The white mage knows all about the angels."

Lwelter stopped cackling. "You didn't say he was a mage."

"He did," Cerryl said. "You have been very helpful. Thank you." He fumbled in his purse and handed a pair of coppers to the younger potter before turning and leaving.

". . . could have gotten us turned to ashes . . ."

". . . never said . . ."

Ignoring the recriminations behind him, Cerryl walked quickly back to the wizards' square.

The dinner bell was ringing as he opened his cell door, and he washed quickly and hurried toward the meal hall. The others who ate there were already seated with platters, and he found himself alone at the serving table.

After taking a chunk of oat bread, some cheese, noodles in white sauce, and a mug of the light ale, he sat down across from Faltar. He absently let his senses range over the food, though outside of the poisoned cider, he'd never found any other sense of chaos in food in the halls.

"Where have you been?" asked the blond student mage.

Beside Faltar, the curly-haired Heralt raised his eyebrows as he chewed some of the tough bread.

"Trying to find out where Quessa is—and Hierna, and Zrenca, and . . ." Cerryl broke off a corner of the bread and dipped it in the white sauce.

"Too bad scriveners can't use glasses like real student mages . . ." came the murmur from Bealtur at the adjoining table.

Cerryl stiffened momentarily, then smiled and turned to Faltar. "For some reason, the honored Jeslek did not want me to use a glass, and I would not think of going against his expressed wishes." His face hardened slightly. "I'm sure he wouldn't like to learn that anyone had suggested otherwise."

There was a satisfying gulp from the adjoining table.

Faltar grinned. So did Heralt, if momentarily.

Cerryl didn't. He had too much drawing and copying ahead. Instead, he took a chunk of the oat bread and began to chew.

LVI

The isle of Recluce was hotter than the Sand Hills raised by the treachery of Nylan, and drier as well, and not even the sorceries of the dark mages nor the fires of Megaera could bring forth water from the dry earth and barren rock.

Children shriveled and died; despite even the spells laid by Creslin upon his followers, more and more voices were raised in anguish and in pain, asking why Creslin had brought them to such a desolate place.

He answered them not, but withdrew into himself, then sent forth ships to plunder the seas. Yet the plunder would not buy water, nor food enough . . .

Why should all the gentle rain fall upon Candar and upon the lands of our enemies, and those who have sworn to destroy us? asked Creslin of Megaera. Why should we not turn the great winds so that the rains return to Recluce as they once must have fallen?

Even the faceless black mages shivered as they heard Creslin's words whisper across the barren rocks and bleached sands.

Yet none would raise his voice when Creslin and Megaera set forth to raise the waters and the skies and fought the winds of Heaven, nor was a word spoken when fires blazed out of the sky and floods of water cascaded across Recluce.

The fires burned across dry Montgren and the crops of Certis. Even the hardy oilseeds withered and dried, and the forests of Sligo blazed through the long summer.

The floods subsided, and rains fell upon Recluce, and Creslin and Megaera rejoiced, never looking into a glass or caring about the destruction which they had wrought upon Candar . . .

Colors of White
(Manual of the Guild at Fairhaven)
Preface

LVII

A woman in green crossed the hall and started toward the courtyard and the front building as Cerryl stepped out of the library workroom with his map in hand—a woman in green with red-blonde hair . . . a young woman.

Cerryl looked for a moment, just looked. Could it be the girl from his glass? She was definitely a woman now.

He glanced toward the steps to Jeslek's quarters, then in the direction she had gone, pursing his lips. After a moment, he turned toward the courtyard. Even with that momentary delay, by the time he passed the fountain and reached the end of the foyer of the front building, she had turned and was headed up the steps to the tower.

Cerryl walked more quickly, holding the map high so that he wouldn't trip or drag it along the polished stones. He dodged around Lyasa, who gave him a questioning look, and offered a harried look that he hoped would cover his action.

Lyasa raised both eyebrows but said nothing.

By the time Cerryl reached the pair of guards at the base of the tower, breathing slightly harder than he would have liked, the young woman in green had vanished. No sound of feet echoed down the steps to the higher levels, either.

He looked at the guard standing on the right. "Hertyl . . . the woman who just went up the steps . . . do you know her?"

"Young ser, it be not my business to know any like her."

Cerryl caught the twinkle in the young guard's eye and grinned. "Nor I . . . but you might know her name."

"I've heard that it be Leyladin. She is a merchant's daughter, but some say she also be a healer." Hertyl nodded toward the steps. "I do not ask where she visits."

Cerryl paused.

The older guard cleared his throat.

Cerryl understood the signal. "Thank you." He looked at the map he held and then at the guards, nodding to both. "Best I be going. Good day."

"Good day to you, young ser."

Cerryl walked quickly, if slightly more deliberately, back toward Jeslek's quarters.

The red-blonde hair—it could be no one else. But what was she doing in the Halls of the Mages? Just a healer? Or something else? His thoughts went back to Benthann's comments—sex? Was she the mistress or consort-to-be of a white mage? Of one of the older mages?

His fingers curled until his hands were almost fists, and he took a slow and silent deep breath, trying to relax. He had no claim on her. He didn't even know her, and she certainly didn't even know he existed. Why was he reacting so violently?

Besides, Jeslek had asked to see the map, and he dared not hasten, not after chasing the woman—*Leyladin, not woman*—practically to the white tower. Another test? Had Jeslek sent her past him?

He shivered but left the front foyer hall and started across the courtyard.

"Why were you in such a hurry?" Lyasa stood by the fountain, clearly waiting for him. Her olive brown eyes pinned him.

"I got flustered . . ." That was certainly true enough. He inclined his head to the map. "Jeslek wants to see this, and I found myself going in the wrong direction."

"In more ways than one." Lyasa shook her head, adding a wry smile. "She's an apprentice healer or some such. You're an apprentice white. You want to kill both of you? Black and white don't mix that way."

"I didn't know." Cerryl could feel his face fall, but a sense of elation followed. Leyladin . . . she probably wasn't a test by Jeslek, at least.

"That's obvious. It's one of the things we have to live with." Lyasa reached out and patted his shoulder. "At least you're not watching Anya . . . the way Faltar does."

Cerryl didn't know what to say.

"You understand that." Lyasa's tone was low and matter-of-fact. "Now . . . if Jeslek wanted you, you'd better hurry. He's not all that patient."

"No . . . he's not."

With an indulgent smile, Lyasa touched his shoulder again, then watched as he hurried across the courtyard and into the hall toward the steps. Again, he was breathing hard by the time he reached the back of the building.

Gostar, the guard outside Jeslek's quarters, nodded as Cerryl approached. Cerryl stepped past the armed guard and rapped on the door. "Cerryl, ser, as you requested."

"Come in." Jeslek's voice resonated through the closed white oak door.

After opening the door and closing it behind him, Cerryl bowed. "I have the map you requested, ser."

"About time."

"Yes, ser." Cerryl bowed again.

"Kesrik, move the glass to the side table." Jeslek nodded to the older student mage, then to Cerryl. "Spread it on the table."

Once Kesrik had removed the glass, Cerryl eased the vellum onto the table, then stepped back as Jeslek studied the map, squinting and shifting his eyes from point to point.

"Tellura . . . Hierna . . . Quessa . . . Kyphrien . . . hmmm."

At the "hmmmm," Cerryl took a slow and deliberate breath. *He's just trying to upset you. Calm, you have to be calm.*

Kesrik continued to display a broad smile as Jeslek pored over the vellum.

After what seemed like eight-days, the white mage straightened and looked at Cerryl. "It's basically accurate. At least it's the best one could expect from a new student, and one who was a scrivener's apprentice." Jeslek nodded. "You may have it put with the others in the racks in the library."

Kesrik did not manage to conceal a smirk from where he stood by the wall.

"Yes, ser."

"You are disturbed? You find my judgment harsh?" Jeslek's tone was light, amused, even as Cerryl could sense the white forces building.

"You are my master, ser, and you know what is best." Cerryl was surprised to find his words level and even, with an unseen barrier between his rage and his words and surface feelings.

"You actually believe that. My . . . my . . . how refreshing." The mage paused. "And very good for you." The sense of power dwindled. "You may go and rack your map. I will see you again tomorrow morning. Immediately after breakfast. Immediately."

"Yes, ser."

"Go."

Cerryl reached forward and gently lifted the map.

Jeslek nodded to Kesrik, who turned toward the small table and the screeing glass.

Cerryl bowed and turned, glad that Jeslek had not found any overt faults in the map. He rolled up the vellum, forcing himself to remain detached and deliberate as he departed, carrying the map.

There was no sign of the blonde girl-woman—or Lyasa—as he walked toward the library.

LVIII

Cerryl walked up to Jeslek's door with a stride more confident than he felt within himself.

"He be expecting you," said Gostar from beside the door, one hand casually on the hilt of the white-bronze shortsword used by the inside guards.

"Thank you." Cerryl knocked cautiously.

"Enter."

The student mage stepped inside and closed the heavy white oak door behind him. The mage stood by the screeing table—alone. With the considerable residue of unseen white around the table, Cerryl could sense that Jeslek had been using the glass recently. "I am here as you requested, ser."

"Your map was good." Jeslek watched Cerryl.

"Ser . . . you did not seem pleased. I will try to do better in the future."

"It was good," Jeslek repeated. "Yet I did not say so. Why might that be?"

"Kesrik was here."

Jeslek nodded. "Have I permitted you to work with chaos-fire?"

"No, ser."

"Kesrik has been a student for nearly four years. He has been working with chaos-fire for over two years. My reasons should be clear to you, if you consider them." Jeslek offered a perfunctory smile. "You are very bright, Cerryl. Perhaps too bright. You also do not understand in your heart what the Guild is, and why it is good for Fairhaven and Candar. With your talent, that presents a problem."

Since Cerryl couldn't say much to that, although he questioned whether he had that much talent, he nodded and waited.

"Sterol and I have agreed on this."

Jeslek's overly polite tone confirmed to Cerryl that whatever they had agreed upon was one of the few areas where the two mages had reached agreement.

"You will see Myral after you leave here. You will work with him to service the sewers until spring . . . or longer, as he sees fit. I have told him to expect you," Jeslek said mildly. "You will not have any more

instruction from me until then. Nor from any other mage except Myral
. . . oh, and Esaak. He has told me you are terribly deficient in your
calculations. Do not bother to try to see the High Wizard . . . about this
or anything else. He and I have already discussed this."

"Yes, ser." Cerryl bowed.

"You have my leave to use your abilities to handle chaos as you
can, but only as directed by Myral—only Myral."

Cerryl waited to see if any other directions were forthcoming.

"And, young Cerryl?"

"Yes, ser?"

"I know you can block your innermost feelings from any mage. So
can I. It is a useful talent, but one best used sparingly. One should not
have too much to hide, especially not a student."

"Yes, ser." What else could he say?

"Think about light while you work in the darkness of the sewers. I
would suggest you think a great deal about it, and do not hesitate to
ask Myral. In such matters, he is a good instructor." Jeslek smiled another of his perfunctory smiles. "You may go. I told Myral to expect you."

"Thank you, ser."

"You are welcome, and some day you may understand exactly how
much. Good day, Cerryl."

Cerryl bowed again before he left.

Almost every time he had met with Jeslek for nearly two seasons,
the mage had unsettled him, and his words this time were no less unsettling. Cerryl walked down the steps and then out of the rear hall into
the courtyard and past the fountain. The wind whipped spray across
him, and it felt like ice on his face.

First, Jeslek had suggested that Kesrik would have used chaos-fire
on Cerryl. Why? Because Cerryl wasn't mage-born? Or from wealthy
parentage? Or for some other reason? Then, Jeslek had implied that
Myral was a good instructor, but not terribly good at other things. But
at what was the balding mage lacking? And finally, Jeslek had flatly
stated that Cerryl owed Jeslek great thanks. For letting Cerryl survive?

The thin-faced young man took a deep breath as he entered the rear
of the front foyer, and several more before he reached the second level
of the white tower.

"Jeslek said to expect you." The older and rotund mage with the
thinning and wispy black hair opened the door before Cerryl could
knock, and gestured for the young man to enter the room.

Myral's quarters were smaller than either Jeslek's or Sterol's, and
one entire wall of the single squarish room was filled with books—
perhaps as many as a third of what was contained in the entire library.
Practically underneath the shuttered windows was a narrow bed, wide

enough for one person, unlike the spacious beds favored by both Sterol and Jeslek. Through the window, Cerryl could see the avenue angling toward the artisans' square.

The wall opposite the bookshelves held two desks and a round table with a screeing glass and four chairs. One of the chairs was occupied— the one on the far side of the screeing glass—by a woman in pale green with red-blonde hair. A large tome lay open before her. Cerryl froze for a moment.

"Ah, you must have seen Leyladin around the halls." Myral made a sweeping gesture from Cerryl to Leyladin as he turned to the young woman. "This is Cerryl. Like you, he does not come from the creche or a magely parent. He was a scrivener's apprentice." The mage smiled, a smile that took in both mouth and eyes. "Now I have to teach him about sewers and wastes."

"It's good to see you here." Leyladin stood, her gaze meeting Cerryl's, a faint and amused smile upon her lips, the hint of a glimmer in her dark green eyes.

"I'm glad to meet you." As he bowed, Cerryl felt she saw right through him, that she knew he'd once screed her through his glass, the glass probably still hidden in the wall at Tellis's place.

"I should go," she said to Myral, stepping away from the table. "Before they—"

"No. This will take but a moment." Myral smiled and turned to Cerryl. "Pay attention to me, if you will, not the young lady."

Cerryl flushed.

"I'm not nearly so gentle to look upon, young Cerryl, but we have work to prepare for."

"Yes, ser."

"Fairhaven has its name for a reason." Myral's voice was high, almost squeaky, and he steepled his fingers, then gestured vaguely in the direction of the door—or the square. "If you travel to most places, they dump their night soil and everything else in the streets, and they stink." The mage wrinkled his nose. "Fairhaven is fair, and one of the tasks before us is to keep it fair . . ."

Myral half-turned toward the books, and Cerryl's eyes strayed again to Leyladin.

Her eyes were so green, like a deep ocean. She pointed to Myral, as if to suggest that Cerryl had best listen.

". . . and we have to work to keep Fairhaven clean. You probably don't know how much work that is. Everyone who has lived here knows some things about keeping a city clean—sewer catches and clean walks—jakes here in the halls and in the greater homes. No rubbish in the streets. The big waste wagons, but much more goes on unseen."

Suddenly, the rotund mage turned and walked over to the book-shelves, pulling out one book, then another and another. He walked back to the table and set five of them down.

"Jeslek says that you read quickly. Can you read these in the next eight-day?"

Cerryl looked at the stack of books, then at the mage. "I think so. If there's not something strange about them."

"Only the subject matter . . . I even wrote one of them." A brief grin followed. "If you can't, come and see me. If you can, study them, and come back here an eight-day from now, immediately after breakfast." Myral paused again. "Study them as if I were Jeslek."

"Yes, ser." Cerryl bowed.

"One other thing." Myral bustled toward the corner of the room, almost behind the white oak door, where he rummaged through a chest of some sort, one with thin drawers that he slid out, one after the other. "Ah . . . this will help."

The white mage rolled a section of vellum into a tube as he headed toward Cerryl. He thrust the tube at Cerryl. Cerryl stepped back as he took it. What was it?

"That? Oh, that's the best map of all the sewers. You need to study that, too. Learn where every sewer runs. You shouldn't have any trouble. Jeslek said you were good with maps. It might help if you took a few walks with it and tried to locate where the main sewers are."

Cerryl felt like he'd been frozen in a different way. First, running into Leyladin, and then being assaulted with a pile of books and a sewer map. A sewer map, for darkness's sake!

"An eight-day from now," Myral said cheerfully as he piled the books into Cerryl's arms. "Best get on with it."

His arms full, Cerryl nodded toward Leyladin. "It was good to meet you."

"I was glad to see you." She smiled an enigmatic and faint smile. "More closely." The green eyes sparkled.

Suppressing a wince at the gentle reminder, Cerryl nodded to her again and to Myral. "An eight-day from now, ser."

The door closed behind him with a *thunk*.

He walked slowly down the stairs, his arms already beginning to ache with the weight of the books and the rolled map, his thoughts spinning. What was Leyladin doing with Myral? It wasn't conclusive, but the pudgy mage had but a single bed, and there had been an open tome on the table.

You hope she's just studying . . . but what can you do if it's more?

And why had she wanted to leave when he'd come in? Or said that she was glad to meet him—more closely? Had that just been a jab, or had she meant it?

He tried to shift his grip on the books and staggered against the wall in an effort to keep his hold on the map.

A sewer map? What was he going to be doing with Myral? What did books have to do with sewers? Or sewers with becoming a white mage?

Another form of test?

LIX

In the late afternoon, with gray light falling through the library windows, Cerryl rubbed his forehead, forcing himself to concentrate on the words on the vellum.

... the heavy greases, be they cooking tallow or renderer's leavings or ... reform in a weak order upon exposure to heat or chaos or heat created by the chaos within chaos-rich wastes ... such scattered blocks of order combine with detritus of a less solid nature to impede the flow of fluids necessary for evacuation ...

He'd thought the histories and the philosophizing of *Colors of White* had been boring and difficult to follow, but they were transparently clear compared to Myral's *The Management of Offal*. The book wasn't even that long, less than a hundred pages. He continued reading and turned the page.

... odoriferous as they may appear, night soil and animal droppings retain but a weak order and will dissolve in the presence of water into a liquid which can be purified through the application of simple techniques ... "

"Cerryl?"

He looked up. Faltar and Lyasa stood by the library table.

"Didn't you hear the bells?"

"The bells?" Even as he asked, he felt stupid. He knew he sounded stupid.

"Those are Myral's books, aren't they?" Lyasa pointed to the volumes by his elbow. "The ones on wastes and offal?"

Cerryl nodded.

"How long have you had them?" she asked.

"Since yesterday." Cerryl massaged his forehead again, this time with his left hand, then the back of his neck, trying to work out the tension.

"How many years did it take Myral to write them?" Lyasa demanded.

Faltar offered an ironic smile.

"He only wrote one. This one." Cerryl glanced from Faltar to the dark-haired student.

"It's the same thing." Lyasa's voice bore a tinge of exasperation. "It took him years to figure it out enough to write it, and you're trying to learn it all in a day."

"I only have an eight-day."

"You have an eight-day to read it—not learn it word by word."

"Cerryl has to know it better than anyone . . . even Myral," said Faltar.

"Says who?"

"Cerryl," answered the blond student mage.

"You two." Lyasa glared at Faltar, then at Cerryl. "Let's go eat."

Cerryl stood, feeling his muscles twinge. How long had he reading?

"Too long," answered Faltar.

Lyasa had already left the common by the time Cerryl scooped up the books from the table and started down the corridor toward the meal hall. He stopped by his cell and quickly set the books on the desk.

"Why do you have to learn everything as quickly as you do?" asked Faltar as Cerryl stepped back into the corridor.

"This is the first place where I've ever been supposed to learn, and . . . I don't know." Cerryl looked down at the polished stone floor tiles, glad he didn't have to scrub floors any longer.

"Why did the scrivener take you on? I mean . . ."

"I was a mill boy without any learning?" Cerryl nodded. "I got the millmaster's daughter to teach me my letters and help me. She gave me books, both in the old tongue and in Temple. They're really not that different."

"You taught yourself to read?" Faltar shook his head.

"There wasn't anyone else." Cerryl glanced around the meal hall, only half-occupied because the full mages ate there intermittently. Kesrik was at a corner table, apparently being lectured by Fydel about something, because his face was more sullen than usual. Lyasa was at the serving table. "And I didn't do it alone. I did have help."

"Darkness," hissed Faltar. "It's the lemon lamb."

The lemon lamb was fine with Cerryl, but he nodded. "It could be worse."

"Cheese in the sewer? It would take that. Oh . . . sorry . . . it'll be my turn next, I suppose."

"You haven't done sewer duty?" Cerryl took a large serving of the lamb and a chunk of dark bread and a too-firm pearapple—none of which showed signs of chaos, and probably never would, but the habit he'd developed early had stayed with him.

"Some people get it early, some late, some—like Kesrik—get it more than once." Faltar took a smaller helping of stew, nearly half a loaf of the dark bread, and two pearapples.

"Kesrik's had two times on sewer duty?"

"That I know of. They say Kinowin did four as a student, and Eliasar three."

Cerryl frowned. The big mage had done sewer duty four times? The arms mage three times?

Faltar inclined his head toward the round table where Lyasa sat alone, and Cerryl followed him.

"I see you two finally got hungry." The black-haired young woman looked up as they sat down.

"For lemon lamb?" Faltar broke off a chunk of bread, then took a swallow of the light ale. "For this I should hurry?"

"Try neruada sometime." Lyasa smiled.

"Neruada?" asked Cerryl.

"Marinated goat stomach stuffed with spices and greenery."

Faltar mock-glared at her. "Lemon lamb is bad enough."

Cerryl laughed.

"It's not funny," Faltar protested, trying to keep from smiling.

Lyasa smoothed her face into a serious expression. "Is the poor student mage so sour that he cannot withstand the additional sourness of even a tender lamb?"

Faltar half-coughed, then choked and sputtered out fragments of bread.

Cerryl grinned even as he ducked.

After he recovered, Faltar took a sip of the ale and glared at Lyasa. "I will *never* say an unkind word about lamb. Ever." He paused. "Until it's served again."

"It could be old mutton." Lyasa shook her head.

Cerryl took a healthy mouthful of the lamb, being careful not to look at Faltar. He didn't want to start laughing and choke, too.

"So . . . you're starting on the sewers?" Lyasa looked down at her empty platter. "I was hungry."

"Interesting phrasing there." Faltar's voice was dry.

Lyasa flushed. "You're . . ."

"Difficult."

Cerryl swallowed quickly.

"You are. You know you are. Wait until you get in the sewers, Faltar."

"Scrivener's apprentice going to get his whites all dirty . . ." Bealtur's voice drifted across the room from where he sat at the same table with Heralt. The diffident Heralt continued to eat without speaking.

"Let him talk," said Lyasa quietly. "He doesn't understand."

Cerryl didn't, either, but wasn't about to admit it. He broke off another chunk of bread.

"You still suffering with Esaak?" asked Faltar.

"Yes. I still have to study mathematicks, even while I'm working with Myral." Cerryl grimaced.

"Numbers and sewers and offal . . . numbers and sewers and offal . . ." offered Faltar in a whispered chant, grinning broadly.

"Enough." But Lyasa grinned.

So did Cerryl, even as he wondered about the sewers.

LX

A narrow cooper's wagon rolled by, carrying but three large barrels, less than three cubits from where Cerryl stood on the west side of the avenue, his white leather jacket unfastened. The driver flicked the reins, careful not to look directly at Cerryl, and the single horse half-*whuffed*, half-sighed.

After the wagon passed, Cerryl turned the map, frowning, trying to hold it against the wind and study the tracery of black and purple and red lines. The two main sewers, the ones that collected wastes from all the others, mostly followed the avenue, each along an alleyway about a hundred cubits back from the avenue. The map showed sewers in three sizes, and from what Cerryl could deduce, there were large tunnels with walkways, smaller tunnels, and then a scattering of covered brick ditches.

Cerryl grinned as he looked from the map to the granite paving stones, and then to the large houses on the east side of the avenue— perched almost above the large sewer tunnels. Then he nodded. Of

course, those with coins got the best waste disposal and the best roads
and were closest to the market and the artisans, and even the grain
exchange.

He walked farther north, past the market square, finding his mouth
watering as the smell of roasting fowl was carried to him on the midday
wind that also held a hint of rain to come. Overhead, thin but dark gray
clouds scudded southward.

"... spices for the winter ... spices for late harvest ..."

"... best roots in Candar ... turnips, beets ... get your roots
here ..."

"Baskets, baskets for storage ..."

Cerryl lurched as a sudden gust of wind jerked at the map, almost
dragging him off the curbstone and into the avenue itself. Since the way
was clear, he rerolled the map and walked across the south side of the
market area.

A girl, perhaps the age of Serai, Pattera's sister, walked around a
blue cart displaying woven blankets, still looking over her shoulder. Her
head turned, and she swallowed as she saw the white jacket and trousers. Before Cerryl could say a word, she ducked back behind the cart.

"A blanket, young ser? A fine white blanket?"

Cerryl shook his head and, rolled map in hand, continued across
the square. He almost stopped at the cart where a thin man roasted
fowl, but thought about the few coppers left in his purse and kept walking. Too bad he had left his silvers behind at Tellis's. Once in a while
he missed them and wondered if he would ever see that much coin
again, but he felt the absence of the amulet more.

He supposed Kesrik would call him stupid for not caring more
about the silvers, but there was little he could do. The Guild had told
Tellis that all Cerryl left belonged to the scrivener, and Cerryl couldn't
very well show up in Tellis's showroom and ask for his silvers back.

After reaching the other side of the square and crossing the eastern
section of the avenue, he headed north again and into the jewelers' row.
Because of the wind, all the doors were closed, but the shutters were
open—enough to show that the metalsmiths were present for any customers.

He paused before a goldsmith's shop with gold-trimmed green
shutters and checked the sewer map again, standing close to the white-
painted bricks of the wall to keep the wind from grabbing the map.
From what he could tell, the main sewers had been built farther from
the avenue north of the market square.

Another gust of wind—colder—whipped around him. When it subsided, he studied the map again, then walked north to the first side

street, where he turned eastward, in the general direction of Nivor's—
the apothecary's—looking for the heavy bronze grill that marked an
access grate to the main sewer tunnel.

The grate was almost flush with the wall of a fuller's shop. Cerryl's
eyes—and senses—noted the chaos bound into the large white-bronze
lock that secured the grate, a square about two cubits on each side.

With his own senses, he could make out a set of narrow brick steps
disappearing into the darkness below. He could also sense that—
again—someone was following him with a glass.

The wind rose, more steadily, and a few drops of something damp
wet the back of his neck. He turned and looked up. The clouds were
thicker, and intermittent white flakes flew by his face. He could sense
the beginning of the headache that always seemed to come with rain or
snow.

Cerryl fastened his jacket and started back toward the tower, half-
wondering who was following him with a glass—and why.

LXI

Cerryl stepped into Myral's quarters, dim in the morning despite two
lit wall lamps. Sleet clicked against the closed shutters, and the shutters
rattled. He could feel a draft around his legs until he closed the door
from the tower landing. His head throbbed slightly, but it always did
during storms.

"Ah . . . a warm winter day in Fairhaven." Myral wrapped the white
wool blanket around his shoulders but remained seated on one side of
the table. He gestured to the seat directly across from him.

Cerryl sat.

"How did you find the books?"

"I read them, but I'm certain I didn't understand everything." Cerryl paused. "I'm sure I didn't."

"I'm not sure I understand everything there, and I wrote one of
them." Myral lifted a mug from which steam drifted upward into the
chill air of the room and took a sip. "You're being put on sewer duty
earlier than most students. Do you know why?"

"No, ser . . . unless it's because I was a scrivener's apprentice." The
remaining draft seeping through the shutters chilled the back of Cerryl's
legs, even through the thick white trousers. He shifted his weight in the
hard wooden chair, smelling the warm cider in the older mage's mug.

"That is one reason. We'll get to the other in a bit." Myral took another sip of the cider. "The important thing to remember is that Fairhaven is what it is because it is an ordered city." Myral smiled blandly at Cerryl. "I use the word 'ordered' advisedly, but it's not something that should be discussed outside the Guild." He paused. "Or even within the Guild, except with me, or if Sterol or Jeslek should bring it up. Never with anyone else."

"Yes, ser."

Myral raised his eyebrows. "There is a difference between thoughts and words. Don't forget that."

"No, ser."

"Just like a healthy person, a healthy city must have nourishment, a functioning structure or body, fresh clean water, and a way to get rid of wastes. The aqueducts supply the water, and the sewers take away the wastes, and the Guild is there to ensure that the rest of the city's structure works. Are you surprised that the Guild is the White Order?"

"Ah . . ." Cerryl wasn't surprised, and he wasn't unsurprised.

"You've had to worry about more pressing needs. I imagine you worried more about food than the place of the Guild. That's one reason why Sterol bent the guidelines to admit you." Myral smiled. "As for order . . . most of the Guild doesn't like to admit it, and they're not exactly pleased to accord some recognition to the blacks. They'll do what they can . . . but you can't separate order and chaos and survive."

Cerryl nodded, not knowing what Myral expected.

"That is enough philosophizing for now. Starting tomorrow, or the day after, if the storm doesn't clear, you are going to be cleaning sewers and finding places in them that need to be repaired. There are several things you need to keep in mind in the sewers." Myral's tone was dry. "First, look both up and down. People don't look when they open their sewer catches. And the brick, even on the walkways, can crumble or get slimy."

Cerryl sat silently. Cleaning sewers? That was sewer duty?

"Also . . . you'll be accompanied by lancers—it's disciplinary duty for them . . . so what kind of guard you get . . ." The older mage shrugged.

Guards in the sewers? Cerryl moistened his lips.

"We do our best to keep the sewers for offal and sewage . . . that's one reason why the sewer catches are so small. We don't want people shoving larger wastes, like branches or bodies, into the sewers." Myral grimaced. "We still find bodies—usually children—and then we have to try to find who killed them. I'll get into that later. If you find a body right now, leave it and send a messenger for me."

Guards and bodies? What lurked in the sewers? The door to the tower stairs rattled, and Cerryl's eyes followed the sound before he turned back to concentrate on Myral.

"Branches and any sort of rubbish that doesn't reflect a crime—it's up to you to dispose of it as you clean the tunnel and the walkway."

Cerryl frowned. "With chaos-force, ser?"

"How else?" Myral offered a broad smile. "How else indeed? You can certainly call it forth." A brief shadow crossed Myral's face, so brief Cerryl wasn't sure he had seen it. "It crackles around you. You see, Cerryl, those with the talent to handle chaos are blessed and cursed. Someone who *might* be a black mage would not suffer should he choose not to use his talent. That is not true of someone with the talent to handle the white force of chaos. Chaos is so powerful that it must be guided and disciplined. If it is not, it will destroy anyone with the talent to channel it. It cannot be ignored. In time, it will destroy even those of us with discipline."

Myral's face turned from an ironic smile to a somber mien. "One either masters chaos, or it masters one. We cannot afford to have even one undisciplined chaos focus in Candar."

Cerryl did not know what to say. He waited.

"You wonder—all young mages wonder—why the Guild suffers no one to survive who is not bound by its disciplines. Are we that power-mad? Are we so insecure that anyone who defies us must be destroyed?" A sadness crossed the round face, and Myral brushed back a lock of wispy black hair, carefully, to cover part of his balding pate. "I fear for the time when there is no Guild, no discipline."

How could there not be a Guild? Cerryl shifted his weight and glanced toward the window, but the closed shutters blocked the view of the avenue stretching northward toward the artisans' square.

"All things pass, young Cerryl, and the Guild will also, as will Fairhaven, and mad chaos-wielders will roam Candar, for the mad attain their powers more quickly." Myral shook his head. "This I have seen . . . but it will be many generations." He reached for the pitcher and poured still steaming cider into the other mug and extended it to the younger man. "I have been remiss, and the room is draft-ridden."

Cerryl sipped the hot cider gratefully.

"What has this meandering of an old mage to do with the sewers?" The sadness vanished with a forced smile. "The sewers are where you all learn to wield and control chaos-force. If you fail, only you suffer."

Cerryl could see that.

"There are two aspects to sewer duty—three if you count maintenance, but there your job is to protect the masons. You must learn to bring forth chaos-force under control, and you must learn to develop a shield against that force—either that which you raise or that raised by others.

"The greatest mages—not the most heralded but the greatest—are those with the strongest shields. I'll leave it to you to figure out why."

All of the mages did that—they left puzzles for the students to figure out. Was that an ongoing test, or just because they were busy doing other things?

"You are *not* to attempt shielding or raising chaos-force anywhere except in the sewers or when directed by me or an overmage."

"Are overmages the ones with the sunbursts?"

"Do you know why none of you are told that? Because the Guild doesn't care much for hotheads." Myral nodded, almost to himself. "Caution is called for when handling chaos." Myral smiled. "Did you know that Anya was sent to scare you?"

"To see if I would flee?"

"And Kinowin was given instructions to let you have the illusion that you *might* be able to escape. He didn't like that."

Cerryl felt half vindicated, half dazed.

"The sewers will be harder than that." Myral lifted the steaming cider. "To a warmer tomorrow."

Cerryl lifted his own mug, inclining his head to the rotund mage, knowing there was little else he could do.

LXII

Under the clear skies and with the bright sun on his back, Cerryl still felt cold because of the chill wind that blew out of the northwest, almost into his face. He and Myral walked westward on the side avenue, followed by two of the white guards.

Next to a blank white granite wall—the side wall of a warehouse of some sort—Myral stopped and knelt by the bronze sewer grate. The older mage fumbled with his purse before extracting a large bronze key.

"Cerryl."

Cerryl bent down.

"Watch what I do with the key. Use your senses."

Cerryl could sense a point of chaos within the heavy bronze lock, and he watched as a darkness built up around the lock before Myral turned the key and opened it.

"Lift the grate."

Cerryl struggled and lifted the grate, discovering that it opened on a pair of hidden hinge pins nearly as thick as his wrists.

"Swing it back against the wall."

When the grate was against the wall, another bronze ring protruding from the building wall extended through the bars of the grate. Myral relocked the grate in the open position and returned the key to his purse. The two guards stood back from the square opening.

"Did you see what I did?"

"You did something with darkness there."

"Exactly." Myral smiled. "All sewer locks are charged with chaos. I'll explain in a moment." He turned to the guards. "Remain here until we return."

"Yes, ser." The older and grizzle-bearded armsman nodded.

Myral stepped onto the top stair within the circular opening and started downward.

Cerryl glanced over his shoulder, back at the bronze grate that Myral had locked open, and at the pair of white lancers guarding the entrance to the main sewer tunnel. A faint smile crossed the lips of the taller and younger guard, then vanished.

Looking back down, Cerryl followed the older mage into the darkness barely lit by the oil lamp Myral carried down the narrow and unrailed brick staircase. Their boots clicked on the hard bricks.

The first odors—a mixture of barnyard and fish and rotten meat, or worse—almost gagged Cerryl.

"You'll get used to it," Myral called back over his shoulder.

Never . . . I hope not. Cerryl swallowed and kept heading downward, trying not to think about the source of the foulness.

At the bottom of the stairs, Myral took several more steps before he turned and waited.

The main sewer was a square tunnel of red glazed bricks whose braced and squared granite arches were a good two cubits above Cerryl's head as he stood at the foot of the narrow staircase. On the left side was a walkway, about two cubits wide, except where the cubit-wide stairs descended. To the right of the walkway was the drainage way that carried the sewage, the surface of the turbid waters another cubit or so below the walkway.

"In storms, the waters can rise halfway up the staircase." Myral paused, then added, "You don't work in the sewers during heavy rains."

The younger man looked back at the stairs, imagining all that filthy water rushing through the tunnels.

"The secondary sewers are just tall enough to walk in—sometimes—

and the collectors for them are little more than covered and glazed brick trenches anywhere from one to two cubits square."

Cerryl decided not to ask how he was supposed to clean the collectors.

"You won't be working the collectors to begin with. You'll start on the secondaries once I'm sure you can handle the work. Now . . . we'll go a little farther, until the walkway starts to get slimy. It doesn't take long down here."

A dozen cubits or so farther from the stairs, Myral halted. "I'm going to demonstrate how to use chaos to clean away the filth. Watch me, with your eyes and your senses."

As the mage turned back toward the darkness, Cerryl could sense the buildup of chaos, a white unseen fire that seemed to flicker around the older mage, yet behind the white of chaos was a dark mist, a dilute blackness, the same as Myral had used with the lock, except there was more of it.

Whhhssttt! A line of flame splashed across the bricks of the walkway. Where there had been green-and-black slime there now were only powdery white dust and clean bricks.

"What did you sense?"

"A black mist and chaos force beyond it, going away."

"The black was an order shield. Unless held back, chaos force will expand equally in all directions. That's why people seldom unlock the sewer grates. Someone usually dies if they do."

"You pack chaos into the lock?"

"People would be using the sewers for everything if we didn't. Now watch again."

Once more, Myral repeated the process, and Cerryl tried to capture the feel of it, the constriction and the release as the chaos-fire arced away from the older mage, leaving another circle of clean brick, perhaps a cubit in diameter.

"You see?"

"I think so."

Myral turned to Cerryl. A tip of flame flickered on his index finger. "We'll start with the shield. Try to replicate the black mist. Squeeze the flame up into a thin line."

Cerryl concentrated. Nothing. Why was he trying to control Myral's chaos force?

"No. Order is not an absence of chaos. Try this. If chaos is fire, flaming where it will, order is ice. You have seen snowflakes, have you not?"

"Yes, ser." Hot in the tunnel despite the cold wind above, Cerryl wiped his forehead.

"If you look at a snowflake, each one is an ordered pattern, a repeating lattice."

Cerryl didn't know what to say.

Myral blotted his forehead, streaming sweat, with the back of his sleeve. Then he sighed. "Pure chaos has no pattern, only power. Pure order is like death or ice, with a perfect structure and no life. Think about a pattern, any pattern. Build it in your mind—a net, a web, a lattice . . ."

Cerryl nodded.

". . . and pattern it around the chaos." Myral continued to sweat as the chaos-flame danced on his fingertip.

The second time, the student mage created the image of a black net, shrinking around the chaos-fire. He blinked as the point of chaos-fire winked out.

"Again." This time Myral manifested a brighter line of fire, bright enough that Cerryl could see the rivulets of sweat streaming down the older mage's face.

Cerryl put his mind back to the dark net—and the light vanished.

"Good. You try it. The *smallest* amount of chaos-fire you can raise. The very smallest."

Cerryl obeyed, trying to form a candle tip of white fire just above his upraised index finger.

The faintest point of light appeared.

"Good. Now . . . try to use order to move it away from you."

Cerryl managed the black lattice mist—and the chaos-fire flicked out. So did the lamp Myral held.

"Order may be harder to hold than chaos," said Myral dryly, "but it is stronger than most white mages realize." The lamp flickered back to life, sparked by a touch of chaos-fire. "Unless they've already run into one of the blacks from Recluce."

Cerryl wiped his forehead, realizing that even the small efforts asked by Myral were tiring. "If order is so strong, why did Creslin leave Candar? I've always wondered . . ."

"And were afraid to ask?" Myral laughed gently. "If the accounts are halfway correct, he was the greatest weather mage ever known and possibly the greatest blade of his time. Yet he ran. Is that what you're asking?"

Cerryl nodded just the slightest bit.

"Because the man had brains, young Cerryl. He'd offended the Guild, with reason . . . How many mages are there in the Guild?"

"I don't know."

"Good. How many do you know?"

"I've seen close to a score, maybe even twice that. I'm not sure."

"And how many mages supported Creslin?"

"One—Megaera."

"Actually, there were two other blacks at first, but it doesn't matter. Would you have stayed in Candar with fivescore times your number of mages seeking you, and all the armsmen east of the Westhorns seeking your head for a price?"

"Oh . . ."

"He was smart. An isle is about the only place that could have stopped that many white mages—all that water, and, worse for poor Jenred, he picked an isle with an iron core." Myral shook his head. "This history isn't improving your handling of chaos-force. A stronger touch of chaos—just a little stronger, mind you."

Cerryl let more chaos-force glimmer from his fingers, until it exuded enough light to match the lamp. Then . . . slowly, he wove his black net around it, turning it into a long glowing taper.

"Now . . . push the force away from you, toward the bricks on the side of the tunnel or the walkway."

Cerryl tried . . . and the wormlike chaos-fire flopped onto the bricks almost at his feet.

Whsst.

"It's harder to propel it away from you. That's why you need to work on the shield first. You can get burned by your own fire."

Cerryl glanced at the small patch of ash and clean brick beneath.

"Chaos-fire is hard on boots—and toes." Myral's voice took on the dry tone again.

The student mage swallowed.

"Again. You need to keep practicing until you hardly have to think about what you're doing."

Cerryl wiped his forehead with the back of his hand, then took a deep breath. He had the feeling the day was going to be long—very long.

LXIII

Cerryl took the large brass key that Myral had entrusted to him, and placed it in the lock, letting the black order rise and gently restrain the chaos-fire that would have burst forth if without the restraint—or order shield.

Order—just to use chaos. The strangeness of it still struck him, almost with a shiver, a shiver compounded by the distinctly foul odor rising from the tunnel below the grate.

"Bad one down there . . ." murmured one of the guards.

"They're all bad when they need to be cleaned," answered Jyantyl, the head guard of the detachment.

Once Cerryl had lifted the grate and relocked both the bronze lock and its chaos force, he turned to the senior guard.

"Jyantyl, I don't know how long this will take." *Is that a true statement!*

"Me and Shelkar will stand by here." A smile followed. "Usually, a season or so. Most give the guards a midday break, and they need it as well."

Cerryl nodded, thankful for the combined reminder and hint.

The other two guards, Ullan and Dientyr, followed Cerryl down the narrow steps to the secondary sewer tunnel. Cerryl almost slipped on the bottom step.

"Hold it."

"Yes, ser." As Ullan stopped, his lance scraped the fired and glazed brick of the wall.

Cerryl looked down at the green slime on the bottom two steps, then at the tunnel. The gray-and-black mass in the drainage way bobbed up and down gently, within a half-span of the walkway. The tunnel walls were coated with slime up to a good three cubits above the water level.

Something was partly blocking the sewer—somewhere.

First things first. He turned. "Ullan . . . back up a little. I need to clean these steps."

The dark-haired lancer guard nodded, the ends of his twig-thin mustache fluttering as he did. He and the sandy-haired Dientyr stepped back up to street level.

Cerryl backed up three steps and looked down. He took a deep breath and concentrated, first on raising the black shield mist and then on pushing forth the chaos-fire.

Whhhssst . . . A glob of fire half-floated, half-fell onto the third step from the bottom and oozed across the two steps below it. Points of fire sparked as the chaos lit scraps of wood or something. Cerryl could feel the residual heat wash over his legs, despite his boots and heavy white trousers.

Darkness, what a sloppy firebolt . . .

In a moment, the steps held only powdered white ashes that sifted off the glazed bricks.

Cerryl took another breath and mustered another shield and more chaos-fire.

This time his firebolt was larger and cleared the walkway for perhaps three cubits. Cerryl stepped down onto the walkway, trying not to gag at the stench that enfolded him.

He glanced at the side of the tunnel by the steps, then repressed a sigh. *Everything* needed fire-scouring. Everything.

As he turned to the wall beside the steps, a gurgling and bubbling came from the drainage way, and he glanced back in time to see a gas bubble pop out of the dark green fuzz on top of the wastewater.

For a moment, he felt he couldn't breathe, and he quickly jumped up two steps and took a gasp of air, glad he hadn't loosed any chaos-fire when the gas bubble had burst.

He shook his head and raised order and chaos-fire again, clearing the tunnel wall. He stepped down to the tunnel and glanced toward the drainage way.

Then he climbed back up the stairs.

". . . up and down . . . up and down . . ."

"Shut up, Ullan . . . be glad it's him and not you. Some'd have you down there in front of him, and you'd not last so long as clean air down there."

Cerryl ignored the byplay and, from halfway up the steps, dropped a firebolt onto the green-and-gray scum-fuzz on top of the wastewater.

Crumpt . . . umpt . . . ump . . .

A line of fire and a series of little explosions ran in both directions from the chaos-fire impact. After a moment, white ash sprayed across the secondary sewage tunnel below, some rising on hot sewer air and gas into the cooler fresh air of the street above.

". . . ugh . . ."

"Ullan," warned Jyantyl.

Cerryl already felt tired, and he'd barely cleared the area around the tunnel entrance. A gust of cold air swirled around him and mixed with the fetid sewer atmosphere.

He stepped down to the walkway. Bits of white ash covered the thick-looking wastewater, but the green-and-gray scum-fuzz had disappeared. Burned off? Cerryl didn't know. More reading, he supposed.

Another firebolt brought more clear walkway bricks. He glanced at the drainage way. Was the wastewater level slightly lower? Had the scum he'd burned off slowed the flow down?

Slowly he walked another half-dozen paces into the darkness, though he could sense things well enough. Something protruded from the drainage way, not a great deal, perhaps a half cubit above the water level, and he thought the water level was lower on the other side. A rubbish buildup?

With a half-shrug, he lofted another firebolt onto whatever it was that rose out of the drainage way.

A burst of flame flared into the tunnel, then subsided, and the protuberance vanished with a gurgling sound. Then another gurgling sound rose, and the water level in the drainage way began to drop.

"Why here?" Then he looked back toward the stairs and the grate above. Of course some good citizen of Fairhaven had probably disposed of something through the bars—something he hadn't wanted to bring to the refuse wagon.

Cerryl wanted to shake his head. Whatever it had been, he'd just destroyed it.

His eyes went to the drainage way, now down to what he thought was a more normal level, and back along the next dozen cubits of walkway that he had yet to clean.

He mustered another firebolt, scouring half the distance to what he'd cleaned previously, but his head was beginning to ache, like it did in a storm, and skies were clear.

How could he direct enough fire to clean anything? He leaned against the just-cleaned tunnel wall for a moment.

Light . . . light . . . Myral kept talking about light. So had Jeslek. That had to be something about it, something he needed to think about . . . if he ever had time and energy.

"Ullan, you and Dientyr can come down now." His voice sounded ragged, but he turned toward the darkness and slime ahead.

LXIV

Cerryl rapped on the door to Myral's tower quarters. Almost immediately, he felt the sense of being watched in a glass.

"Come on in, Cerryl."

As the sense of being scanned vanished, the student mage opened the door and entered, closing it behind him firmly. "I'm here, as you requested, ser."

"Yes, you are here. That's good." Myral stood from the chair by the round table. "It means that you got the lock open and closed. I would have heard if you hadn't gotten that far. Jyantyl also would have reported if you hadn't been able to clean anything." The round-faced mage pointed to the chair. "Have a seat. You'll be on your feet all day. Would you like some hot cider?"

"Yes, please." Cerryl waited until Myral poured another mug of the steaming liquid and had reseated himself. He could see the faintest of white chaos residue around Myral, far less than he sensed around Jeslek or Sterol. *Do other mages sense that around you?*

"You were up in the old tanners' section, along the old warehouses."

Cerryl nodded, taking a quick sip of the spiced cider, so much better than the water or ale that were the morning choices in the meal hall.

"It's been a while since it's been scoured. How was it?"

"The drainage way was clogged, not more than a dozen cubits from the steps." Cerryl managed another sip, despite the heat of the beverage.

"That happens a lot. People push things through the grates. The rubbish flows some distance, sometimes quite a distance, before it catches on something and creates a block." Myral cocked his head slightly. "Did you find out what it was?"

"No, ser. I didn't figure that out until I saw something sticking out of the scum and fired it. Then it was too late."

"It burned, I take it."

"The scum burned off and so did whatever jammed the drainage way."

"It could have been worse. You can get quite a jolt if you hit polished iron or steel and you're not expecting it. Quite a jolt." Myral fingered his bearded chin thoughtfully. "Have you reached that cluster of third-level inlets on the south side?"

"No, ser."

"How far did you get?"

"Not very far, ser. Yesterday, I'd guess maybe forty cubits. The slime was almost shoulder high on the walls."

"That secondary hasn't been thoroughly cleaned in three or four years, I believe. The cluster should be another fifty cubits or so beyond where you are now. When you get there, spend some time cleaning the inlets as far back as you can press with your chaos-fire."

"How far should I be able to reach?"

Myral shrugged. "You have just begun to handle chaos-fire. I don't have any idea. You ought to be able to press it fifteen or twenty cubits back, and the steam should clean it even farther. You can use the steam to your advantage, you know? Block the conduit with your shield, and the steam can only go the other way."

"Ah . . . yes, ser. I hadn't thought of that." How much else hadn't he thought about?

"You'll learn. You have to do things to learn." Myral smiled politely and stood. "Oh, there's one other thing I forgot to tell you. Never use all the chaos force you have."

Cerryl nodded.

"No. I mean it. You can feel the force build up within you, right? Before you release it?"

"Yes, ser, in a way."

"If you spray out everything each time, you get tired quickly. Also, unless you're like Jeslek—with so much power to spare that it doesn't matter—you'll find that your ability to handle chaos diminishes over time."

"Won't holding chaos back . . . ?" Cerryl wasn't certain exactly what he wanted to say.

"Mayhap . . . I didn't say that as well as I could have. Use the force you have, but don't strain. Don't try to push that last bit out that you may not have."

That made more sense.

"Well, best you get to work. Stop by tomorrow—every morning, in fact—and give me a report."

"Yes, ser." Cerryl stood.

"Think about what you do. Do not just act." Myral inclined his head toward the door.

Cerryl nodded and left, closing the door behind him and starting down the stairs, then pausing as he heard boots coming up from below.

He stepped back up to the landing as a blonde-haired figure in green appeared. "Good morning." He eased to one side of the landing to give the green-eyed young woman access to Myral's door.

"Good day." Leyladin smiled pleasantly but made no move to enter Myral's quarters or to continue up the steps.

Cerryl felt tongue-tied, wanting to say something but not knowing what he could say—or dared to say. Finally, he forced a smile and said, "Good day." He headed down the steps, conscious of her eyes on his back, wishing he had said something more profound—or less banal.

He'd dreamed of her for years, and all he could say was "Good day." He looked back up the steps, but she had gone into Myral's quarters. He took a deep breath. He had sewers to clean.

LXV

Cerryl trudged down the corridor toward his cell, feeling that his shirt, tunic, and trousers smelled of sewer, even though he'd washed thoroughly and brushed the surface of his garments with the hint of chaos-fire before redonning them—a trick he'd picked up from watching Myral. Then maybe the smell of sewage was too deeply imbedded in his nostrils for one stop in the washroom to rid him of it.

He'd been working nearly an eight-day on the one secondary sewer, and he'd cleaned the space between two access grates—all of perhaps three hundred cubits, more or less. The section he'd worked on had only a handful of small collectors entering it, and that was fine because he wasn't very good at pushing chaos force away from himself and through the buried small glazed brick conduits. The slime and grime were coated on the brick walls more than half a handspan thick in some places, and Cerryl had to wonder when the collector had last been scoured.

He didn't stop by his cell, knowing he was close to being late for the evening meal. As he stopped outside the meal hall, he felt again— as he had more and more frequently—that someone was watching him in a glass. But who?

He squared his shoulders and stepped into the room, glancing around and seeing Faltar and Lyasa at one of the round center tables. Lyasa was the one who motioned for him to join them.

". . . the sewer student . . . say he's spent an eight-day between two grates—two nearby grates." Kesrik looked up and smiled blandly. Beside the stocky blond sat a redheaded youth in a new student mage's tunic, the red stripes at the end of the sleeves bright and fresh. On the other side of the new student sat Bealtur.

Cerryl smiled back at Kesrik and continued toward the serving table. His stomach growled after the long day.

". . . be a long year for him." Bealtur didn't bother to look in Cerryl's direction.

". . . supposed to clean at least one collector all the way," murmured Kesrik. "At least one."

Myral hadn't mentioned that; he'd just told Cerryl to clean it out as well as he could and stop by every morning to report on his progress.

Every morning, the rotund mage had answered Cerryl's few questions and repeated the same instructions, not appearing either pleased or displeased.

Cerryl concentrated on filling his platter with stewed fowl, still checking for chaos in the food and finding none. Then he stepped toward the table with Faltar and Lyasa.

"They say you're having a hard time of it," Faltar said quietly as Cerryl slipped onto the stool.

"Trying to . . ." Cerryl paused, wondering if he should even mention the means. "Yes, it's hard, harder than I would have thought." He took a bite out of the hot crusty bread.

"No one has an easy time in the sewers," said Lyasa. "I didn't."

". . . finding that out . . ." mumbled Cerryl, finding himself gobbling down his food.

"It takes a lot of energy, and you're going to be eating a great deal more."

Faltar glanced from Cerryl to Lyasa.

"It just does," said Lyasa. "You'll see."

Cerryl would have smiled, if he hadn't had a mouthful of stewed fowl, at the way Lyasa also avoided mentioning the use of chaos-fire.

"It's hard work, and I imagine Cerryl got the filthiest secondary in the system." Lyasa popped a last morsel of bread into her mouth.

Faltar brushed blond hair off his forehead. "You two are keeping secrets. I can tell."

"When you go to work on the sewers, you can judge that." Lyasa turned to Cerryl. "Did you know that the Council has worked out a trade agreement with both Certis and Sligo?"

Cerryl decided that Lyasa wasn't just changing the subject, but thought he should know about the trade agreement, not that he knew anything about trade. "And? The way you say that means there's something unusual about it."

"They've put a tax on goods from Recluce—wool mostly, I'd guess."

That didn't help Cerryl much.

"We don't need their wool," said Faltar. "Montgren has plenty of sheep."

"Spidlar doesn't. Gallos doesn't. Kyphros does, but not northern Gallos."

Cerryl broke off a chunk of the still-warm bread, then took a sip of the ale. "That should mean something."

"Geography . . ." suggested Lyasa.

Cerryl mentally called up the map Jeslek had required. "Gallos doesn't have any ports—except Ruzor, and that's a long way from Fenard."

"The south is Kyphros. It may be part of Gallos, but the Kyphrans don't think so. Anyway, Ruzor's no good except for the south, and they don't need wool there anyway, not a lot. Besides, the Analerians have their own sheep." Lyasa shrugged, as if the implications were obvious. "Sterol and Jeslek both spoke in the meeting . . . that's what I overheard."

"They're worried about Recluce."

"Cerryl, the Guild has been worried about Recluce since the time of Creslin and Jenred the Traitor." Faltar laughed, then turned to Lyasa. "What about Recluce?"

Lyasa lifted her shoulders again, then dropped them. "I don't know. Not for sure, but the prefect of Gallos doesn't listen much to Sverlik, and the Spidlarian Traders' Council has never allowed a white mage into Spidlaria. Not in years, anyway."

"Trouble in the west, then?" asked Cerryl. "With the traders preferring to use the sea and Recluce?"

"And not to pay road taxes to Fairhaven," suggested Faltar.

"I don't know for sure."

Cerryl had a feeling Lyasa did, but he didn't press the issue as he looked at his empty platter. He stood. "I still have to study for Esaak."

"You have to study while you're on sewers?" asked Lyasa, pushing jet-black hair back over her ears.

"The most honored Jeslek informed me that I was woefully deficient in mathematicks." Cerryl laughed softly. "I still am, Esaak informs me."

"He so informs all," said Faltar dryly.

"Even so . . ." Cerryl gestured toward the corridor to his cell.

As he left the meal hall, he could hear Bealtur murmur, "Yes . . . go study, for all the good it will do . . ."

Once in his cell, Cerryl picked up *Naturale Mathematicks* and dutifully opened the book, taking out the slate and chalk stick. Three pages and a dozen problems were all he managed before his head was swimming.

He closed the book and stood. He began walking in a narrow circle in his room. He was tired but not that sleepy, and if he tried to sleep, he'd just wake up in the middle of the night. Besides, he still hadn't followed up on Myral's—and everyone's—suggestions about light and chaos-fire. He paused. That wasn't right. Various mages had suggested he study light. None had linked it with chaos-fire. Was that another of the unmentioned links or bits of knowledge that he'd assumed were tied together?

Light, trade, Recluce, sewers, mathematicks, Recluce . . . Cerryl found himself rubbing his forehead. His eyes went to *Colors of White*, then toward the *Mathematicks* book. Finally, he lifted *Colors* and slowly opened it.

Light? What did it say about light? He flipped through the sections, trying to recall what he had read, the pages that had dealt with light. He found one section and read it, then frowned.

Cerryl studied the words again . . . There was something there.

> . . . light, being the spirit and manifestation of chaos, has neither order nor more than minimal cohesion . . . but embodies all the power of primal chaos in a manifestation that must be weaker than its source in order for those objects on which it falls to survive . . .

That made sense . . . in a vague sort of way. He closed his eyes and tried to think, then opened them as he found himself jerking as if he were about to fall asleep.

Darkness knew, he was tired enough. He read the next few lines.

> . . . the challenge facing any mage is to strengthen the power of chaos embodied in light without reducing light to mere streams of color without true power . . .

Mere streams of color without power . . . did that mean some streams of colored light had true power? How could that be? His eyes closed, and he forced them open.

The implication was that light from the sun was less powerful than it could be . . . and somehow that was tied into separating—or strengthening light by separating it into different beams of color.

Maybe tomorrow . . .

He barely managed to pull off his boots and hang up his whites before collapsing onto his bed.

He didn't remember waking up or even eating before he went to the secondary collector to begin his cleaning duties once again, but was that because he had been so tired?

Still . . . he found himself back underground, standing in a long and slimy sewer . . . a secondary collector, and the oozing scum from the drainage way seemed to grab at his boots, with armlike branches that clutched.

Cerryl tried to wield chaos-fire, but his firebolts were but small globes of flame that sputtered across the greened bricks without searing them clean. Each step found him trying to yank his boots free. Even when he did not move, he had to lift his boots and kick them free of the clutching ooze and slime.

He glanced over his shoulder, but the white lancers had vanished, and so had their lamp. And the grate at the top of the steps was again closed, locked with a bronze lock that bore double order and chaos twisted around it.

Cerryl felt heat at his back, and he turned to the space he had been cleaning. A fireball of chaos abruptly swelled up before him on the brick walkway. Lines of light, light that burned like chaos-fire, but more brightly, flared from the chaos ball, and his tunic burst into flame, and he could feel his face blister and the lances of light rip through him like spears of fire.

Cerryl bolted up in his bed abruptly. Sweat poured from his forehead. It had only been a dream, a realistic dream, but only a dream.

Still . . . he could feel chaos—and something else—nearby. His eyes and senses scanned his cell, but no one was within the room. He massaged his forehead. It had to be the dream.

After a moment, he padded barefoot across the cold stone to the door, lifted the latch, and eased the door to the corridor barely ajar. His eyes said that no one was about in the darkness well before dawn, yet his senses indicated that *someone* was, just past his door. Then Faltar's door eased open and closed.

Cerryl swallowed. He had seen no one, not even Faltar. Yet someone had passed. He sniffed the air. A scent . . . a faint fragrance . . . somehow familiar . . . sandalwood and something.

The only mage who wore any fragrance was Anya—at least the only one he knew. But . . . Anya—going to Faltar's cell? Why? Faltar was only a student mage, and probably a good year from becoming a full mage, perhaps longer, since Faltar had been in the halls longer than Cerryl but still hadn't even done anything in the sewers.

Anya . . . why? Why was she bedding—or seeing—Faltar in secret? And what else had he missed? Cerryl rubbed his chin, feeling a few signs of the beard he had wondered if he would ever grow. What had Anya done to avoid being seen?

Light? Had she used order to wrap light around her?

Abruptly, he realized his feet were chilled and getting colder, and that he stood with his door ajar. He eased the door shut and the latch back in place as silently as he could, and climbed back into his bed, his thoughts spinning.

Every time he turned, there was light—some aspect of light—and he still didn't understand . . . not well enough. *Colors of White* offered oblique hints . . . and little more. Myral offered hints . . . and little more.

With a sigh, Cerryl pulled the thin blanket around him.

LXVI

Cerryl glanced through the gloom of the secondary sewer tunnel at the line on the bricks where the slime began, then concentrated on raising his order shield and then channeling chaos. His nose twitched at the noisome odors rising from the scum on the section of drainage way to his right.

As in his dream, a globule of chaos-fire barely arced out before him, burning clear a patch of bricks no more than two cubits across, leaving the slightest of white residues. *If you can't do better than that, it will be a long day, and seasons in the sewers.*

He straightened his shoulders and took a deep breath. The second time, he forced his shields down at an angle.

Whhssstt! The chaos-fire sprayed across the bricks, almost like liquid, scouring a patch nearly twice the size of the first.

Behind him, Ullan nervously clunked his spear butt on the bricks of the walkway, and the muted *thunks* echoed around Cerryl. The student mage paused, not wanting to say anything . . . but the sound was distracting.

"Stop it," whispered Dientyr to Ullan.

Cerryl waited until the echoes died away, and then turned the chaos-fire on the tunnel wall across the drainage way.

Whhhssttt! This time the fire arced too low, barely scouring the bricks a cubit above the water level.

Cerryl frowned. He'd done so much better before he'd started thinking about how to handle and direct the chaos-fire. Why was that? He knew he didn't want to spew fire wildly—or even half-wildly. He'd seen how little good that had done for the fugitive back at Dylert's mill.

"Less order . . . more chaos . . ." he murmured, and tried a third time. The results were better but not much—a patch on the walkway perhaps three cubits long and one wide.

Doggedly, he kept at it, slowly scouring the bricks on the walkway and the wall. When he had a section nearly ten cubits long cleaned, he turned the fire on the scum in the drainage way. A quick-running fire burned across the surface, leaving the turbid and slow-flowing water free of the scum and an odor that mixed ashes, dung, and worse.

Slowly, he cleared the bricks, noting almost absently that he had to take longer and longer breaks between each effort . . . and that Ullan had started tapping the lance on the bricks again. He glanced back at Ullan for a moment.

"Sorry, ser." Ullan bobbed his head, and the thin mustache twitched.

Without speaking, Cerryl turned back to the work at hand.

Once, as a firebolt seared a chunk of branch, Dientyr whispered to Ullan again. "Stop banging that lance. He's no Jeslek, but he's got enough flame to fry us."

No Jeslek? Not yet. Cerryl tightened his lips for a moment, then just let the fire fly.

WHHHSSSTTTT! The fire cascaded into the tunnel wall across the drainage way and splattered in all directions, scouring clear an irregular patch nearly ten cubits long and half again as high.

"Ulppp!" The gulp from Ullan was followed by stillness.

Cerryl smiled to himself, but the expression faded quickly. Somehow . . . somehow, he had to manage to combine control with the relaxed flow of chaos . . . somehow. And that was hard when he still didn't really understand what he was doing.

Recalling what Myral had said, Cerryl tried to concentrate on separating chaos into a stream of red light and one of green . . . but that wasn't what he got. Instead, three separate beams flared—yellow, blue, and red—flashing across the slime on the walkway, leaving a hint of steam but not scouring the glazed bricks clean.

" . . . was that?" murmured Ullan.

"Shut up . . . don't know, and don't want to find out," muttered Dientyr. "Get us both turned into ash."

"Ooooffff."

Even without turning, Cerryl had the feeling that Ullan had gotten an elbow, or something, in the gut. He glanced at the faint miasma of steam that dissipated as he watched. Three colors?

He took another deep breath and faced the wall across the drainage way.

LXVII

Esaak's fat hand flew across the slate, leaving behind a line of numbers. "You see? If you take the area of the cross-section . . . Bah!" Esaak stared at Cerryl. "Do you not see?

Cerryl was having great trouble, not with understanding why it was necessary, but with Esaak's explanations.

"You do not see why the study of mathematicks is necessary . . . despite all I have said . . . despite the evidence of Fairhaven." The heavyset mage gave a deep sigh, and his wattled jowls wobbled.

"Ser . . ."

"You are cleaning the sewers, are you not?"

"Yes, ser."

"Does the water, when the sewer is clean, not flow below the drainage way?"

"Yes, ser."

"How did the engineer who built that secondary tunnel know how big to build it? Did he just guess?"

Cerryl felt blank. He knew that the engineer couldn't have guessed. Esaak wouldn't have asked the question, but why was the older mage asking such an obvious question? "He used mathematicks."

"Brilliant. Now . . . how and why?"

How? That Cerryl didn't know. "He used mathematicks to make sure it didn't fall apart or wasn't too small. I understand that, ser. It's the formulas and the way to manipulate numbers I have trouble with."

"Cerryl . . . you are so bright, and so stupid." Esaak wiped his sweating forehead. "No . . . no one ever taught you anything, did they?"

"No, ser."

"How did you learn to read? Jeslek and Sterol say you read well—at least history and maps."

"I persuaded a tutor of my master's daughter to teach me the letters, and I worked at her books—those she would lend me. Tellis the scrivener helped me some later."

"It is too bad they taught you nothing of numbers. What a waste. We will do our best, though it is late in your life for such." Esaak paused. "This formula—it shows . . ." Esaak paused. "You know a watering trough? Well, the bottom of the sewer tunnel is like a trough . . .''

Cerryl forced himself to concentrate, hoping that he would still understand after he left Esaak's chambers and headed out to the sewer again.

LXVIII

Cerryl rapped on the brass-bound white oak door.

"You may come in, Cerryl," called Myral.

As normal for cold mornings, the older mage was sipping hot spiced cider from an earthenware mug. The shutters were closed, but wispy glimmers of bright sunlight flickered through hairline openings in the frame, glimmers that seemed to move with the breeze that brushed the tower. Myral had a white woolen lap robe across his knees, although Cerryl felt the days were getting warmer.

Myral followed Cerryl's eyes to the lap robe. "The days might seem warmer, but I'm colder. I'm tempted to ask Sterol to send me to Ruzor, except . . .'' He shook his head and forced a smile. "It's warm there all year.''

"Some would say it is hot there." What had Myral almost said?

"These bones could use some heat. At times I would not mind the heat of the Stone Hills." Myral took another sip of cider.

Cerryl glanced at the small hearth, where a handful of coals still glowed.

"The coals provide more lasting heat than a fire." Myral cleared his throat. "Your progress?"

"Another thirty cubits yesterday, ser, more or less." Cerryl stopped, then added, "I had a problem the other day."

"With the lancers or you? Be precise, Cerryl." Myral frowned. "What kind of problem?"

"With me. I was trying to be more exact. I was trying to direct the chaos-fire, and the harder I tried, the less force I had." Cerryl swallowed. "Ah . . . then I tried to think more about light . . . the way you said, and I got three flashes of light at the same time—red and yellow and blue. They barely scorched the slime. But whatever it was I did, I couldn't do it again."

"Mmmm." Myral sipped his cider, glanced at the door behind Cerryl, then coughed. "What happened to your chaos-fire?"

"I lowered my shields and didn't think much, and there was plenty. But the colored shafts bothered me. Chaos-fire arcs and falls eventually, but these didn't, and . . ." Cerryl stopped. Had he heard footsteps on the stairs? Leyladin?

Despite what Lyasa had said, he still wondered about the healer. Why couldn't blacks and whites be lovers—without danger? And was Leyladin really a black? Was she Myral's lover?

The faintest scraping penetrated the room, and Cerryl could sense someone standing outside on the landing.

"Ah . . ." Myral glanced toward the heavy white oak door. "That is something you will have to work out yourself, young Cerryl. Each mage must, you know. Chaos handling is not like mathematicks, where each number always has the same value."

The younger mage suppressed a frown. Force was force . . . Somehow Myral's words seemed wrong, but Cerryl could not say why.

"Think about the light. You might reread *Colors of White*—even more carefully."

Cerryl nodded, suppressing his immediate need to protest that he had already done so, many more times than anyone suspected.

"You may go," Myral said, with another glance at the door.

"Yes, ser." Cerryl stood.

"Tomorrow."

After a nod of acknowledgment, the younger man turned and walked to the door, opening it and stepping outside onto the landing, a landing occupied by another.

"Good day, Leyladin." Cerryl offered a smile, broader than he'd intended as his eyes took in the oval face, the blonde hair that was faintly red and tumbled not quite to her shoulders, the green eyes that sparkled even in the dimness of the landing, and the lips that were full, but not too full.

"Good day, Cerryl." She returned his smile with one that was friendly but not inviting. "Be careful in the depths."

"Thank you." Now what? He wondered, but got no further, as she opened Myral's door and stepped inside, closing it, and leaving him standing on the landing.

With a shrug he really didn't feel, Cerryl started down the stone steps to the foyer, passing the guards at the lowest level and then hurrying down the steps to the foyer. He had managed a few more words, a very few, but he still felt tongue-tied around her. She was truly beautiful.

He crossed the foyer, pausing when he turned toward the rear of the hall as a redheaded figure approached. He bowed. "Greetings, honored Anya."

"I'm not that much your elder, Cerryl." A warm and white-toothed smile flashed across Anya's face, a smile Cerryl distrusted even as he admired its effectiveness. "If you keep working, you'll be up before the Council within the next few years ... and then we'll be working together for a long time."

The scent of sandalwood, mixed with roses or another heavy floral essence, enfolded him, almost cloying.

"I am yet in the sewers," he pointed out, "but you are kind."

"You are cautious, an admirable attribute." Her smile turned even more perfunctory. "Do your best in the sewers."

As Anya gave a parting nod and walked across the high-ceilinged foyer toward the steps to the tower, Cerryl turned toward the courtyard and the lancers' barracks beyond, where he would again meet Jyantyl and the other lancers assigned to his charge, although he was certain Jyantyl was reporting on him as well as supervising the disciplinary detail.

The sun seemed slightly warmer on his face as he entered the courtyard. Was winter really coming to an end? Had he been in the Halls of the Mages nearly a year? By spring, it would be a year.

So much had happened ... and so little. So many hidden tests—and pitfalls. After nearly a year, he still had no idea whether the poisoned cider had been a test or an attempt to kill him, though he suspected more and more it had been a crude attempt at murder by Kesrik or Bealtur. But that was something he couldn't prove and dared not mention ... because ... if it had been a test ... He shook his head. His logic was weak, but his feelings were strong. Mentioning the cider would do no good, especially since Myral was the only one who drank cider all the time, and he doubted strongly that Myral would stoop to poison. And Kesrik didn't seem smart enough to think or try something like that on his own.

So had someone been trying to get rid of two people? *More feelings you can't prove?*

Like mathematicks, and chaos-fire ... he just didn't know enough.

The warmth of the sun was countered by the chill of the spray from the fountain, and he continued through the rear hall into the next courtyard and toward the barracks.

"We be ready, ser." Jyantyl straightened as Cerryl neared.

"Good." Cerryl turned toward the avenue, Jyantyl walking beside him, the other four lancers two abreast behind them.

The secondary sewage collector tunnel Cerryl had been assigned was more than two kays from the mages' square, two kays very slightly uphill along the main avenue.

Cerryl's thoughts seemed a jumbled mess as he marched along the avenue. Why did chaos-fire arc and fall? Light followed a straight path. But chaos-fire burned, and light didn't. Cerryl's lips tightened, and then he licked them. The colored light beams had burned—just not so much as chaotic white light. And sunlight didn't burn, unless it was concentrated with a glass or one stayed in it all day at midsummer. So it wasn't the color of the light, but the chaos of the light.

How could one separate color from chaos? Cerryl frowned as he kept walking quickly northward on the avenue.

"He's in a hurry this morning," muttered Ullan.

"Most mages are," answered Dientyr.

"Quiet," snapped Jyantyl.

The five continued along the avenue, passing the market square, the jeweler's row, and the artisans' square, until they were within easy sight of the northern gates, before turning left.

Once beside the warehouse wall, Cerryl unlocked, lifted, and relocked the bronze grate in place, then started down the brick steps to the walkway. Even after the eight-days he'd spent chaos-scouring the secondary, the slime had not reappeared where he'd begun.

Behind him, Dientyr lit the sewer lamp, and he and Ullan followed Cerryl into the depths.

Cerryl stood for a time at the edge of the bricks he had already chaos-scoured, staring into the slime-filled darkness that stretched toward the main sewer tunnel west of the avenue, his thoughts still swirling. Find his own way? How? Could he somehow let chaos flow without restricting it, but use order to separate and guide it?

Somehow . . . that was the way. How . . . that was another question.

Finally, he took a deep breath and just let the chaos flow, barely shielded, observing as much as controlling.

Whhhsttt! Red-tinged white flared everywhere, then faded, followed by minute white ashes swirling up in the dim light of the lamp held by Dientyr, standing perhaps four paces behind Cerryl.

After gathering himself together and taking a full breath, Cerryl stepped forward another several paces to the edge of what he had just scoured. After a moment, Dientyr followed with the lamp, and the muted *thump* of Ullan's lance told Cerryl that the lancer had restationed himself.

Standing in the noisome depths, Cerryl tried to form the idea of a glass hanging before him in the air, the kind that would split the light the way a wedge of clear glass did, into colored streams. Slowly, he let the chaos summoned from somewhere—exactly from where he still wasn't certain—he let it flow through the chaos lens.

The three streams of light played across the slime of the walkway. Steam rose, and the slime blackened but did not burn.

Cerryl took a deep breath. Splitting the light shouldn't necessarily weaken it—should it?

He tried again. Again he got colored light lances that steamed and blackened the slime but did not clean.

He had the feeling that he was missing something, but he didn't know what, and that meant another long day beneath the streets of Fairhaven—perhaps many more, too many more, long eight-days.

LXIX

Outside the mages' tower, the cold early spring rain beat on the stones and shutters, and occasional chill gusts sifted past the closed shutters. Inside, the heaped coals imparted a welcome warmth to Myral's room.

Cerryl sat on the hard chair.

"You look troubled." Myral lifted his steaming cider. "Have some."

"Thank you." The younger man poured a half a mug from the pitcher, half-scanning it for chaos, then took a sip of the warming liquid, hoping it might lessen his headache.

"What is the difficulty?"

"Sometimes, I seem to be able to clean large sections of the bricks easily, as if . . . as if I had been doing it for years. But at other times, or at almost any time I try to focus the chaos-fire on anything, it sort of just . . . dribbles out. Or it's like a ray of light that warms the bricks but doesn't scour. Sometimes, I can get it to blacken the slime—"

"The fire like a light ray?" asked Myral.

Cerryl nodded.

"That's what you should work on . . . if you can."

"If I can? Can't all mages—"

"No." The older mage shook his head. "The ancients of Cyador all could, if one can believe the old writings, but few can today. Very few. It would be good if you could."

"I don't know. There's a lot of order use it takes . . . I think." Cerryl wondered at Myral's diffidence, at a subtle wrongness, and yet Myral was clearly concerned for Cerryl. Again . . . what was being withheld?

"Cerryl," said Myral mildly, "you can use chaos without being of chaos."

That was a clear, direct, and truthful statement, and the younger mage swallowed as Myral continued.

"The world is filled with order and chaos. Some floats free; some is mixed with the elements of the world. There is chaos in the molten rock of the fire mountains, and chaos feeds the waters of hot springs. Order is bound into iron. Chaos is not bound into you—or me, or Jeslek. We direct the chaos—that is, gathering it from the world around us. I have told you this before. It is written in *Colors of White*. But you need to understand this. When you marshal chaos fire in the sewers, it does not come from within you but from the world. You do not have to make it part of you. Some do." Myral smiled sadly. "They die young."

"But . . . why?"

"It is easier at first to let the chaos flow through you and be part of you." Myral offered an ironic smile. "Most of the time, in whatever trade one engages in, true skill takes greater effort and time to develop. You are struggling between trying to channel chaos outside yourself and letting it flow through you. You get better results now, if it goes through you. Is this not true?"

"Yes," Cerryl admitted.

"The choice is yours." Myral stood. "I have no special tricks to offer you, no easy steps to control, just observations." He gestured toward the door. "And you need to keep working at it in the sewers, for so long as it takes until you can handle chaos consistently and with control."

Cerryl hurriedly swallowed the last of the cider, wincing as the hot liquid seared his throat, then eased back the straight-backed chair and stood.

"I am not hiding a secret from you," Myral added. "I can tell you what is, but you have to find out how to make it work for you."

"Yes, ser."

"Cerryl." Myral's voice hardened. "You can honestly try to understand, or you can pretend you do and fail or die young. You choose." He nodded to the door once more.

As Cerryl left and started down the stone steps, the sound of the white oak door's closing still echoing in his ears, his throat still burning, he felt like screaming. If he didn't have the ability to muster strong chaos force, he would be at the mercy of the Kesriks of Candar. If he didn't get control of the chaos force outside himself, he'd die young. If he didn't keep some ability to handle chaos, he'd fail and die.

But . . . Myral was suggesting that the ways that Cerryl *knew* would work were wrong, and that the ways he couldn't even see how to master were right, and then Myral had the coldness . . . the something . . . not even to offer a single practical piece of advice.

The young would-be mage shook his head as he walked down the steps, thinking of another long day in the sewers, fumbling and scrambling with his uncertain control of chaos-fire . . . and his all-too-uncertain life in Fairhaven.

LXX

Behind Cerryl, back up the tunnel toward the steps to the street and the bronze sewer grate, Ullan's lance tapped nervously, then stopped, as if Dientyr had jammed an elbow—or something—into the other lancer.

Cerryl could sense that the day was getting late. He was sweating, and his tunic probably reeked from sweat and fear and sewage, so much so that he smelled nothing.

He had tried everything he could think of, but still the only way he could seem to manifest a decent amount of chaos-fire was to let it flow through him—half-instinctively. Yet Myral had been quite clear that such was far from the best way.

Cerryl wiped his forehead with the back of his hand, looking almost blankly into the darkness. His eyes were tired, and the darkness seemed to flash at him in waves.

For a moment, he closed his eyes, trying to think. What was he overlooking? He had to be missing something. Maybe there wasn't enough chaos close enough to him to channel. Did one have to gather chaos? How?

There had to be a way. Myral's words still rang in his ears. ". . . use chaos without being of chaos . . . gathering chaos from the world around us . . ."

What drew in chaos? Sunlight?

Cerryl nodded, imagining himself as a huge flower, drawing in chaos as a blossom drew in sunlight, turning that sunlight into flame, and directing it toward the slime on the bricks . . .

Whhhsssstttt . . . A line of golden white flame—a *line* of flame flashed from the air before Cerryl down the tunnel . . . not touching the green-coated bricks until—who knew how far away?

Cerryl stood motionless, unable to believe what he had seen. Had he really seen it?

Again, after another deep breath, he tried to replicate the sense of gathering chaos as the flowers gathered sunlight, and to let it flow around him—not through him—but around him and slightly down.

Whhsttt!

The golden white flame lance seared a line across the bricks.

A wide grin spread across Cerryl's face, and he felt like jumping up and down in joy. Instead . . . he tried to replicate the feeling, the actions, again.

Whhhsstt!

For the third time, the flame lance flared down the tunnel, at a flatter angle that seared away even more of the scum and slime.

The young mage, unable to keep the grin off his face, kept looking into the darkness as he took another long breath. He was winded, and tired, but he had something, something he wasn't sure he'd seen elsewhere. But would Jeslek or Sterol have showed all they had?

He shook his head.

Behind him, Ullan's lance tapped nervously, once, twice.

"Not now," hissed Dientyr.

Cerryl turned, wiping the grin off his face. "Ullan . . . I know it's uncomfortable down here, and I know you don't like it, but when you keep tapping that lance, it distracts me, and that means whatever I'm doing will take longer." He paused. "I'd appreciate it if you'd make a bigger effort not to tap it on the bricks."

"Yes, ser." Ullan's voice squeaked on the "ser," and the thin dark mustache bobbed, and sweat streamed down his forehead.

"Good." Cerryl turned back to the tunnel, wanting to see how much more progress he could make while refining his new technique.

"Lucky . . . Ullan . . . real lucky," whispered Dientyr.

Cerryl forced himself to concentrate, to ignore the rising sense of elation that had begun to fill him.

LXXI

As he stepped through the squared archway into the foyer of the front Hall of the Mages, Cerryl wiped the dampness from his forehead, part sweat from the rapid walk down the avenue until he had parted from Jyantyl and the lancers at the edge of the square and part dampness from the spring drizzle that cloaked Fairhaven, so fine that his head almost didn't ache. His eyes blinked to readjust to the dimness inside the building. After a moment, he started toward the back of the hall and the courtyard. The evening bells had not rung, and that meant he had time to get washed up before eating and not be one of the late arrivals.

A motion caught Cerryl's eyes, and he stopped just inside the foyer. Eliasar marched quickly from the tower steps through the foyer. The arms mage wore a huge white-bronze broadsword in a shoulder harness, and a shortsword from a belt. A lazy smile flickered across Eliasar's face as his fingers touched the hilt of the shorter blade.

Cerryl frowned but followed Eliasar toward the courtyard. When Cerryl had reached the fountain, though, the arms mage was out of sight. With a shrug, Cerryl circled the fountain, avoiding the wet stones near the basin, and entered the rear hall, then turned toward the washrooms.

For once, even after cleaning up, Cerryl got to the meal hall before most of the other students or the handful of mages who ate there. Esaak sat alone in one corner, perusing a book of some sort, and another apprentice—Kochar—sat at one of the larger circular tables. Kochar's eyes went to the table's surface as Cerryl glanced toward the younger redhead.

"Young Cerryl!" called Esaak.

"Yes, ser." Cerryl turned and started toward the older mage.

"You can eat. You young men are always starving. I was once. Remember, I want the best you can do on those cross-section and flow problems tomorrow."

"Yes, ser."

"Good." Esaak waved. "Go eat."

Cerryl headed back toward the serving table, getting there just as Bealtur came through the archway. Cerryl filled his platter with lemon creamed mutton chunks over hard bread, grabbed two pearapples to balance the heavy meat and thick sauce, and added the mug of ale. He made his way to one of the empty circular polished white oak tables.

Bealtur stood back, fingering his dark and wispy goatee, until Cerryl left the serving table.

Cerryl ate slowly, silently, his mind flitting between the cross-section problems he had not finished working out and his efforts, unsuccessful so far, to split the golden lance light into the colored beams and still have them retain enough power to fire-scour the slimed bricks.

Bealtur joined Kochar, and the two began to talk, but in voices low enough that the sounds did not carry to Cerryl nor interrupt his thoughts about chaos-fire and light.

Did trying to order light, so to speak, mean that the power of chaos was weakened in the light? Or was it the way in which he was trying to order it? Cerryl shook his head abruptly. How many times had he argued those points in his head? And how many times had he not found an answer there, or in *Colors of White*? How many answers had he sought and not found—beginning with the death of his aunt and uncle? Deaths he was more convinced than ever had been caused by chaos-fire.

"Cerryl?" Faltar stood by the table.

Cerryl glanced up with a sheepish smile. "Sorry. Sit down. I didn't see you. I was thinking about the problems I have to do before tomorrow for Esaak."

Faltar slid onto the stool across from Cerryl, his blond hair drifting across his forehead. "You're always thinking about something."

"I suppose so. There was a time when . . . never mind." Cerryl laughed self-consciously, then grinned. "Has anything interesting been happening around here?"

"Broka says I haven't learned the bones of the body well enough. Derka doesn't think my hand is good enough for a mage. He keeps telling me that no one could read what I write. You're lucky you were a scrivener, that way." Faltar took a bite of pearapple and chewed it, then looked at the yellowed white sauce on his platter. "Mutton . . . again."

"I hadn't thought being a scrivener's apprentice was good for much." Cerryl took a swallow of ale, a draught that helped cut the greasiness of the lemon sauce. "This is greasier than usual."

"You should listen to Derka about writing," said Faltar sourly. "The mutton is always greasy."

Cerryl paused. "I saw Eliasar wearing a lot of weapons, just before I got here. He looked happy." He gave a low laugh. "He likes weapons. I had to wonder where he was going."

"Haven't you seen?" Faltar took a quick sip of the amber ale. "They're readying a whole force of white lancers. They're all going to Certis—Jellico, from what I've heard."

"From whom?" asked Cerryl quietly. "No one seems to tell anyone anything. Especially us."

A quick blush passed across Faltar's face, a flushing that Cerryl ignored. "I've just listened," Faltar finally said. "You aren't around here enough to overhear things."

"That's probably true. "I'm down there struggling along in the tunnels." Cerryl offered a smile. "Did you hear why Eliasar and those lancers are going to Jellico? I thought we had an agreement with Certis."

"I think it has something to do with the problems in Gallos." The blond student shrugged. "You know about the new prefect there?"

His mouth full of lamb and lemon-sauced bread, Cerryl nodded.

"He's claiming that the agreement about the Great White Road was made when his sire was ailing, and that it doesn't bind him to collect the road tariffs for us."

"That's almost half the road's length," mumbled Cerryl.

"It's worse than that, Derka says. The prefect's claiming that we have no right to tax any of the other roads we built, and that includes the main road from Jellico through Passera to Fenard." Faltar lowered his voice. "They're going to have a meeting about it—all the full mages." Faltar lowered his voice. "That was what Lyasa told me."

Yet Eliasar was already on his way to Certis. To ensure that the viscount stayed loyal to Fairhaven? Was the White Order's hold on eastern Candar that fragile?

"That doesn't sound good," murmured Cerryl. "I wouldn't know, but if there is going to be a meeting . . ."

"That's what . . . Well . . . no . . . I don't think so, either." Faltar glanced nervously around the meal hall.

"Isn't there a mage in Fenard? We saw him here once, I think. Can't he do anything?"

"I don't know." Faltar finally looked back at his platter. "About the mage, I mean. There's a mage in all the places where there's a ruler. Except Spidlar and Sligo, and they have a Traders' Council or something."

"If they want us to know, they'll tell us." Cerryl laughed. "Otherwise, what can we do? I've still got sewer duty. You've still got to improve your hand, and I've still got to do cross-section problems for Esaak. Tonight," Cerryl added as he stood.

"Tonight?"

Cerryl nodded and turned toward his cell, hoping he wouldn't be working too long into the night.

LXXII

Cerryl woke almost clutching at his throat, feeling, sensing chaos everywhere. Sweat rolled down his forehead, and he had a hard time swallowing for a moment.

His eyes traversed the darkness of his small cell, but it remained as always—the desk with the books, the stool, the table, the unlit lamp, and the cold stone floor—all empty.

He swallowed again, then eased from under his blanket toward the door, standing with his hand on the latch, shivering in his smallclothes.

After a moment of thought, he decided against opening the door but just listened.

Had he heard the whisper of footsteps on the polished stone of the corridor? Or was that the wind outside the halls?

He sniffed. Even through the door he could smell the faint odor of sandalwood and flowers, and his senses told him that someone in the corridor had warped or twisted light somehow.

The faintest *snick* of a lifted latch—had he heard that, or was it his overactive imagination?

Anya? Visiting Faltar again?

Briefly, the corners of his mouth lifted in the darkness as he thought how he would react if someone slipped into his room. Say someone like Leyladin . . .

He swallowed and pushed that thought away as he sensed, almost like a white shadow, a looming but partly shielded chaos presence, farther away—where, he couldn't sense, but not too far. And that chaos presence was definitely watching.

Cerryl swallowed. Anya was visiting Faltar, and Cerryl had no doubts about what kind of visits the redhead was making, and someone was watching Anya, and both were hiding their presence.

The thin-faced—and cold-footed—young man slipped back from his door to his bed, easing his blanket back around him, trying to let his feet warm up as his thoughts swirled in his head.

What did Anya want of Faltar—a mere student? Mere sexual pleasure? Somehow, recalling Anya's smile and the coolness beneath it, Cerryl doubted that.

Should he tell Faltar? How much should he say? Or should he just wait? *What else can you do but wait. Wait and learn . . . and hope.*

He turned over, wrapping the blanket tighter about him, but sleep was long in returning.

LXXIII

H ow did those mathematicks problems go with Esaak?" asked Faltar, taking a swig of ale from his mug, then following it with a mouthful of the crusty hot bread.

"I managed to figure out most of them." Cerryl sipped the mug of water. Ale was something he couldn't swallow in the morning. Cheese and bread were bad enough, but trying to handle chaos fire on an empty stomach was worse. He broke off another chunk of bread and ate it slowly, his eyes on the oiled and polished white oak table that had turned a burnished gold over the years.

"Esaak wants everyone to know how much water the sewers can carry and how you determine how strong a wall or bridge is."

"Walls and bridges?" blurted Cerryl.

"Those are next," affirmed Faltar, attacking another chunk of hard yellow cheese. "He says being a mage isn't just wielding chaos-force. Oh, and Derka says I'll start doing sewers pretty soon, maybe before you finish. He has to talk to Myral."

"It's not exactly fun," demurred Cerryl.

"That's what he says."

As he chewed the fresh bread, Cerryl looked at Kesrik, not so much with his eyes as with his senses. The stocky blond sat at the corner table with the red-haired Kochar and the goateed Bealtur, and at that moment, none were looking toward Cerryl or Faltar. Then Cerryl turned his scrutiny to Kinowin, who stood over the table where Esaak had been eating alone.

Cerryl blinked, then looked more at Esaak. Clearly, a far greater chaos power surrounded Kinowin—although far less than Cerryl would have guessed—than the other two, and even the aging Esaak blazed with power compared to Kesrik. Cerryl glanced at Faltar the same way.

"What's the matter? You have a funny look," mumbled Faltar.

"Just thinking."

"About what?"

About chaos power and who shows it. "All sorts of things. Esaak, Kinowin, Kesrik."

"Sometimes you think too much." Faltar swallowed the last of the ale in his mug.

Cerryl tried not to wince at the thought of starting the day with ale, glancing at Lyasa, who walked into the meal hall with Leyladin. Lyasa, like Faltar, showed a modicum of chaos. The red-golden–haired Leyladin flickered with what Cerryl sensed as flecks or streaks of white that seemed to swirl in and through an unseen black mist that enshrouded the blonde. Was that what a black mage looked/felt like? Black mists? Cerryl quickly looked down at his platter as Leyladin's eyes swept toward him.

"Too bad she's a black," murmured Faltar.

"I thought you were more interested in Anya," countered Cerryl in a low tone.

Faltar flushed.

"She's beautiful," agreed Cerryl. *But so are lances and daggers.* "Anya, I meant."

"I got who you meant."

"Even if I were a full mage, I think I'd walk carefully with her," Cerryl murmured.

"I didn't ask . . ." Faltar looked hard at Cerryl. "You aren't a full mage."

"You're right." Cerryl forced a smile. "Anyway . . . different women appeal to different men." He paused. "It's your choice. When the time comes, Faltar, the best of luck to you."

"Oh . . . thank you. I'm sorry. I must have . . . never mind."

"It is one of those mornings, I think. Have you heard about any more lancers going places?"

"No one's saying, but there aren't many left in the barracks out back." Faltar mumbled through a mouthful of bread. "I overheard Kinowin talking about some armsmen from Hydlen. I thought he said twenty score."

"Twenty score? That's a lot. It seems like a lot to me."

Faltar laughed. "You know Eliasar took twice that with him? And that doesn't count the lancers in the south barracks outside Fairhaven. There are ten times as many there as here."

"A good number." Something like four thousand white lancers? No wonder Fairhaven needed the road tariffs.

"That's why we need the tariffs. Fairhaven is what holds Candar together, and the Guild holds Fairhaven together." Faltar nodded sagely, blond hair flopping onto his forehead and spoiling the effect. He stood. "I have to meet with Broka. Bones and more bones."

Cerryl stood more slowly, his eyes drifting toward the table where Lyasa and Leyladin sat. Neither glanced toward him as he left the meal hall.

As he walked across the courtyard, past the fountain and the spray that seemed chill with the wind, despite the bright spring sun, he had the feeling that every time he learned more about Fairhaven, there was more to learn, and so much no one talked about. So much wasn't in the books, either, like the amount of chaos that surrounded some people.

Lyasa and even Faltar—even the new student Kochar—showed far more chaos power than Kesrik. Yet Jeslek seemed to favor Kesrik.

Cerryl made his way through the front hall, past the closed doors to the meeting hall, across the foyer to the tower steps and past the pair of guards. Hertyl gave him a faint smile, and Cerryl smiled back.

At the second landing, Cerryl rapped on Myral's door.

"Come in."

Cerryl opened the heavy door, smelled the spiced cider, and closed the door behind him.

Myral sipped his usual steaming cider, though the room was comfortable, at least to Cerryl, and the shutters were half-open, showing a sunlit view of Fairhaven to the north of the tower.

Cerryl glanced from the window to the wall of bookshelves and then to the older mage, seated at the table.

"Have some cider."

"Thank you." Cerryl slipped into the chair across from Myral, pouring cider into the spare mug and taking a sip. Cider was far better than plain water or ale in the morning.

"How are you coming?"

"Another few days, and I'll have finished the secondary to where it joins the western branch of the main tunnel."

Myral's eyebrows lifted. "You're moving faster."

"Yes, ser. It's been hard work."

Myral nodded to himself, sipped his cider, coughed, and cleared his throat. "Have you found anything else interesting?"

"Besides branches near the grates, a few soggy chunks of vellum scraped clean . . . no."

"No bodies . . . weapons, or scrap iron?"

"No, ser." Cerryl frowned. "Scrap iron?"

"Sometimes it happens. Don't use chaos-fire on it. You're not ready for that." Myral set down the mug and stretched. "These old bones get stiff. I'll be glad when summer comes. I might even want to go to Ruzor—for a visit—or somewhere warm."

"Ruzor?"

"Everywhere east of the Westhorns where there's a port, there's a member of the brotherhood and a detachment of lancers. Ruzor gets a great deal of trade from Southport and Summerdock, even from Recluce. Especially from Recluce." Myral's eyebrows waggled.

"Ser . . . everyone talks around Recluce. Why? I mean, Eliasar laughs about Recluce. He says they have no warships, and they haven't ever—I mean, according to the histories—they haven't tried to send armsmen to take things here, not since Creslin the Black raided Lydiar, and that was a long time ago . . ."

"Two hundred eighty-seven years ago at the first turn of summer, according to the records."

"Oh."

"It's in the Guild records, the sealed ones, but you can figure it out from the histories." Myral's eyes hardened and focused on the younger mage. "Cerryl . . . power is measured not solely by warships and armsmen." Myral coughed again, almost rackingly, cleared his throat, and sipped more of the hot cider. "Fairhaven maintains armsmen and lancers, and they are paid in part by the trade duties on all the roads Fairhaven has built, but especially on the Great White Highways, and in part from the levies on the trades here in Fairhaven itself. Have you asked what happens if Recluce sends cheaper wool—or better wool for the same coinage for a stone's bundle of wool—to Tyrhavven or Spidlaria? What if the traders of Gallos or Spidlar buy their wool from Recluce instead of Montgren? Or pearapples or oilseeds from Recluce instead of from Certis or Hydlen?"

"Not so many traders use the roads?"

"Exactly." Myral set the mug on the table with a thump. "Less traders on the Great White Roads means fewer road tariffs and fewer coins to pay our lancers."

"Could we not tariff the cargoes from Recluce?"

"Ah . . ." Myral smiled. "Someone could . . . but the port of Spidlaria does not owe allegiance to Fairhaven. Lydiar and Renklaar do, and we could insist on tariffs there. But . . . say you are a trading captain, and the taxes raise the price of your cargo in Lydiar but not in Spidlaria, would you not increase your price less than the tariff and—"

"Port it in Spidlaria?" asked Cerryl.

The older mage nodded. "It is more complex than that, young Cerryl, and something you need not worry about yet, but that was exactly why Creslin the Black raided Lydiar those long years ago. He needed ships and freedom to trade. Now . . . Recluce has both." Myral smiled sadly. "Sterol is talking about how we may need to place mages aboard our ships—and those of our friends and allies—to protect them. I hope it does not come to that, but it may."

"Eliasar said we were building warships," Cerryl prompted.

"We have always had warships. A land that cannot protect its traders upon the seas soon has no traders. Now . . . enough of that. You need to get to work if you are to complete your duties as you plan."

"Which sewer tunnels did Kesrik clean?" Cerryl asked after a moment of silence.

"Does it matter?" A soft smile crossed Myral's lips, one that bothered Cerryl. "You all clean secondaries."

"I was curious." Cerryl forced a shrug. "Did he—I guess it doesn't matter."

"It matters to you, or you wouldn't have asked." Myral's tone was dry.

"Yes, ser."

"You know, Cerryl . . . you blaze too much."

Cerryl's mouth started to open, and he swallowed, almost choking on the bit of cider he hadn't swallowed.

"This should come later, but, if I don't tell you now, you may not be around later." Myral took a deep breath and glanced toward the tower door. "Jeslek has gone to Gallos, and Sterol and Anya are otherwise occupied—for the moment.

"When a mage feels strongly or is about to gather chaos and does not shield himself, the chaos around him flares—or blazes. That's one reason why Jeslek always seems so powerful. Chaos almost radiates from him. Sterol is almost as powerful, yet he seems mild, withdrawn. He shields his power, much as you shield yourself from chaos in the sewer—or maybe it's better described as ordering chaos so that it is held rather than dispersed." Myral shrugged. "Right now, you're like a young Jeslek, spraying power everywhere. If you hadn't been an orphan or a scrivener's apprentice, where no one thought to look, Sterol would have slapped you into the creche years ago—or had you suffocated."

Cerryl waited.

"Sterol's worried about Recluce—again, and for the reasons I just told you. You can thank the blacks and the new prefect of Gallos for your survival, I suspect. But . . . you're a possible rival to Jeslek. Once Sterol goes, Jeslek won't want you around."

"Me, ser?"

"I said possible. Right now, Jeslek would snuff you out like a candle. You have no shields to speak of, and you still haven't figured out how to use your power. It's not easy, as you're finding out. Some mages finish sewer duty almost burned out; they exhaust themselves rather than learn. In any case, why do you think Sterol wanted you in the sewers? It was Sterol's idea, not Jeslek's, no matter what the great Jeslek said." Myral wiped his suddenly damp forehead.

"So I could learn?"

"So you would have to learn." Myral's tone turned dry again. "Let us hope you have. And, by the way." Myral stood and walked to the bookshelves, where he extracted a rolled scroll. He carried the scroll back to the table where he unrolled the sewer map. "Here are the two collectors that Kesrik was told to scour the last time." The rotund mage leaned over the unrolled map and pointed.

Cerryl fixed the locations in his mind.

"I didn't tell you. And I can lie convincingly, even to Jeslek. It's one of my few strong abilities." Myral smiled bitterly. "Now . . . on your way. And work upon shielding just how much power you have—if you want to keep it."

"Yes, ser." Cerryl stood, almost in a daze.

The entire walk to the secondary collector was like another dream, though he remembered talking to Jyantyl and feeling the cool wind that blew down the avenue out of the north.

He barely recalled unlocking the bronze grate and descending into the all-too-familiar odors of the tunnel.

Cerryl looked into the darkness of the collector tunnel. In a way, it seemed like no matter what he discovered, he was still always looking into the darkness. Was life looking into the darkness?

He blazed too much . . . and it was important enough that Myral had told him—told him while being most nervous. He blazed too much, and Jeslek would snuff him out like a candle. He blazed too much.

If he blazed, as Myral put it, was that because he was still holding too much chaos within and around himself? Could he do otherwise? Could he not do otherwise . . . if he wished to survive?

Cerryl took a deep breath and looked once more into the darkness of the tunnel . . . a darkness that stretched well beyond where the secondary tunnel met the main tunnel.

LXXIV

Emerging from the secondary tunnel slightly earlier than usual—he hoped—Cerryl turned to Jyantyl. "You and the guards go on back from here. I have to check something for Myral." He brushed his fine hair off his forehead, vainly, because the light gusting wind immediately blew it back across his eyes.

"Ser?"

Cerryl offered a smile. "I still have to be back in the halls." His eyes went to the east, where the hazy clouds were thickening into a deeper gray.

"We could accompany you."

Cerryl shrugged, deciding that it wasn't a battle that needed to be fought. "If you think it better. I just have to check the level of sewage in two secondaries. It shouldn't take long, but I didn't want to keep you . . ."

Jyantyl smiled, clearly an expression of relief. "Not so late as usual, ser. Where to?"

"We can take the warehouse road south from here, and then, after one check, go east toward the avenue. We'll have to cross the avenue to get to the second, but it's not too far."

"As you say, ser." Jyantyl nodded, and Ullan and Dientyr fell in behind the other lancers, another pair Cerryl didn't know, since those who remained on the street with Jyantyl changed almost daily, while

Ullan and Dientyr always accompanied Cerryl. He wondered for what they were being punished, but didn't think it was his place to ask the head lancer.

Ullan's lance dragged intermittently for a time, until Jyantyl glanced over his shoulder. Always it was Ullan's lance, never Dientyr's.

Cerryl almost missed the first secondary grate he was looking for because it was actually in a niche in the wall, as if the stable wall had been extended almost to the edge of the sewer tunnel.

Cerryl knelt and turned the bronze key, smelling both manure from the stable behind him and the odors of sewage drifting up from the grate. Ignoring the smells, he confined the chaos around the lock within order and unfastened the lock. He lifted the heavy grate and locked it open before starting down the brick steps.

Even before he had taken three steps into the gloomy secondary tunnel, he could sense a strong residual of chaos everywhere. The steps were still clean, as were the walkways and the glazed brick walls.

At the bottom of the steps, recalling his subterfuge, he turned and examined the level of sewage in the drainage way—flowing smoothly a good two spans below the edge of the walkway.

With a nod, he turned and walked back up the steps, where he reversed the process to relock the grate in place, ensuring that the chaos protected the relocked grate. Even in the brief time he had been underground, he could feel that the wind was stronger, and somewhat cooler, although the coolness was welcome after the early spring heat of the past few days.

"One more," he said to Jyantyl. "Across the avenue and then two long blocks east of here." After a pause, he added, "I'm sorry."

"This be no problem, ser. A few extra steps, we can do that." Jyantyl shook his head.

Two women bearing baskets of laundry on their heads looked at Cerryl and the lancers and darted into an alleyway.

Cerryl smiled faintly—amazed that an orphan mill boy could generate concern simply because he wore a white tunic trimmed in scarlet. Was that power? Or did people do the same when the carriage of someone like Muneat passed?

He studied the side street as they crossed the avenue, realizing that, although it was not all that far from Tellis's shop, he had never walked down the narrow street before. How many streets and places were like that? So close and yet unvisited?

All the shops seemed to be either those of weavers or basketmakers, and cloth of all shades hung in unshuttered windows. A bolt of bright green was in the third window, and for some reason, it reminded Cerryl of Leyladin.

He tightened his lips and kept walking. The grate he wanted was off the second side street from the street of weavers, not more than fifty cubits south.

The second tunnel was like the first, nearly immaculate except for the excessive residue of white dust, and reeking of chaos. Cerryl walked along the walkway southward nearly a hundred cubits from the steps— well into the darkness, but with the leftover chaos, his senses let him see almost as well as in full light.

Scattered raindrops began to splat on the stones of the street and the white-plastered walls as he finished relocking the sewer grate. "Back to the halls. That's it."

"Not a moment too soon . . ." came a mutter from the rear of the lancers.

Jyantyl stiffened but did not turn.

As they rejoined the avenue on the side street that passed just south of the grain exchange, Cerryl tried to keep his face blank.

Both tunnels reeked of chaos, so much so that he knew Kesrik could not have scoured them—not the Kesrik that Cerryl knew. While Cerryl couldn't be sure, Kesrik didn't feel the way Sterol did, and that indicated to Cerryl that Kesrik probably wasn't shielding his control of chaos.

So . . . who had cleaned the tunnels—and how and why? How had Kesrik managed to avoid having the guards see whoever it had been?

Cerryl almost groaned as it hit him. Anyone strong enough to use that much chaos was probably able enough to use the same technique Anya had in visiting Faltar's cell.

That raised a few other questions, but all of the questions Cerryl had were not ones he dared surface, not while he was but a student and Kesrik was Jeslek's favorite.

Once back in the Halls of the Mages, Cerryl stopped by the washroom, where he stripped to the waist and scrubbed off the grime and odor from his hands and face and arms. A touch of chaos helped remove some of the odor from his tunic and trousers.

Cerryl was actually entering the meal hall when the last bells announcing dinner rang—off-key and jarring. Kesrik's stocky blond form was at the serving table already, but no one else had been served.

Heralt and Faltar were lined up at the serving table, and Cerryl slipped in behind them.

"You're early." The curly-haired Heralt turned.

"Sometimes it happens."

"Not often," said Faltar with a grin. The grin faded as he regarded the bowls and the steaming pot presided over by a serving boy. "Soup?"

"Barley and mutton, ser. Mostly barley." The youth offered a smile of sympathy.

"Barley? What have I done to deserve barley?"

"You're a student mage," suggested Heralt.

"You're a glutton," added Cerryl.

"What have I done to deserve friends like you?" Faltar filled a mug with the lighter ale. "I've been faithful and good."

His words were so mock-plaintive that both Cerryl and Heralt laughed.

"And you laugh at me." Faltar turned and walked to one of the circular tables.

"You laugh at us," countered Heralt as he followed Faltar.

Cerryl took a healthy chunk of the dark bread, then filled his own mug before joining them.

"I don't like the damp." Heralt shivered.

"None of you Kyphrans do." Faltar took a sip of ale.

"How did you get here?" asked Cerryl. "I didn't know you were from Kyphros."

"Kyphrien. My father was a wool merchant there. I went with him one day when he went to sell some white wool to the white wizard who was the advisor to the subprefect." Heralt shivered again.

"And he saw you could handle chaos, and packed you off here?" asked Faltar. "What did your father say?"

"He wasn't allowed to say anything." Heralt broke off a piece of bread. "It's better than dying."

Cerryl nodded, then took a spoonful of the hot soup, grateful for its warmth after the damp of the rain. Spring was like that—too hot and then too damp. His eyes flicked to the table where Kesrik sat alone.

As Kesrik ate, Bealtur slipped into the hall, but instead of heading directly to the serving table, he went straight to Kesrik and whispered something. The stocky blond student nodded once as Bealtur finished, then shrugged.

Cerryl kept his head down but watched. Kesrik didn't look directly at Cerryl but glanced across the hall toward Esaak for a long moment. Bealtur walked quickly to the serving table, brushing by Faltar.

"I wonder what that was all about," said Heralt.

"Who would care?" answered Faltar after swallowing a mouthful of the barley soup. "Kesrik acts like he's already been up before the Guild and as if Bealtur is his student."

"That's Bealtur's problem." Cerryl took a sip of the light ale, more than welcome after his day in the sewers.

Lyasa eased her lithe form onto the last stool around the circular table, her eyes going to Cerryl. "I heard you're almost through with your first secondary."

How had she heard? From Leyladin? "Almost. Myral thinks I may have to do another."

Lyasa nodded. "That can happen."

Faltar's eyes flicked back and forth between them. "You two are always leaving things out." He slurped some of the barley soup, then broke off a chunk of bread and shoved it in his mouth.

"You'll learn why. I also heard that it won't be more than a few eight-days before you start in on the sewers."

"So tell me what you're leaving out."

"After you start in the sewers," answered Lyasa.

"You're not fair."

"You think chaos is fair?" countered the slender black-haired young woman.

"Or order?" added Heralt.

"You're all against me," complained Faltar, spoiling his words with a wry smile.

Cerryl half-listened, watching as Bealtur returned to eat with Kesrik, but neither student spoke, and both ate quickly and left the hall.

"Cerryl . . . are you here?"

"Oh . . ." He turned to Lyasa. "I'm sorry. I was thinking."

"About what, I wonder?" Faltar grinned. "Or should I say who?"

"Better not," countered Cerryl, "or I'll talk about your dreams."

Faltar flushed.

"Look at him . . . look at him." Heralt smiled broadly.

"What . . . about . . . your dreams?" Faltar jabbed, bread still in his hand, toward Lyasa.

"My dreams are mine. And they remain mine." She raised both eyebrows in high arches.

Cerryl couldn't help grinning.

"All of you . . . all against me . . ." protested Faltar.

"Poor Faltar . . ."

Everyone laughed, even Faltar.

Later, well after dinner, Cerryl sat on the stool at the desk in his cell, looking blankly at the open pages of *Naturale Mathematicks*. The formulas and numbers in the dark iron-gall ink seemed written more in the evanescent white of chaos than in solid ordered black ink.

The more he learned the less he knew.

Anya was visiting Faltar in the darkness, shielding herself with or-dered chaos . . . and Cerryl couldn't see why. Faltar didn't have a wealthy family like Kesrik, and he wasn't powerful like Jeslek or Sterol.

Add to that that the collector tunnels Kesrik was supposed to have cleaned had been cleaned by someone else.

Then . . . Myral had warned Cerryl about radiating too much chaos, and then told him about the sewers assigned to Kesrik. The old mage had also told Leyladin about his progress. Had she asked?

A faint smile crossed Cerryl's face, but he shook his head. She'd been nothing more than friendly. Nothing more than friendly, and somewhat standoffish, he reminded himself.

But what could Cerryl do? How could he protect himself?

Myral had talked about mages burning themselves out, and others like Sterol shielding their chaos powers. Why couldn't he do both? Let others think he had burned out some of his powers . . . but conceal what he could do? Could he do it?

He swallowed.

But why shield? He nodded. Shielding was necessary because mages essentially carried chaos within themselves—or around them. Better to call on chaos or channel it from elsewhere . . .

"Large words and thoughts . . ." The words almost dribbled from his lips and he glanced around the dark cell. Conceiving of the idea was easy. Working it out in a way convincing to others was a harder problem.

Another smile crossed his lips. He had an entire new sewer collector tunnel to work on, and no one to observe closely.

LXXV

The struggle between the white and the black, between the way of rightness and the powers of darkness, will continue so long as the world endures, for even as the Guild has banished one twisted vine of darkness, yet another springs from the wickedness of the world.

When the ancient white mages had imprisoned the dark forest of Naclos and created the great and peaceful land of Cyador, they believed that they had banished darkness forever, but the demon powers reached and drew mighty champions from far beyond the world, and the black mage Nylan sundered the prison created by the righteousness of Cyador and freed the dark forest.

When Westwind sundered the lands of the west, the white mages of long ago rebuilt the lands of the east into a bastion of light and prosperity, and founded the city of light itself, a beacon unto all the world that light, like the sun from which it comes, always conquers the darkness.

Then, after years of struggle, the white brethren of the Guild at last overthrew the tyranny of Westwind. Yet before the last stone had fallen, before the last female demon had fallen on those defiled heights, the black wind wizard Creslin created another haven for darkness upon the barren isle of Recluce.

In the fullness of time, when Recluce is sundered and split in twain, then, too, will yet another black fortress arise, for never can darkness be overcome, but only conquered and held at bay so long as the right-thinking continue their efforts . . .

Yet, we should not consider such efforts as futile, for with each effort, the powers of light have increased and grown more able to provide peace, prosperity, and the providence of life to those who follow the path of light.

> *Colors of White*
> (Manual of the Guild at Fairhaven)
> Preface

LXXVI

Cerryl trudged up the avenue in the midsummer heat, leading what amounted to his own procession, as he had for almost every late afternoon for more than two seasons. He still found himself struggling somewhat with keeping chaos out of his body, and he had to concentrate to make sure that he drew chaos from around him and did not store it within him the way Jeslek did.

He wasn't sure, but he thought he felt less tired. That also could have been because he had gotten more in the habit of trying to use the appropriate form of chaos for scouring—the golden yellow light lance for broad expanses where more power was needed, and shorter bursts of the tricolored light lance for corners and angled sections of the tunnels.

Once in a while, he still used firebolts, but those exacted more effort, if more spectacular looking.

A hot summer breeze blew at his back, out of the south, as he put one white-booted foot in front of the other, ignoring for a moment the rivulets of sweat oozing down his back under the too-heavy wool of the white trousers and tunic.

Cerryl glanced to his left, at the green sign outside an open door—a sign showing a white-bronzed ram with curling golden horns. He licked his lips, thinking how good a cool mug of ale would taste. The sounds of drinking and disjointed song from The Golden Ram swirled around him as he passed the doorway, and he frowned as the song called up a brief twinge, not quite a headache. Headaches from storms he understood, but from songs?

After Cerryl had finished fire-scouring the first secondary tunnel Myral had assigned him, the older mage had selected a second, east of the avenue, and to the south, south even of where Nivor the apothecary's shop was. While his new assignment was not as slime-covered as the first, it smelled even worse.

Behind Cerryl, Ullan's spear half-tapped, half-dragged on the granite paving stones of the avenue walkway.

"Hot, ser . . . real hot," observed Jyantyl. "Be much longer afore you finish this tunnel?"

"I don't know. This one turns ahead of where we've gotten. I'd say a few more days, maybe an eight-day. That depends on how bad the collectors that are coming up are." Cerryl wiped his forehead. "There's also another secondary that joins—it must have been added later, because it's not on the map. I'll have to ask Myral about that."

"Yes, ser."

A covered wagon groaned past the group, and Cerryl's eyes followed it momentarily, noting that it held full barrels of something. Ale? Beer? Wine? The dampness at the edge of the wagon bed indicated some liquid that had spilled or overflowed within the wagon.

"Do I need to finish soon?" Cerryl asked.

"Some of us . . . they be talking about sending us to Jellico or Rytel."

"Rytel?"

"Only talk around the barracks, ser." Jyantyl shrugged. "Some say Axalt is allowing all the free traders to cross into Spidlar that way. Maybe even traders' guild types."

Cerryl nodded, not sure he understood but not wanting to confess his ignorance. "So the trouble there . . ."

"I don't pretend to know, ser . . . just that there be a storm rising in the north." The older guard's eyes flicked toward the wizards' square, then toward the tower.

"I don't either, Jyantyl." Cerryl nodded to the guard. "Until tomorrow."

"Yes, ser." Jyantyl and the four lancers marched past the front entrance and around the north side of the building.

Cerryl turned and climbed the steps, his legs aching.

So . . . there were rumors about Axalt? Cerryl frowned. He knew nothing about Axalt, except its location. Then, there were so many places in the world about which he knew nothing. He laughed to himself. There was so much that he did not know about Fairhaven . . . or women . . . or power.

Once inside the front Hall foyer, he started toward the rear court-yard, then stepped aside for a slim hurrying figure in white.

"Cerryl . . ." Anya glanced at Cerryl, almost as if puzzled, then abruptly made a face. "You need the attentions of the washroom, Cerryl."

"Yes, ser. I know."

"You don't have to address me like Sterol, Cerryl. Anya is fine." Again, she offered the blazingly warm smile he distrusted.

"Yes, Anya." He returned her smile with one he hoped was friendly and pleasant.

"Later," she said enigmatically.

Cerryl kept from swallowing as she nodded and headed past him in the direction of the lower steps to the tower. He continued on to the washrooms, arriving as the first bells of evening rang.

He hurried through his ablutions and started for the meal hall.

Even from the archway, he could see that dinner was plain roasted fowl and boiled potatoes and bread—bread baked earlier in the day and already partly stale.

Lyasa and Faltar sat at one of the round tables, and Kesrik, Kochar, and Bealtur at the one almost adjoining. Lyasa motioned to Cerryl, and he nodded in response as he loaded his platter. Plain food or not, he was hungry.

As Cerryl neared the table, Lyasa glanced at him, then toward Faltar, then back at Cerryl.

"What's the matter?" he asked.

"Are you all right? The sewers . . ."

"You mean," he asked wryly, "have they had a 'diminishing' impact? Probably, but I suppose that's the price you pay for control. Or the one I'm paying."

Cerryl could sense Kesrik's eyes on his back—or perhaps Bealtur's.

Lyasa nodded tightly. "I'm sorry."

"Don't be. Myral does fine." Cerryl wanted to smile but kept his face as expressionless as he could as he set the platter on the table beside Lyasa.

After he seated himself, he could feel Lyasa's hand under the table, briefly touching and squeezing his upper leg, a gesture of reassurance and sadness, all in one. He wanted to tell her that it was all right, but steeled himself and murmured, "It's hard, but it happens." In a way, the words were true, just not in the way Lyasa would take them.

Faltar looked up from his fowl, a puzzled look crossing his face.

"You'll understand later," murmured Lyasa. "How long have you been in the sewers? One eight-day?"

"Almost two. I'm not moving very fast." Faltar shook his head and pulled a long face.

"Most don't," said Lyasa. "Not at first."

". . . can say that . . ." mumbled Faltar.

"Have you heard anything new about Gallos or Spidlar?" Cerryl asked quickly.

Lyasa glanced back over her shoulder, toward the table that Kesrik and Kochar had just vacated. Her face clouded momentarily. "Ah . . . no. I mean . . . nothing's changed." She lifted her mug and winced.

"What's the matter?" Cerryl asked, his eyes following Kesrik, wondering what Lyasa had seen—or heard.

"Kinowin has taken over showing students about arms. He stuffed me into full armor and then beat me around some."

"To show you what guardsmen and lancers go through," said Cerryl. "Eliasar did that to me."

"I certainly don't want to be a lancer." Lyasa laughed. "The black angels were crazy in more ways than one."

"The ones from Westwind?" asked Faltar. "They supposedly knocked everyone else around. I can't believe it, though."

"You don't think women are tough enough?" Lyasa's eyebrows rose.

"I didn't say that," answered Faltar quickly.

"You didn't have to say it."

Cerryl held back a grin.

"You know a good number of the blades on Recluce are still women. So are some of the white lancers."

"I shouldn't have said anything."

"So you did say something?" Lyasa kept a straight face.

Faltar sighed, despondently, almost in the exaggerated fashion of a traveling minstrel. "Go ahead, flame me. Beat me . . . anything you wish . . . for I am in pain and misery . . ."

"Next time . . ." Lyasa laughed.

"There won't be a next time," Faltar promised.

Cerryl laughed at his plaintive tone.

"Why did you ask about things?" Lyasa turned back toward Cerryl.

"Jyantyl—he's the head guard for my sewer work—he said there were rumors about more guards and lancers being sent to Certis, and something about Axalt." He paused. "What do you know about Axalt?"

"It's an old walled city. It used to be on the main trade road from Jellico to Spidlar—until the Great White Road was completed through the Easthorns. It's not quite a land, but it owes no allegiance to any other ruler."

"Maybe we'll all be mages before it comes to war," suggested Faltar.

"Maybe." Cerryl wasn't sure that was good. He broke off a chunk of bread.

"War doesn't make sense," said Lyasa.

"Many things don't make sense," pointed out Faltar, mumbling through his food again. "Why should war?"

Thinking about Anya's reaction when he'd entered the Hall, and so much that had occurred, Cerryl had to agree with Faltar. But there wasn't much he could do, and he lifted his mug and enjoyed a swallow of cool ale.

LXXVII

Cerryl stepped into the tower room, glad that Myral had the shutters open and that a breeze blew in—except that the breeze stopped when he closed the heavy brass-bound door.

From his seat by the table, where he sipped cool cider, Myral studied Cerryl. "You've been working on not holding chaos within yourself, have you not?"

"I've tried to follow your instructions and suggestions," Cerryl admitted. "It's hard."

"Anything done well is often hard." Myral smiled briefly. "Those to whom power comes naturally have difficulty understanding such until it is oft too late."

Cerryl refrained from noting that parables weren't exactly going to help him, and eased into the chair across from the older mage.

"How is the cleaning on this one coming?"

"Not too bad," Cerryl said, "but there's a place just ahead where another tunnel seems to join, and it's not on the map."

Myral frowned, then rose and half-walked, half-waddled to the bookcase. Cerryl didn't recall the older mage being so ponderous before, but said nothing as Myral returned to the table and unrolled the map scroll.

"Where?"

Cerryl pointed. "About there, right before that turn when it joins the eastern main tunnel."

Myral's eyebrows rose, and his face cleared immediately. "Oh . . . that. It's not a collector tunnel. Years and years ago, there was a group of ruffians—they called themselves traders, but they decided to use the sewers as a way out of the city to avoid the guards and the tariffs, and they built an entrance from the lower level of their building. That tunnel was never fully bricked up underground—just from the building side. If you followed it, you'd come to a brick wall. There was another bricked-up tunnel exit all the way out by the spillway, but that was filled in with rubble." The older mage smiled. "They got away with it for almost a year." He paused. "I told you how the sunlight striking the water on the spillways cleans the sewer water before it reaches the lake . . . ?"

"Yes, ser. You took me out there and showed me how the sludge is trapped in the first basin, and then—"

Myral waved vaguely as he straightened up and rerolled the scroll. "No sense in telling you what I've told you. These days—maybe I always did—I repeat myself too much. Happens when you get old."

"Old? You don't look old."

"I'm old, Cerryl. Old, old, old for a mage. I have my vanities, and Leyladin helps me with them, but I'm an old man, good for telling about sewers and refuse and such, and little else." Myral plopped back into his chair, breathing heavily. After a moment, he glared at Cerryl. "Go on. You go scour the sewer, and I'll sit here and look important to myself."

Cerryl stood.

"When you get to the smugglers' tunnel, be careful. You'll have to clean that out, or it will mean the secondary will have to be scoured sooner. But there's no telling whether their workmanship was any good. You may have to get masons. Just let me know." Myral laughed, then coughed. "It's not as though I'll be traveling far."

The younger man nodded again, then left, meeting Jyantyl and the lancers outside the barracks at the rear of the halls as usual.

The morning went quickly enough, if not so swiftly as Cerryl had hoped, since he found another set of small collectors on the east side. One was nearly totally plugged, and he'd had to use firebolts and steam to bore through the sludgy mass.

Even after he and the lancers had taken a midday break, Cerryl still felt tired, but he again unlocked the bronze sewer grate and nodded to Ullan and Dientyr, then started down the steps. At least in summer the tunnels were somewhat cooler than the streets.

He tried not to breathe deeply at first, until his sense of smell was partly deadened. The odors were far worse in summer and would get even worse as the heat drew on toward harvest. Cerryl ignored the omnipresent stench and let his senses range up the sewage tunnel to his right. Somewhere ahead was the bricked-up smugglers' tunnel.

The wastewater flowed down the bottom of the sewer, below the slimy walkway . . . but there was something about it . . . a hint of turbulence . . . something.

Cerryl let a small lance of the golden chaos light flare along the top of the water. A line of fire flashed even beyond the limits of his light lance. Something in the sewage was burning—an oil? He tried to sniff but could smell nothing. Where would oil come from?

He loosed another bolt of chaos along the tunnel wall closest to him, but all that resulted were cleaner bricks and white ash. In the lingering flash he could see as well as sense the curve of the secondary tunnel.

A brief tapping on the bricks echoed down the tunnel. Cerryl turned.

"Sorry, ser," squeaked Ullan.

Cerryl returned to scrutinizing the tunnel ahead, frowning not only because of the smell of burned oil but because of something else.

Ullan clicked or tapped the lance again.

Cerryl ignored the tapping, trying to press his senses into the darkness of the tunnel.

A scraping rose over the burbling of the drainage way.

Suddenly, Cerryl could sense someone—something around the corner—waiting in the supposedly bricked-up tunnel. He began to gather chaos to him as he heard boots on stone.

A faint light oozed out from the side tunnel, and two men appeared, dim shapes, shapes not clear even in his senses, let alone to his eyes. Cerryl blinked in spite of himself.

One hung a bronze lamp from a hook on the wall, a hook Cerryl hadn't noticed. Both men carried shields—large and dark glowing iron shields. They also bore dark iron blades that glowed with the reddened black of order, and moved silently and slowly toward Cerryl.

Behind him, Cerryl could hear the two white lancers easing backward, almost silently.

Myral had said the guards might not be much help. He'd also said that firing chaos against iron would jolt Cerryl.

Cerryl stepped back slowly, trying to think. What could he do?

The armed men moved toward him, shields forward.

Whhhstt!

Cerryl released a golden firebolt—not aimed at the leading man's shield, where it would do little good, but at the sewer water directly before and beside the man.

A second firebolt followed the first, and a third and a fourth.

Cerryl held his shields against the chaos steam, keeping it confined, trying to direct it toward the armed men even as he backed away from them, but they continued to advance.

He angled a gold lance light low—toward the leading man's legs. It missed, but the second man jumped and crashed into the tunnel wall, staggering there for a moment, his shield low.

Whhhhsttt! Cerryl flared another lance of the golden light into the man's exposed face.

"Aeei—" The choked scream died as the armsman clutched at his charred face and throat, then toppled slowly forward.

As he cast another firebolt at the sewer water, the young mage backed away from the first armsman.

The armsman rushed forward, then half-flung, half-pushed the iron shield at Cerryl, lifting the iron blade and scrambling the few remaining cubits between them.

With a calmness he did not feel, even as the heavy shield crashed into him, Cerryl loosed another firebolt.

The man plummeted forward, his body a charred mass.

Cerryl pushed away the heavy shield, conscious that he would have burns on his hands. In several places, his white tunic was charred from the impact of the iron.

He had to reach out and steady himself on the wall. His head ached, and his stomach churned, and he stood there, gasping, the darkness seeming to recede and flash toward him.

Finally, he straightened and began to walk toward the steps. Dientyr stood there.

"Ser?" The white lancer looked at the walkway.

"Where's Ullan?"

"Ah . . . I don't know, ser."

Cerryl kept walking until he reached the steps, where he sat down in the pool of light cast from the grate opening above. He didn't care if his whites were filthy. He needed to rest.

"Dientyr? Have someone get word to Myral . . . brigands in the sewer. They're dead, but I'm supposed to let him know."

"Yes, ser."

Cerryl ignored the relief in the guard's voice and the rapid scramble up the steps. He just kept trying to catch his breath. Was it that he'd thrown so much chaos in such a short time?

When he finally felt less shaky, he eased his way back up the tunnel slowly, looking through the darkness. But there was nothing left—except two partly charred figures, two iron shields and blades, and the smell of burned oil—and slime and sewage. Of Ullan there was no sign, either.

He turned back to the steps to wait for Myral.

Dientyr and another lancer preceded Myral down the steps. A messenger in blue followed.

"Cerryl?"

"I'm here. There's nothing here except me—and the bodies."

"Bodies?"

"Two armed men—I don't know why."

"Best we see." With the guard leading the way, and the messenger trailing, the two walked the few dozen cubits to the scene of the attack.

"Two of them." Myral studied the two forms—the mostly charred one and the partly uncharred one. His face hardened as he used the white-bronze knife in his hand to lift one of the shields, but his breath rasped heavily as he straightened.

Cerryl tensed. What had he done wrong?

"It is not you." The rotund mage turned to the messenger in blue. "I would have the honored Sterol meet me here."

"Yes, ser." The messenger left, almost as though fleeing.

"Maker's marks . . . on the shields." Myral continued to breathe heavily. "They're from Gallos . . . only one trader in arms licensed to Gallos . . . shouldn't be too hard to find who brought in iron weapons."

"I didn't think iron weapons were allowed here."

"A few uses only . . ." Myral panted.

"Ser . . . the steps back there. They're clean. You could sit there."

"Not . . . a bad idea."

Cerryl led Myral back to the steps up to the grate.

Even without Myral's orders, the lancers stood guard over the charred shapes sprawled on the walkway. Another group had joined Jyantyl on the street above in guarding the grate.

"Does this happen often?" Cerryl finally asked.

"Every once in a while. That's why we provide guards." Myral took another deep breath. "People think the sewers are out of our sight. Sometimes, they're right. We can't watch everything. The locks help, but some people tunnel in, like those smugglers." After a moment, he added, "After Sterol comes, we'll check that old tunnel they built. I would gather that your attackers unbricked part of it. What happened to Ullan?"

"I don't know. He was gone by the time I finished with—" Cerryl gestured up the tunnel.

"Most interesting. A missing guard, and an attack late in the day."

Late in the day? When someone knew a young mage would be tired? Cerryl hadn't thought about that.

Myral stood slowly. "The mighty Sterol is taking his time. While we wait, we might as well check that tunnel. You can clean some more if it's too slimy."

Cerryl felt like groaning but didn't. His left shoulder ached where the edge of the shield had struck him, and he felt exhausted.

They walked slowly over the bodies to where Cerryl had reached in scouring the walkway, trying not to touch either corpse, but the walkway was too narrow to walk around the dead brigands. Myral turned to Cerryl, eyebrows lifting.

Whhhst!

Cerryl used as little of the golden lance flame as possible in clearing the fifty cubits of walkway that curved to the rough aperture of the smugglers' tunnel, a rough archs lightly less than four cubits high.

Cerryl stepped into the side tunnel gingerly, feeling the clay underfoot give slightly. Less than twenty cubits farther on, the tunnel ended in a wall—except in the middle of the wall was an open doorway.

Myral stepped up and closed the door.

Cerryl took a deep breath. The back side of the door had been painted to resemble bricks.

"Someone has been using this again. Clever of them." Myral turned. "No one is around now, and I'd rather leave this to Sterol. You don't want to know where that door leads, not until you're a mage, anyway." The heavyset older mage puffed slowly back along the secondary until he reached the stairs to the street, where he carefully settled himself on the second step.

How long they waited, Cerryl wasn't sure, except that the sound of more armsmen and weapons echoed down the steps even before a handful of guards appeared, followed by the High Wizard.

Sterol appeared out of the dimness, a glowing presence of chaos, with a squad of guards before him and with Kinowin flanking him. "Your summons was not precisely convenient, Myral."

Myral heaved himself to his feet. "Yes, High Wizard." Myral gestured into the darkness toward the two bodies. "Young Cerryl dispatched these two malefactors. I would request that you examine the bodies for yourself."

Sterol nodded. Kinowin's face was blank.

"You might also note the side tunnel beyond the bodies. There is a door painted to look like bricks."

Sterol stepped past the two, and followed by Kinowin, he marched down the tunnel. Cerryl noted that while Sterol did not blaze chaos energy the way Jeslek did, he definitely radiated chaos—as did the rugged Kinowin, if to a lesser degree.

The High Wizard stopped by the bodies and bent over. After a moment, Sterol straightened. "I see what you mean." With a gesture, he pointed toward the figures, and the tunnel filled with blinding light.

Cerryl blinked. When the stars cleared from his eyes, all that remained were white dust, two iron shields, and two blades.

Wearing heavy white gloves he had pulled from somewhere, Kinowin lifted both shields and handed them to one of the lancers. Then he lifted the blades and carried them toward the steps with the lancers, leaving Sterol with Cerryl and Myral.

"Also," said Myral, "one of the lancers guarding young Cerryl fled somewhere into the tunnels." The older mage glanced to Cerryl.

"Ullan," Cerryl supplied.

"Ullan is doubtless hiding somewhere in the sewer. You have leave to destroy him." Sterol's eyes flashed as he looked at Cerryl. "In fact, you are to destroy him immediately—without mercy. You have the power to do so." Sterol glanced around the tunnel. "Do you understand?"

Cerryl nodded.

"Good." The High Wizard turned to Myral. "We have some work to do." Then he turned back to Cerryl. "Continue to seek Ullan and carry out my orders. We will not expect to see you before the evening meal. If you find him, do what else you can here. If you cannot find him—or if you do—see me after you eat."

"Yes, ser."

"You had only two guards, did you not, young Cerryl? Down here with you?"

"Yes, honored Sterol. I sent Dientyr to fetch Myral; Ullan disappeared when I was struggling with the . . . malefactors."

"You remained here?"

"Yes, ser."

"Good. Better and better." Sterol gestured. "Luyar, pick enough guards to watch all the grates on the secondary and the western main tunnel. If they catch Ullan, have them hold him for Cerryl."

The lancer leader nodded and walked back up the steps to the street above.

"If the lancers find him first . . . you will be notified, and your task will be to execute the deserter with chaos-fire—right where he stands when you find him."

"Yes, ser."

Sterol nodded in a peremptory fashion, turned, and started up the sewer steps. Myral puffed up behind the High Wizard.

Cerryl looked down the tunnel, past the stairs and away from where the bodies had been, then shrugged. Ullan had gone away from where Cerryl had fought the armsmen, and the entrance, and the lancer hadn't gone up the steps.

After a moment, Cerryl started down the tunnel slowly, heading back through the area he had scoured earlier, watching his feet nonetheless.

Behind him followed the pair of lancers. Were they watching him as much as guarding him?

He passed one set of steps, dappled with light from the grate overhead, then a second, and finally a third. The tunnel was silent except for the muted gurgle of sewer water in the drainage way and the sound of boots on damp brick.

Close to the fourth access steps, Cerryl paused, listening, looking into the darkness, letting his senses pick up something . . . someone . . . hiding in the darkness behind the stairs.

He turned to the guard with the light, whispering, "I think he's up ahead. Stay back here a bit. I can't follow him and worry about you."

Surprisingly, the guard nodded.

Cerryl eased along the edge of the tunnel, knowing that the back and upper sleeve of his tunic were hopelessly stained with slime.

A set of boots scraped on the bricks . . . as did a spear.

Cerryl waited, gathering chaos energy from around him. "Ullan . . ."

Only the sewer water in the drainage way burbled.

"There's nowhere to go."

The indistinct figure of the lancer slid along the side of the steps, lifting the white-bronze spear.

Cerryl focused the chaos energy—the white-golden lance.

Whhsttt! The chaos bolt shivered the spear and turned it into flame. Ullan dropped it . . . his hand and lower arm also a mass of flame.

The lancer reached for the shortsword at his belt.

With almost a sigh, Cerryl loosed another targeted firebolt, one that caught Ullan in the midsection. The lancer staggered, seeming to fold before sliding onto the bricks.

Cerryl stepped forward. "Who set it up?"

Ullan lay sprawled on the slimed bricks, his midsection blackened, eyes avoiding Cerryl.

Cerryl focused another chaos bolt on the lancer's foot, then let it fly. The odor of burning flesh rose over the smells of sewage and mold.

"Aeeei . . . no . . . no . . ."

"Who told you to keep tapping that spear?"

"Don't know, ser . . . swear I don't . . . Someone in white . . . short . . . never saw his face . . . soft voice . . . slim . . . wore scent."

Cerryl let a blaze of fire glimmer from his fingertips.

"Honest . . . honest . . . ser . . . threatened to kill me if I told . . ."

Cerryl could sense the truth, and the despair. For a moment, he hesitated, then let the fire flare across Ullan.

He swallowed, trying to hold in the nausea—and succeeding, barely.

After a time, he turned away from the white ash that sifted across the walkway.

The two lancers waited, their lamp a puddle of light in the darkness. Cerryl walked past them silently, back toward the unfinished cleaning of the secondary tunnel.

LXXVIII

Every eye looked at Cerryl as he stepped into the meal hall, then looked away, almost in relief, it seemed to the thin-faced student mage. He was late, later than he should have been because, even with chaos, cleaning the grime off his tunic had taken longer than he had expected. Surprisingly, he'd even managed to deal with the dark grease that he'd thought had burned the white cloth.

Bealtur and Kochar kept their eyes down, fixed on the polished white oak of the table. The meal hall was silent, students looking at the entrance archway every so often. Unlike at most meals, no full mages were in the hall.

Cerryl walked through the silence to the serving table and helped himself to the mint burkha and noodles, to a healthy chunk of bread, and poured a full mug of the light ale, carrying it all over to the table where Faltar and Lyasa sat.

"You missed everything," Faltar whispered.

"I have sewer duty. I miss a lot," Cerryl said dryly. He sniffed. Did his tunic still carry the faint odor of sewage? "What happened?"

"You don't know?" asked Lyasa.

"I was told specifically to stay in the sewers until mealtime," said Cerryl. "The orders came from the High Wizard. In person. I wasn't about to do otherwise."

The black-haired Lyasa's mouth formed an O.

"Sterol came into the common with some guards." Faltar lowered his voice to almost a whisper. "They had iron shields. You know that's trouble. Iron deflects chaos, you know?"

"I have learned that."

"Sterol had Kinowin and Fydel with him, and even Myral."

Cerryl took a bite of the bread, trying to quiet his empty stomach. "For what?"

"You should have seen Kesrik." Faltar glanced toward the table where Kochar and Bealtur sat. "Sterol threw an iron shield—he had to wear heavy leather gloves, but he did throw it—right at Kesrik, and he asked him something about recognizing it . . . about maker's marks and authorized traders with Gallos."

Lyasa nodded.

"Marker's marks? Why would Kesrik have anything to do with traders?" Cerryl paused. "You think that this has to do with Kesrik's family?"

"It makes sense," Lyasa murmured. "Kesrik doesn't like you. His family has access to golds and armsmen, and weapons."

"Jeslek wasn't around either," added Faltar.

Nor Anya, thought Cerryl, glancing at the blond Faltar.

"Kesrik—he turned white, and then it looked like he tried to throw chaos at Sterol." Lyasa glanced at the silent Kochar and Bealtur.

"That wasn't smart," said Faltar.

"He tried to throw chaos? With those three standing there?" Cerryl took a mouthful of the spicy, brown-sauced burkha and noodles.

"Well . . . there was chaos-fire everywhere. Kinowin raised his shields first," said Lyasa, "and then someone threw chaos-fire at him, and he fried Kesrik. I think he was the one. It happened so fast."

"And then?" Cerryl chewed on a piece of bread to relieve the heat of the spiced burkha.

"Sterol looked around and he said something like, 'Scheming is not appropriate in the Halls of the Mages.' "

"Then they all marched off, and a couple of the lancers picked up the iron shields," Faltar concluded.

"So . . ." Lyasa's eyes fixed on Cerryl. "What was Kesrik doing? Why were you in the sewers so late?"

"A pair of men with iron shields and blades attacked me," Cerryl admitted.

"How did you stop them?" pressed Faltar. "Myral and Derka have both been telling me how dangerous it is to cast chaos against iron, especially polished iron."

Cerryl forced a laugh. "Steam . . . mostly. I turned the water in the drainage way into steam."

Lyasa smiled. "You thought quickly. How did you manage that?"

"I don't know." Cerryl had to shrug. "I knew I couldn't use chaos against iron. I had to do something." He took another mouthful of burkha, feeling slightly deceptive and taking refuge in eating.

"How did they get down there? All the grates are locked and sealed with chaos," Faltar pointed out.

"They used an old smugglers' tunnel. Myral knew about it, but it had been bricked up years ago. They unblocked part of it."

"How did they know . . . ?" Faltar's forehead furrowed.

"That's easy," said Lyasa. "Cerryl walks down the streets every day. There are sewer grates every few hundred cubits. Anyone could figure that out."

Cerryl wondered. That was true enough . . . but why had he been assigned the secondary tunnel that already had an old smugglers' tunnel? Someone wasn't telling the truth, but who? Myral had said he could lie convincingly, and that meant other mages could as well. Despite the maker's marks on the shields, Kesrik or his family paying to have armsmen attack Cerryl didn't make sense, especially after Ullan's words about a slender mage. But Anya wasn't from a trader's family, not that Cerryl recalled. And why would Sterol have turned Kesrik to ash, if the apprentice mage hadn't been guilty? All that meant there was even more that Cerryl didn't know.

LXXIX

The two guards nodded as Cerryl passed them and started up the tower steps. The nod from Hertyl was more deferential, Cerryl thought. Myral's door was closed, and his room felt empty to Cerryl as the younger man passed the landing. Before he had reached the third level, his steps lagged, and he was breathing heavily when he stopped at the open landing of the uppermost level of the tower.

"Come in, Cerryl," called Sterol through the white oak door that was not quite closed.

Cerryl took a deep breath, squared his shoulders, took another deep breath, and opened the brass-bound white oak door. He stepped into Sterol's apartment, turning and closing the door to the position in which he had found it.

"You can close it all the way." Sterol sat behind the desk, centered between the white oak bookcases filled with leather-bound volumes. The High Wizard gestured to the straight-backed chair before the desk.

Cerryl closed the door, then walked across the room and around the table that held the circular screeing glass to take the proffered seat.

"You found the missing guard." The High Wizard's hair glinted a reddish iron gray in the light of sunset that streamed through the open tower window at his back.

"Yes, ser. He hadn't gone that far. He was hiding to the south, where the next secondary joined the main tunnel, behind a set of steps."

Sterol nodded. "There was no one else with him?"

"No. He was alone. At least, I didn't hear or see anyone else." Cerryl added carefully.

"Did the guards see you flame him?" The High Wizard shifted his weight in his chair, but his eyes remained on Cerryl.

"I don't know how much they saw, honored Sterol. They saw me use flame. They had to have heard Ullan scream."

"He screamed? Good . . . excellent. That will suffice. No white guard or lancer must ever be allowed to desert his post or duty." Sterol frowned. "Why did he scream?"

"He had a lance, and I struck his arm and the lance with the first firebolt."

"You went in front of the guards?"

"I wasn't supposed to be, ser?"

"Ah, young Cerryl . . . the bravery of youth. That story will indeed serve you—and the Guild—serve us well." Sterol laughed, but the laugh faded as the High Wizard studied the younger man. "I had hoped . . . but you retain enough force . . . more than enough . . . and you are bright . . ." A quick nod followed as though Sterol had reached a conclusion about something.

Cerryl waited.

"I take it this . . . Ullan said nothing?" Sterol's voice sharpened.

"He begged for mercy."

"Anything else?"

Cerryl frowned. "He mumbled something about being afraid . . . that someone had approached him. That might have been Kesrik . . . but he said he didn't know, only that whoever it was happened to be short." Cerryl smiled apologetically. "I hope you don't mind, ser, but since someone was trying to injure me, I wanted to know if he knew anything. I did flame him, as you ordered."

"Short . . . hmmmm . . ." Sterol smiled broadly. "I will pass that along to Jeslek . . . another confirmation that Kesrik was involved. His family has been asked to leave Fairhaven, you know. They had to have supplied the coins paid to the two men you killed."

"Yes, ser."

"Now . . . do you remember what I told you when you first came to the tower?"

"Yes, ser. That I was to watch and to say nothing and to tell none but you . . . and not until you asked."

"Good." Sterol's face hardened. "Do you honestly think that Kesrik could have set up the attempt on you?"

"Ser . . . I do not know Fairhaven or everything about the Guild. I had some doubts, but when one knows so little . . ."

Sterol laughed, a short bark. "You know far more than you let any know, even me, and that is wise, so long as you remember who is High Wizard."

"Yes, ser."

"What do you know about Recluce?"

"Nothing except what is in the histories and the old stories, ser. I have overheard that Recluce is trying to trade with Gallos through Spidlar and that such will not help Fairhaven."

Sterol leaned back in his chair slightly, but his face remained stern. "Men are weak, Cerryl. They will seek coins and personal gain, even if it will ruin their children and their children's children. Even white mages can do the same, and that can be even more dangerous, for they do not have to worry about their children. Chaos provides great power, and great power can create great corruption. That is why Kesrik died."

Cerryl didn't conceal the puzzlement he felt.

"No," Sterol answered the unspoken question. "Kesrik was not powerful. He was weak, too weak to resist the corruption of chaos. He saw the great power wielded by Jeslek and would do anything if he could have possessed like power." The High Wizard straightened and the red-flecked brown eyes bored through Cerryl. "Do you understand that?"

"I understand that he wanted power, ser. He tried to control the other students."

Sterol nodded. "That is one reason why you found brigands in the sewer, seeking your death. Where chaos can be manifested, so can corruption and evil. The same is true of great order, and that is why Recluce is corrupt. Far too much order has been concentrated on that isle. Now . . . why do you suppose so many mages are not in Fairhaven?"

Cerryl blinked. He'd known there were mages outside the city, but Sterol was suggesting there were far more away from Fairhaven.

"Too many mages means more concentration of chaos." Sterol offered a wry smile. "That is also why I had you made a student—and years back, Kinowin, and later young Hcralt. But those are points for you to consider in the seasons ahead." He placed the fingers of each hand against each other in a pyramidal shape. "What have you observed here in Fairhaven?"

Cerryl swallowed. "Ah . . . I have observed much, ser. I have noticed that most of the mages do not teach so much as force me to answer questions and to undertake tasks."

"That is because that is what I have told them to do. All young people, even student mages, ignore or resist what they are told by their elders. They learn best by thinking and doing. What else have you observed?"

"I don't know what else to say, ser. There is so much, so many things I had not considered. I never would have thought sewers so important, or paved streets and walks or clean water . . ." Cerryl looked almost helplessly at Sterol.

The High Wizard nodded, almost to himself, then glanced toward the door, then back at Cerryl. "Well . . . you need some rest, and you have a sewer to finish cleaning, I believe?"

Cerryl nodded, then stood.

"And . . . Cerryl . . . best you be most careful out in the streets. We are not as loved or respected as should be, and Kesrik's family was well connected."

"Yes, ser."

After he closed the tower door to the topmost landing, Cerryl walked slowly down the tower steps. Sterol had been pleased, but Cerryl wasn't sure he liked the idea of his actions being passed to Jeslek. Nor did Sterol's parting caution help, although it was clear he needed to be careful just about everywhere.

Also . . . there was one other thing that worried him—worried him a great deal. While he suspected Kesrik had been a poor mage, Cerryl doubted that the blond student would have tried something as involved as hiring bullyboys to kill Cerryl in the sewer. And Sterol's questions confirmed that—in a roundabout way.

Was this another convoluted test—or did someone else want Cerryl out of the way? And why? And if that happened to be so, why had Myral assigned Cerryl the sewer with the smugglers' tunnel? Or had that been Myral's choice? Was Myral right—that Jeslek himself viewed Cerryl as a rival?

And why had Sterol talked about chaos power corrupting? Cerryl was only a poor student mage . . . not exactly a respected and powerful mage like Jeslek or Kinowin. Despite Sterol's avuncular performance,

Cerryl doubted that Sterol had said all that just to further educate him, and that left Cerryl more worried than ever.

Still, he had managed to survive, and that was something for the orphaned son of a white fugitive.

So far, he reminded himself. *So far*.

LXXX

Cerryl opened the door and stepped into Myral's room. The heavyset mage finished a sip of cider and pointed toward the chair. Cerryl left the door ajar, hoping Myral wouldn't mind, but he wanted the breeze that existed with the open door. He eased into the chair and waited.

After a moment, Myral cleared his throat. "How long will it take you to finish that secondary tunnel?"

"Two, perhaps three days."

"I need to inform Sterol about that." Myral took a sip of cider. "Your meeting with him last night went well." The older mage smiled as Cerryl raised his eyebrows. "No, I have not talked to the High Wizard. After yesterday, had it not gone well, you would not be here today. Jyantyl did tell me that you were forced to deal with Ullan, and that you handled his execution well."

Cerryl swallowed slightly.

A series of coughs racked Myral, and Cerryl leaned forward in his chair.

The balding mage raised a hand, as if to insist Cerryl remain seated, coughed several times more, then took a very small sip from his mug. "Chaos dust does not do the lungs well, but when one is a mage, the dust follows wherever one is, and I'm not one for wasting away on a breezy hilltop." Myral snorted. "You need to keep working on whatever you're doing to keep the chaos out of your system. It's effective, it appears, but sometimes you flicker very brightly. Do you understand?"

"I take it that flickering that way is not good?"

"Not if you are a very young mage, it's not."

"I'll keep working on it."

"Good. I will see you again tomorrow morning."

Cerryl rose.

"And, Cerryl?"

"Yes, ser?"

"You can close the door all the way when you leave. I'm not as hot-blooded as you are."

Cerryl flushed as he closed the door behind him. On the way down the steps, he took several deep breaths, then nodded to Hertyl. He went down the stairs to the foyer quickly and turned left toward the courtyard and the rear barracks, where he usually met Jyantyl.

At the doorway to the courtyard, he saw a blonde figure in green. Leyladin smiled as he neared. "Good day, Cerryl."

"Good day, Leyladin."

She stopped, as if she wanted to talk. So did Cerryl.

"Cerryl . . . ?"

"Yes?"

"How did you find Myral this morning?"

Cerryl kept his pleasant smile in place. "He was in good spirits. He gets tired more quickly now, I think."

"More quickly than when you first began to work the sewers?"

He nodded.

"That has been less than three seasons." She frowned, then smiled gently. "He is older than he looks, and I fear for him. I suppose all healers worry about those they tend."

Cerryl repressed the exuberant smile he felt. "He has said that you help him, but he has never said what it was that you did."

The young healer glanced around the foyer and lowered her voice. "All mages who handle chaos . . . the chaos ages them faster, even those like Myral who are careful. I can help restore a little of the order—only a little, because too much order is worse than too little. It helps—or it did. Now I worry."

Cerryl could sense no one was near or watching them in a glass. "Thank you."

Her brows knit in puzzlement. "For what?"

"For not mentioning that I once saw you in the glass."

Leyladin laughed, a warm laugh, a soft sound, and her eyes sparkled enough that Cerryl could see the amusement. "Oh . . . Cerryl . . . I never knew you were the one. I thought . . . after I first saw you . . . but you never said anything."

"I only tried twice," he confessed.

She shook her head; then her face turned calm. "I thank you, ser."

Cerryl nodded as he heard the footsteps, even before he saw Bealtur. "You are most welcome. May your healing continue to bring results."

With a quick nod, she was gone.

Bealtur kept his eyes from meeting Cerryl's, and continued toward the tower, following Leyladin up the steps from the foyer.

Cerryl hurried through the courtyard, glad for the brief cooling afforded by the fountain and the light breeze before he entered the rear hall on his way to the rear barracks. But most of all, he was glad he had told Leyladin. He'd hated carrying that as a secret, and her reaction had relieved him . . . at least somewhat.

Waiting outside the weathered granite building with Jyantyl were four lancers Cerryl had never seen before.

"Good morning, ser," offered the weathered lancer.

"Good morning." Cerryl's eyes took in the new guards. "What about Dientyr?" he asked quietly. "I would not—"

"He would be glad that you thought of him." Jyantyl gave a quick smile. "His punishment is over, and he has returned to his company. They are departing for Jellico tomorrow."

"Are you? You had mentioned something . . ."

Jyantyl lifted his shoulders, then dropped them. "Some day soon, but no one has said."

More and more lancers heading west, reflected Cerryl as the group of six started southward and out to the avenue. Something was definitely happening.

The light breeze ruffled Cerryl's fine hair, and he brushed it off his forehead, glancing up at the morning sky. The faintest haze of high clouds tinted the green-blue sky, imparting a slightly bluer cast to the heavens.

Cerryl walked in silence, conscious of the heavy tread of the lancers' boots as they turned onto the avenue and continued southward.

As they passed the row of inns that catered to the richer travelers, he glanced down the side avenue that led to the traders' square to the southwest. Was it less crowded?

Ahead on the paved sidewalk, two women eased toddlers into a shop—a wine cooper's shop.

Cerryl frowned. Why would they go there? He tried to catch the sense of the words from the women and the cooper's assistant gathered under the overhang of the shop entrance.

"Student mage or not . . . red stripe . . . still kill a man as look at him . . ."

". . . not so much as a reason . . . threw Kelwin and his folk out of the city . . ."

". . . chaos . . . dirty way to fight . . . not like a blade or a lance . . . them's clean at least . . ."

Cerryl wanted to answer all of them, but he kept a smile plastered on his face as he strode toward the last sewer grate. He hoped the grate was the last, and the collector the last he had to scour, but he supposed he could be like Kinowin had been, spending more than a year beneath the streets of Fairhaven.

He repressed a shudder. *I hope not. I hope not.*

LXXXI

Cerryl slipped into the chair across from Myral, blotting his forehead from the warmth that would certainly intensify as the late summer day went on. Somehow, it was still hard to believe that another summer had nearly passed, and that he had been in Fairhaven almost a year and a half.

"I went back as you said, and checked everything yesterday. The tunnel is clean." Cerryl paused. "They haven't bricked up that door yet."

"I know. Your successor, young Faltar, will take care of that."

"My successor?"

"I have talked it over with Sterol. You have cleaned elaborately and well two secondary sewer tunnels, and you have proved that you have the minimal ability to use chaos to defend yourself. There's nothing more you need learn about the sewers or the use of chaos-fire to clean them." Myral smiled blandly. "Jeslek has summoned you. You are to replace Kesrik as his assistant."

"I thought Bealtur or Kochar . . ."

"Neither is as accomplished nor as far along as you are."

"I do not understand. I don't think Jeslek even likes me."

"Nor should he. You respect his ability, but you do not worship the ground on which he treads." Myral's tone was dry. "Respect will suffice for now, but never forget to respect the overmage. Remember that."

Cerryl nodded.

After a sip of cool cider and a silence that the creaking of a noisy wagon on the avenue broke, Myral turned back to Cerryl. "Cerryl . . . times are getting . . . interesting." The older mage coughed, the same racking cough, despite the warmth of the room, covering his mouth with a grayish cloth.

"Are you all right?"

"As well . . . as possible." Myral folded the cloth.

"Ser, if you would explain why times are interesting . . . I did not have the privilege of growing up in the creche."

"I'd not call it a privilege." Myral laughed, a laugh that turned into another racking cough. The older mage blotted his mouth once more.

"Are you sure you are all right, ser?"

"Nothing wrong with me but age . . . and the ills that brings a mage." Myral took a sip from the mug on the table. "You know about Gallos, do you not? It stretches from where the rivers join in the north all the way south to Ruzor. The distance is vast enough that it has never been measured accurately, Esaak notwithstanding, but Gallos extends well over eight hundred kays, perhaps a thousand from north to south, and it is a rich land."

"Yes . . . I have heard such."

"Too rich. The prefect is another descendant of Fenardre the Great who would emulate his ancestor. He is young, and he is cunning, and he does not like the road taxes or the traders' guild or us. He toys with Sverlik."

Sverlik—Cerryl had heard the name somewhere.

"Sverlik is the mage who represents Fairhaven in Fenard. He's close to my age, and he can't last forever, either. This young prefect—Lyam is his name—he wants to take over Certis and Spidlar. The Spidlarian Council of Traders, and all Spidlarians are traders of one sort or another, those who are not mercenaries . . . where was I? Oh, the Spidlarians are turning to more trade with Sarronnyn and Recluce, and Gallos is buying most of that. The traders think it is greed on Lyam's part, but greed is only the beginning. . . ." Myral coughed again and fell silent.

"Ser . . . does that mean the lancers must go to Gallos?"

"I cannot say what Jeslek and Sterol will decide. They will decide something. Jeslek has hinted that he *might* be able to develop another course of action. He has not said what that might be. You will be there to assist him."

"Ah . . . when do I see him?"

"Now. You might as well get on your way. I have little enough else to teach you, though I doubt I have taught you so much as you have taught yourself." A brief smile flitted across the lined round face.

"Ser, you have taught me much."

"Don't protest too much." Myral waved toward the door. "On your way, young Cerryl, old as you are beyond your years. On your way."

Cerryl rose. "Yes, ser."

"And do close the door. There's nothing more susceptible to chill than an old and tired mage."

"You're not that old and tired."

"You're kind but inaccurate. Best you get off to serve Jeslek . . . and Cerryl?"

"Yes, ser."

"He will be High Wizard one day. So be most careful."

Cerryl nodded. He had no intention of ever being other than most careful where Jeslek and Sterol—and Anya and Kinowin—were involved. He closed the door firmly, but not hard, and took a deep breath. What would being Jeslek's assistant involve? After a moment, he shrugged and started down the tower steps.

The foyer was empty, except for the tower guards. Was it his imagination, or were all the Halls of the Mages more deserted? Just because mages wanted out of the summer heat? Or because of the troubles that Myral had mentioned?

Cerryl paused in the courtyard, beside the fountain, and blotted his forehead, lingering in the fountain's spray to cool off before he marched toward the rear hall.

At the upstairs rear of the hall that contained his own cell, Cerryl paused at the door where the guard, a lancer in white he did not know, rapped on the white oak.

"Send Cerryl in."

Cerryl stepped into Jeslek's quarters. The white mage seemed to blaze with power.

Cerryl halted, not even closing the door.

"You can close it."

Cerryl complied.

"I will not cross words with you, young Cerryl." Jeslek's golden eye glittered. "You are here as Sterol's tool to watch over me as much as assist me. You know that, and I know that."

"The honored Sterol did not tell me such, ser."

Jeslek snorted. "He does not have to tell you such. How can you not answer his questions?"

"He is the High Wizard, ser." Cerryl felt as though he walked the edge of a cliff.

"You would pay such allegiance to any who might be High Wizard?" A slow smile crossed Jeslek's face.

"Would I have any choice, ser?"

Jeslek laughed. "I said I would not cross words with you, and yet you cross words with me. For a student mage, you are dangerous, young Cerryl."

Cerryl waited, feeling silence was his only response.

"I know you can wield more chaos than you manifest. How much more, that I do not know, save that it is nowhere near what I could bring to bear upon you. Do you understand that?"

"Yes, ser."

"And I can tell that is a truthful answer. That will suffice." Jeslek pointed to the chair beside the scrying table. "As my first assistant, you may sit. Kochar will be taking your place, and he, like you did, has much to learn." The white-haired wizard seated himself.

Cerryl sat as well, but slightly forward on the chair.

"Sterol should have told you about the intolerable situation in Gallos. Has he?"

"He and Myral told me about the new prefect, and about how the traders of Spidlar are taking goods from Recluce."

Jeslek nodded. "And you know that we have sent close to four thousand lancers to Certis to support the viscount, and to move them closer to Gallos?"

"I knew that most from the southern barracks had been sent, but not how many."

"I am glad Sterol has informed you somewhat." Jeslek pulled at his chin. "We will be going to Gallos, but not for a handful of eight-days. We will be addressing the prefect's problems." A grim smile followed. "Not in exactly the way he would prefer. In the meantime, we have some last chores to consider, including cleaning the aqueduct." Jeslek stood. "You will certainly handle some of the work, but I will be supervising as well. It matters not if sewage isn't perfectly clean, but water is something else."

Jeslek pointed to the glass. "Can you call up an image?"

"I have not tried since I came, ser."

"We won't spend time on your experimenting here. You have my leave to practice, but you are not to observe through the glass any full mages. I would strongly suggest you attempt to use the glass to locate places along the Great White Highway in Certis and Gallos."

"Yes, ser."

"You may take a glass from the storeroom and practice in your cell until you are proficient. Meet me here tomorrow right after breakfast." Jeslek stood.

So did Cerryl. Then he bowed and left, closing the door quietly behind him. He had leave to use the glass—really for the first time. A smile crossed his face as he started down the corridor.

LXXXII

Cerryl set the small glass on his desktop and pulled up his stool, looking blankly at the silver surface that reflected the books on the shelf.

What did he know? Know well enough to call up in the glass?

Cerryl concentrated on Dylert's mill, trying to envision the barns and the mill and the house, trying to draw that image from the light that was chaos and permeated all the world.

The glass seemed to shiver before it clouded with white mists. Slowly, slowly, in the middle of the mists, appeared the door to the mill and a wagon on which a red-haired man loaded timbers from the lumber cart. Cerryl concentrated on seeing the redhead, and the image grew until only the man, the lumber cart, and the side of the wagon filled the glass.

Brental's face bore lines Cerryl did not remember, and the once-bright red beard was filled with white streaks. He did not smile as he lifted timber after timber, almost mechanically.

Cerryl found sweat oozing from all over his face, collecting in the thin wisps of hair on his jaw and chin that might become a beard someday. Then he let go of the chaos light he had focused on the glass, and took a deep breath.

How long had it been since he had seen Brental in person—more than four years? Enough to bring white to his beard?

Cerryl took another slow and long breath, this time trying to recall and focus on the kitchen and the long trestle table where he had eaten so often.

The second image came more easily, but Cerryl was still sweating as the silver mists formed and then ringed the view in the glass.

Dyella stood by the hearth. Her once-brown hair was streaked with silver. Beside her stood a young woman, a woman with a round face and black hair woven into a single braid wound into a bun on the back of her head.

Four places were set at the table.

Cerryl frowned as he released the image. The black-haired woman had to be Brental's consort. Matters could not be going well for Dylert— not with Brental's haggardness. Yet there was nothing that Cerryl could do. He had no coins beyond a silver and a handful of coppers, and no way to help the mill master. He thought of the four places at the table and swallowed.

He studied the blank glass again, feeling helpless.

Jeslek had suggested that he attempt to use the glass to find images along the Great White Highway. How should he start? How could he start?

He thought about Tellura, the town that he hadn't known about that had resulted in his having to draft the map of eastern Candar for Jeslek. Then he squared his shoulders and concentrated once more.

All he got was a set of swirling silver mist in the glass—and even hotter. He let the mists vanish and got up from the stool, then walked to the bed, where he stood on the end and tried to push back the shutters even wider to get some air, but the day was so still that not a breath of air entered the small cell.

He went back to the screeing glass and sat down. He tried to call up the image of the white road into Fairhaven. While slightly blurry at first . . . that effort worked, and he let the image lapse.

Cerryl wiped his forehead again, trying to keep the sweat from running into his eyes. He blinked. His entire head ached. He closed his eyes and sat before the desktop for a time, until the sharpest of the twinges had subsided. Then he opened his eyes, stood, and stretched. He couldn't go back to using the glass immediately, even if he were far, far from the expertise that Jeslek wished.

After opening the cell door and stepping into the cooler corridor, he walked slowly down the corridor toward the commons, which was empty, except for Bealtur, who sat alone at one of the tables, poring over a thick volume Cerryl didn't recognize. Cerryl turned toward the open windows, which offered no breeze, blotting his still wet forehead with the back of his forearm.

"Cerryl?"

Cerryl turned. "Yes, Bealtur?"

"I'm sorry." The hazel eyes twitched, and Bealtur's hand went to the thin dark goatee. "I didn't know Kesrik meant something like that."

Cerryl forced a pleasant smile. "I do not think many expected that. I didn't."

"Well . . . I am sorry. I wanted you to know that." Bealtur looked almost like a whipped dog.

"I understand." *Believe me, I do.*

"Cerryl? What are you doing here?" Faltar trudged into the commons, a set of books under his arm.

"What are you doing here? I thought you were out in the sewers."

Faltar gave a grim smile and lifted the leather-bound books. "Esaak and Broka prevailed on Derka and Myral. One morning a week for them. That's today." He slid into the chair at the table next to the one used by Bealtur. "Esaak even said continuing studies had benefitted you . . ."

Cerryl gave the blond student a wry smile. "I'm sorry."

"I don't know which is worse—mathematicks and anatomie or the sewers."

"The sewers," suggested Cerryl. "The sewers."

"Cerryl is right," added Bealtur. "Especially now, when it is so hot and the odor in the tunnels leads you to retch. I was there last summer." He shook his head.

"You two are so cheerful about studies." Faltar sighed and looked down at the books. At the sound of steps, his eyes turned. Leyladin, Lyasa, and Anya walked by the archway to the commons together. A smile crossed his face.

"I can tell where your thoughts are," said Cerryl.

"And yours aren't? You're smiling, too."

"There's not much I can do about it. I'm only a student. Besides, I suspect that those who are in higher places have a greater claim." Cerryl tried to keep the bitterness out of his voice.

"With Leyladin? Neither Sterol nor Jeslek could touch her. Maybe not Fydel or Myral, either." Faltar grinned. "It's good to see that you are like the rest of us—just that you don't show it."

Cerryl frowned. "But she's pretty. Why couldn't they?"

"She's a black or gray—healers have to be. Touching, and you can't take a woman without touching her, would be pretty painful—for both of them." Faltar winced. "They're filled with chaos."

"They say old Chystyr was into that, but he looked like he had lasted three generations, and he didn't have forty years when he died two years ago," Bealtur added from the adjoining study table.

Cerryl felt his heart sink. Did it have to be that way? He groped for words. Even though he already knew the answers, he had to say something. "Then . . . why does Myral instruct her? Or Sterol allow her around?"

"Someone has to instruct her, and Myral is the one who probably has the most experience. Sterol . . . how could he do otherwise?" Faltar glanced toward the corridor. "I'm hungry. Do you want to see if there's any bread left out?"

"They had two dark loaves a while ago," suggested Bealtur. "I had some."

As his stomach growled, the young mage nodded to himself. "That sounds good." He still had to practice with the glass, but that could wait, would have to wait until after he scrounged something to eat from the meal hall. He turned down the corridor, thinking again about the glass and how much he had to learn.

LXXXIII

As the chestnut carried him back toward Fairhaven, and the Halls of the Mages, Cerryl rubbed his forehead, which ached, because he couldn't message his posterior, which also ached from all his bouncing in the saddle. Sitting in the hard leather saddle, he still felt very high, and very exposed, even after almost ten kays of riding to and from the water tunnel. He kept having to relax his fingers because he found them gripping the leather of the reins far too tightly.

Eliasar had stuck him on a horse several times, but that hadn't prepared him for the five-kay ride out to the point north of Fairhaven where the aqueduct went underground and became the main water tunnel for the city. He glanced ahead at Jeslek, and Leyladin, who rode silently beside the white mage with an ease Cerryl envied. Even Kochar, riding beside Cerryl, seemed relatively at ease on horseback. Cerryl shifted his weight. The saddle felt hard, and it had felt hard from the first few cubits the chestnut had carried him right after breakfast.

He glanced to the west, where the sun hung over the hills, then to the white granite road that sloped gently toward the north gates of Fairhaven.

Cerryl still had to wonder why Leyladin had been required. He could sense as well as she had the residual chaos of sludge and mold in the cracks in the stone of the tunnel that could have poisoned the water had it been allowed to grow.

Before they had left the Halls, Jeslek had said, "There's a difference between what you might call honest chaos and the kind of chaos that poisons the water. That's something that usually only healers can feel."

For all of what Jeslek had said, cleaning the water tunnel had been little different from cleaning the sewers—except for checking more carefully to ensure there was no sign of slime or mold. Yet Jeslek had insisted that cleaning the aqueduct required a black or gray mage who was a healer. Cerryl wondered why—he had sensed the flux type of chaos that Leyladin had pinpointed. He frowned. Could it be that neither Jeslek nor Kochar had? He couldn't very well ask.

Cerryl massaged his left shoulder with his right hand, hanging on to the front rim of the saddle—and the reins—with his left.

By the time they passed through the north gates, Cerryl's thighs were cramping. The even half-score of white lancers followed the group down the avenue, and despite the late afternoon sun, Cerryl could feel even more sweat oozing down his back. The day had been hot, though much of it had been spent in the comparative cool of the water tunnel, and forecast a warm harvest season indeed.

He glanced ahead again at Leyladin, still riding easily beside Jeslek, then at Kochar. The redheaded student looked over with a smile and said in a low voice, "Remember, relax. Don't fight it."

How did one not struggle to stay in the saddle? Cerryl wondered. It was easy enough for Kochar to say, but another thing to manage. Cerryl took a deep breath and tried to study the grain exchange building as they rode past. Only a single carriage stood by the mounting blocks, cloaked in the building's shadow.

Nor did the artisans' square look any different from any other afternoon, with a handful of buyers, and a single apprentice running up the side street in the direction of Tellis's shop.

Before long, Cerryl reined up and glanced wearily around the front of the stables. Jeslek, Kochar, and Leyladin had already dismounted. A pair of stable boys led Kochar's and Leyladin's mounts into the stable, and they walked back around the north side of the stable toward the eastern courtyard.

A white-bearded man in blue stepped out from the late afternoon shade of the overhang. "You getting off that mount, ser?"

"Oh . . . yes." Cerryl swung awkwardly out of the saddle, and his legs almost buckled as his feet came down on the hard stone of the courtyard. He looked back at the big chestnut dubiously, wondering if he would ever get used to riding, then followed the others back to the east side of the stable.

"So you decided to rejoin us, Cerryl?" Jeslek did not smile as he spoke.

"I'm sorry, ser. I'm not as good a rider as you are." That was certainly true.

"Well, you're all here, and you did a good day's work—all of you." Jeslek's youthful face, as always, belied the white hair and the sun-gold eyes. "Right after breakfast again tomorrow."

Kochar took a deep breath. Leyladin and Cerryl exchanged glances as Jeslek turned and left.

Then, with a nod, Kochar also turned and left.

"You haven't ridden much, have you?" Leyladin smiled sympathetically. At least Cerryl hoped the smile was sympathetic.

"No. Eliasar stuck me up on a gentle beast a couple of times and let me ride around the streets. That was about it." Cerryl glanced toward the entrance to the courtyard, the one leading back to the main section of the Halls of the Mages, then at Leyladin. "Ah . . . I had a question."

She smiled. "No . . . I'm not Myral's lover. Nor Jeslek's. Myral's a sweet, but not to my taste. Jeslek's not to my taste, either, but that wouldn't stop him. I'm a gray, almost a black, and that does stop him because that wouldn't work."

"Ah . . ." Cerryl found himself flushing furiously. "That wasn't . . . my question."

"That may not have been the question you were going to ask." She grinned. "But it was on your mind." She waited. "Wasn't it?"

Cerryl found himself blushing again.

"I'll take that for a yes. Now . . . what was the question you were going to ask?"

"I could see the kind of chaos you were finding in the tunnel. Can't all whites?"

The blonde shook her head. "Myral could. Faltar *might* be able to. You clearly can. Once a white mage surrounds himself—or herself—with chaos, it's really hard for most of them to sense lower amounts of pure physical chaos, like the stuff that grows in the sewers or the water tunnels." She cocked her head and looked at Cerryl, almost as if she had not quite seen him before. "That could be a useful thing for you. I wouldn't tell anyone, though."

"Thank you." He gestured toward the archway. "Would you like to eat . . . ?"

"I would." Leyladin smiled. "But it will have to be another time. Tonight, I promised my father I'd have dinner with them. It's his natal day."

"Well . . . I hope you have a good meal." Cerryl offered a smile in return. "It's probably better than in the halls." He paused. "You don't have to eat here, do you?"

"No. And I sleep at home. But I can't be a full member of the Guild, either, not as a gray or black."

"Oh . . ."

"Like everything, it has its advantages and disadvantages." She nodded. "I do have to go."

Cerryl watched as her green-clad figure vanished through the archway that led to the southern part of the avenue. Why had the glass drawn him to her, so many years earlier? He was drawn to her, like iron to a lodestone, and even now, he wasn't quite sure why. It wasn't lust. *Not just lust . . . anyway . . .*

He watched where she had gone. Then he turned and walked slowly toward the meal hall, conscious that his thighs still ached. So did his rear, and his head.

More riding tomorrow? He winced.

LXXXIV

Several large droplets of water splatted from the overhead arch of the water tunnel onto Cerryl's already damp hair and oozed down his forehead toward his eyes. He blotted them away with the back of his forearm and watched Leyladin's gesture.

"There's some of the dark chaos along this joint," said Leyladin.

Cerryl studied the polished stone of the tunnel walls, the damp gray broken by a line of dark green.

Whhsst! He eased a firebolt onto the slime that coated the mortar, a firebolt because he didn't wish to use the fire lances when Jeslek was watching—or anyone who might report that ability to the overmage. Ashes flaked into the damp air of the water tunnel. Both Leyladin and Cerryl coughed.

Under the light of the bronze lamp carried by the lancer, as the ashes flaked away, the surface of the mortar appeared, yellowed with age, and with a long crack, still dark-looking.

"There's more . . ."

"I know," Cerryl said tiredly. "I can see the dark stuff there." He did not glance over his shoulder, sensing Jeslek's presence with every bit of chaos he channeled into destroying the flux-causing natural chaos in the decayed joints of cracked granite tunnel walls. Making sure he revealed nothing of his own abilities to focus chaos into light lances made the job even harder, but he trusted Leyladin's suggestion that he reveal nothing he did not have to.

After a deep breath, Cerryl half-dropped, half-arced another firebolt against the mortar. This time the darkness—and the flux chaos—vanished in the swirling white ashes.

Cerryl found himself taking another deep breath, leaning forward, and trying not to pant.

"Kochar, you see what Cerryl is doing. The next one Leyladin finds, you clean it up." Jeslek's voice was crisp and impersonal. "Stand back."

WHHHHSSTTT! Once again, another wall of flame flared down the tunnel, scouring most of the surface of the granite, leaving just the rough patches not touched by Jeslek's flame blasts.

Cerryl coughed again as the ashes and white fire dust settled and as the drier air came through the tunnel vent opened by the lancers who followed along the top of the stone tunnel.

"Here." Leyladin stepped forward another half-dozen paces—followed by a tall lancer with the bronze lamp—and pointed, then stepped back.

Whst. Kochar's small fireball plopped onto the dark patch on the side wall.

"Another one, please," requested the blonde.

"Keep at it, Kochar." Jeslek's voice was hard. "We need to finish today. The reserve tanks are almost empty, and we need to reopen the tunnel."

". . . trying . . ."

Cerryl almost felt sympathy for the redhead.

By the end of the day, when Cerryl stepped out of the tunnel access building into the late afternoon sun, into the dust and heat, he had somewhat less sympathy, since Kochar had lost all ability to raise chaos halfway through the afternoon, leaving Cerryl to handle all of the rough patches and cracks.

Heat waves shimmered off the side road. Slowly, he heaved himself into the chestnut's saddle, trying not to grunt. Leyladin and Jeslek mounted easily, as did Kochar and the half-score of white lancers.

The saddle remained hard as he tried not to bounce on the ride back into Fairhaven. He still had to work on relaxing his fingers. When he didn't think about it, they tightened around the leather of the reins until his hands were almost cramped.

In the west, the sun burned over the hazy hills, and heat waves rose off the white granite of the road. Sweat began to seep down Cerryl's back, and he almost wished for the dampness and cool of the water tunnels.

He was soaked when he reined up before the stables. Jeslek, Kochar, and Leyladin had already dismounted, even before he had stopped.

Cerryl swung his leg over the saddle, almost catching his boot on it. Then he stood wavering on the hard stone of the courtyard, his hand reaching out for the chestnut to steady himself.

Jeslek stepped forward, his eyes raking the three and settling on Cerryl. "That's all the work we'll do on the tunnel this season. I'll see you and Kochar tomorrow after breakfast." He did not smile as he turned and walked toward the Halls.

Kochar looked at the departing overmage, then trudged after him. Cerryl took a deep breath and looked for Leyladin, but she, too, had vanished. With a shrug, he walked slowly to his cell and then to the bathing chamber.

His stomach was growling by the time he finally reached the meal hall, right after the bells rang. Even so, Kochar had a full platter already and was walking toward the table where Bealtur and Heralt ate together in the corner. The redhead sat down with them.

Cerryl walked slowly from the serving area toward one of the empty round tables, where he sat. He glanced at what was supposed to be lemon-creamed lamb, then across the table, unmindful of the soreness in too many muscles from riding to and from the water tunnel for three days, scrambling through the slippery tunnel, and feeling Jeslek watching over his shoulder every moment. The more he was around Jeslek, the less he trusted the overmage, despite Jeslek's apparent straightforwardness.

"Might we join you, ser mage?"

Cerryl looked up at the warm voice to see the blonde hair and green tunic, then staggered to his feet. "Of course."

"Sit down," Leyladin added. "If you're as tired as I am, you don't need to be jumping up for people."

Leyladin and Lyasa sat down on the other side of the table.

Cerryl sat and absently fingered his chin.

"You know, you'd look better if you didn't try to grow a beard."

Cerryl blinked, refocusing on the blonde.

"You're like all the other young mages, growing a beard to look older."

Cerryl's mouth opened.

"You'd look much better without it," she continued, breaking off a chunk of fresh dark bread.

"Iron irritates me," Cerryl said. "Even a sharp iron blade does."

"It does many of the whites. There are answers to that. I'm sure you'll find one. Besides, you'll look old and distinguished soon enough." Leyladin's eyes twinkled, and her voice lowered. "It's always better to be underestimated when you don't have as much power, and everyone knows it.

That's why I laugh a lot. Laughing mages can't be taken seriously."

"Nor women," added Lyasa.

For some reason, Cerryl's thoughts went back to Benthann and her comments about women always being considered for what they provided in bed. "The Guild allows women to be full mages. What about Anya or the older woman in Ruzor that Myral was telling me about?"

"Shenan," mumbled Lyasa. "Think she's Myral's younger sister. He doesn't say."

Leyladin frowned. "He's never mentioned her."

"There's usually something most mages don't mention." Lyasa took a long swallow of ale. "That tastes good."

"What were you doing today?" Cerryl glanced at the black-haired student.

"Anya and Whuyl were showing me how to use a dagger—in close. It's a lot of work."

Cerryl took a mouthful of the lamb, dry despite the thick sauce. "No one's taught me about daggers."

"Anya says a female needs that kind of knowledge."

"She'd know," suggested Leyladin quietly. "If it can kill, she's looked into it."

"I don't know that she has a choice," pointed out Lyasa. A wry smile crossed her lips. "You can't use your body for everything."

Cerryl almost choked, especially when he saw Falter at the serving table.

"We'll behave," promised Leyladin, her eyes sparkling.

Cerryl wasn't quite sure he wanted her to behave. Even Lyasa snorted.

After a moment, he finally asked the question he'd wondered about for over a year. "Why do you spend so much time with Myral? He doesn't need that much healing."

"Myral is old, very old for a white mage, Cerryl. He must be three-score, and most whites don't live much past two score." Leyladin lifted her shoulders and dropped them. "I'm a healer, and that's what he needs."

"That's all?"

"Handling chaos is hard on the body. You should know that. Especially after today."

Cerryl gave a rueful smile. "But Myral?"

"I'm a healer, Cerryl. Myral's not too proud to ask for my help, unlike Sterol or Esaak. And I can learn from him. He knows a lot." Leyladin studied him. "You . . . you're actually jealous."

Cerryl looked down, then forced himself to meet the laughing green eyes. "Yes."

"And honest."

"I try," he said. "I don't know how honest."

"You're honest. That's one reason why Myral likes you."

"Honesty isn't enough around here."

"No," interjected Lyasa, "it's not enough. But all the other stuff you need to know isn't enough without it, either. Not over time."

"My . . . we're all so philosophical . . ." Leyladin laughed.

Both Cerryl and Lyasa joined her laughter.

LXXXV

M atters have worsened in Gallos." Jeslek paced around the table, then glanced to the rear window of his quarters. "Even the High Wizard is concerned." His eyes went to Cerryl, then to Kochar. "We will be traveling to Jellico the day after tomorrow. Get together what you will need for a long trip."

"Yes, ser," said Kochar.

Cerryl nodded.

"There will be other mages and apprentices. You may bring your own glass, but no books. Not a word of the journey outside the Halls. From either of you." This time, the mage's golden eyes rested on Kochar. "You may go."

At least that meant that Cerryl didn't have to worry about Esaak and mathematicks. He bowed and turned, following Kochar through the door.

As Cerryl stepped out of Jeslek's quarters and down the corridor, he had to move aside as Kinowin strode past him. The tall mage with the purple-blotched cheek was aimed like a quarrel toward Jeslek's door.

The slender student mage walked slowly down the corridor. What did he need for a journey? What kind of journey was it going to be? He wished he'd asked more, but Jeslek somehow discouraged questions, without even saying a word.

At the foot of the steps, he glanced around, then walked slowly toward the commons but found it empty, except for Bealtur poring over a thick tome. Cerryl turned. Leyladin might have been able to give him an idea, but he hadn't seen her.

Who else might help—who would be around? He nodded, then turned and walked swiftly back down the corridor and out into the courtyard. Light rain joined the fountain spray in cooling the enclosed space, and Cerryl hurried into the foyer of the front hall and then up the front steps to the tower, past the silent guards.

He tried not to cough at the fine white dust raised by his boots as he trudged up the levels to Myral's room, where he stood for a long moment on the landing, listening, hoping he wasn't interrupting the older mage. Finally, he knocked gingerly on Myral's door.

"Yes, Cerryl. You can come in." The old mage sat in his chair by the table, but his feet were resting on a stool. "Too much chaos in the legs. It pools in the feet by late in the day, and I must elevate them to let my body redistribute it."

Cerryl nodded.

"Now . . . young fellow . . . why are you here?" Myral raised his mug, almost as if in a salute.

"Ah . . . ser . . . Jeslek is taking us to Jellico . . . and told us to make ready. I thought you would know if there happened to be anything I should take beyond clothes."

Myral laughed. "I can see Jeslek has once again assumed that all know what he does. You have not traveled much, have you?"

"No, ser."

Myral nodded. "On the third shelf there, you see the matched boxes?"

"Yes, ser."

"Open the one on the right. There should be several small jars of ointment inside."

Cerryl opened the box, holding the oak lid, carved in a pattern of interlocking triangles, in his left hand.

"You may take one of them."

"Ser?"

"It relieves the rawness of where the saddle rubs you—or anything else. Use it sparingly."

"Thank you, ser."

"Also, make sure you have a heavy jacket and an extra blanket for your bedroll."

Cerryl nodded. He was ashamed to admit he had not even thought of the bedroll.

"And, if you can talk Yubni out of it, an oiled waterproof to wrap your bedroll in would also help."

"Is there anything else you would advise?"

"Not traveling, but that be not your choice." Myral took a swallow of the ever-present cider. "An extra water bottle would not be amiss, if you can obtain one, but be careful of how and where you fill it." He coughed several times, and Cerryl wondered if the racking coughs would follow, but Myral merely continued. "Oh . . . you can use chaos to heat water to boiling. If you do that and let it cool, it will keep the other kinds of chaos, the kinds that cause the flux, from the water. You can also send the tiniest fragments of chaos after bed vermin." Myral smiled grimly. "There are always vermin when you travel. Especially in Certis."

"Why in Certis?" Cerryl blurted.

"That I could not tell you." Myral shrugged. "Save many have died from flux and vermin chaos there. Take care what you drink and eat in Jellico, though with Jeslek I am certain all will be well."

Was there a slight irony in Myral's words? Cerryl wasn't sure, but he nodded.

"If you have other questions, you can come back. I am not likely to be traipsing around Fairhaven much, not unless your friend Faltar runs into trouble in his sewer duty."

"I hope he doesn't."

"I doubt he will. Even if there are smugglers around, they know to avoid another student mage right now."

"You think there are others?"

Myral laughed. "Cerryl, we impose tariffs and road duties. Goods are not made with tariffs attached to them, like wool to a sheep. So there will always be those who would avoid taxes and tariffs, even in Fairhaven. Not all the chaos-fire you or even the great Jeslek can cast will stop those who live for silver and gold." He pointed to the door. "Go and get what you need, and you can tell Yubni, for what it's worth, that both Jeslek and I think you ought to be well prepared for your journey."

"Thank you."

"It be little enough." Myral coughed, but only once, and smiled briefly.

Cerryl eased down the tower steps slowly, hoping he would be able to follow Myral's suggestions, carrying the box of ointment back toward his cell.

Bealtur nodded as the two passed in the corridor by the commons, but the goateed student mage did not speak, and Cerryl didn't feel like always being the one to offer greetings first.

Cerryl eased down the corridor and slipped into his cell, still feeling somewhat stiff and wondering how long before he'd really get used to riding. He stepped over to the desktop.

A soft gray leather case lay there. With a frown, he opened it, then began to smile as he lifted out the white-bronze razor. Then he laughed. "She does care." *And she has a sense of humor in making her points . . .* He laughed softly again as he replaced the razor in the case.

LXXXVI

A light wind blew out of the northwest, right into Cerryl's face, carrying faint bits of dust and grit raised by the riders in front of him. He shifted his weight in the saddle, wishing he could get more comfortable on the big chestnut, then glanced westward.

Jeslek rode at the front of the column, bareheaded, his white hair almost glistening in the late morning sun. Beside him rode the lanky Klybel, the white lancer captain. Behind them rode the red-haired Anya, and beside her, the square-bearded Fydel. Behind the two mages rode the three students—Cerryl, Kochar, and Lyasa. Following the mages was a detachment of white lancers—more than fourscore, Cerryl thought, although he hadn't tried to count them.

The only sounds were the breathing of the horses and the clopping of hoofs on stone. Again, Cerryl shifted his weight in the saddle in an effort to get less uncomfortable. Riding he could do without, save that it was faster and easier than walking.

The wind that blew out of the clear green-blue northwestern sky carried a chill that suggested the coming winter, though the sun was warm, warm enough that Cerryl was still sweating slightly.

Abruptly, Jeslek leaned toward Klybel, then lifted his arm.

Klybel turned his mount out to the raised shoulder of the road and ordered, "Lancers . . . HALT!"

Cerryl found himself reining back the chestnut, then almost lurching forward in the saddle into his mount's mane.

Jeslek then circled around Anya and Fydel and eased his mount up beside the apprentice mages. "You see the road?"

"Yes, ser," answered Kochar and Cerryl. Lyasa nodded.

"Do you not think it is somewhat . . . exposed?" A smile crossed Jeslek's thin lips.

"Anyone can see it," offered Kochar quickly.

Lyasa remained silent. Cerryl nodded, barely.

"You do not agree, Cerryl?"

"It is exposed, ser. I do not know if that is good or bad. It is good for someone who wishes to avoid brigands, but it could be bad for other reasons."

"You are cautious. Why?"

"Because I do not know. I have not lived in Fairhaven all my life, and I have not studied all that you and the other mages have."

"At least you know your limits. Unlike some." Jeslek laughed, then turned to Kochar. "You think the road would be better were it less exposed?"

Kochar tried to conceal a frown. "If it were less exposed, the white lancers could move without all Candar knowing where they went."

"That is true." Jeslek smiled. "Yet we are within a dozen kays of Fairhaven, and here it scarcely matters."

Kochar's face became stolid.

"On the other hand, beyond the Easthorns, where the road stretches across the plains of Gallos—that is another question. And that is why we may be headed there." His smile faded. "In the meantime, I want you to use your senses to understand how the road is built and how it is held together. How a road feels is as important as all the calculations Esaak would have you make."

Gallos?

They had yet to reach Certis, and Jeslek was talking about Gallos?

"Stop scaring them," said Anya with a laugh as Jeslek turned his mount around and rode past the other two mages.

"You would do well to study the roads as well, Anya. Given your . . . inclinations," suggested Jeslek with a smile. "You as well, Fydel. We will have much to do." He eased his mount past the other two mages and rejoined the lancer captain. Klybel raised his arm again, and he and Jeslek resumed riding as if nothing had happened.

"We're going to Gallos?" whispered Kochar.

"It would seem so," suggested Lyasa.

Cerryl frowned, wondering why Jeslek had stopped the column. The white mage could have made his suggestion without halting the lancers, yet had made a point to do so, and to offer barbed comments to Anya and Fydel.

Belatedly, Cerryl flicked the reins and lurched in the saddle as the chestnut started up again.

LXXXVII

As the column rode across the wide stone bridge that spanned the River Jellicor, Cerryl's eyes went to the walls that lay less than half a kay north of the bridge. Jellico was a walled city—a well-walled city with smooth stone ramparts that rose at least forty cubits above the level of the road that led to the gates.

On the western shore, the highway turned almost northeast for a few hundred cubits before arrowing straight toward the walls. The huge red oak and ironbound gates were open, but well-oiled iron grooves showed that they could be closed rapidly.

Armsmen in gray-and-brown leathers and with armless green over-tunics were stationed by the gate. Jeslek and Klybel halted, as did the three students and the lancers who followed.

"The overmage Jeslek, to visit the viscount," announced Klybel in a deep voice that echoed off the granite walls of the city.

The head armsman glanced nervously from Jeslek to the next two mages, then to the students, and then at the column of white lancers.

"Ah . . . you are most welcome, overmage. You know your way to the palace?"

Jeslek nodded. "I am sure we will find it."

Cerryl looked up. Archers in green with bows—some strung and some unstrung—watched from the ramparts above, but none seemed terribly interested in raising their weapons.

"The viscount is particular about who he lets enter, but not about us," suggested Anya.

Cerryl wasn't sure he cared that much. The inside of his thighs felt raw, and every muscle in his legs seemed ready to cramp.

"Most rulers in Candar are," said Fydel in a low voice that barely carried to Cerryl.

A messenger in green mounted a gray and quick-trotted down the avenue before them, vanishing from sight even as Jeslek nodded again to the guards and urged his mount through the archway and inside the walls of Jellico.

Houses and shops of fired brick lined the street, wide enough for perhaps four mounts but far narrower than the avenues of Fairhaven.

The buildings were higher, often three stories, and seemingly older and less kempt.

Two shaggy brown dogs ran out of a side alley to the right, in front of Jeslek and Klybel, and disappeared into the alley on the left.

"Like as they stole something," said Kochar.

"Probably," agreed Lyasa. "There's more theft here."

How would dogs know? Cerryl sniffed, noting the sour odor of Jellico, an odor compounded by the smells from the open sewers running next to the buildings on the right of the street, and by other odors, including burned grease and tanning acids, plus some Cerryl could not identify.

"Smells . . ." murmured Kochar.

Cerryl nodded, wondering if every city in Candar but Fairhaven did. He tried to shift his weight in the saddle again, in a way that wouldn't rub his legs, hoping that they didn't have to ride that much farther.

The viscount's palace stood at the west end of the city on a small hill. The granite walls were even smoother and more polished than those of the city, if not so high, and the gates were open. Only two pair of guards were stationed by the gates, but above them on a false rampart was a full squad of crossbowmen.

Hoofs echoed on the stones as the group rode slowly through the long archway that was almost a tunnel, and low enough that Cerryl could have reached up and touched the damp stones overhead.

Inside the courtyard, Eliasar waited, only a pair of guards in green beside him.

"Greetings, honored Eliasar." Jeslek reined up.

Eliasar's eyes ran over the group, pausing ever so slightly at Anya and then at Cerryl. "You brought quite an entourage, Jeslek. Three apprentices?"

"One for each full mage," answered the white-haired wizard.

"Well . . . we can get everyone settled in the guest barracks—except for you. You'll have the guest quarters down the hall from me—and from Shyren." He pointed to the west, at another archway, smaller, from the courtyard that barely held all the mounts of the lancers. "The guest stables are through that arch. Klybel, you'll have to stable the lancer's mounts in the stable beyond that. It's closer to the barracks, anyway."

"Yes, ser." Klybel's tone was formal.

Eliasar walked beside Jeslek's mount, as if leading the white-haired mage to the stable. His voice was low enough that Cerryl could not hear what either man said.

"Who is the viscount?" Cerryl finally asked Lyasa in a low voice. "His name, I mean. I know his rank . . ."

"I understood what you meant." Lyasa grinned. "His name is Rystryr. He's been viscount for ten years or so. His older brother and his consort and son—the brother's consort—died of the bloody flux." Lyasa raised her eyebrows.

Cerryl wondered what poison created the effects of the bloody flux . . . or could some indirect application of chaos?

"That was right after Shyren became the mage to Certis, wasn't it?" asked Kochar.

Cerryl mentally confirmed his thoughts about how Rystryr became viscount.

"I believe so." Lyasa's voice was flat. "I'll be glad when I can get off this horse and get cleaned up."

Once Jeslek reined up and dismounted in the second courtyard, a square a good hundred cubits on a side surrounded by window-studded stone walls rising a good five stories, Cerryl struggled out of the saddle, clinging to it for a moment as his legs threatened to buckle.

"Feels good to stand up," said Kochar.

Cerryl nodded, flexing one leg and then the other. Behind him the lancers continued onward through another archway, leaving just Eliasar, Jeslek, Anya, Fydel, and the three student mages and their mounts in a rough semicircle around a dark opening a good ten cubits wide.

"This is the guest stable . . ."

Cerryl hoped he wouldn't get lost in the viscount's keep or palace. Every building seemed to join every other one, and all looked about the same from outside—flat stone walls with small windows. He took a slightly deeper breath and decided that the keep didn't smell any better than the city.

Eliasar turned from Jeslek. "Fydel and Anya, you two rate captain's rooms, and the apprentices each get an undercaptain's room."

"Don't get any overlarge ideas of your worth. Certis has a great number of captains," added Jeslek with a broad smile. "Get your gear off your mounts. The ostlers will stall them."

Mechanically, Cerryl unstrapped his bedroll and pack, then followed the others through a weathered bailey door and up two flights of steps, then along another narrow stone corridor and around a corner. Their boots echoed in the empty corridors.

"The first two rooms are yours." Eliasar nodded to Anya and Fydel.

"Thank you for your kindness," Anya offered graciously, her voice melodious and modulated. The tone sent shivers down Cerryl's back, so much did he distrust it.

Fydel merely inclined his head.

Around yet another corner, Eliasar pointed out three more doors. "You all are expected for dinner at the second bell in the small dining hall. Take the stairs at the end to the first level and cross the third courtyard. Ask the guards."

As Jeslek and Eliasar walked away, Cerryl stepped into the room between Kochar and Lyasa. He lowered his bedroll and pack onto the bare stone floor and studied the barracks room—several cubits larger than his cell in Fairhaven, with a single window, shuttered. The furniture consisted of a narrow pallet bed, a battered wardrobe, a washstand and pitcher, and a lamp on a brass bracket. A heavy door bar lay propped against the wall behind the door.

Were undercaptains so disliked they needed to bar their rooms? Or just in Certis?

After washing his hands and face and arms and everywhere he could easily reach, Cerryl again applied some of Myral's ointment. It helped reduce the rawness and soreness, and his legs and thighs seemed to be getting tougher.

He shook his head. He couldn't believe that in the rush to leave Fairhaven, he'd forgotten the white-bronze razor from Leyladin. He thought he'd put it in his pack, but it was nowhere to be found. The only real gift anyone had given him in years, and he'd forgotten it. And from Leyladin, no less. He wanted to bash his own head, but that would have only added another area of soreness.

Instead, he used a touch of chaos to clean his clothes before dressing, finishing as the bell rang.

Kochar was waiting in the corridor, somewhat stained and disheveled. His eyes widened as he saw Cerryl. "You . . . your clothes . . . you weren't carrying that much in your pack."

Cerryl smiled. "Something I learned in the sewers. I'm sure you will, too."

Lyasa joined them, looking even more fresh than Cerryl. Kochar shook his head.

"Let us go," said a fourth voice that echoed down the corridor—Anya's. She and Fydel stood at the end of the corridor. "We should not keep the overmage or the viscount waiting."

Cerryl noted the slightest of emphasis on the word "overmage" but walked quickly toward the steps where the two full mages waited.

"Have you seen anyone else?" Kochar asked in a low voice, glancing forward to Anya and Fydel.

"Seems rather empty," Cerryl agreed blandly.

Anya turned her head. "Observations by junior mages are best made silently, especially in the keeps of other lords."

Kochar flushed. Fydel grunted. Cerryl kept his face expressionless.

Once Anya returned to her low conversation with Fydel, Lyasa offered a bemused smile.

"Better to be here now than in winter . . . All this stone gets cold . . ."

"Better sleeping here than on the road," answered Fydel, "no matter what the season . . ."

The guards on the far side of the next courtyard barely nodded as the group of mages passed, but as Anya led them up the steps, Cerryl strained to hear the few words that passed.

"All that white . . . only means trouble . . ."

At the top of the steps, the decor changed. Instead of bare stone corridors, the hallway was wainscotted in pink marble, and gilt frames held pictures of men in green uniforms on horseback. The brass lamps were polished and lit, and their glass mantels sparkled. Guards in green and gold were stationed every dozen cubits, and the scent of cooking meat and flowers mixed.

An open archway at the end of the short corridor revealed a dining hall, though one Cerryl would not have called small, as it was a good fifty cubits long and half that in width.

Eliasar and Jeslek stood near the head of the table, talking with a younger man in a gaudy green-and-gold tunic. Rystryr was a big and broad-shouldered man, almost as tall as Kinowin, with ruddy cheeks above a bushy beard and under thick blond hair. With the three at the head of the table, was another mage in white—clearly Shyren, the only mage in the dining hall Cerryl had not met.

In a corner by the unlit marble fireplace at the foot of the table were gathered a number of Certan officers. They fell silent, and the viscount glanced up, raising his eyebrows as Anya led in Cerryl and the others. "With such an assembly of mages, we scarcely might need food." Rystryr's voice was as big and hearty as he was, and he followed the words with a broad smile. "Welcome to Jellico!"

"We thank you," answered Jeslek. "You are and have always been most hospitable."

"With all the guests present, I suggest we eat." Rystryr made a sweeping gesture toward the table.

Cerryl looked blankly at the long table, wondering where he was to sit and how to determine that.

"Look for your name on the place slate," whispered Anya before smiling broadly and stepping forward.

Cerryl's bronze-framed place slate—bearing a statuette of an undercaptain—was more than halfway down the long walnut table and read in a chalked old tongue script, "Carrl." Jeslek and Eliasar sat on the right and left of the viscount, while Shyren—an older and heavier man—sat to Eliasar's left. Anya sat beside Jeslek, while Fydel sat below Jeslek. Then came an officer in green and gold, and beside him Klybel.

"You ever used a blade, young ser?" asked the dark-haired under-captain across the table from Cerryl.

"Only enough to know that I'd make a poor armsman," Cerryl admitted. "I'm Cerryl."

"Deltry, undercaptain of the Fourth."

"Slekyr, undercaptain of the Second." The older undercaptain who sat beside Cerryl and toward the head of the table had streaks of gray in his trimmed beard.

"Lyasa."

"Kochar," gulped the redhead, who sat below two other undercaptains.

After a moment of silence, Deltry took the pitcher and filled the goblets of those around him with the red wine.

"Thank you," said Lyasa.

"My pleasure, and for that I would beg you clear up a question for me. It's said that a white mage can still kill an armsman, even one with an iron blade," offered Deltry as he broke a chunk of rye bread from the loaf in the basket and handed it to Lyasa. "I don't see how, myself, especially if the armsman had mind enough to carry an iron shield."

Lyasa smiled, taking the basket.

"You smile, apprentice mage," noted Slekyr, his eyes meeting those of the dark-haired young woman. "Know you for a fact any mage who has confronted cold iron one on one and survived?"

Cerryl looked down, fearing what was coming.

"Yes. Cerryl there was attacked by two men with iron blades and shields. He killed them both."

Slekyr turned and studied Cerryl. "Is that true?"

"Yes." Cerryl looked up and met the other's eyes.

"Yet you are not a full mage yet?" asked Deltry.

"No." Cerryl wanted to say "no, ser," but knew that doing so would undermine the status the three students had been granted. He added, "undercaptain," belatedly. "Mages have to learn much."

"So it would seem." Slekyr laughed. "I'm just as glad that our viscount counts himself a friend of Fairhaven."

"So are we," answered Cerryl, reaching for the bread.

"You really killed two men armed with cold iron?" pursued Deltry.

"Three, actually," added Lyasa. "Cerryl tends to be modest."

"And they . . . just stood there? I am not sure I understand." Deltry's voice was easy, warm, conversational.

"I . . . came upon them in my duties in the tunnels," Cerryl said carefully. "The first two attacked. I had no choice, since they would have killed me."

"But what did you do? Turn them stone?"

"No. I can't do that. I turned them into ashes with chaos-fire." Cerryl felt a twinge in his skull at the exaggeration. He'd merely killed them, while Sterol had turned them into dust and ashes.

Deltry swallowed.

"You had to ask, didn't you?" commented Slekyr into the silence, his voice slightly ironic.

Deltry offered a smile, both to Slekyr and Cerryl. "My apologies, ser."

Cerryl returned it with a smile he hoped was almost shy. "I understand. Four years ago I would not have believed it, either."

"You are not from Fairhaven, then?" asked Slekyr.

"No. I came from Hrisbarg and was apprenticed to a scrivener in Fairhaven."

"Some have said that all mages come from higher birth . . ."

"I am afraid mine was not high, nor that of some others," Cerryl replied, glancing toward the platter of meat making its way down the table and trying not to drool.

"Some mages come from high families," confirmed Lyasa, "others from where their talents are discovered. The skills are rare enough that the Guild does not waste them."

"Even women mages, I see." Slekyr's eyes lingered on Lyasa for a moment.

"They are fewer, but still number among the Guild." Lyasa's head inclined toward the head of the table. "Anya is one of the more powerful mages, and she is most definitely a woman."

Both Deltry and Slekyr nodded politely.

"We hear that the prefect of Gallos has begun to make life difficult for some in Certis," suggested Lyasa, taking the half-empty platter and serving herself some of the brown-sauced meat.

"Mostly talk," suggested Slekyr easily. "We can sell our oilseeds to Hydolar as easily as to Gallos."

"Just not for as much, perhaps," suggested Lyasa with a smile.

"There is that, but the viscount is hardly likely to go to war over a few coppers' difference in a barrel of seed oil." Slekyr took a deep swallow of wine.

Cerryl took little more than a sip, then concentrated on serving himself and eating the half-tough meat and the not-quite-dry rye bread.

"And wool?" asked Kochar politely.

"Many would sell us wool." Slekyr reached for the wine pitcher and refilled his goblet.

"Are you from Jellico?" asked Lyasa.

"Me? No. I come from Rytel . . . and most of the family's still there."

"How did you get to be a captain?"

"I'm not . . . yet . . . but an armsman. Well . . . like many a thing, I didn't quite plan it that way . . ."

Cerryl ate and listened, listened and ate, occasionally looking toward the head of the table, where Jeslek listened and ate, ate and listened to Shyren and Rystryr.

LXXXVIII

Under the early harvest sun, Cerryl fidgeted in his saddle again, a saddle that seemed as hard as the glazed bricks of the sewer tunnels, and as unyielding. He knew that for all his efforts he still swayed and bounced far too much.

The western side of Certis was hillier, but the oilseed fields were interspersed with meadows where grazed small herds of cattle. Not sheep? Then, the meadows were more lush than those of Montgren. Scattered stone houses reared out of the green hills, located seemingly without pattern.

Cerryl wondered why they had even gone to Jellico. It was more than four days out of the way, since they were headed to Gallos on the Great White Highway, and all they had done was stay for two days and ride off.

Then, he had no idea exactly what Jeslek and Eliasar were conveying to Rystryr. A show of magely force? A trade agreement?

He shrugged. Who knew? No one was telling him—that was certain. His eyes went to the way before them. Ahead on either side of the Great White Highway, looming into the western sky, lay the Easthorns. Even in late summer, the tops of the peaks were crowned in snow, and by harvest time, snowfalls had resumed on the higher slopes.

Despite the heat, as he glanced toward the mountains, swaying in the saddle, Cerryl shivered. He had no doubts that the road through the Easthorns would be cold.

"More snow than usual," commented Fydel from his mount in front of Cerryl. "It could be a cold winter in Candar. There are times when it would help to have weather mages."

"Not like the accursed Creslin, thank you," said Anya.

"Megaera was red-haired, you know." Fydel laughed. "I wonder if, way back, you might be related."

Fire flared from Anya's fingertips, lancelike fire. "Would you like to see how I am otherwise like her, dear Fydel?"

Cerryl could sense Fydel's order shields rise, and perceived that the square-bearded mage's shields were nowhere strong enough to contain the power that rose around Anya. He swallowed, half-wondering if Faltar had any idea of the power Anya could raise.

"I think that the overmage would be less than pleased if we turned chaos-fire among ourselves." Fydel's voice bore an edge.

"The overmage will find much work for your chaos, Anya." As Jeslek turned the saddle, his voice was mild, but the sun-gold eyes burned. "And your other talents."

Anya smiled, more brightly than normal, and more falsely, the chaos-fire lance gone as though it had never been. "I am here to do your biding, honored Jeslek."

"Good. And I hope all of you are using your senses to study the road." Jeslek turned and resumed his conversation with Klybel.

Lyasa coughed, lightly, and Cerryl looked to his left. The black-haired student lifted her fingers in imitation of Anya and then raised her eyebrows, mouthing the words "Did you see that?"

Cerryl nodded.

"What are you talking about?" asked Kochar abruptly.

"The snow," answered Cerryl, grasping for the first words that crossed his mind that made any sense. "Fydel was saying that it might be a cold winter with all the snow up there already. Lyasa wanted to know if I'd seen where he pointed."

"Oh . . ."

"I have the feeling the way is going to get colder."

"Fine by me," suggested Kochar. "I'll take cold over heat any day."

Cerryl wasn't so sure, although his face was sunburned and his legs ached, cramping so fiercely that he knew that when he did dismount, he would barely be able to stand for several moments after he did.

"You haven't felt the mountain cold," added Lyasa.

Cerryl wasn't certain he wanted to, not as he recalled how cold his winters with Dylert had been. He shifted his weight in the saddle again, his eyes traveling to the Easthorns once more, then to the shadows cast by the chestnut on the white granite of the road, the hard white granite of the road. Only slightly past midday, and that meant a great deal more riding.

He took a deep breath, trying to relax.

The Great White Highway seemed endless, and they had yet to reach the base of the Easthorns.

LXXXIX

Cerryl wrapped the heavy white leather jacket around him, and stood in the stirrups to try to warm up his legs. In the early morning, his breath puffed out like a cloud. Although the sky was clear and it was well past dawn, the sun had yet to clear the eastern edge of the gorge through which the Great Highway ran.

The sound of hoofs echoed through the stillness, stillness broken abruptly by the shrill *ye-aah!* of a vulcrow that flapped off a dead pine limb and into the middle of the artificial canyon that contained the highway.

"Amazing," murmured Kochar, a smile upon his face, as if the cold bothered him not in the slightest.

Cerryl ignored the redhead's comment and settled back into the saddle, rubbing one thigh, then switching the reins to his left hand and rubbing the other. The chestnut *whuffed* once.

In places, the gray stone of the cliffs seemed to have been peeled away as if by a mighty knife. Cerryl nodded to himself. Even he could sense the residual chaos of that effort of centuries past.

To the left of and below the wall separating the highway from the lower section of the gorge was a stream of cold and tumbling water, violent enough even in harvest season that light spray occasionally cloaked Cerryl and the chestnut, spray that felt like ice. Small patches of ice had formed during the night on the stones next to the wall, where the late afternoon sun had cast shadows the day before.

"Amazing . . ." mumbled Kochar once more.

"The cold or the highway?" Lyasa's voice was sharp.

"The highway. It is made of order, yet formed by chaos . . ."

Even Cerryl understood that whatever was built lasted longer with greater order. Chaos had great power, but it was the power of destruction. The great whites of the past had cut the granite with chaos, but the masons had joined the stones with skill and order. While the slope of the pavement was gradual, it was continuous, and the ancient stones still held flush.

Cerryl could sense some areas of greater residual chaos, places where he suspected the highway had been repaired—or rocks that had fallen from the cliffs had been removed.

"The Guild maintains it by chaos," said Lyasa. "Fine, but I'm still cold. I'm from Worrak. It's not this cold in midwinter even in the Lower Easthorns."

"Gallos will be colder than Certis," said Fydel, turning in his saddle. "It is past the peak of harvest there—in the north where Fenard is. That's because it's between the Easthorns and the Westhorns."

"Even young Cerryl knows that," said Anya. "He created a most accurate map."

"He doubtless needed to," said Fydel.

"Fydel." Anya's voice was as cold as the ice beside the stone highway wall.

Fydel turned abruptly, his eyes on Jeslek's back.

Lyasa coughed.

Cerryl glanced at her, catching her mouthed words: "Watch out . . ."

He nodded, understanding all too well. If Anya happened to be too interested in him, he needed to be careful—most careful. "It should get warmer once the sun hits the road."

"I hope so," answered Lyasa.

"Amazing," whispered Kochar to himself.

Cerryl shook his head, trying to ignore the chill in his thighs and his frozen ears, hoping Anya would confine her overt attentions to others.

XC

Cerryl swayed in the saddle as the chestnut carried him up the winding trail away from the Great White Highway. Ahead rode Jeslek and the other mages, and behind followed the students, with the line of lancers stretched out after them on the narrow mountain trail for hundreds and hundreds of cubits.

A light layer of fresh-fallen snow covered the rocks and mountain grasses between the scattered junipers and low pines, but the sunlight had been strong enough to melt the snow off the trees—at least on the sunny side. The chestnut carried Cerryl by a pine leaning over the trail so low that he had to duck, a pine so twisted and buffeted by the mountain winds until only the limbs on the southern side had retained needles.

Although there was still some snow on the trail before Cerryl, he had no doubt that the way behind him was rapidly becoming sloppy, since the lancers' mounts would churn damp earth and clay and snow into cold mud. He hoped Jeslek had another way back. He took a deep breath, but the midday was warm enough that he didn't puff a cloud of white when he exhaled.

Lyasa rode before Cerryl and Kochar behind him. Jeslek disappeared as his dusky-white mount carried him out of sight and down from the ridgetop that Cerryl's and Lyasa's mounts still climbed.

Cerryl sniffed the breeze, detecting a faint odor of brimstone that strengthened as the gelding carried him over the ridge and downward. Below, in the small valley steamed a small lake, surrounded by greenish blue ponds, from which also rose steam.

"Here lies the key to our future in Gallos." From where he had reined up his mount on a hillock overlooking the lake and hot springs, Jeslek gestured toward them.

Cerryl had to work to keep from wrinkling his nose at the odor of brimstone. He glanced over his shoulder, back along the winding trail.

"Smells," murmured Kochar, reining up beside Cerryl and Lyasa.

"Of course it does. It's a chaos spring," answered Lyasa from where she had reined up beside Cerryl.

"Chaos spring?" asked Kochar, brushing ice crystals off his red hair.

"The water flows up from where chaos has gathered closer to the top of the ground. Haven't you read your books?"

"Oh . . . yes . . . I never thought of that here." Kochar bobbed his head.

According to *Colors of White*, the entire center of the world was filled with chaos, just like the sun. Cerryl nodded to himself as he recalled what he had read. It made sense that some of that chaos might be closer to the surface of the ground.

"Cerryl," Jeslek called, "you should be able to trace the fire of chaos that feeds the springs. You also, Lyasa."

"Yes, ser." Cerryl straightened himself in the saddle, trying to ignore the chill that burrowed through the white leather jacket as he attempted to let his senses flow into the rock and heat beneath the ground.

"And, Kochar . . . try to follow what they're doing."

"Yes, ser."

Cerryl let his senses flow across the small pond less than fifty cubits downhill, picking up a diffuse and wavering line of . . . something. Letting his senses follow the unseen reddish white line, he could feel a darker and deeper whiteness that oozed around the rocks below the pond, and beneath the greenish blue of the larger lake to the west.

Another probe—one more like a huge battering ram—rumbled by his and arrowed toward the depths. Cerryl felt like a fly brushed aside by a diving vulcrow, shivering as he sat astride the chestnut.

Kochar shook like a gray winter leaf in a gale. Even Lyasa swallowed.

Cerryl wiped his forehead, suddenly damp despite the chill. Beneath him, he could sense Jeslek's powers rearranging the vague patterns of darkness and reddish chaos that lay beneath the earth, rearranging them so that a fountain of reddish white bubbled through the spaces between the rocks and oozed up underneath the spring to the south of the lake.

The ground trembled again.

From his mount Jeslek smiled . . . smiled as steam geysered from the spring into a plume that rose nearly a hundred cubits into the green-blue sky of Candar.

Rain, hot rain, cascaded down across the greenish blue lake, and then droplets fell on Cerryl and the others, and even on the lancers farther up the trail.

"That! That is but the beginning," said Jeslek as the plume subsided into a three-cubit-high fountain of boiling water.

"How . . ." murmured Kochar under his breath.

Beside Jeslek, overcaptain Klybel's eyebrows rose momentarily.

Jeslek smiled. "You all doubt, but there will be no doubt. The very earth will break Gallos, and you will see." His hand jabbed at Anya and Fydel. "Put down your shields and protect the ground beneath you. For I will lift the chaos under you and fry you if you do not."

"Jeslek . . ." Anya's voice was calm.

"I will do this, and you cannot stop me. Even Sterol could not. Now . . . do as I say."

"As you wish, overmage," conceded Anya.

"As you wish," echoed Fydel.

Cerryl watched with eyes and senses as the unseen darkness concentrated in the rocks beneath the two full mages and as the reddish whiteness rose from the depths, rose and spread around them—one tendril seemingly drifting sideways, uphill toward the stone underneath the students.

Without a word, Cerryl began to create his own shields. As he did, he could feel another presence beneath the ground, and his eyes went sideways. Lyasa nodded. Neither spoke.

A sense of heat built up around him, and the chestnut gelding side-stepped, tossing his head slightly and *whuffing* twice. Cerryl absently patted his mount's neck. "Easy . . . easy."

Trying to hold an order shield was never easy, and doing so on horseback while the earth rumbled was even more difficult, but Cerryl had no doubts that Jeslek was either testing them—or trying to set up an "accident" to remove one student mage. Either way, it didn't matter.

He focused on channeling order around them and chaos back toward the massive concentration that Jeslek raised from deep beneath the ground, so far down that Cerryl could not even sense from where Jeslek gathered such forces.

Rrrrrrrrr . . .

The chestnut whickered and tossed his head, stepping sideways once more, toward Anya's mount, a black mare that bared her teeth at the gelding.

"Easy . . ." murmured Cerryl. "Easy."

"Darkness . . ." whispered Kochar. "Darkness on us all."

"Chaos, more likely," replied Lyasa tartly. "Keep working on your shields if you don't want to roast."

Slowly, the underground chaos concentration shifted westward, away from the lake, and the fountain in the spring dropped to mere seething bubbles, even as the concentration itself swelled. Cerryl's head was throbbing, yet he dared not release the shields, not with all the power raised by Jeslek.

He darted a glance sideways, catching sight of sweat streaming down Lyasa's face, and a grim expression on Anya's more distant face.

Gurrrr . . . rrrrr . . .

Cerryl's mouth opened as the ground trembled, and then trembled again. His eyes went beyond the immediate hillside to the west of the lake toward the lands of Gallos—except a line of hills seemed to be rising more than a kay away. Were they actually rising? Rising above the once-higher nearer hills?

He swallowed. The ground *was* rising, and steam billowed from cracks in the rocks wide enough to swallow a mount and rider.

His senses went full back to the shields, now an intertwined effort of both full mages and the three students. The more distant line of hills continued to rise, and the ground around the lake began to ripple ever so slightly.

Another geyser spurted skyward from the center of the lake below, then collapsed as suddenly as it had risen. A sickening, sucking gulp followed, with a curtain of steam clouding the lake momentarily. More hot rain cascaded around Cerryl, then dispersed, as did the mist, to show an empty and steaming lake bed—rent by a fissure a half-dozen cubits wide.

Still the hills to the west continued to rise, groaning, trembling, thrust up skyward by the welling of chaos from beneath, that chaos loosed and chevied earthward by the overmage.

Jeslek and his mount were like a statue, a statue frozen by the power of the forces welling from and around the white-clad and white-haired mage.

Rivulets began to gurgle down the hillside to the north of Cerryl, rivulets formed from the quick-melted snow. The ground rumbled once more, and to the south, the misted hills lurched upward.

Cerryl drew from the chaos that flowed away from the central tap, drew and channeled it around him and the others, funneling it back toward the overmage in an effort to push chaos away from the order shield that he and the others—mostly Anya and Lyasa—held.

The Highway trembled ever so slightly, as the hills to the north of them shuddered upward, as chaos and steam twisted together and wreathed the new mountains-to-be.

The late afternoon sun was almost touching the tops of those steam-shrouded hills before the shaking of the earth subsided to a mere grumbling.

Cerryl's head ached, and stars flashed before his eyes, half from the effort of holding shields and half from struggling with his mount. Not that he blamed the chestnut, not as scared as he had been, wondering whether he would see another sunrise.

"Eat something from your pack, you idiot," hissed Lyasa, "before you fall out of your saddle." Her face was pale.

"You better do the same," he answered in a raspy voice, grasping for the small ration pack.

The hard cheese and dried bread helped—after he moistened his mouth and lips enough to be able to swallow. The flashing stars before his eyes slowly vanished, but he was conscious of being light-headed, and the food didn't remove that sensation.

Jeslek, who had remained almost like a statue, abruptly turned his mount as though no time at all had passed. "You see, Anya, Fydel—it's not all that difficult to raise chaos through the ground, and mountains with it. Still . . . we must protect the highway—and that will be your task—and that of the students." Jeslek's sun-gold eyes flashed at the three younger mages. "For a first try, your shields were not bad, but you'll all have to do better than that." Jeslek turned to Klybel. "Now, overcaptain, let's return to the Highway. We will proceed into Gallos."

"He's not going to raise more mountains, is he?" asked Kochar.

Both Lyasa and Cerryl stared at the redhead.

Kochar swallowed and looked down at his mount's neck and mane.

Cerryl glanced around. To the north and east, all seemed as it had been, but to the west . . . low mountains that had not been there before stretched a dozen kays or more toward the horizon.

Yet, the Great White Highway remained—untouched, if dwarfed by the new heights.

Had Jeslek called forth chaos—and shielded the highway? Why? With such power, surely he could have used the stuff of chaos to cut a new passage through the uprisen rock. Cerryl scratched his head, aware suddenly that his face felt flushed, almost burned.

Then . . . was not chaos like the light of the sun? He glanced at Lyasa as she turned her mount. The black-haired student's face seemed more olive-tanned than before. Kochar's cheeks and forehead were bright red.

Cerryl turned the chestnut, aware that his thighs were close to cramping once again.

"Back to the Highway!" Klybel's order rang out over the hissing created by steaming rocks and the places where the meltwater ran into the heated lake bottom and spring.

Standing momentarily in the stirrups helped relieve the incipient cramping, but Cerryl was all too aware of the stiffness and soreness that would not be relieved.

XCI

In the dimness, away from the cookfire, Cerryl pulled off his white leather boots, coated in chaos dust but free from mud, and stretched out on his bedroll, his eyes on the white silk tent where Jeslek reclined on a cot. "Ohhhh . . . darkness . . ."

To the east, a faint glow lighted the horizon, the red-limned light from the scattered lines of molten rock that had burst from the ground with the hills Jeslek had raised into small mountains.

Cerryl took another long breath.

"Even the ground feels better than a saddle," Lyasa said wryly.

"It's hard," complained Kochar, sitting disconsolately on his bed-roll, his boots still on. "Too hard to sleep on."

"Try it," suggested Lyasa.

"I'm going back to the fire. I'm cold." Kochar stood and ambled back in the direction of the silk tent, its white sides an orange from the light of the slowly dying cookfire.

The rustling murmur of lancers preparing their bedrolls and the muted talking they did conveyed a sense of the summer that had already passed in Gallos, a sense of summer dispersed by the chill breeze out of the northwest, a breeze bringing the odor of damp and decaying grass.

Lyasa eased her bedroll closer to Cerryl's, then removed her boots and pulled her blanket up to her shoulders. "This way we can talk, and no one will think anything."

I'm sure they'll think something. "I doubt that." Cerryl shivered, despite his double blankets. Feeling guilty, he eased the edge of the top blanket over Lyasa.

"That's even better. And warmer." The black-haired woman laughed softly. With her lips less than a span from Cerryl's face, the laugh tickled his left ear. "They will think but of two apprentices taking comfort where they may. Jeslek and Anya both are used to such, as both couple like hares, given the chance."

"You know this?"

"I have been spared, saved only that I am beneath him. None are beneath Anya, not if it will serve her."

"I know." Cerryl thought of poor Faltar, who saw nothing but Anya's beauty and wonderful and false smile. "I know." After a moment, he added, "Why are you telling me this?"

"Who else dare I tell? I am a student mage also, and any full mage who wishes me . . . I cannot leave . . ."

Cerryl's throat tightened. "I'm sorry. I didn't . . . I thought I was the only one . . . like that."

Lyasa offered another soft laugh, half-sweet, half-bitter. "I know that as well. We are alike, you because you have no family, and I because I am a woman with a talent for chaos. As for you . . ." Lyasa's voice held a regretful shrug. "I was wrong. I would be your friend. I would always be your friend, and I will give you my body, if you wish it."

"I do not understand. I have not asked . . ." Cerryl swallowed.

"No. Nor will you, and you and I both know the reason."

Cerryl was afraid he did. Leyladin. Yet he had never done more than speak with the green-eyed gray mage. "You said . . ."

"I did, and I was wrong, and that is why I am your friend, and your ally. If you can survive Sterol, and Jeslek, and Anya, you will save us all."

Cerryl shook his head. "I'm still a student, and every time I look, Jeslek is trying to test me in some other way."

"He is not testing you. He is trying to get you to make a mistake that will kill you. He dares not kill you outright, and you must be strong enough to withstand him when he succeeds Sterol as High Wizard."

Jeslek as High Wizard? How could he not become High Wizard with the power he already commanded? And how could Cerryl withstand that kind of power?

Lyasa reached out and gave him a one-armed hug. "You don't have to do it alone."

Her words echoed in his ears even as he drifted off to sleep, savoring the comfort of her closeness, and only her closeness. "You don't have to do it alone. You don't have to do it alone."

Even so, a blonde mage with red highlights in her hair filled his dreams, and as he seemed to watch her walk through endless corridors, corridors he could never quite enter, he half-dreamed, half-wondered if he would ever see Leyladin again. And what he could do about it, if ever he did.

XCII

Cerryl refastened the white leather jacket against the damp wind out of the north. His eyes went back along the column of lancers stretched eastward on the Great White Highway, reined up and waiting.

Ahead, Jeslek gathered chaos around him, so much that his jacket and trousers seemed to glitter silvered white under the midmorning gray. A light misting rain swept from the low clouds.

A trumpet sounded, faintly at first, then more loudly. A row of armsmen in purple appeared on the hill to the north of the Great Highway.

"So . . . the Gallosians have decided upon a show of force." Jeslek laughed, and his laugh carried easily to Cerryl. "Much good it will do them."

Beside the overmage, Klybel remained silent as the armsman in dark purple rode down the hill and toward the mages. He bore a polished iron oval shield, the blue-trimmed messenger's pennant drooping from the staff rising out of the lance holder. Scattered raindrops slid across the cold metal as he reined up a good thirty cubits from Jeslek.

Cerryl massaged his neck. So far the headache was but faint.

"You bring a message?" asked Klybel.

"I am bid to tell you that the way of the road is yours, o mages, but only the way of the road."

Jeslek glanced from the messenger to the mass of armsmen on the rolling hill to the north. A crooked smile crossed his thin lips, and the misting rain swirled away from him. "You may bid your captain that the way of the road is indeed ours, and all that it takes to protect the

rights of trade upon the road. And the rights of Fairhaven, long established in Candar, and respected by those of wisdom and power."

The messenger frowned. "I will so relay your message."

"You may also tell your captain that it would be to his advantage
to proceed eastward with great care and reflect upon what he will find
there." Jeslek's eyes flashed.

The messenger's face was like stone, stone damp with the mist that
coated all the riders. "He will hear your words, o mage."

"He had best think upon them long and hard," said Jeslek. "Most
long and hard. You may go."

The messenger nodded, his jaw tight as he turned his mount and
rode northward up the gentle slope to the waiting Gallosian force.

"Your words will not please them," offered Klybel.

"I do not intend to please them. How many tens of years have we
labored and poured gold into the Great White Highway to ensure that
Candar will be strong and united?" Jeslek's eyes blazed. "Now that the
road has reached the Westhorns, this . . . puppy of a prefect would seize
it for his own use."

"They outnumber our lancers greatly." Klybel's eyes remained on
the Gallosian host.

"Numbers . . ." A broad smile revealing yellowing teeth crossed Jeslek's face. "You will not have to concern yourself with numbers, Captain
Klybel."

"As you say, ser."

"I do say." Jeslek watched as the Gallosian force began to move
northward, almost paralleling the line of white lancers but riding eastward, rather than westward.

Once the purple-clad lancers had vanished behind them, Jeslek began to probe the ground again with what felt to Cerryl like tenuous
darts of chaos. "Indeed, they will find much to reflect upon, and even
more should they return. Even more." He lifted his eyes and glanced
at Anya, Fydel, and the three students. "This afternoon will we raise
yet another set of hills to join the first." The sun-gold eyes fixed on the
square-bearded wizard. "Fydel, you are charged with following the Gallosians through your glass. I wish to know if that group of armsmen—or
any other—nears us."

"As you command, overmage." Fydel inclined his head.

"I trust all this will meet the approval of the High Wizard," Anya
said mildly.

"I was sent to use my discretion as overmage," Jeslek returned
pleasantly, although chaos boiled unseen around him.

Unseen but not unsensed, and Cerryl shivered in the rain, and not
from the cold . . . or the weather.

XCIII

When the winds warmed and the rains and snow fell less heavily upon the Westhorns, fewer needed the protection of Westwind, and the summer heat prostrated those of the chill heights, and their crops and their flocks.

Lacking the dark talismans of order borne off to Recluce by Creslin, the Marshal of Westwind attempted to persuade the folk of Sarronnyn and Southwind to stand behind her and to offer more coins to her.

As they feared the double-edged twin blades of the Westwind guards, those of the lands beyond the Westhorns pledged their allegiance yet again to the Marshal.

Yet even as they pledged, they gathered together in the darkness they had brought to the once-fair lands of the west, and they plotted as how they would bring down the Marshal and split the plunder laid up over the generations upon the Roof of the World.

For honor had they none, even after all the years that Westwind had protected their dishonor from the efforts of the Guild to redress the ancient wrongs.

Following their custom of dishonor, they invited the Marshal to Southwind, where she might receive gold and tribute and grain. The Marshal traveled from her black tower to the great banquet, and flower petals rained upon her, and then arrows from behind the screens of flowers.

The Marshal had not been without forethought, and had left upon the Roof of the World her daughter the Marshalle and the mighty arms master of the guard. And the Marshalle gathered together all the guards of Westwind and vowed that those responsible for the devastation would pay.

As the Marshalle prepared her retribution, there came a traveling minstrel to Westwind, a minstrel known of old as of trust and worth—save the minstrel, for all that his face was of old and his voice as well, was not as he had been, but enslaved to the tyrant of Sarronnyn.

As he sang, the minstrel lit a candle, a marvelous candle wrought as a model of Westwind—and then the candle exploded with the ancient fires of the West, and claimed the Marshalle and the arms master, and the senior guards of Westwind.

Yet this treachery did not repay the tyrant, for the remaining guards, they packed the treasures of Westwind, and they took their blades and cut a trail of blood to the sea.

There they seized a ship and forced it to Recluce, where they laid all the coins of centuries at the feet of Creslin and swore their blades to his service ...

> *Colors of White*
> (Manual of the Guild at Fairhaven)
> Preface

XCIV

The rain, a cold drizzle earlier in the day, had become a hot, afternoon, chaos-heated mist that cloaked all the mages—and their mounts. The white lancers walked their mounts and those of the mages through the hot mist and along the road to the east of where the three mages and students struggled with the chaos deep below the high plains of Gallos. The horses skittered sideways intermittently, demanding attention and reassurance as the ground rumbled, as irregular screaming bursts of steam perforated the rising hills less than two kays to the north.

"Keep the chaos below the upper rocks!" snapped Jeslek—the first time Cerryl had heard any sense of urgency in the overmage's voice. "Keep it down!"

The wavering wall of order darkness that spread to the north of the road flexed under the rising and expanding globule of reddened-white chaos.

"More ... all of you," grunted Anya. "You don't ... give more ... Fydel, and I'll let you fry first."

The darkness thickened.

Cerryl glanced down the road, where Jeslek stood alone, a point of white amid the chaos that shimmered like light reflected from a still sea at twilight, except more brightly. As he watched, the light around Jeslek brightened even more.

The ground rumbled with a thundering from below, shuddering so much that Cerryl could feel it through his boots.

One of the mounts held by lancers somewhere behind them screamed.

"Hold, you ball-less beast! Hold!"

Cerryl took a quick step forward, trying to keep his balance and his concentration on the interworking of order and chaos.

"Demon damn him . . ." muttered Anya, half under her breath. "Demon damn him . . ."

"Quiet . . ." grunted Fydel.

Sweat, the leftover moisture from the rain, and the hot mist combined in streams of water that poured down the mages' faces, even down the creamy chiseled features of the redheaded Anya, plastering her hair down across her forehead.

The smell of brimstone raised with the steam that escaped the shifting and rising ground drifted from the north and the west across the mages and toward the lancers.

Cerryl swallowed, trying not to gag at the odor.

Behind him, Kochar retched.

"You . . . haven't time to retch. . . . Keep holding the . . . barrier," demanded Anya.

Kochar retched again, but then an additional sense of order joined that of the others.

The sounds of other disgruntled horses, not quite screams, punctuated the rumbling from the depths and the rippling of the ground that had been the low hills of the high grasslands.

Gurrr . . . rrrrr. . . .

Cerryl blotted his brow with the back of his forearm sleeve and continued to concentrate on channeling chaos back into the depths under the rising hills and away from the road. For him, channeling was easier, and seemed more productive than straining to hold order barriers against the heat and reddish white power loosed by Jeslek.

"Getting it . . ." Anya's voice was hoarse.

"If . . . he doesn't loose . . . more chaos . . ." replied Fydel.

"Still . . . holding . . ."

The brown-haired and thin-faced student mage turned another wave of chaos back, back toward the upwelling that had already become a small mountain two kays and more north of the Great White Highway.

"No more chaos . . . now," called Jeslek. "Just . . . hold for a bit . . . not too long."

"Easy . . . for him . . . to say," whispered Lyasa, the words barely reaching Cerryl.

He nodded briefly, silently.

Slowly, the pressure of the chaos faded . . . subsided.

"Keep holding!" ordered Jeslek.

Cerryl blotted away more sweat, but not enough to keep the salty stuff out of the corners of his eyes, which burned anyway.

A light gust of hot wind carried another gout of brimstone, and he swallowed back the bile that threatened to climb into his throat—or higher.

"Better . . ." said Fydel. "Better."

Anya straightened. "All right. You can rest."

Jeslek turned and began to walk, ever so slowly, back toward the other mages. He stopped and bent slightly, breathing hard, as if trying to catch his breath.

"Even Jeslek . . . pushed too much."

"Won't see that happen much," answered Fydel.

Kochar and Lyasa exchanged glances.

Jeslek stopped a dozen cubits from the group of mages, brushed back overlong white hair. "That's a good start for the prefect. It will give him something to worry about."

Gurrrr . . . rrr . . .

As if to emphasize Jeslek's words, the ground trembled . . . and rippled, even as the low hills to the north continued to shudder their way upward, cutting off the direct late afternoon sun.

The smell of brimstone continued to drift over Cerryl both from the north and the west as he studied Jeslek.

For the first time, the overmage looked exhausted, his face drawn, almost pinched. The white hair that usually sparkled was dull and lifeless, and his face was covered with a gray stubbly beard.

Cerryl slumped onto the wall at the side of the road, hot from chaos and indirect sun, faint stars flashing before his tired eyes, eyes that burned. After a moment, he lifted his head, wishing he had taken his water bottle when he had dismounted.

Lyasa sat beside him, offering him some of her water.

"Thank you. I wish I'd thought of it."

"I'll take some of yours later. There won't be much water around here for a while."

After taking a long and welcome swallow, Cerryl nodded. Any streams had to have been dried up or diverted or turned to steam. Heat continued to well off the high hills, or low mountains, that stretched on either side of the flat beside the Great Highway.

Klybel rode up from the east, reining up short of Jeslek.

"We still lost almost a dozen spare mounts. The smell and the unsteady ground spooks the most excitable ones. They broke their leads."

"We will get spare mounts." Jeslek nodded. "Yes, you will have those spare mounts."

The lancer captain glanced toward the northeast, where another bank of lowering clouds promised a return of the rain. "The Gallosians will return, you think?"

Jeslek turned toward Fydel, who stood beside his mount. "Fydel, find out where the Gallosians are."

"Yes, overmage." Fydel heaved himself to his feet and walked slowly toward the lancers who held the mages' mounts.

"We need water for the mounts," continued Klybel. "Your mountains have moved the streams away."

The white-haired mage glanced toward the clouds. "The drainage ways beside the Highway here will be full of water before long. Let it come to us."

The lancer captain frowned momentarily. "As you command."

Jeslek watched as Fydel concentrated on the small glass he had set on the road wall.

"The Gallosians are encamped ten kays to the east," Fydel finally reported.

"They will be back in the morning," predicted Jeslek. "We need some rest and food."

"Here?" asked Klybel.

"None of the mages—or the students—have the strength to move. If your lancers need water, send them in detachments to the southwest. That's the only safe place besides here right now." Jeslek coughed. "Or back toward the Gallosians."

"The southwest." Klybel turned his mount.

Cerryl sat on the side wall of the Great Highway. Like Lyasa and Kochar, he was breathing hard, still trying to catch his breath.

"Derka . . . said this couldn't be done." Lyasa moved closer to Cerryl.

"He . . . was wrong." In how many other things was Jeslek going to prove the older mages wrong? Cerryl wondered.

After a time, he stood and limped on feet sorer than he would have imagined toward the chestnut that held biscuits and hard cheese. He needed to eat something. Anything.

XCV

Cerryl sat on the wall and sipped from his water bottle—filled with rainwater that he had chaos-fire boiled, following Myral's directions, and then let cool overnight. His headache had faded somewhat with sleep. Breakfast, if only of hard cheese and stale road biscuits, had helped—enough to reduce the throbbing but not eliminate it.

The day was cool, the early morning sun filtered by high and hazy clouds drifting out of the south from the heat of Kyphros and the southern ocean.

"We're going to have to get supplies somewhere," predicted Lyasa. "The packs on the supply mounts are near empty."

"No," said Kochar dryly, "Jeslek will insist that the student mages form chaos into food. That's something that any good mage should be able to do."

At the mimicry of Jeslek's tone, both Lyasa and Cerryl laughed. Then all three glanced down the road where Fydel stood over a screeing glass set on the road wall. Jeslek waited behind Fydel, and Anya watched from the other side. All three faces were grim.

"I don't like that," murmured Lyasa.

Cerryl didn't, either. "Gallosian armsmen, you think?"

"That's what he's been tracking with the glass," pointed out Kochar.

"I can't wait." Lyasa snorted.

Cerryl decided he could.

"Klybel!" called Jeslek.

Anya motioned for the student mages to join the group.

"Told you," muttered Lyasa as the three walked the thirty cubits or so toward the full mages.

Klybel rode past them and reined up short of Jeslek.

"The Gallosians are riding westward again," Jeslek announced, even before the younger mages reached the group. "Toward us. They're still a good five kays east, and perhaps a kay south of the highway on a older track."

"How many lancers are there?" asked Klybel.

Jeslek glanced to Fydel.

"I would judge twenty score, more or less."

"Twenty-score Gallosian lancers," Klybel said mildly. "We have less than four score."

"Can you deploy your forces so that most of the Gallosians will be in one place? Or close to it?" asked Jeslek, massaging the back of his neck with his left hand.

"All I have to do is to leave us on the Great White Highway over there—where the ridge line from the south intersects the road. They'll have to come across the ridge. They won't take the road because it's too narrow, and you mages could pick them off a few at a time."

"Good."

"If you cannot stop them, of course," Klybel added, "all of us will die."

"We will do more than stop them." Jeslek offered a yellow-toothed smile. "You will need to place your lancers before the road wall on the hill, to ensure we have time to use the chaos-fire against them as they advance."

"We will do so." Klybel inclined his head. "With your permission, I will place a company on the road—both to the east and west. They should be sufficient to protect the flanks—at least until your mages can react."

"As you see fit, Captain. We will make ready."

Klybel turned his mount and headed eastward to where the main body of white lancers had been breaking camp in the sheltered area beside the Highway and under a low bluff.

"Another day of hard work." Jeslek stretched and glanced at Anya, then Fydel. "The Gallosians will attack. Stupidity . . . but they will attack."

"You are convinced?" Fydel shook his head, glancing to the hills south of the Great Highway, hills not yet raised into mountains—unlike those to the east and north.

"They wanted only an excuse to attack the day before. Now that they know we have raised mountains, they have such."

"But . . . raising mountains? Will they not think?"

"It has been many years since any have faced the true power of the Guild. A single aging mage in Fenard . . . does not show such power." Jeslek shrugged. "They will demand something impossible—perhaps that we restore the land. Then they will threaten, and then they will attack."

"But why?"

"Because they have been ordered to. Enough questions." Jeslek pointed westward to the ridge line that intersected the south side of the Great White Highway. "Let us proceed. Leave your mounts."

Cerryl took another swallow of water and walked behind Fydel, who carried his screeing glass and case. Lyasa and Kochar flanked Cerryl, and the three students walked quietly.

"Why would they be ordered to attack us?" Fydel asked in a low voice, looking to Anya.

"Jeslek is right." Anya's voice was also low, but loud enough for the overmage to hear. "Fairhaven has not shown enough power in recent years, and so the prefect believes such power does not exist."

Lyasa tapped Cerryl on the shoulder, and as he turned, rolled her eyes. Cerryl smiled ironically in return.

"They're stupid," Kochar mumbled. "People are going to get killed."

Stupidity usually got people killed, reflected Cerryl, but the ones who got killed weren't always the stupid ones.

The high and hazy autumn clouds had slowly thinned, and the

south wind had risen, bringing a hot dry breeze that combined with the strengthening sun to warm the granite of the road.

Cerryl glanced across the empty ridge line, wondering how soon it would be filled with mounted armsmen. He could feel the sweat collecting under his tunic as the day continued to warm.

Jeslek stopped and gestured. "Klybel says that the Gallosians will ride across the ridge. We will cast firebolts from the higher end here. Fydel—you and the students will be farther eastward, by that clump of brush there, just in case they try to use the road. If they do, use your first firebolts to bring down the lead mounts. That will slow everyone down, and even a student mage should be able to cast chaos-fire at an armsman who cannot get out of the way." The overmage gestured to Anya, and the two sat down on the road wall, talking in low voices.

"This way. It's shady there anyway." Fydel shrugged.

The three looked at one another, then turned and followed the square-bearded and broad-shouldered mage back along the white granite paving stones, back eastward, until they stood in the shade of the bluff.

"Now . . ." began Fydel, "Jeslek and Anya will certainly bring chaos-fire upon the mass of the Gallosians. None of you have their strength. So you must watch the battle and cast your firebolts at individual armsmen who may threaten them or you, or who look to be attacking places where our lancers are beleaguered."

That made sense to Cerryl.

"That's all you can do." The older mage nodded. "You wait here. I will be screeing for them to see where the Gallosians may be." He turned and walked back down the road.

Klybel rode past Fydel, and then past the student mages, eastward to where the lancers waited, some mounted, others preparing weapons or mounts or both.

Cerryl offered his water bottle to Lyasa.

"Thank you." She drank, then looked southward. "I didn't expect we'd get caught in a battle."

"We might not," suggested Kochar.

Lyasa and Cerryl looked at him.

"I guess we are, aren't we?"

"Neither the prefect nor the overmage is likely to back down," said Lyasa.

Cerryl took another drink from the bottle, then glanced farther eastward, where three lancers had tied the students' mounts and watched them. His chestnut sidestepped and lifted his head, as if to indicate unhappiness with the situation. Cerryl agreed with the gelding's unvoiced feelings.

The Gallosian armsmen appeared well before midmorning, the lead riders bearing purple pennons, and all riders bore polished oval iron-faced shields that shimmered in the sunlight. Heavy shields, Cerryl suspected from his own brief attempts to bear weapons. Besides the shields, each had an iron-tipped lance in a holder.

Again, an armsman rode forward under the messenger's blue-trimmed pennant. The pennant fluttered in the hot light wind that swirled across the ridge and the highway, a wind not strong enough to bend the knee-high and browning grass.

Jeslek mounted his off-white horse, and with an escort of a half-score lancers, rode forward onto the ridge and reined up, waiting for the messenger.

The messenger inclined his head. "I bring you the words of the prefect under the flag of truce."

"We listen under the flag of truce." Jeslek waited, his white hair glittering almost silver in the bright sunlight.

"You have abused the right of the road and profaned the lands of Gallos. You must return them to the grasslands they once were, and pay the prefect three thousand golds in penance."

Jeslek's eyebrows rose. "Your prefect has a rather high opinion of the value of those worthless grasslands. He also has an excessive opinion of himself."

"Are you refusing to undo the damage you have caused? If so, I am bid to tell you that you will suffer the prefect's wrath."

Jeslek offered a bland smile. "We look forward to seeing his wrath. It could be amusing."

The messenger swallowed. "So be it, mage." He turned his mount, riding quickly back toward the massed horsemen.

"They'll charge quickly," Klybel said. "Stand ready!" His voice rose as the order was echoed down the ranks of the white lancers.

"Stand ready!"

Fydel carried his screeing glass toward the spot where the student mages waited, his eyes darting back toward the Gallosian ranks.

"Arms ready!"

From the south sounded two trumpet notes, then two more.

A wave of dark shafts appeared in the green-blue sky, seemingly from nowhere, dropping into the ranked white lancers. At least three lancers sagged in their saddles.

"Archers! Hidden on the left," called Fydel, standing on the road wall and yelling the directions back to Jeslek.

His face twisted in annoyance, Jeslek turned and lifted what seemed like a wave of fire that arched over the white lancers and surged over the north side of the ridge line.

Fydel gave a nod and slipped the glass into its leather case, then almost ran back to the students. "Start raising chaos!"

Cerryl watched the Gallosians but could not see where Jeslek's fire tide had gone, only feeling that it had swept through a group of men.

"Aaeeeiii..." Screams—brief, muted screams—followed the fire wave. No arrows did.

Jeslek stood bent forward, his hands on his knees, his face somehow both pale and flushed.

A mass of Gallosian horses charged across the ridge line, straight at the outnumbered white lancers, lances leveled.

The front line of Klybel's lancers spurred their mounts forward, but slowly.

Whsst! Whstt! Whsst! Three quick firebolts from Anya splashed across the front of the Gallosians, and two mounts dived into the damp ground, snarling a half score of riders who followed.

Whhsst! Fydel lifted a larger firebolt that arced into the left center of the purple-clad armsmen, bringing down more mounts and men.

Still, a good score of the Gallosian riders reached the white lancers, and white and purple overtunics mixed together in a swirl, and the off-tune striking of lances on shields, blades on shields, and blades on blades drifted toward the younger mages.

Whst! Whst! Whst! Three more firebolts sailed over the nearer combatants and into the waiting ranked line of Gallosians.

The trumpet sounded again, and all the purple-clad figures surged forward.

Jeslek straightened, as though he had taken a deep breath, and around him rose another cloud of sparkling fire. That cloud sprayed into fragments and foamed above the few fighters remaining near the front of the white lancer line, then flowed into the front ranks of the charging Gallosians.

Cerryl swallowed—hard. The entire front two ranks of the purple riders went down in a charcoaled and flaming heap, and at least another two ranks ended up either on the burning grass or turning into each other, dropping lances, and otherwise rendering each other ineffective.

Whst! Whst! Two more firebolts from Anya dropped into the confused mass, incinerating even more armsmen.

Whhsst! A single fat fireball from Fydel soared behind Anya's, then dropped and flattened into a half-dozen points of single flame, each point a dying armsman.

"To the east!" called someone. "On the highway."

Cerryl glanced down the Great Highway to his left—eastward—to see a short column of purple-clad lancers charging toward them.

"Fydel! You and the students! Stop them." Jeslek's voice was loud—and hoarse.

Stepping up and standing on the road wall, Cerryl turned eastward to face the riders—still almost half a kay away, but closing the gap rapidly.

Whhsttt!

A pale-faced Fydel lifted a fireball into the leading rider, turning man and mount into a flaming mass. The rider to the right pulled up, trying to beat out flames crawling across his tunic and snarling those behind him.

Those on the left poured past the charred mass and the burning armsman, the hoofs of their mounts pounding on the white granite paving stones of the road.

Whhssst! Another firebolt from Fydel flared into the granite before the oncoming Gallosians, splitting their force around the chaos-fire.

Whsst! A small firebolt from Lyasa arced into the purple-clad rider next to the road wall on the northern side. His chest a mass of flame, he sagged in the saddle, then toppled over the wall into the puddled water in the drainage way.

Cerryl lifted a firebolt across the two leading lancers, and both went down in a flaming heap. Two more riders plowed into the dead armsmen and their struggling mounts, and the charge stopped—momentarily.

Fydel took advantage of the congestion to loft another fireball into the riders blacked behind the fallen and still-struggling mounts.

"First and third squads—to the left flank on the road!" Klybel's order rose above the confusion. Hoofs on stone sounded behind Cerryl and Lyasa.

Cerryl glanced eastward beyond the milling Gallosians. Another score of purple-clad riders rode more slowly from the east, and they bore neither lances nor blades but curved staves—bows.

"Archers on the left road flank!" called Cerryl. "More archers!" As he spoke, he arched a firebolt over the mass toward the oncoming archers, but it splashed on the granite short of them.

Kochar tried the same thing, with the same results.

"Too far," muttered the redhead.

"Get the closer ones!" snapped Fydel. "You can do that."

Cerryl's eyes inadvertently flicked to the south, where yet another rank of mounted Gallosians thundered over, through, and around their fallen comrades toward the white lancers, who used blades against the handful of Gallosians from the first two attacks who had survived the fireballs.

An arrow clattered on the stones beneath Cerryl, and he jerked his eyes back to the Great Highway.

A good dozen archers remained mounted, loosing shafts.

Cerryl glanced to his left and right. No one was watching. Gathering chaos as he had in the tunnels, he focused it into a golden lance that flew straight—straight through the lead archer, who flew from his mount in flames.

Whhstt! One of Lyasa's firebolts took out an archer on the flank.

Fydel lifted another fat fireball that exploded in the midst of the archers, leaving but two mounted. One turned his horse and started to ride away.

Whhsttt!

The thin student mage mustered more chaos and released another light lance, effective at downing the last archer moving forward.

Behind the archers rode another company of the purple-clad arms-men bearing long iron blades that glittered in the midday sun.

Fydel staggered and reached out to grasp the road wall.

Cerryl glanced toward the riders, then tried to spray chaos across the front rank, the way he once had in the sewers.

A flare of light washed across the Gallosians, and the four riders and their mounts slowly tumbled into a blazing line of fire, a line that nearly engulfed the next set of riders.

Whsstt! Lyasa's firebolt scored more riders, and even a smaller blast from Kochar splashed into those who followed.

The road cleared—almost. Out of the smoke came a single rider. The lancer bore down on Cerryl, the long gray blade swinging straight at the student, even as the armsman tried to shield himself behind the smallish oval shield.

Whhst!

A flare of golden light—like an arrow—speared the lancer, who looked dumbfounded as he pitched back out of the saddle onto the ground.

Cerryl glanced around. The road was empty, except for a handful of white lancers, the mages, and burned heaps that had once been men and mounts.

Lyasa stepped up beside Cerryl and glanced at the circular hole in the beaten leather armor of the Gallosian. She glanced at Cerryl, then cast a small fireball onto the corpse.

"Why—" Cerryl broke off his question.

"Better this way."

"Thank you."

Lyasa smiled. "There will come a time . . ."

Cerryl nodded. He would pay his debts.

They turned. The ridge was a sea of swirling smoke and dark heaps. To the west, Cerryl could see a handful of riders in purple, moving slowly. On the ridge line remained only the white lancers—perhaps two thirds of them.

Jeslek sat exhausted on the road wall, his face so red that Cerryl could see the color from more than a hundred cubits away. Anya sat beside the overmage, her back to Cerryl and Lyasa.

Kochar stepped up beside the two student mages and looked at the charred corpse of the last lancer. "Oh, you two did stop him."

"We managed," Cerryl said. "I needed some help from Lyasa."

"At least he admits it . . ." Fydel's words drifted with the wind and the smoke from the intermittently burning grass and low brush toward Cerryl. The bearded mage also sat on the road wall, leaning forward, forehead resting in his hands.

Cerryl swallowed, trying not to smell the odor of smoldering brush and burnt flesh, wondering what and how much he would have to keep hidden in order to survive.

"Let's look at that arm," demanded Lyasa.

Cerryl glanced at his arms, first one, then the other. His sleeves were smudged with dirt, soot, and grime, but he didn't think he'd been wounded. He felt stupid as he realized Kochar had been hurt, and he watched as Lyasa lightly bathed the slash in chaos—one of Broka's techniques, he recalled—and then bound it.

Around them, white lancers began checking corpses for weapons and coins.

Cerryl looked at the last lancer he had killed.

"Go ahead," said Lyasa. "His purse is yours."

Cerryl forced himself to cut the thongs and take the purse, only lightly burned. It held two silvers and three coppers. Was that the worth of a man's life?

He put the coins in his own wallet, trying not to shake his head. He glanced upward. Was it midafternoon already?

Behind them, Fydel slowly stood and walked westward, toward Jeslek and Anya.

"I don't understand." Kochar checked the dressing on his arm. "About Jeslek. He can raise mountains, but those Gallosians, they almost got us."

"It's simple." Lyasa sighed. "Chaos-fire is pure chaos—it's concentrated chaos. It takes more effort. When Jeslek raises the hills, he's moving and directing a lot of chaos in the ground that's already there. When you cast a firebolt, you have to separate the chaos from the world and force it somewhere. That's harder." She looked at Kochar. "How do you feel right now?"

"Like horse droppings," admitted the redhead.

"Look at all three of them." She gestured toward the section of road wall where the three mages sat, talking in low voices. "I couldn't raise a chaos-fire ball the size of my fingernail. I'll bet they couldn't either."

Cerryl kept his mouth shut, just nodding. "Maybe we should join them."

The other two walked alongside him as the three made their way toward the full mages.

XCVI

In the gray of dawn, Cerryl finished his cheese and biscuits with a swallow of water. Then he walked down to the drainage way, where a thin stream of water flowed and refilled the bottle, concentrating on channeling chaos heat into the water until it boiled. The heat wasn't the hard part. Wrapping the bottle in order to keep it from breaking was.

He couldn't drink the water until it cooled, and he walked back to where the chestnut was tethered, easing the bottle into the straps.

A faint orange glow filled the sky above the newly raised hills to the east, but the morning was silent—only the scattered chirping of insects. The light wind carried the odor of death, and Cerryl was glad that they would be traveling on, but worried. How long before the prefect decided to sacrifice more men?

Cerryl was well aware that twice as many Gallosians might have carried the skirmish or battle, and he wondered if Jeslek had understood that also.

A hundred cubits or so west of Cerryl, Jeslek stood beside Klybel, and the two talked in low voices. Klybel nodded, reluctantly, and turned. He mounted his horse and rode past Cerryl, back to where the lancers had camped.

"Cerryl?" called the overmage.

Cerryl walked quickly toward Jeslek.

The older man's face was shadowed, and lines radiated from his eyes, lines of age that Cerryl had not seen before. His sun-gold eyes still glittered, and the dullness had left the white hair.

"You saw how the Gallosians received us yesterday?"

"Yes, ser."

The overmage cleared his throat, then fixed Cerryl with his eyes. "Cerryl, all students must undertake a task—a thing to be accomplished alone—before they are accepted into the Guild. The task is set before each in a manner to ensure that the mage-to-be indicates utterly his devotion to the Guild."

Cerryl didn't like what he knew was coming, even if he had no idea of what task Jeslek was about to lay upon him.

The gold-eyed mage smiled. "Many have questioned your devotion, and I have set you a task after which none can gainsay your right to the Brotherhood."

"Yes, ser."

"You are to remove the prefect of Gallos."

Cerryl swallowed, as much because of the growing chaos that swirled around Jeslek as because of the task. Was that because Jeslek expected him to refuse?

"Ser?"

"Why do I task you, is that what you wonder?"

"Not exactly, ser. You have the power to destroy massed armies . . ." Cerryl wanted to know more, even if he were in no position to refuse the overmage.

"Ah . . . and I could ravage the lands, you think."

"You have that power. Of that, after yesterday, there is no doubt."

"That is indeed true." Jeslek stroked his chin. "Therein lies a problem. If I did indeed ravage Gallos—then who would farm the land, or cut the timber—or collect the road duties? Likewise, if the removal of the prefect is accomplished by a lesser mage . . . then who will refute the wisdom of acquiescing to the 'requests' of Fairhaven?"

"And how am I to accomplish this, ser? I cannot very well walk up to Fenard—"

"You will be sent with a lancer guard as an assistant to Sverlik. He, of course, as an envoy, could not act overtly against Lyam." Jeslek shrugged. "How you deal with Lyam, that I leave to your discretion, save that you must vanish from Fenard and return to Fairhaven without knowledge of any in Gallos. A simple enough task for one who would be a mage." Jeslek smiled.

"How am I to deal with those armsmen who escaped, ser? They will claim we attacked them."

"You have been most creative so far. I am sure you will find a way." Jeslek shrugged, and the chaos continued to build around him. "Captain Klybel is forming your escort right now. He will also provide some extra rations for you. It is best you do not have to forage. I would like you to leave as quickly as possible." Another false and quick smile followed. "We have made our point, and will also be returning to Fairhaven shortly."

Cerryl preferred the more direct speech Jeslek had used when Cerryl had been a more junior student mage.

"Best you prepare," Jeslek suggested pointedly.

"Yes, ser." Cerryl bowed and turned. Even before he was a dozen steps away, Jeslek had summoned Anya.

"Anya . . . I'd like you and Fydel to ride south—just a kay or so—to the end of that ridge, and study the area. Have Fydel scree it for Gallosians. I'll need to trace the chaos lines there. I'd like you to leave immediately . . ."

Cerryl frowned as he walked back toward where he and the other students had camped and where the chestnut was tethered.

"What was that about?" asked Lyasa. "Should I ask?"

Cerryl glanced around. Kochar was nowhere in sight. "Jeslek has insisted that I go to be an assistant to Sverlik in Fenard. I have to do something for him and Sverlik. As a test."

"After this?" Lyasa also glanced around, then back to Cerryl, her olive-brown eyes filled with concern.

"After this. One does not argue with an overmage." He glanced along the road to where Jeslek had dismissed Anya. "I would like another favor. Jeslek says you're headed back to Fairhaven before long. Would you tell Myral? Just Myral?"

"I can do that." Lyasa paused. "I'd rather tell Leyladin, and let her tell him. I don't see him often, and people would notice. I can trust her."

"If you think so." He smiled as he strapped his pack on the gelding. "All right. Thank you."

Klybel rode past, leading a line of lancers—doubtless Cerryl's escort. The captain did not look at Cerryl.

"You be careful," cautioned Lyasa.

"As careful as I can be."

"Cerryl!" called Jeslek.

The student mage untethered the chestnut and began to lead his mount toward the group around Jeslek.

"Good luck," whispered Lyasa.

"Thank you."

All of the lancers were mounted, save one—an armsman with a single silver bar on his left tunic collar who inclined his head.

"This is Undercaptain Ludren, young Cerryl," said Klybel. "Your escort will be a half-score. That should be large enough to deter brigands and small enough not to alarm the people of Gallos." The lancer captain leaned forward and extended a folded parchment square. "This is a map of the main roads of Gallos. We trust it is accurate."

Cerryl took the map with a nod. "Thank you."

"If you are attacked, you have leave to defend yourself, but I would encourage you not to use your powers against any except those who do attack you." Jeslek's voice was mild, reasonable, and Cerryl could sense that the chaos around the overmage had begun to subside.

"I will use what powers I have," Cerryl answered as he mounted the chestnut, "only if attacked."

"Good."

Ludren remounted, then looked at Cerryl.

"Whenever you are ready, Undercaptain."

Ludren nodded and turned his mount westward on the Great White Highway.

Cerryl's lips tightened as he could sense a screen of chaos rising behind them, one that doubtless blurred his departure. *Sterol has set you as a check to Jeslek, and Jeslek wants you removed in a manner not to be traced to him.*

Still, there was nothing he dared do. Not yet. His lips tightened. Perhaps not ever, but definitely not yet. He flicked the reins and let the chestnut pull alongside the undercaptain and his mount.

XCVII

Through the day and a half since Cerryl and his escort had left the main body of the Fairhaven forces, the twelve had ridden alone westward on the Great White Highway, not encountering anyone, in and out of intermittent cool rain and chilly breezes. Puddles collected next to the granite road wall, and their mounts occasionally splashed through flat sheets of water running off the nearly level granite paving stones.

"Empty, it is," Ludren said once more, as he did every few kays.

"Not a soul in sight," answered Cerryl. The only living thing outside his group was a single black vulcrow that flew ahead of them and waited, then watched as they passed, and flew farther ahead—either looking for scraps or for someone or some animal to keel over and die.

Ahead, Cerryl could see a side road—one that crossed the Great Highway, or that the Highway crossed. As they neared the crossroads, he could make out a single kaystone with two arrows. One pointed south with the name Tellura—one of the names that had led to his mapmaking. The north-pointing arrow bore the name Fenard.

"Toward Fenard." Cerryl turned the chestnut off the Great White Highway and onto the clay-packed trail that bore hoofprints—not terribly recent prints.

"Here's where it may get rough, ser," said Ludren.

"Do you think that the Gallosians would wait on the side road this far from Fenard?" Cerryl doubted it very much. They might run into a company of armsmen closer to the capital. Might? He held back a laugh, since Ludren would have taken it wrong.

Ludren frowned, then nodded slowly. "You might be right, ser."

"I don't know. I'm new to this," Cerryl said as the chestnut carried him along the narrower packed clay road. "I would think that the armsmen who survived would probably ride to Fenard to tell the prefect."

"Like as not, he won't be wishing to see us."

"No." That was an understatement. Jeslek had clearly set Cerryl a near-impossible task, doubtless in hopes that someone would kill him. More than a day of riding, and Cerryl still didn't have a good idea of how he was going to get into Fenard, let alone kill the prefect and get out.

Half-surprisingly, the thought of killing the prefect didn't bother him. Was that because what everyone had said and what he had seen gave the impression of a very unpleasant character? What if Lyam weren't as pictured?

Cerryl glanced back over his shoulder at the white lancers. The pair behind him—Jubuul and Zusta, he thought—rode silently and dejectedly. The mage wondered what they had done to displease Klybel and Jeslek.

"Ludren?"

"Yes, ser."

"What were you told about escorting me to Fenard?"

"Well . . . ser . . . I can't say as I was told much. The captain said I was to get you there, and then we were to try to catch them on the Great Highway, and if not, to rejoin them at the South Barracks."

"You weren't supposed to carry any messages or supplies to the mage Sverlik or back from him?"

"No, ser. We were to escort you to the prefect's palace and then return."

Cerryl nodded. "How long have you been a lancer?"

"Nigh on ten years, ser. Glad I was that the captain and the overmage offered this. Otherwise, it might have been another ten afore I made captain. That's why there be no silver on my tunic—just the rank bar."

"It must take a while to make rank."

"Depends, ser. Huylar made undercaptain in six, but he was in the

Sligan campaign—the one where they put down the timber camps and the traders so as they'd listen to the Brotherhood. To make rank, you take chances or time."

The Sligan campaign? "When was that?"

"Three, four years ago. Huylar's been 'round longer than me."

"Were you involved in the Sligan campaign?"

"Me, ser? No. I was part of the mage's guard in Hydolar, like Viurat is in Fenard."

"I don't know Viurat," Cerryl said pleasantly, his eyes on the road ahead, and where it wound to the left around a long hill that flanked the road on the east.

"Viurat's my cousin. No reason as you'd know him, ser."

"How long has he been in Fenard?"

"Must be five years now. Brought Ryentyl—she's his consort—he brought her with him." Ludren laughed. "Lancers aren't supposed to have consorts unless they're officers, but no one really looks. Not that hard. Guess they like Fenard. He's still there."

Cerryl steered the chestnut around a particularly deep-looking pothole filled with dark and muddy water, glancing at the sky to the north. The clouds were dropping and darkening, foreshadowing another storm, if not for another few kays—and more headaches.

"Storm coming," the undercaptain added. "Might keep those purple lancers from looking for us."

"I doubt they're looking for us. Not here." Of course, any Gallosians who saw them might well want to eliminate anyone from Fairhaven, especially a student mage, but Cerryl doubted anyone was actually out searching. Not yet. That might change after the survivors of Jeslek's fire attacks reached Fenard.

"Hope you're right, ser."

Cerryl nodded, his mind more on what awaited him. Even assuming he could get into Fenard, assuming he didn't have to evade or flee Gallosian armsmen, Jeslek had said he was to remove the prefect and to leave Fenard unseen. How? The only way he could be unseen was to cloak himself in light, as Anya had done in visiting Faltar, and Jeslek knew Cerryl hadn't ever done anything like that.

Could he channel light around himself the way he could channel chaos? He ought to be able to—light was a form of chaos. Still, what he ought to be able to do and what he could do might be very different.

He concentrated . . . and found himself blind—enclosed in darkness. The chestnut half-whuffed, half–whimper-screamed, as the darkness surrounded them. Cerryl quickly released the light-shifting screens, or whatever what he had done was called. The gelding stepped forward and sideways for a moment.

"What was that?" Ludren leaned forward. "For a moment, you were not there."

Cerryl forced a quizzical expression. "You must be mistaken. I have been here all along. My mount . . . something spooked him."

"I would have sworn . . ."

"Still say he disappeared . . ." came the mumbled words from Jubuul. ". . . trouble with mages. . . . never where you think they are."

Cerryl licked his lips. He needed more practice, but it wouldn't help much to practice while riding with the lancers. He forced a laugh. "Isn't that true about most things?"

"What, ser?" asked the earnest Ludren.

"Oh . . . nothing's exactly what or where you think it is."

"If you say so, ser."

A long ride to Fenard, a long ride to certain trouble, trouble he wasn't even quite certain he could avoid or master. Cerryl did not shake his head but kept his pleasant smile in place.

XCVIII

Cerryl peered through the cool fall drizzle, wishing he'd brought a true waterproof. The leather jacket was hot, and tended to soak up the misting rain after a time, but the rain was too cool to ride through in just his shirt and white tunic.

Ahead, to the north, a narrow stone bridge arched over the river. Beyond the river, a wagon drawn by a single horse creaked past the browning grass of the roadside meadows toward still-distant Fenard.

The student mage eased out the map and looked at it. "That's the River Gallos, I think."

"Is that close to Fenard?" asked Ludren.

"Not that close," Cerryl said. "We'd see more people on the road. Fenard is a big place."

Cerryl wasn't looking forward to reaching Fenard. He couldn't afford *not* to succeed because if he survived without carrying out Jeslek's charge to him, Sterol would say that Cerryl should have confronted Jeslek immediately. But Jeslek would have tried to destroy Cerryl, and Cerryl wasn't certain he was strong enough yet to hold off Jeslek's power.

He laughed softly to himself. Who was he deceiving? Jeslek would have turned Cerryl into ashes if he'd refused to undertake the task—

and then told everyone that Cerryl had attacked him, or some such. There was a reason Anya and Fydel weren't anywhere around when Cerryl left. Doubtless, Jeslek would claim that Cerryl had run away—or something. As for the lancers, they were the ones no one would miss—probably listed as lost on a scouting mission. Lost to hostile Gallosians, providing another reason for bringing the force of Fairhaven to bear on the prefect.

"Ser? Begging your pardon . . . ?"

"What's so funny? Nothing, really, I guess." Yet it was all absurd. Once he got close to Fenard, he'd have to rely on the invisibility trick to get into the city. He'd tried it at night, when the lancers weren't looking, and he thought he had it mastered, although he worried that the shield might cause the air to waver, like the one time when he had seen Anya use it. Yet . . . he had no other alternatives.

If he could get inside Fenard, he'd need some kind of cloak to cover his whites . . .

Cerryl shook his head. At the moment, he wasn't certain how close he could even get to Fenard before the Gallosian lancers or armsmen or whatever showed up. He looked at the bridge, then at the map. From what he could determine, they were still a day and a half from Fenard.

"Another two days, almost." He rubbed his chin, conscious that he had a beard, but one all too scraggly—and no razor. No razor from a certain gray/black mage . . . that might have been the last thing he ever received from her. He pushed away the thoughts.

"Like as we'll never catch Klybel, then, on the return." Ludren sounded discouraged.

Cerryl wondered how the overpromoted undercaptain would feel if he knew he was never supposed to catch the rest of the white lancers. "So long as you get back to Fairhaven, it doesn't matter, does it?"

"I suppose not, ser. And what about you, ser?"

"I have a task to carry out. Then we'll see." *See what? How you can manage to get back to Fairhaven and manipulate Jeslek and Sterol into making you a full mage? Why?* Because the alternatives were worse, at least over time. Fairhaven controlled or would control all the lands east of the Westhorns, and those to the west hated white mages, as did Recluce.

Cerryl imagined he could live out a life somewhere as a peasant, but it would be a short and miserable life, and he'd seen enough of poverty.

So . . . you'll take on the Guild? And probably get killed in the effort?

He laughed softly again.

"Ser?"

"Nothing. I'm not thinking too well, I guess." Cerryl folded the map and replaced it inside his jacket. "We've a ways to go."

XCIX

The green-blue sky was clear, and the midday sun warm, but not too warm. A light wind, with a hint of chill, blew from the west, from the unseen Westhorns, ruffling the roadside grass, including the few tufts that grew out of the old road wall on the west side of the packed clay, a road wall little more than stacked gray and black stones.

Something did not feel right, and Cerryl reined up abruptly. A small cot stood less than a kay to the west, and rows of cut stalks lined the field beyond the strip of meadow that bordered the road. A man gathered and bound the straw, not looking toward the road or the travelers.

A small river meandered from the northwest, and another stone bridge crossed it perhaps three hundred cubits down the road from where Cerryl had stopped. On the far side, low-lying fields, almost like marshes, stretched nearly another a kay before reaching the reddish granite walls of Fenard. A long and low dust cloud rose from the road on the north side of the river, a dust cloud coming from the city.

Cerryl glanced down at the road, its dust damped by the intermittent fall rains, then across the bridge. Dust meant a lot of riders, and a lot of riders meant lancers.

Cerryl glanced to his left, toward a low and rolling hill. Several horsemen appeared on the crest, their purple overtunics visible clearly in the sun. He almost sighed as he heard the fumbling and clanking behind him. As he had suspected, his escort did not contain those lancers most accomplished in arms.

"Ludren! Take your men and ride south—as fast as you can."

"Ser?"

"Ride south as fast as you can," Cerryl said. "If you hurry, you might outrun all those lancers."

"But . . . we're not to the gates."

"If you don't mind, neither do I. Otherwise, we'll all look like Eliasar's straw targets."

"The overmage and Klybel said—"

"Ludren—you stay with me, and you're dead. *You may be anyway* . . . Please just go." Cerryl tried to keep the exasperation from his voice as he looked at the oncoming lancers and watched the archers on the hill begin to string their bows.

"Ah . . . yes, ser. Good luck, ser." Ludren wheeled his mount. "The mage says we're done, boys, and it's time to go. Best we hurry."

"Now he tells us . . ."

"Move!" Ludren gave a half-salute, then spurred his mount.

Within moments, Cerryl flung the cloak of light or darkness around himself and the chestnut. Using his feel of where order and chaos fell, he could sense his way slowly toward the scrubby tree at the edge of the unfenced meadow land.

Wheeee . . . whuffff . . .

"Easy . . . easy." Cerryl patted the chestnut on the neck, trying to calm the gelding as he walked his mount slowly off the road, across the shoulder, and through the twisted and browning grass.

The ground vibrated with the hoofbeats of the Gallosian lancers approaching. He hoped that the faint wavering that appeared—as it had around Anya—with the light cloak would be masked by the wind and the fluttering gray winter leaves of the tree beside which he and the gelding waited.

There was no point at all in trying to use chaos-fire against the Gallosian horsemen. There were too many, and using flame would alert everyone to the fact that there was a white mage around. *Better no one knows you're here.*

As the hoofbeats gradually faded out, Cerryl waited in his self-created blindness and darkness, hoping he could sense the approach of twilight, and worrying about Ludren and the other lancers. He'd needed the diversion, but he hadn't liked using them. *You didn't hesitate there.*

In all likelihood, many would have died in combat somewhere . . . *Are you sure? Or did you choose what benefited you?* He nodded. He'd chosen what helped him, and nothing was going to change that. He just hoped he didn't end up like Jeslek and Sterol.

Although the road seemed silent, Cerryl waited a time longer, conscious of the sweat that oozed down his back. Finally, he released the shield and quickly studied the road and the cot.

The peasant had disappeared, and smoke rose from the earthen-brick chimney of the cot. The sun hung over the hills to the west, those low hills that led to the Westhorns.

The road was empty, except for a cart that creaked southward, already past Cerryl and heading toward Southbrook or Tellura or some other town that Cerryl and the lancers had skirted on their ride toward Fenard. No lancers waited on the hilltop.

Cerryl waited, sipping his water until the sun dropped behind the hills. Only then did he urge his mount toward the river to drink, and then he waited until the sky was nearly full dark before traveling the last kay or so toward Fenard, halting in the gloom several hundred cubits from the gates.

A half-squad of armsmen or lancers stood under the torches by the gates, waiting, their posture signifying boredom.

"Someone's out there . . ."

Cerryl eased the light shield around him and the chestnut. Did he dare try to walk through the gates—just shielded? Virtually half-blind?

He sat on the gelding . . . waiting . . .

"Don't see a thing. You get jumpy every time a rat climbs out of the sewer ditches." One of the guard's voices drifted through the darkness.

"I did see something."

"Any of you others see anything?"

Cerryl held his breath.

"See, Nubver . . . there's no one out there. Overcaptain Gysto and his lancers even chased out the rats."

Laughter echoed from the walls.

The guards chatted, but no riders or wagons moved along the road. Finally, bit by bit, Cerryl eased the chestnut, now more at ease in the darkness of the light shield, forward along the road, moving more slowly, more deliberately, once the gelding's hoofs clicked on the paving stones of the causeway that began a mere hundred cubits from the guards. He tried not to think about the madness of what he attempted.

One of the guards turned. "You hear something? Like someone walking on the causeway?"

"I don't see anything. You and Pulsat want to go check . . . go check. Probably a rat."

Another wave of laughter followed.

"Pulsat, come on."

Cerryl swallowed, not knowing whether his shield would hold if the guards got too close. He concentrated, then arced a fireball at what felt to be a pile of rubbish to the west of the guards.

Whhssttt! Light flared up.

"See! There was something."

Four of the guards pulled out blades and eased toward the flickering fire that remained near the base of the walls.

"Looks like rubbish . . ."

"Maybe a rat set it on fire . . ."

A step at a time, Cerryl guided the chestnut by sense and feel toward the gates and past the remaining pair of guards, both of whom were more interested in the fire than the seemingly empty gates.

"Nothing here."

"Who set the fire?

". . . someone drop a torch from the walls?"

"Why?"

"Who knows? Report it to Delbur in the morning."

With the sweat seeping down his back, Cerryl guided the gelding into the streets of Fenard, turning abruptly at the first corner into a narrower way. Another hundred cubits onward, he released the light shields and just sat on the chestnut, shivering. The street smelled like the sewers of Fairhaven, if not so strongly. The only light was that of the stars and a smoky torch perhaps fifty cubits farther along the street.

He was in Fenard, with no idea of where the palace or anything was. He wore white garments that would make him an instant target in daylight, and he had but two silvers and a handful of coppers in his purse.

Cerryl had few doubts that he would find any trace of Sverlik—dead or alive. He also had strong suspicions that Jeslek had already figured that out, well before the overmage had sent Cerryl on his "task."

"Out! Out before you wreck it all . . ."

The junior mage glanced up where a tall figure staggered out into the street by the torch.

"A weighty man was he . . . was he . . . a weighty man was he . . ."

Thud . . . The sound of a door closing echoed down the street, followed by a brief rustling that Cerryl suspected signified rats.

". . . and a weighty man . . . am I . . . am I . . ."

The shadowy figure waddled toward Cerryl, who could see that the drunkard was both tall and broad, twice his own bulk, and wearing a capacious cloak. Cerryl had no weapons to speak of, save the short white-bronze knife. Should he turn? But that might put him in view of the gate guards.

He sat on the chestnut and waited.

As the reveler staggered toward Cerryl, Cerryl drew the light shield around himself and the chestnut—then released it when the man was less than three cubits away.

"Weighty . . . man . . . am I—where did you come from, fellow?"

Cerryl recloaked himself and his mount, easing the chestnut sideways slightly, so that the reveler would walk by, rather than run into the horse. He drew out his knife. The heavy man stood there for a moment, then scratched his head. "If that's how . . . you want it . . ." He started past the concealed mage.

As he passed, Cerryl reached down and grabbed the long cloak, slicing the ties.

The heavy man turned, coming up with a truncheonlike club, but Cerryl and the cloak had vanished.

Cerryl rode slowly down the street, past the smoking torch, and turned left at the next, and broader, way where he stopped and fastened the long cloak over his white jacket. The long cloak covered his upper body and most of his trousers.

Then he urged the chestnut on. The buildings were mostly of two stories, with plaster and timber fronts, and the second stories protruded a cubit or two farther into the street than the ground-floor levels. A foggy mist swirled around the buildings, a mist that bore the odor of open sewers and fires.

Someone was ahead. Cerryl swallowed, and gathered chaos, hoping he did not have to use it.

The small figure scurried down a side alley, and Cerryl took a deep breath. The next block was not quite so dark, though there were no lamps or torches hung, because blotches of light fell into the street from the windows or shutters of the dwellings on the left.

The scrape of boots on the cobblestones brought his attention closer. Two figures darted from the shadows of the alley on the left that he had not really noticed.

"Fellow . . . you'll be surrendering that mount—and your purse."

Cerryl glanced at the pair. Both wore tattered shirts and trousers, and wide belts with scabbards. Both bore midlength iron blades. No others were near them. "I'm sorry."

"Not so sorry as you're going to be." The bigger man, nearly as tall as Kinowin, laughed.

Cerryl smiled sadly, gathering chaos.

Whsst! Whsst!

The big man toppled. The smaller man stood for a moment, his mouth opening

"White—!"

Whhhstt!

Cerryl swayed in the saddle, then forced himself to dismount. He glanced up and down the alley, but the narrow way was dark and empty—with only a hint of a lamp or torch reflected on the corner of the building nearest the main way.

Splushh . . . His right boot went into the sewer ditch. "Darkness . . ."

His chaos-aided night vision helped as he stripped the smaller man and cut both purses and took a scabbard and blade he could scarcely use.

He kept looking around as he dusted the ragged trousers with chaos and then pulled them on over his own white trousers, but no one appeared. After belting the scabbard in place and sheathing the blade, careful not to touch the cold iron, he cleaned his boots as well as he could and remounted. Then, still scanning the area, he checked the purses. Three silvers and a handful of coppers.

That the two would have killed him was clear, but that he had profited from their deaths nagged at him—and such a little profit. Was a man worth more than a pair of silvers? Yet Jeslek had sent him off to certain death, one way or another, for less than that. And had sent Ludren as well.

Yet, was Cerryl any better? He'd used the lancers as a decoy. Still, they had a chance. He'd given them that, a better chance, he hoped, than Jeslek had given him.

He took a deep breath and resumed the ride down the larger street, trying to be more careful, until he reached the main road again, where he turned right and continued toward the middle of Fenard.

The main street had more traffic—men with guards and lamp bearers, a carriage with guards—but no one really scrutinized the thin cloaked figure. Cerryl finally found what he sought.

The signboard bore an image illuminated by a single torch—that of a yellow-colored bowl. Cerryl rode past the door and toward what looked to be an archway to a courtyard and a stable.

"Ser? Late you are."

"Aye . . ." Cerryl roughened his voice. "Late . . . any man would be in this warren."

The stable boy shrank back as Cerryl dismounted.

"There's room here?"

"Was last time I heard, ser."

"Good." Cerryl flipped a copper to the lad. "That's for you, if you take good care of him. If you do, there's another. If you don't . . ."

"Thank you, ser. Thank you. I'll call Prytyk."

Cerryl unfastened the pack and bedroll.

The stable boy whistled, twice, and by the time Cerryl had his gear in hand, a squat figure in soiled gray had appeared under the lamp by the stable door.

"A room? This late?"

Cerryl's eyes blazed.

The squat man backed away, his eyes going from Cerryl's face to the blade at the young mage's hip and back to his face. He swallowed. "Tonight?"

"Tonight and tomorrow. Alone."

"A single—that be a silver a night."

"And fare?"

"And fare, but no drink."

Cerryl nodded and extended a silver. "The rest when I leave."

The innkeeper's eyes went to the blade again, then to Cerryl's face. "Guess I can trust you."

"That you can, innkeeper." Cerryl forced confidence into his voice but kept it soft and low. "So long as you keep yours."

"You . . ."

Cerryl looked into the muddy brown eyes, raising chaos as he did.

"Yes, ser."

Cerryl smiled. "Thank you."

He followed the innkeeper through the side door.

"Public room be that way. Stairs here."

He followed the squat man up the narrow steps.

The end room on the single upstairs corridor that was now more than two cubits wide had a battered gold oak door, and Prytyk pushed it open. "This be yours. Not much fare left this late, but you come down and I'll have Foera get you the best we can."

"I'll be there shortly."

"No bare iron in the public room."

Cerryl nodded.

Once Prytyk had left, Cerryl glanced in the wall mirror. The face that looked back at him was drawn, lightly bearded, and blood-streaked. The crooked smile that greeted him seemed almost cruel.

"Well, without a razor . . ." How would Leyladin have found The Golden Bowl? He didn't doubt it was beneath her, well beneath her.

He used the washbasin to remove the blood, still wondering how he ended up with it on his face, and the worst of the grime, then slipped off the cloak, the white leather jacket, and the red-striped overtunic. A plain white shirt, travel-stained, and brownish trousers—and a blade—scarcely the picture of a mage. The jacket and tunic went in his pack. He left his borrowed cloak on the wall peg and eased the pack and bedroll against the wall on the far side of the bed, out of easy sight, not that there was much of value there, except the jacket, but wearing it close to people would cause too much notice.

The public room was smoky from a low fire in the small corner hearth, with grease in the air, and loud chatter. Twelve tables were situated haphazardly, and all but two were taken—a round one still bearing empty mugs and dirty platters, and a small square one against the wall. Cerryl took the small table, turning the chair so that he could watch the archway without seeming to do so.

". . . care where you get wool . . ."

". . . you think she cares . . . All she wants is silks from Naclos . . . and a larder full of spices and a matched pair of milk cows . . ."

". . . young fellow . . . there . . . just came in . . . another bravo . . . Prytyk said he'd like as kill . . ."

". . . doesn't look that bad . . ."

". . . blood on his face . . . some on his blade, Prytyk said . . ."

"...worry...not here. If he be a real bravo...safe enough... don't do their work where they stay. Now...wouldn't want to be down at The Black Kettle..."

Cerryl glanced up as the serving girl, thin, harried, and wearing a stained apron, eased by the adjoining table.

"Ser...you're the one Prytyk said came in late?"

Cerryl nodded.

"Best we have is the stew and a leg from the fowl. Bread, a course."

"That's fine. What to drink?"

"The good ale is two, the red swill one."

"The ale." Drinking anything called swill didn't appeal to Cerryl.

The brown-haired serving girl was gone as quickly as she had come. He glanced at the corner table, the one where the conversation had been about him. Three older men sat around the battered and whitened circular table, nursing tall mugs. A single basket of bread sat in the middle.

Cerryl turned his glance to the table where a blonde woman of indeterminate age, but not profession, sat with a gray-haired and heavy man in rich browns. He wished a certain blonde mage had been sitting across from him. Since she wasn't, his ears picked up the conversation from the corner.

"...see what you mean...looks right through you..."

"...coulda taken him...years ago..."

"It's not years ago, Byum. Ha!"

A faint smile creased Cerryl's lips.

"Here you be." The bread and ale arrived with the thin server, a half-loaf of rye and a tall gray mug of dark ale, smelling strong enough to chew. Cerryl laid out two coppers and took a careful sip. At the prices in Fenard, he'd have to be careful—and quick.

The bread was moist, at least, moister than that in the Halls of the Mages, and by the time the platter that held a single fowl leg and a chipped brown crockery bowl of stew appeared, Cerryl had finished half the bread.

"Here you be."

"Thank you." Cerryl knew he needed to give her something. He fumbled out a copper.

"Thank you, ser." She flashed a professional smile and slipped away.

The stew was peppery, hotter than burkha, and Cerryl didn't care, but he listened as he ate.

"...a lot of lancers going out the east gates these days. Don't see so many coming back..."

"...know a good cabinet-maker? She says we need a dowry chest for Hirene..."

"... good riddance to him ... mages nothing but trouble ..."

Cerryl's ears burned, but he took another sip of ale, another mouthful of bread, and then more stew.

"... say the white devils are raising mountains to the east ..."

"Ha! Even they can't do that ... more stories ... Like as not, next they'll be talking of the black angels returning to Westwind. Or the great white birds landing on the plains of Kyphros ... Don't believe all you hear."

"Don't hear much about the black isle these days."

"Good that we don't. Got any ideas of whether Frysr do a better job on that chest than Donleb?"

"Frysr be a better crafter, but he'll be costing twice what Donleb will."

"She'll say Frysr—only the best for Hirene."

"Lucky you."

Cerryl looked at the bowl and platter. He'd finished it all—and probably too quickly. With another glance around, he slipped away from the table.

No one seemed to notice—not obviously—when he left, and the hall upstairs was empty but not silent. A bed creaked repeatedly as he passed the door adjoining his.

His room seemed untouched, and there was no sense of chaos or disruption.

Cerryl dropped the bar in place. He brushed the bed with chaos, hoping that would remove most of the vermin, then took off the blade and sword belt, both sets of trousers and tunic and did the same with them.

He stretched out on the bed, feeling his eyes close almost immediately. Darkness, it had been a long day.

C

Cerryl woke with the gray light that filled the room even before dawn. His head ached, and his back and legs were sore. One arm itched with several small red bites—despite his efforts of the night before with the vermin.

He swung his feet over the side of the bed and just sat there for a time, slowly massaging first his neck and then his forehead. Finally, he stood and walked to the basin, where he washed up as best he could.

After that, he pulled on his boots and the sword belt. The tunic and jacket had to stay in his pack.

In the wavering image of the wall mirror, thin-faced and drawn, he looked like anything but a well-fed student mage—or a mage of any type. More like a brown-coated weasel or something, he decided, or even a bravo down on his luck—as if he could do more than hack with the blade at his belt.

He definitely missed the razor—and the lady who had given it to him. Would he see her again? Would she care?

Don't think about it . . . You have a task to finish.

He left his pack beside the bed and went downstairs to find something to eat. The hearth in the corner of the public room was cold, with the smell of ashes. The tabletops were covered in a thin film of whitish dust, and the only table taken was filled by the same three older men that had been there the night before. The three looked Cerryl over, nodded to themselves, and resumed their low conversation.

". . . still looks like a bravo . . ."

". . . you figured out the materials, yet, Byum?"

". . . get to it . . . You know that . . ."

". . . figures out everything but the important stuff . . ."

A single serving girl—portly—stepped out from the kitchen and looked at Cerryl. "Breakfast don't come with the room."

"How much for some bread and cheese and ale?"

"Three."

Cerryl nodded and sat down at the same table where he'd eaten the night before.

A scrawny white-bearded man shuffled in and sat down at the round table in the corner, not looking at Cerryl or the other three. The older man waited, head down, until the heavyset blonde brought him a mug. He slurped it slowly, holding it with trembling hands.

Thump. "Bread and cheese, dark ale." The blonde's voice was hard, as if she wished she didn't have to serve him.

Cerryl handed over the three coppers. The serving girl vanished through the door to the kitchen. The three men continued talking in their low voices as he ate a half-loaf of the day-old rye bread and some hard white cheese, washing both down with ale. When he had finished, more quickly than was polite, but in character for a bravo, the headache had begun to fade. Did using chaos too much take extra food?

He swallowed the last of the ale, rose, and headed back up to his room, where he used the chamber pot and set it by the door. Then he donned the too-large cloak before picking up his pack and bedroll.

The bed in the room adjoining his was creaking once more as he passed.

Exactly what type of inn had he chosen? He shrugged. At least it wasn't the kind where everyone looked cross-eyed at strangers. Maybe he'd been lucky in that respect.

Out in the dusty courtyard, the stable boy looked at Cerryl and his pack and bedroll. "You not coming back, ser?"

"Would you leave your gear there all day?"

The dark-haired boy grinned. "I'll get your mount. The chestnut, right?"

"That's the one." Cerryl glanced back toward the inn but didn't see Prytyk, which was just as well. A thin line of smoke rose from the chimney, and the smell of something baking drifted into his nostrils, a scent far more pleasant than his stale breakfast or the smell of the streets. Overhead, puffy white clouds, with barely a touch of gray, dotted the green-blue sky.

The stable boy had brushed the chestnut. That was clear enough from the sheen of the horse's coat. "I gave him some grain. Not supposed to . . ." The boy glanced toward the stable, then over Cerryl's shoulder toward the inn door.

Cerryl smiled and slipped the youth another copper he couldn't afford.

"Thank you, ser." A pause followed. "Some say you're a bravo . . ."

"You wonder if that's true?" Cerryl smiled as he began to strap his pack and bedroll on the chestnut, unwilling to leave them behind, even for the day. "I can't give you an answer you'd believe. If I am, then I won't say I am, and if I'm not, I won't say I am." He laughed, pleased at his answer.

"I don't think you are."

"Probably not in the way you mean." The mage swung up into the saddle, half-amazed that he'd finally gotten somewhat graceful at mounting the big horse. "Tonight."

"Yes, ser."

Cerryl hoped he didn't have to stay another night, but he had no idea of what to expect in Fenard—or if he could even get close to the prefect. Or if the prefect even happened to be in Fenard.

The Golden Bowl looked even more dingy in the morning light, yellow plaster walls grayed and chipped, roof tiles cracked, with some missing. One shutter beside the front door hung tilted from a single bracket. Cerryl held in a shiver, noting that it was probably a good thing he hadn't been able to see the place well the night before.

He guided the chestnut out onto the narrow street and west, toward the main avenue, through the sour odors of a city with too many open sewers. There, even in the early morning, a line of carts trundled to his right, north, in the direction he hoped led to the central square or what passed for such.

He'd only ridden a block or so when he had to guide the chestnut around a cart that had collapsed, one wheel snapped in half, the cart tilted, and baskets of potatoes half-emptied into the cart bed—and into the street, and even the open sewer ditch.

A half-dozen urchins were scooping up the tubers into their ragged shirts, then scuttling down the alley. Cerryl swallowed as he watched one scoop two potatoes out of the filth.

"Out ! Leave a poor farmer alone!" The carter lifted a staff, and the urchins suddenly vanished.

Cerryl kept riding, his eyes never stopping their study of the surroundings, even when he passed a set of ancient rock pillars and looked into the central square—just a cobblestoned and open expanse filled with carts and wagons and hawkers. Most of the wagons were of bare wood, brown or gray, not like the painted carts in the market square in Fairhaven.

To his right, standing on an empty mounting block, an urchin with cold eyes studied Cerryl, then looked away.

"You!" snapped the mage.

"Ser? I didn't do nothing. I didn't."

"Which way to the prefect's?"

"You? They won't let you in the gate." The urchin gave a diffident sneer.

"My cousin's in the guard there."

"Up the hill past Gyldn's. The goldsmith."

"Thank you."

"Frig you, bravo." The urchin spat.

Cerryl urged the chestnut into the square, eyes traveling across the carts, the women with baskets, and the two wagons tied on the other side, opposite what looked to be a warehouse. Two men lugged bundles wrapped in gray cloth from the wagon through the open door.

"Spices! Best winterseed this side of the Gulf . . ."

"Ser! Flowers for your lady!"

Cerryl shook his head.

"Then she be no lady!"

The young mage half-grinned, looking for the goldsmith's as the chestnut carried him around the square. A signboard with a golden chain against a green background caught his eye, and he made for the place, and the street that seemed to slope gently up past three-story buildings that bore shops on the main level and dwellings above.

"Scents and oils . . . scents and oils . . ."

". . . harvest-fresh roots . . . fresh roots . . ."

Once out of the square and on the cobblestones of the upsloping side street, he could make out the walls ahead on his right. The prefect's palace was indeed walled, and the walls were a good ten cubits high. Two hundred cubits uphill on the paved street was a gate—or the first gate. While the two wrought-iron gates were open, the four guards were alert, one studying Cerryl as he rode by. Cerryl ignored the scrutiny and continued past the gate, a gate made up of interlocking iron bars forming rectangles that afforded a view of an empty paved courtyard.

Should he be cautious?

He shook his head. There was a time to be bold and a time to be cautious. Mostly, in the past, he'd had to be cautious, and that had to be what Jeslek was counting on. Despite Sterol's advice about there being no old bold mages, if he weren't bold, he'd never have the chance to get old. The sooner he removed the prefect—if he could—and returned to Fairhaven, the better . . . before Jeslek's stories could get out of hand.

On the cross street, at the top of the hill was another gate, but it was locked, and chained, and looked not to have been used in some time. On the north side of the walls was a third gate, where several wagons were lined up—the tradesmen's gate, Cerryl guessed as he rode by. The bottom gate, less than a block from the square but north of the street he'd taken first, offered entry, from what Cerryl could tell, only to the guards' barracks, and but a single guard lounged by the guardhouse.

That meant that the southern gate was the one that led where he needed to go. He rode slowly down another side street, trying to find an avenue that angled back toward the gate he wanted. The simplest thing would be to cloak himself in the light shield and follow someone, or someone's carriage, into the palace—but what would he do with the chestnut?

He smiled—why not just tie the horse somewhere? No one was going to kill a horse. His rider perhaps, but not the mount. They might steal the mount, but the chances were less if he tied the gelding somewhere fairly prosperous looking. He shrugged. If someone stole the gelding, he could find a way to steal another horse. After what he had to do, horse theft couldn't make it any worse if he were caught.

He rode down several streets and had to retrace his way several times before he finally found what he was looking for—several well-kept shops in a row—not more than a block and a half from the palace walls. The first shop was that of a silversmith—attested by the painted silver candlestick and pitcher that adorned the purple-bordered signboard by the door. The second was some sort of weaver's or cloth merchant, with bolts of cloth shown behind real glass windows. The third was a cooper's, with a small half barrel set on a bracket on the left porch post.

Two stone hitching posts with iron rings were set against the cooper's open wooden porch. Cerryl glanced around, but the cooper's door was shut, although he could hear muffled hammering within.

He dismounted quickly, tied the gelding, and slipped around the corner of the building and down the short alley to the side street that led to the perimeter street that flanked the southern gate to the prefect's palace.

Don't run . . . Don't hurry . . . Just look as though you have business to take care of . . . The side street curved slightly, and Cerryl stopped at the corner, just back of a large rain barrel that was held to the timber walls of the dwelling with an iron strap. His hand brushed the iron, and he felt a tingling, but the iron didn't burn. *Not yet . . .*

Leaning against the wall, in the morning shadows and out of sight of the gate guards, Cerryl watched the street running up from the main square.

After a while, after a cart and two men bearing something wrapped in cloth on a long pole between them had passed, an officer with a single gold slash on his sleeve made his way up the street, his mount's hoofs clicking on the cobbled paving stones, so much rougher than the smooth blocks of Fairhaven's avenues. The officer barely paused as he rode through the gate. Cerryl strained to hear the exchange between guards and officer.

"Good day, Undercaptain. Here to see Captain Yurak?"

"If he's in."

"He's there."

As the sorrel carried the captain across the courtyard, one guard turned to the other, but from behind the corner, Cerryl could not catch the words.

He waited. The sun got warmer, and the sky clearer. Another officer, a full captain, rode through the gate, but the guards did not speak.

Cerrly continued to wait as scattered riders and a cart, then a wagon, passed. Three women bearing laundry walked out of the side street, right past Cerryl, ignoring him, and down toward the square.

". . . Elva . . . too good to do her own laundry . . ."

"Would I had her coins, and I wouldn't either."

Cerryl drew himself up. A carriage—a dark carriage—had started up the street, and both guards had stepped forward, stiffening into positions of attention. Whoever it might be, the guards expected the carriage, and it might be his only chance for some while.

Cerryl slipped the light cloak around him and eased across the street. Despite his care, since he could only sense things in rough terms, he almost tripped on the uneven stones. He stopped against the wall on the north side of the gates, where he could slip behind the coach and walk in after it. The coach slowed as it approached and turned through the wrought-iron-gate–flanked entry. Cerryl walked quickly, almost abreast of and between the back of the rear wheels, glad that the coach was not the kind with footmen.

"Good day, ser."

There was no answer from the carriage to the guard's pleasantry, and the coach continued to roll slowly through the courtyard and then under another archway. Cerryl found he was panting when the coach creaked to a halt, and he forced himself to breathe more deeply and slowly.

Which side should he take? Cerryl eased up next to the right rear wheel, listening as the coach door opened and a man stepped out onto the mounting block.

An officer, perhaps the same undercaptain who had entered the palace earlier, stood in the archway above the steps. "The prefect is waiting in his study, ser."

"Very well." The voice was modulated, and bored. "I will see him before I deal with Overcaptain Taynet. Would you inform the over-captain that I will be there presently, and that I expect him to await my arrival."

"Yes, Subprefect, ser." The officer's boots clicked on the stone.

Cerryl reminded himself to step lightly as he followed the dignitary. He walked carefully behind the guards who trailed the subprefect, trying to keep his steps in the same rhythm as theirs, hoping no one stopped too quickly.

The journey was surprisingly short, just into a foyer, and then down a corridor for perhaps fifty cubits, and then up three flights of steps, and back down another corridor for another fifty cubits or so. The entourage halted before a set of double doors guarded by a pair of arms-men.

Cerryl stopped as they did, amazed that no one had looked around, but, then, perhaps everyone felt watched or followed in a palace.

"Subprefect Syrma, at the prefect's request."

"We will inform him, ser."

The doors opened and closed.

Cerryl eased up closer to the guards, standing to one side, wagering that they would not accompany Syrma into the study.

The study doors opened again. "The prefect will see you, ser."

The guards stepped to the left, and Cerryl barely managed to slip around them to the right, and then inside. He swallowed and stepped wide around another set of guards, glad he was almost right behind the subprefect. One of the guards stiffened as his eyes flicked around, then slowly relaxed.

Cerryl edged along the bookcases to the left of the door before the guards closed them with a firm *thump*. He kept sliding along the bookcases and around a table to the left of the broad wooden desk behind which sat the prefect. At least he hoped the figure behind the desk was the prefect. That was the problem with navigating totally through chaos senses.

"You requested my presence, Prefect."

"Syrma . . . you have deigned to appear. How kind of you." The voice was resonant and cruel. Lyam didn't seem that much older than Cerryl, although Cerryl could not see him, properly speaking. "Why were you delayed?"

"There was a report of a white mage in the city last night."

Cerryl's heart seemed to contract as he waited in the dim corner behind the table.

"The fellow was drunk, but he swore he saw a man all in white on a horse, and the fellow disappeared and took his cloak."

"You cannot be serious." Lyam began to laugh. "You would bother me with such nonsense?"

"You asked to be told of all reports of what the whites might be doing . . . sire."

"I was talking about matters that were real—like those mountains, and those mages who slaughtered that idiot Jerost's whole force, or that squad of white lancers south of here. What happened to them, anyway?"

"We killed them, as you instructed. They must have been scouts—just an undercaptain and ten armsmen."

Cerryl winced but kept silent, standing in the corner formed by two of the ceiling-to-floor bookcases, hoping no one looked his way and noticed the slight wavering of the air that often accompanied the light shield.

"They weren't any trouble, unlike the old mage." The subprefect bowed, but only slightly.

"The mage wasn't that much trouble—just heavy iron-tipped arrows from a distance . . ."

"It took a dozen, sire, and we lost half the bowmen. He was casting fire even with all that cold iron in him. You underestimate the wrath and the ability of the mages."

"Oh? He's dead, isn't he?"

"So are six good bowmen, sire."

"Nasty people, those whites. We're better off without the mages. All of Candar would be."

Cerryl frowned. So how was Lyam any different from Jeslek? Or did all those with power just think they were better than anyone else at ruling?

"What of the receipts from the Spidlarians?"

"Two hundred golds this season . . . so far, and the tax levies on the merchants in the city are fifty golds higher."

"That's almost a thousand golds a year, plus what we saved from not paying Fairhaven. Scoundrels—every last one of the whites. Their precious road isn't worth that." Lyam laughed once more, the same cruel laugh.

"They think so, and it has been unwise to mock them in the past. Ask Viscount Mystyr."

"He's dead, Syrma. What riddle is this?"

"He died rather soon after he began to oppose the road duties. His brother pays the road duties most faithfully. Viscount Rystryr now receives support in terms of white lancers."

"I don't envy him for such *support*. Nor should you, Syrma."

"As you wish, sire. I stand at your command."

"Good. Inform me of any other developments with the whites. I'd also like to know when the next lancers will be ready to ride for Yryna."

"You will be informed."

"Leave me."

"As you wish, sire." The older man turned and stepped out of the room. The doors closed with a dull thud.

Two guards remained, flanking the inside of the doorway.

Cerryl studied the room with his senses. There was a railed balcony, but it was three stories up, and from what he could sense, there was no way off it—except for a twenty-odd-cubit fall.

That left nothing but the obvious.

Cerryl gathered chaos around him, then dropped the light shield and let the first bolt of lance fire take Lyam in the face and upper chest.

"Aeiii . . ." The scream gurgled off into silence.

Cerryl turned. The second bolt got the first guard. The third bolt went wide as the second guard jumped aside, then flung the door open and ran out into the corridor yelling, "Chaos wizard! Chaos wizard! Frigging chaos wizard!"

Cerryl ran to the balcony door. Pushing back the hangings around the door, he threw it open and stepped out onto the balcony. There he struggled to get the light shield back around him, before easing back around the hangings and into the paneled study.

"He killed the prefect and ran for the balcony . . ."

"Seal the courtyard! Close the gates. Let no one out." A figure glittering slightly with random chaos burst into the study, followed by a half-dozen guards.

Recognizing the modulated voice of the subprefect, Cerryl used his senses to ease his way along the walls toward the double doors. He slipped out the still-open door and onto the polished marble of the corridor. Darkness, he was tired. He just wanted to rest, but that wouldn't have been a very good idea. Syrma had too good an idea of what mages could do, and Cerryl wasn't even a full mage.

He stayed next to the marble balustrade all the way down to the courtyard level, then hugged the wall as he retraced his steps, half by feel, half by chaos sense, all the way back to the second courtyard.

Guards milled around the courtyard, and the subprefect's carriage remained where it had been. Slowly, carefully, managing to hang on to the light shield, Cerryl made his way along the walls, back through the archway and into the first courtyard.

Surprisingly, while the wrought-iron gates were closed, only a single pair of guards remained there.

Should he wait? No . . . he was too tired. He edged along the wall on the north side, away from the guards, until he reached the gates. He could climb them, if he didn't get too tired. He couldn't afford to get too tired. He couldn't.

The gates weren't so high as the wall, and they were crossbarred. He took the first step up to the gate, and his hands tingled as they closed around the crossbars. Each time his fingers closed over the iron bars, the iron burned. Because he'd been using so much chaos? Because he wasn't channeling it properly? He didn't know, only that it hurt, and it was hard because each level up had to be silent and each bar burned.

Finally, he reached the curved top of the gate and swung himself over.

Clung! His boot slipped and struck one of the side bars.

"Who's there?" Boots echoed on the courtyard stones.

"There's no one there. One of the beggar kids—throwing stones at the gate again."

"Enough troubles without them. Wish I'd get my hands on one of them. Teach them a lesson."

The steps receded. Cerryl waited, his hands burning, his lungs rasping, before he began to lever himself down. His entire body was aching and trembling before his boots touched the street outside the walls. He forced himself to cross the street with care and slip into the side street, behind the rain barrel, listening until he could hear no one.

He released the light shield, and the afternoon sun struck him like a blow, and he staggered, putting a hand out to the wall. He just leaned against the wall, panting, aware that his hands burned and his head ached. Finally, he straightened and walked slowly down the narrow street, the sun at his back, toward the cooper's.

A woman stepped out of a door, saw him, and stepped back inside quickly.

Wonder of wonders, the chestnut was still tied there. He began to untie the reins.

"That your mount, fellow?"

Cerryl continued to unfasten the reins as he turned. "Yes."

A heavyset man with a leather apron stood under the overhanging eaves that formed a porch of sorts. "Those hitching rings are for customers."

"I'm sorry. I didn't mean to cause you any trouble." Cerryl fumbled in his wallet. "I don't have much. Would a copper help?"

"Wouldn't help me. I gave your mount some water. You shouldn't have left him so long."

Cerryl looked down. The cooper was right, but Cerryl wasn't sure he'd had that much choice. His head still ached, but he looked at the gray-bearded man. "I'm sorry. Are you sure I couldn't give you something?"

"No." The bearded man laughed generously. "You don't look as you'd need a barrel or even a hogshead. Keep your copper; spend it on grain for your beast. Just remember that Mydyr is the best cooper in Fenard—and when you do need barrels, I'd like to see you."

"Mydyr—I'll remember."

"What's your name?"

"Cerryl." Cerryl knew no one in Fenard knew his name, and there was no reason to lie about it. "Thank you. I've got to get going." He mounted quickly.

"Don't forget, now."

"I won't, ser." His knees were trembling, and he hoped the cooper didn't see that, or his reddened and burning hands. "I won't."

He mounted and rode slowly down the side street, and then around the square, hoping he didn't get lost, and managed to find the main avenue again. It was beginning to fill with carts departing Fenard, and he rode slowly behind a cart with mostly empty baskets, except for one half-filled with maize.

His legs hurt; his vision kept blurring, and his head throbbed. His hands still burned, feeling both hot and as though they had been bruised. But trying to ride faster would only call more attention to him, and he wasn't sure he could handle any more attention.

As he neared the gate, he wondered whether he should try to use the light shield to get out of the gate. He shook his head. That would slow him down, and the sooner he was outside the walls the better. If the guards challenged him . . . then . . . then he would do what was necessary. *As you have all along . . . no matter the cost to others . . .*

He swallowed and kept riding.

The guard waved the maize cart and driver through, then looked at Cerryl lazily. "Where to, fellow?"

"Tellura . . . then maybe Quessa, depending on . . ."

"Go . . . better you be there than here." The bored-looking fellow waved Cerryl on.

Was that all there was to it? Was there a chance he would get back to Fairhaven and Leyladin? Would she even care?

Once past the low-lying fields and over the bridge, he looked back, but the gates remained open, almost as though the city were oblivious to the death of its prefect.

Although his head felt as though it were being ripped apart by Dylert's big mill saw, he kept riding as the sun dropped behind the western hills, and the sounds of insects rose above the whisper of the wind at his back, a wind that carried the scents of damp autumn earth and molding grasses, and the chill of the winter yet to come.

CI

Cerryl glanced at the still-steaming heights ahead—the hills that Jeslek had raised into mountains. He patted the chestnut on the neck and glanced along the empty Great White Highway.

After more than five long days, he was back on the Great Highway, and back in the whites of a student mage. He hadn't changed out of his "bravo" disguise until he'd finally been on the Great White Highway for more than a day, but he kept the darker cloak strapped on top of his pack—just in case he ran into some Gallosian armsmen.

The clouds that moved slowly out of the northeast were thickening, and darkening. He looked up, judging that rain would not fall until midafternoon, and hoping it would not be heavy.

His hands still hadn't healed totally, and his headache, while it had faded, had not disappeared, and a rainstorm would just make that worse. His thighs threatened to cramp, but hadn't, perhaps because he was getting more used to riding. His neck was stiff—probably from looking over his shoulder to see who might be pursuing him.

Better think some about what's ahead . . .

His stomach growled, reminding him that he needed to stop and eat something, not that he had all that much to eat. He'd spent most of the remaining coins on travel food at a small town just short of the Great Highway—hoping that the hard cheese and road biscuits would last until he returned to Fairhaven.

On the road to Tellura, he'd encountered some travelers, but the highway had been vacant, totally vacant. Was that because traders loyal to Fairhaven couldn't sell their goods at a low enough price to compete in Gallos? And because the disloyal ones hadn't paid road tariffs and feared using the roads after Jeslek's destruction of the Gallosian lancers? Or did they fear the prefect's wrath?

Cerryl held the reins loosely—very loosely. His hands remained tender, especially across the palms, where he'd gripped the gate bars tightly.

Touching iron didn't usually burn him. Was that because he'd been using chaos energies? Would that bar him from Leyladin? He winced at that thought. *Something else you really don't know . . .* He sighed. There was so much he didn't know, and he wondered if he would ever learn all that he needed.

His eyes went to the empty road ahead, stretching like a white ribbon into the ugly darkness raised by Jeslek.

Some things just didn't seem to make sense. How had he been able to kill Lyam so easily? Why hadn't anyone even looked for him? The sometime wavering of the light shield was a giveaway. *If anyone knew what it meant . . .*

He nodded. Was that why the Guild sought out all those with chaos or order talent? To keep the rest of Candar from knowing exactly what the white mages could do? Or had the secrecy just happened and been discovered to be beneficial?

About the only thing most people knew was that mages could use the screeing glasses to see things and that they could throw chaos-fire— and that black mages could sometimes heal.

Cerryl laughed. Now they knew that mages could raise mountains. But that was so rare and improbable that in generations to come no one would remember. Cerryl couldn't imagine that the world produced many Jesleks, or very often.

Again . . . the rules of the Guild made sense, although he didn't have to like the way some, like Jeslek, used them to their personal advantage.

Could you do better?

Cerryl laughed at the thought. He'd like to try, but the chances of an orphaned scrivener's apprentice becoming an overmage, or especially High Wizard, weren't exactly overwhelming.

The chestnut *whuffed,* and Cerryl patted his neck again. "We'll stop for water before long. You can have the last of the grain."

The gelding didn't look that thin, but Cerryl wondered. He'd managed to stop where there had been some lush grass, but he doubted that grazing was enough, and he'd not been able to afford as much grain as he'd have liked. He'd tried not to push the pace, letting the gelding carry him easily, knowing that he didn't really know enough about horses, either.

He held in a sigh, then took a deep breath.

Jeslek had wanted him to fail. Why? Had Myral been right? That Cerryl was a threat? But Cerryl didn't really want to be High Wizard. He just wanted people to stop trying to get rid of him or push him around. *Is that so much to ask?*

For some people, apparently it was.

Cerryl frowned. What had saved him was what Jeslek had not known—like Cerryl's awareness of the light shield or his own mastery of targeted fire lances. Jeslek was far more powerful . . . but he didn't know everything. Knowledge was a form of power. Not the only kind of power, as witness the mountains that the overmage had raised, but the kind of power Cerryl could master. Would have to master—for many reasons, one of them who wore green and whose green eyes danced in his thoughts and memories.

CII

Good day." Cerryl waved to the merchant on the wagon seat as he eased the chestnut around the big wagon drawn by a four-horse team.

"Good day to you, young ser." The gray-bearded and trim man in green who held the reins in his right hand nodded pleasantly. "You think it be raining afore long?"

The guard beside the merchant smiled.

Cerryl glanced at the clouds overhead, dark gray, and tried to gain a sense of the weather. He could feel the churning chaos and the black order bands within the gray, so low were the heavy clouds. "Not right now, but not too long."

"Darkness . . . hoped we could make it farther."

Cerryl glanced back at the covered wagon. "What have you there?"

"Mostly carpets, but some hangings—good pieces out of Sarronnyn. Hard to come by these days. Lot easier before the prefect and those traders in Spidlar decided they knew better than all of Candar." The trader spat to the side, behind Cerryl. "Fairhaven your home? You headed back?"

Cerryl slowed his mount slightly out of politeness, pacing the wagon. "Yes." Fairhaven was his home, more than any place, despite Jeslek, and the overmage's struggles with Sterol. Fairhaven was where Myral was, and Lyasa, Faltar, and Heralt, and, especially, Leyladin, all • the family he really had, now that his aunt Nall and uncle Syodor were dead—for reasons he still didn't understand. *Except you want Leyladin to be more than just a relative* . . . "Fairhaven's home."

"Musta been an eight-day back, maybe not quite, saw a bunch of lancers and mages headed back. One of the lancers said they'd beaten a big Gallosian force. You think that was true?"

"It was true." Cerryl smiled. "I was there. I had to do something else before I returned."

"Might teach that prefect not to be so self-mighty." The gray-bearded merchant offered an ironic smile. "Then . . . some folk never learn. Well . . . won't be keeping you, young mage. Have a safe trip."

"Thank you." Cerryl gently urged the chestnut on, on toward Fairhaven.

The merchant's parting words echoed in his ears. "Some folk never learn . . . never learn . . ."

But who is to say what learning is? Cerryl had learned that all too often, when people talked about learning, they wanted you to see things their way. Except maybe Myral, or Dylert . . . and, he hoped, Leyladin.

CIII

Rather than take the avenue, Cerryl rode in the back streets to the stable on the west side of the Halls of the Mages. He'd also camped outside Fairhaven the night before, wanting to be more rested and also wanting Myral to be more rested. If he were to have any chance, he'd have to meet with Myral before he met with Sterol, and especially before he confronted Jeslek, not that he wanted a confrontation, but it might happen whether Cerryl wanted it or not.

The autumn wind was chill, under partly clouded sides, but not cold, and swirled across him in gentle gusts. His eyes flicked past a bronze grate on the side of the paved road, and his lips quirked, thinking of all the time he'd spent in the sewers. As he took a deep breath, he compared Fairhaven to Fenard—and there was no comparison.

Fenard smelled of sewers and smoke and dirt, and Fairhaven smelled of clean granite and trees and grass, and occasional clean odors of cooking and women's scents. In Fenard, buildings were dirty and crowded on top of each other. Fairhaven's stone structures were solid and clean and left enough space for people to breathe. In Fenard, there were open sewers and starving urchins and brigands. While there might be a few beggars and smugglers in Fairhaven, there were certainly far fewer ruffians and hungry folk—far fewer. And there was Leyladin. Fenard had nothing like her. Perhaps no city did.

Cerryl squared his shoulders. Jeslek was *not* going to take Fairhaven away from him, either through death or exile. Whatever it took, Cerryl intended to survive and prosper. *Whatever it takes . . .* He frowned. Yet that was exactly how Jeslek was—doing whatever was necessary. How could Cerryl survive and not be like the overmage?

He shifted his weight in the saddle. There had to be a way. He was still frowning when he rode into the back courtyard of the Hall of the Mages that held the stable from where he had set out more than a half-season before. He dismounted slowly, bouncing slightly on his legs, legs that were sore but no longer cramping every time he rode.

A stable boy stepped out into the courtyard, frowning momentarily as his eyes took in the disheveled Cerryl. "Ser?"

"I'm the last of the Gallos group. The overmage asked me to do something that took longer."

"Your mount looks a little thin, ser."

"I ran out of grain on the way back. I tried to find good grass." Cerryl unpacked the cloak, pack, and bedroll.

"He's just a little thin, ser. We'll take care of him."

"You're sure he's all right?"

"Yes, ser." The stable boy led the chestnut away.

For some reason, Cerryl felt somehow disappointed, let down. Because he and the horse had been through so much together? Because he'd been dismissed by a stable boy, who cared more for the mount than the man who rode him? He wasn't sure whether to smile or sigh. So he took a deep breath, then began to walk toward the hall that held his cell and the commons.

Cerryl looked forward to bathing, really bathing and shaving. He'd wished all along that he'd taken the bronze razor Leyladin had given him, but all that would have to wait. He needed to get to Myral—and a few others—speedily.

Once he entered the hall, he moved quickly, dumping his pack and gear in the corner of the commons. He'd thought about using the light shield, but that could have been construed as an admission of guilt and allowed Jeslek, should Cerryl have run into the overmage, to attack immediately.

Heralt stopped Cerryl outside the commons as he headed toward the fountain courtyard. "Cerryl . . . I heard you'd disappeared . . ."

"No. That was what Jeslek wanted everyone to think. He sent me on a special task." Cerryl pointed toward the courtyard. "I have to report. If you want to walk with me . . ."

Heralt eased beside him as Cerryl crossed the courtyard. The wind whipped chill spray over both students.

"I had to go to Fenard . . . the Gallosians managed to kill most of my escort, and it took a while to get back. I was supposed to give Sverlik a hand, but the perfect killed him before I got there." Cerryl glanced at Heralt. "Please don't tell anyone this—except Sterol, if he asks."

"I can live with that." Heralt smiled. "I'd better let you tell him." The curly-haired student stopped at the archway to the front hall and the foyer that led to the mages' tower.

Cerryl stepped inside. The foyer was empty, and he crossed it and went up the steps to the bottom level of the tower. He marched past the guards, and the messenger from the creche in red, not even looking at them, and up the steps toward Myral's quarters. He'd figured that Jeslek wouldn't have told the guards anything, particularly since they reported to Sterol—or maybe Kinowin. He wasn't totally sure, but he doubted he'd find Jeslek in the tower.

Panting heavily after his quick climb, he rapped on Myral's door. There was no response. He rapped again.

"Cerryl?"

"Yes, ser." Cerryl stepped inside without waiting for an invitation, closing the door behind him.

Myral looked up, his round face annoyed. He sat by the table, stripped to the waist, and Leyladin was massaging his shoulders. "You could have waited . . ." The older mage cleared his throat. "Cerryl . . . I had not heard that you had returned . . ."

"You are the first to know. Jeslek gave me a test."

"He said you vanished."

"I am not surprised." Cerryl snorted. "I thought that might be the case." The younger man glanced at Leyladin, his eyes meeting her green orbs. He swallowed, almost feeling as though he were falling into her eyes, then pulled himself more erect.

Myral laughed. "The great Jeslek is always doing things his way." He pulled his shirt and tunic back into place. "Leyladin told me you had set out to become an assistant to Sverlik. How did that go?"

"I didn't tell Lyasa the whole story. Jeslek instructed me to become Sverlik's assistant so that I could kill the prefect. He said it was a test I needed to pass before I became a full mage." Cerryl's smile was bitter. "One that would prove my devotion to Fairhaven."

"You believed him?"

"No. I believed I had no choice. And after briefly overhearing Lyam, I have to admit that the overmage was right about the prefect."

Leyladin watched Cerryl intently, concern in her green eyes.

Myral sat up straight and scratched his head, then looked at Cerryl. "And the prefect?"

"He's dead. I killed him with chaos-fire, as Jeslek instructed me. But he—the prefect—had Sverlik killed before I reached Fenard. After I left my escort, the Gallosians killed them, too." Cerryl worried at his upper lip with his teeth. "I didn't expect . . . so much death."

"Where Jeslek is concerned, that seems to occur." Myral coughed, and Leyladin leaned forward intently. After several not-quite-racking coughs, the older mage straightened. "Age and chaos . . . not good for the health. Nor surprises."

"I'm sorry. It wasn't my idea. I mean, coming to you was, but it was Jeslek's idea to have me kill the prefect."

"How would you deal with this?" asked Myral, his tone even, not judgmental.

"I would like you to see if we could meet with Sterol. Jeslek, I hope, doesn't know I'm back yet."

"You didn't walk through—"

"I took some precautions, but I didn't see him. I couldn't very well stop him from screeing me, if he chose to do that."

"No . . . you couldn't, but you're probably well beneath his sight. Now . . . I wasn't clear, and I want to be sure. This test of Jeslek's—that was . . . ?"

"To remove the prefect of Gallos."

"Oh, dear. He actually said that was the test? And you were successful?"

Cerryl nodded.

"That will cause problems—but not so much as your surviving." Myral heaved himself to his feet, then glanced at Leyladin. "Best you go your way for a while, young lady. My shoulders are better, and this young fellow doesn't need to be distracted by your presence." The older mage laughed. "Don't think I don't see things when they're right before my eyes. Black and white . . . bah . . . it's not that simple, not that I'd be telling either the High Wizard or that overbearing clod Jeslek."

Cerryl swallowed.

"You think I don't know." A wry smile crossed Myral's face. "I can tell you what I think now. You'll either be accepted as a full mage before the day is out, or we'll both be dead. Makes no difference either way."

Leyladin opened her mouth and then closed it.

"Off with you, young lady."

"Yes, Myral."

"Dear Leyladin," Myral said mildly, "I don't intend for us to be dead. Jeslek might, but Sterol trusts me, and probably Cerryl, far more than he does Jeslek."

"Be careful . . . please . . . both of you." Leyladin offered a smile after her words.

Cerryl noted, though, that the smile was for him, and he smiled back as she slipped out. He fancied he could hear her boots on the stone stairs of the tower.

Myral waddled toward the door. "Sterol is yet up in the High Wizard's quarters, and so we will make our way there."

A single guard stood outside the High Wizard's quarters. "Myral and Cerryl to see the High Wizard, and it is important."

The guard knocked on the door, then announced, "Myral and Cerryl to see you. The mage Myral states his call is important."

The door opened, and a thin, red-haired apprentice mage—barely more than a girl, and one Cerryl did not know—scurried out and down the steps, followed by Bealtur.

"Come in." Sterol's voice was cold and formal. Once the door had closed, he turned to Myral. "Is the return of this deserting apprentice so important?" His eyes fixed on Cerryl. "Have you come cowering back . . . to beg mercy?"

"No, ser. I never left. Jeslek set me a task in Gallos. I did it, and I returned—as he told me. After all I have seen, honored Sterol, I would not desert Fairhaven and then return."

"A task, you say?" Sterol's eyebrows lifted.

"You say, young Cerryl, that Jeslek told you this task was a test?" Myral asked yet again, as though Cerryl had said nothing previously.

"Yes, ser. One that I had to pass to become a full mage." Cerryl left his shields down, including the barrier that would have kept Sterol from sensing whether he told the truth.

"Jeslek told you this, and you believed him?"

"Yes, ser . . . that is, he told me such. I did not fully believe him, but he had sent Fydel and Anya out scouting, and he raised chaos and was ready to destroy me if I questioned him."

"If you doubted him, why did you undertake the task?" asked Sterol, his voice still cold.

"How could I defy him?" Cerryl asked. "Also, after the actions of the prefect's troops, it appeared as though the removal of the prefect might indeed be the will of the Council."

"The prefect's removal? You have said nothing of that."

"That was the task. I was sent to become Sverlik's assistant and then to assassinate Lyam. That didn't work because the prefect had already had Sverlik killed."

"How? He was a strong mage." Sterol's brow furrowed.

"I heard a conversation . . . they used iron bolts. Sverlik still killed half the bowmen. That was what the subprefect said."

"And you let him live?"

"High Wizard," Cerryl said carefully, "Jeslek told me to do only that with which I was tasked, and my task was to be Sverlik's assistant, to remove the prefect, and to return to Fairhaven. I could not serve as Sverlik's assistant because he was dead before I arrived. I sneaked into the palace and killed the prefect with chaos-fire—the overmage was most insistent that I use chaos-fire. Then I sneaked out and rode home."

"And no one even chased you?"

"They sealed the palace, and they had guards running everywhere, but I climbed over a gate no one was watching closely enough. I did dress as a bravo to ride out of Fenard. I even kept the blade and trousers and cloak I used. They're in my pack."

Sterol bobbed his head up and down, and the gray hair glinted in the dull light that came through the window from the cloudy day outside. "You have taken pains to reach me undetected. What if I just removed you?"

"Not totally undetected." Cerryl swallowed, thinking that the High Wizard would have no compunctions about removing witnesses. "I doubt it would be in your interest to remove me and those few who know. It is clear that I have followed your directions. Others have not. You told me to report to you, and I have."

Sterol laughed, a braying laugh that ended abruptly.

"He tells the truth," Myral added.

"I know. That is the most disturbing of all." Sterol nodded once more. "I think we should call the great Jeslek—after we summon Kinowin and Derka." Sterol nodded. "It would be best if you both waited here with me."

Cerryl walked to the window while Sterol rang the bell he carried to the door. A misting rain was beginning to drift across Fairhaven, bringing with it the twinge of an incipient headache for Cerryl.

One of the youngsters from the creche, attired solely in red, appeared and stepped into the High Wizard's quarters. "Honored ser?"

"Have the overmage Kinowin and the mage Derka attend me here. Immediately. Then return."

"Yes, High Wizard." The brown-haired youth bowed, then scurried down the steps.

"Young Cerryl . . . I am curious about a few details."

"Yes, High Wizard."

" 'Ser' will do. I doubt that you were particularly well coined for this venture, nor heavily provisioned."

"No, ser. I had two silvers and some coppers. I stole the cloak from a drunkard in the street at night. Then a pair of brigands attacked me in Fenard. I had to use chaos-fire, but no one saw, and I took their purses, and a blade and some clothes." Cerryl licked his lips, feeling as though he were treading on the edge of a cliff.

"Wait . . ." Sterol moved to the door and motioned Kinowin into the room. "Continue."

Kinowin offered a faint smile, an ironic expression, as he saw Cerryl and Myral.

"What I took really wasn't enough. I haven't eaten much in the last few days, and the stable boy said the chestnut was thin. He's all right, but . . ."

"You didn't 'forage' in Certis or Fairhaven?"

"No, ser. Not in Gallos, either, not after I left Fenard."

Sterol held up his hand and opened the door again.

Derka stepped into the room, his deep-set eyes taking in the others. A knowing nod followed.

"So . . . let me get this straight. Jeslek set you the task of killing the prefect of Gallos. He told you that you had to do this to become a full mage. You distrusted him, but he raised chaos and effectively threatened you with no one around—"

"He didn't threaten me, ser. He sent everyone else away, and he raised chaos, and I felt threatened—"

"Wise of you," murmured Kinowin.

Sterol glanced sharply at the tall overmage, then back at Cerryl. "And you rode to Fenard alone—"

"No, ser. He gave me an escort, a half-score of the lancers Klybel didn't want."

"Did you know that?" Sterol pursued.

"No, ser. I felt it. He made the escort leader an undercaptain just before we left, and we were sent off before Anya and Fydel returned."

"Who was this undercaptain?" asked Kinowin.

"His name was Ludren, ser."

"That's enough for me, right there." Kinowin offered a tight smile. "Ludren is a good man, but he can't lead."

"Ser . . . after they left me . . . or I left them, the Gallosians got them. I found that out later."

"How did that happen?" asked Kinowin.

"We were almost surrounded. I told Ludren to take the men and ride away, that thcy couldn't help me, and I wanted to give our lancers a chance. They—the Gallosians—were bringing up archers..." Cerryl shrugged. "I rode until it got dark and I could hide. I hoped they'd get away."

"Then what did you do?" asked Myral quickly, for which Cerryl was grateful.

"When it got dark and there was a diversion, I sneaked into Fenard."

"A diversion?"

Cerryl offered a guilty smile. "I used chaos to make a big fire out of some rubbish not far from the gates. They all went to look, and I rode into the city. Maybe someone saw me, but not too close."

"I've heard enough." Kinowin turned to Sterol. "What do you want?"

"I think that we should hear what Jeslek has to say."

Cerryl's heart sank, but he kept his face impassive.

Sterol rang the bell again, and the same messenger arrived. "Summon the overmage Jeslek. He is to appear here immediately."

"Yes, High Wizard."

"He will appear and charge us all with attempting to entrap him," said Derka after the boy had left.

"Of course." That was all Sterol said.

The silence stretched out in the tower room.

"Derka... why don't you attempt to scree who might be prefect of Gallos now?"

The stooped and silver-haired mage stepped over to the table with the glass, then concentrated.

Cerryl watched as the mists formed, then swirled away to reveal the image of an older man, standing by the desk Cerryl recalled.

"You know the man?" asked Sterol.

"I think he might be Syrma... I didn't see him well... but he was the one who arranged for Sverlik to be murdered. The room is the prefect's private study. That's where..."

"Where you destroyed Lyam?"

"Yes, ser."

"That is the current prefect," Derka said quietly.

"It's not Lyam," said Sterol. "So you, young Cerryl, are convinced you killed Lyam, and Lyam is dead." He nodded. "Not all bad, by any means."

"It may give Gallos some pause," suggested Kinowin.

"It will take more than that, unhappily," answered Sterol. "In that, our friend Jeslek is correct. But it is a beginning, and one that has not cost too dearly. Not so far."

After another period of silence, the door burst open.

"Sterol . . . I am not . . ." Jeslek bowed. "Fellow mages . . . I am surprised . . ." His eyes glittered as he beheld Cerryl, but showed none of the surprise he had mentioned. "So . . . the deserter has returned. I say that he should have no mercy."

Sterol smiled, a chill expression that did not include his eyes. "Young Cerryl has been telling us an interesting tale, Jeslek, one that other events have confirmed. He says that you set him the mage's task, and that he removed the prefect of Gallos as that task and returned."

Jeslek bowed. "I must beg to differ. I would not have sent Cerryl out on such a test. His mathematicks are deficient, and he has not been a student nearly so long as necessary. And I would not have done so without informing you."

"The prefect of Gallos is dead," said Derka.

"And I knew of this so-called test long before Cerryl returned," Myral added mildly.

"You said nothing." Jeslek glanced from Sterol to Myral.

The older balding mage smiled crookedly. "What could I say? I could do nothing. If Cerryl failed to return, he would not have suited the Guild. In that, you were correct, Jeslek. But now that he has, I see no sense in wasting his talent, especially since he has resolved the problem of Lyam."

"Why would I have set such a preposterous test?" Jeslek glanced at Sterol, then at Cerryl, ignoring both Derka and Kinowin. "This puppy has no real ability . . ."

As Jeslek gathered chaos, Cerryl focused not on repelling or blocking the force, but on channeling it around him.

Whhhstt!

Cerryl shivered but held as fire sheeted around him and vanished.

Chaos filled the room, Kinowin raising almost the power of Jeslek, his gray eyes as hard as the granite stones of the tower.

"Enough!" snapped Sterol. "Enough of this charade."

Cerryl wanted to protest that Jeslek's chaos had not been a charade but a last-moment effort to destroy him. Instead, he waited.

"I said enough, Jeslek." An aura of menace and dark red chaos enfolded Sterol—and Kinowin and Derka, and even Myral. "He has shields enough to stop your incidental rage, and that's more than most of the young mages. You have just proved that he belongs in the Brotherhood. Again."

Jeslek's eyes hardened, even as he bowed.

Cerryl couldn't escape the feeling that in some way Sterol had set him as a weapon against Jeslek. *Maybe that's what you've been all along.*

"For once, Jeslek—you have gone too far. Cerryl may indeed be deficient in his mathematicks, as you have alleged. And he may not be the most powerful of the younger mages with chaos. But he can stand up to you for at least a while, and his actions prove he has ability and he is loyal to Fairhaven—and, unlike some, he has never lied." Sterol laughed. "It would not hurt to have a young mage you cannot intimidate. Not at all."

Jeslek's sun-gold eyes raked across the group. Then he laughed.

Cerryl's eyes crossed Jeslek's, and at that moment Cerryl *knew* that Jeslek had known Cerryl had succeeded, and would return to Fairhaven.

"Ah . . . loyalty over ability," Jeslek said. "Was it ever thus with you, Sterol. Still . . . you are the High Wizard, and you are supported."

"Yes. I am." Sterol's smile was full and cold. "Cerryl *will* be inducted as a full mage at the next meeting, and so far as I'm concerned already has those privileges. The rest of us will discuss how to proceed to salvage the situation in Gallos." Sterol glanced toward Cerryl. "You may go. You could use some food and some cleaning."

Cerryl inclined his head. "Thank you, honored Sterol. And you, Myral."

Jeslek's eyes glittered. "Good day, mage Cerryl."

"Good day, overmage Jeslek." Cerryl smiled faintly. "I thank you for all that you have taught me."

"Good day."

Cerryl bowed to the older mages and slipped out through the iron-bound oak door and onto the landing. His legs were not quite shaking as he made his way down the stairs.

Leyladin and Lyasa found him in the commons, where he was gathering himself together.

"When did you get back? What happened?" demanded Lyasa.

Leyladin merely smiled gently.

"Please sit down." Cerryl gestured to the empty chairs across from him. "It's almost impossible to explain." He smiled. "Thank you both for getting word to Myral. Without that, things might have been . . . more complicated . . ."

"You still haven't told me what happened."

How much should he tell? Finally, he began, just as Lyasa opened her mouth to prompt him once more. "You know that I was supposed to be Sverlik's assistant and then do something, and that it was a test."

"You told me that in Gallos."

"What I didn't tell you was that the task was to kill the prefect of Gallos."

"You? Why you?"

"I don't know. I can guess, but I don't know."

Lyasa turned her head to Leyladin. Leyladin smiled briefly at Cerryl.

"You did it, of course." Lyasa's voice was matter-of-fact.

"The prefect had Sverlik killed, and a detachment of our lancers, and you were there when he sent an entire force against us."

"I heard about that," Leyladin said quietly.

Bealtur stopped dead in the archway to the commons, on his face an expression of alarm and consternation.

"I suppose you heard I had left," Cerryl called to the goateed student. "That was just a story to cover the task Jeslek set for me." He offered a broad smile.

Bealtur bobbed his head. "I am glad to see you have returned."

"So am I. The last eight-days have been hard." Cerryl smothered a grin as he glanced at Lyasa.

"Ah . . ."

"Don't worry, Bealtur. I won't be too much of a problem." Cerryl grinned.

Bealtur bobbed his head, then turned.

"No," said Lyasa. "They'll have to make you a full mage."

"That's what I'm hoping for," Cerryl admitted, deciding that he should not reveal too much.

"That's all?" asked Lyasa. "You just killed the prefect and walked away?"

Cerryl sighed. "No. I sneaked in and out of Fenard. I ran out of coins. Most of the Gallosian guards were after me." His stomach twinged at the exaggeration, and he added, "Those around the palace, anyway. The stable folk complained that I let the horse get too thin, and Jeslek wanted to say that the test wasn't enough because . . . just because."

Lyasa nodded. "He doesn't like you."

"He doesn't like anyone who doesn't think he's really the High Wizard," suggested Leyladin, "and that's most of the students and mages."

Lyasa stood. "I have to meet with Esaak. He's not pleased with my mathematicks. Again."

"Good luck," said Cerryl. "He was never pleased with mine, either. He still isn't."

"Lucky you." The black-haired student walked away.

From across the table, Leyladin looked directly at Cerryl.

Cerryl took a deep breath. "It has been a long few eight-days. Very long." His eyes went to Leyladin's, and he just looked into their depths for a time.

"You've learned a great deal," Leyladin said quietly. One hand reached across the table and covered his. "I wasn't sure you could. Or that you'd want to."

"I had some encouragement. I can't tell you how much encouragement." He grinned, then glanced down. His trousers were filthy, and his boots needed work. He didn't even want to think about how he looked. "I need to clean up and then get something to eat."

Leyladin slid a leather pouch across the table. Cerryl's eyebrows rose as he recognized it. He peered inside to check. The white-bronze razor glittered against the dark leather. "Is this a hint?"

"No. It is a strong suggestion."

They both laughed.

CIV

Cerryl fingered his clean-shaven chin, then glanced across the front foyer, wondering why the Council was taking so long. Or was it just that it seemed long to him?

"I can't believe this," said Faltar, his eyes on the archway to the Council Chamber.

"*You* can't believe it?" asked Lyasa.

A heavyset figure waddled through the archway and across the polished stone tiles of the foyer. "Well, you three," said Myral, a wide smile on his round face, "are you ready?"

The three exchanged glances.

"We're ready," Cerryl finally answered.

"So am I. Just follow me, and do what Sterol says." Myral turned back toward the archway. "It's a good idea, anyway." After a pause, he added, "That's a joke."

Cerryl and Lyasa followed Myral; Faltar followed them. All four walked through the archway and under the pillars that flanked the sides of the Council Chamber. Each circular pillar was gold-shot white granite, fluted, and apparently flawless. Red hangings swept from the top of one pillar to the next, in effect cloaking the capital of each. The base of each was a cube of a shimmering gold stone Cerryl did not recognize.

The floor of the chamber was comprised of polished white marble tiles that held golden swirls. An aisle led up the center of the chamber. On each side of the aisle were gold oak desks, each with a gold oak chair. Each chair had a red velvet cushion. At the eastern end of the chamber was a low dais, a mere cubit above the floor of the chamber. The dais was of the same gold-shot marble, and totally bare.

Sterol stood in the center of the dais. To the right of the High Wizard, and two steps back, were Jeslek and Kinowin, standing side by side. Cerryl caught a glimpse of Anya's red hair somewhere among all the white robes and tunics in the seats to the left of the aisle that the three student mages walked down. Even in a crowd, she stood out— and still made him wary.

In the row of desks before Anya sat Fydel, beside a mage Cerryl did not know. The unknown mage was talking in a low voice. ". . . don't understand it . . . took me years . . . scrivener's apprentice . . ."

Cerryl smiled to himself.

"Bealtur was here before him . . ."

"You want Bealtur at your elbow?" asked Fydel. "Cerryl's solid."

That surprised Cerryl, but he kept walking toward Sterol.

The High Wizard actually smiled as Myral stepped aside.

"High Wizard, I present the candidates for induction as full mages and members of the Guild." Myral inclined his head, then took another step backward.

Sterol let the silence draw out for a moment, then nodded. "Cerryl, Lyasa, Faltar . . . you are here because you have studied, because you have learned the basic skills of magery, and because you have proved you understand the importance of the Guild to the future of all Candar . . ."

Cerryl wanted to nod at that. After seeing Fenard and Jellico, he definitely understood what Fairhaven and the Guild offered for the future of Candar.

"We hold a special trust for all mages, to bring a better life to those who follow the white way, to further peace and prosperity, and to ensure that all our talents are used for the greater good, both of those in Fairhaven, and those throughout Candar." Sterol paused, surveying the three.

"Do you, of your own free will, promise to use your talents for the good of the Guild and for the good of Fairhaven, and of all Candar?"

"Yes," answered Cerryl. What else could he do, being who he was?

"Yes."

"Yes."

"And do you faithfully promise to hold to the rules of the Guild, even when those rules may conflict with your personal and private desires?"

"Yes," answered the three, nearly simultaneously.

"Do you promise that you will do your personal best to ensure that chaos is never raised against the helpless and always to benefit the greater good?"

"Yes."

"And finally, do you promise that you will always stand by those in the Guild to ensure that mastery of the forces of chaos—and order—is limited to those who will use such abilities for good and not for personal gain and benefit?"

"Yes," replied Cerryl. *Yes!*

"Therefore in the powers of chaos and in the sight of the Guild, you are each a full mage of the White Order of Fairhaven..."

A shimmering touch of chaos brushed Cerryl's sleeves ... and the red stripes were gone—as if they had never been.

"Welcome, Lyasa, Cerryl, and Faltar..." Sterol offered a broad smile and looked across the assembled group. "Now that we have welcomed the new mages, our business is over, and all may greet them."

Murmurs, and then conversation, broke out across the chamber.

Sterol glanced at the three. "I'm very pleased that all of you have succeeded. You have very different talents, and in the troubling days ahead, we will need each of those talents, I fear." The High Wizard's eyes were, for once, reflected Cerryl, warm and friendly.

"Congratulations!" Kinowin stepped up and clasped Cerryl's shoulder. The big mage smiled warmly. "You must know I have personal sympathy for anyone who comes from the background we share."

"You mean the lack of background?" replied Cerryl with a laugh.

A broader smile crossed Kinowin's face, then faded. "It doesn't get easier, but if you need anything, I'm here." He patted Cerryl's shoulder and slipped away.

Lyasa touched Cerryl's forearm, and he turned.

"Good," said Jeslek. "Before you are flooded with well-wishers, I wanted to let you know some things quickly. Each of you now has quarters in the second rear hall, on the second level—there is a bronze plate on each door." The sun-eyed overmage smiled. "Best you move your things and get settled quickly. There are some youngsters from the creche who would trade their red for white trimmed with red. You can still eat in the hall, but that is your choice now. You, as do all full mages, receive a stipend of one gold an eight-day. Not extravagant, but since the Guild supplies all your raiment and equipment and lodging, it's generally enough for modest pleasures. You will be assigned more permanent duties sometime in the next eight-day, after the High Wizard, overmage Kinowin, and I review the Guild assignments." Jeslek flashed a broad smile, the one Cerryl still mistrusted. "Now ... enjoy yourselves." The white-haired overmage nodded and slipped across the dais.

"Congratulations!" Anya appeared and offered Faltar a warm hug, then turned to Cerryl. "And to you, too. And to you, Lyasa."

"Thank you." Cerryl inclined his head.

Fydel stepped forward. "Congratulations, all of you." His eyes went to Cerryl. "You've proved you belong here, more than most." With a smile, he was gone.

"Lyasa!" Esaak lumbered forward, something cradled in his arms.

Cerryl glanced at the dark-haired new mage beside him, watching her eyebrows rise as the older mage extended the thin, freshly bound volume. "Since you will not take my tutoring seriously . . . this is a copy of *The Mathematicks of Logic.*" A broad smile crossed Esaak's face. "Your very own."

Lyasa bent forward and hugged Esaak.

Cerryl stepped back and turned to Myral. "Thank you . . . I haven't said it, but I mean it."

The older mage smiled. "Don't thank me. You worked for it, and you will make the Guild proud. I *know* that. Now . . . enjoy the day."

Another mage—one Cerryl didn't know—stepped up to Faltar. "Congratulations."

"Thank you." Faltar inclined his head.

As the crowd of mages finally filtered away, Cerryl leaned against one of the white stone pillars at the side of the chamber. He glanced at Faltar, and then Lyasa.

"Is it what you expected?" asked the black-haired mage, her olive-brown eyes resting on Cerryl.

"I don't know. I didn't let myself think about it," he confessed.

"Sterol gave part of it away. None of us would be mages this soon if things weren't getting bad." Lyasa laughed softly. "I wouldn't be a mage at all if things weren't getting bad. I don't use my body the way some do."

Faltar raised his eyebrows.

"It doesn't matter now," Cerryl said quickly. "We're mages, and not students, and I'm glad."

"So am I," added Faltar. "What are you going to do now?"

"Move," said Cerryl. "Find those new quarters. Then take a walk and have something to eat for dinner—outside the Halls."

Lyasa laughed. "I'll bet dinner tonight is really bad."

"I'll worry about that later." Cerryl straightened and eased out into the foyer, now almost empty. He made his way toward the second rear hall, looking around, but he didn't see who he sought.

Cerryl's new quarters were as far as one could get from the main hall, in the building even behind the one in which Jeslek had his apartment. But the overmage had been correct—there was a bronze plate by the door, and the old tongue script spelled out "Cerryl."

Still, Cerryl allowed himself a smile as he glanced around the room, the most spacious he had ever had, with real shuttered windows—two of them—and a wide desk and a chair with cushions . . . and a full-sized bed with cotton sheets and a red woolen blanket, and even a rug by the bed. And his own washstand—and an empty bookcase against the wall.

His eyes went from item to item. Hard as it was to believe, he was a full mage—admittedly over Jeslek's machinations and reservations, but a full mage—all he—or his father, had ever hoped for, and far more than he could have reasonably expected.

Yet . . . nothing was certain. War loomed with Gallos—and perhaps with Spidlar and even Recluce. Jeslek was even more angry at Sterol, and Sterol was using Cerryl against Jeslek, and Anya . . . well, Anya was playing an even deeper game, and one Cerryl didn't understand the reasons for, only that she did play such a game. Then, Myral, who had helped him in so many ways, was not in the best of health.

Still . . . he was more secure, and more able, than ever before in his life. He had a place and a chance at being what he could be, and a chance at happiness . . .

Thrap!

He turned.

"Very nice quarters." Leyladin stood in the open doorway, a broad smile on her lips.

"I . . . just got them."

"I know." The bright green tunic and trousers shimmered, and she seemed especially alive.

Cerryl studied the blonde young woman with red highlights in her hair, taking in the dancing green eyes. He couldn't help smiling.

"I wanted to see your new quarters." She smiled back.

Perhaps more than a mere chance at happiness. He crossed the room and took her hands.

After a moment, still smiling warmly, her green eyes melding into his gray eyes, she tightened her fingers around his hands.

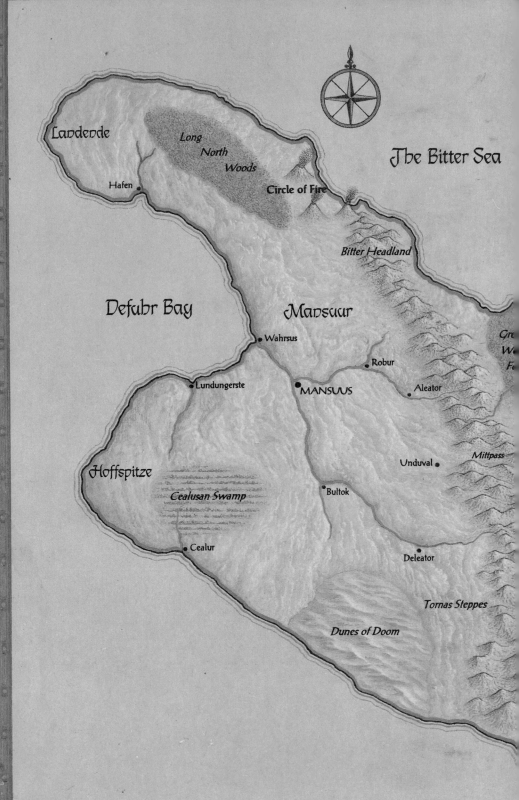